CW00519976

Stillwater

Sarah Anne Moore

Stillwater © 2021 Sarah Anne Moore

All rights reserved. This book or any portion thereof may not be reproduced or used in any manner whatsoever without the express written permission of the publisher except for the use of brief quotations in a book review.

ISBN (Print): 978-1-09835-574-6
ISBN (eBook): 978-1-09835-575-3

Contents

Chapter 1—Awakenings

Annie[1] woke to the early morning glow, enhanced by the amber color of the tent.

Sean[2] was still asleep with his lips parted so he could breathe in the bitter cold of the night air. A faint vapor formed above his face as he exhaled warm, moist breath from his lungs.

She hated to leave the warmth and smell of his body, but her bladder said otherwise. As she rose naked and exited the tent, she could feel the moistness between her legs and the coolness of the night air as it enveloped her body. Her nipples responded to the cold and hardened to the point of pain.

She found the light outside to be much dimmer than inside the tent. Being afraid of the dark and wondering if any other living thing—maybe a hungry grizzly bear—was also out at that hour, she did not stray too far from the tent. As her warm urine splashed on her inner calves and flowed toward the downslope arch of her left foot, she could smell the aroma of their bodily fluids, hers and his. It was a sweet perfume and uniquely theirs. She lingered for a few moments to allow for evaporation.

For the field geologist, the experience of a long day of hiking and mapping in steep, high terrain, leaves the upper thigh muscles weak

---

1 Sarah Anna Moore, "Annie" to those closest to her. Annie was born and raised in the southern part of the US and has a "Texas" accent. Professor of Geology. She is a fictional character loosely based on an amalgam of women in the author's life.

2 Sean Michael Anderson, Annie's best friend and lover. "Seani" to his field buddies and classmates. He was born in New Zealand but studied in England for many years, so he speaks with a variation of British and New Zealand accent. Professor of Geology. Sean is also a fictional character based on a dossier written by a friend.

and the body slightly dehydrated. The sweat from physical exertion evaporates instantly and leaves a residue of salt on the clothing and body as the only evidence of the process.

Deodorant is a luxury, and it is not recommended in terrain frequented by predators. After several days, the hair usually needs to be washed before it is necessary to clean the body.

Women geologists must wash their nether regions more frequently than males, so Annie carried a squirt bottle filled with water to ensure proper feminine hygiene. At that moment, however, she was not concerned with cleanliness as much as getting back to their sleeping bag and the sweet essence and warmth of their bodies.

She entered the tent and knelt for a moment to watch him as he slept. *Ah, love… it feels unreal that you find me special…you should love me?*

Sean was a strikingly athletic and handsome man, an imposing presence in the world of academia, admired by many women and men alike. But, at that moment, he lay with his mouth open, snoring quietly and looking particularly vulnerable and ordinary. He was Annie's lover, soulmate, and best friend, who never saw himself as anything special, except in Annie's eyes.

They shared more than just physical intimacy. Both were academics who shared common interests in the earth and space sciences. On a cosmic and spiritual level, they could sense each other thousands of miles away, and seemed to be familiar with one another—perhaps through space and time.

Unfortunately for them both, they did not find each other until later in their lives, and only after each had married and settled with their own families. When the two first met in that corridor at the *Field Station and campus in the Rockies,*[3] they recognized each other

---

3   The Rocky Mountain Field Station and Campus is a fictional dormitory setting where field camp students reside during their field mapping course in geology.

instantly. The cosmic connection was realized, and their lives would never be the same.

First Meeting -- the "Knowing"

Professor Sean Michael Anderson arrived early to greet his students as they arrived for the dorm check in procedure.

As he waited for his students to finish getting their keys and moving their belongings, he leaned patiently against the wall of the darkened corridor. He could see the entrance and the front office from his venue and was sure to see everyone who entered.

His attention heightened as a group was returning, presumably from one of the field areas he would soon investigate.

The students appeared dirty, hot, and tired as they wearily exited the vans and strolled into the opposite end of the dormitory building.

A young woman with long curly chestnut-colored hair split off from the group and walked toward the camp office. As she approached the outer glass doors of the building, he felt an unexpected excitement, as he seemed to recognize her. *Did he know her? Who is she? Perhaps they had met before?*

Anna[4] was returning from the field with some of her students, and they were covered in dust and salt from the excessive heat of the late June day of mapping. She was wearing a body leotard under a white sleeveless tank top and green field shorts. Around her neck she wore a white bandana to protect the delicate skin of her throat and chest. A small hand lens dangled from a leather cord that hung over the bandana and gently rested on her well-covered bosom. Her arms, thighs, and calves were deeply tanned and covered in dust, and her feet were protected with nylon and wool socks and sturdy

---

4   Annie's given name, Sarah Anna Moore. A character named after the woman who inspired this story.

leather hiking boots. A white cotton shirt was tied around her waist to shield her arms and upper torso during the extreme UV exposure time of the afternoon sun. For added protection, she also wore an Australian field hat and prescription sunglasses. Despite her dirty face and legs, she was a handsome, thin, muscular woman in her mid-thirties, all of one hundred and thirty pounds, and standing at five feet six inches tall.

As she entered the shadowy hallway, she stumbled over a doorstop and dropped an armload of maps and other field supplies, as well as her backpack, which she had carelessly slung over one shoulder. As she squatted down to collect the articles, she noted a tall male figure approaching from the darkened hallway.

The person seemed oddly familiar to her. He was wearing a pale blue T-shirt, khaki shorts, and leather hiking boots, with the same thick nylon and wool sock combination. Around his neck was the telltale sign of a serious field geologist—a rather large hand lens. He had dark brown hair with a few streaks of gray, a neatly trimmed salt-and-pepper beard, and a deep tan above his socks and below his shorts.

Anna could not help but notice how his leg muscles flexed as he walked in her direction and then knelt in front of her. She experienced feelings she'd never felt before, and was frightened, embarrassed, and strangely excited by this man kneeling before her.

"Please allow me to help ya," he said in a deep voice with an accent that was difficult to place—perhaps Canadian, she guessed.

She felt very uncomfortable, as he seemed nervous, and she noted her own extraordinary feelings. Anna wanted to bolt and run, but instead responded awkwardly and shyly, "No, that's okay, I can get it."

"Are ya staying in this dorm?" he asked.

"Yes," she replied.

"Ya have way too much stuff for one trip, so let me help carry some of it to yer room. Is that okay?"

She started to say that she was fine but stopped in mid-sentence and quietly said, "Okay then. Thank you."

They each experienced an instant memory of intimacy—physical, spiritual, sexual. It was not love at first sight. It felt more complex... deeper. Somehow, they knew each other.

At the door to her room, she nervously and politely held out her hand. "Thank you so much. I'm Anna, Anna Moore," she said with a shy smile.

"I'm Sean Anderson," he said as he took her hand in his. "I am a professor with one of the other field camps, and we just arrived. It is a pleasure to meet ya. We'll be here for six weeks, so I expect there will be time to get to know one another."

"That would be nice," she said, as he continued to shake her hand, and included a second hand to the hold. "I'm an instructor with the field camp from *Modavi State University (MSU) out of Mudfence, Texas.*" [5]

"Mudfence?" queried Sean, "That's a place I have never been but would love to visit one day; beautiful *pre-Cambrian*[6] *granites*[7] in that region... ancient rocks indeed, not to mention the volcanic complex to the west of there in the Big Bend area."

Forgetting she was embarrassed, Anna excitedly answered, "Oh, you've never been? You would just love that country. I am

---

5   A fictional place in Texas suggested by fellow author and friend, Jerry Moore. The use of the place is not meant to depict any real place past or present.

6   Precambrian – earliest era of earth's history before the Paleozoic, from 570 Mya to 4.6 bya.

7   Granites are igneous rocks which have cooled slowly from a magma (molten rock material below the earth's surface) for a long period of time. The slow cooling allows minerals to grow large enough to be seen with the naked eye and with the hand lens. Granites tend to make up the basement rocks of most continents and roots of mountain belts and are made up of light elements, like silica, oxygen, sodium, potassium, and aluminum.

particularly fond of the *Davis Mountains*[8] and the *rhyolites*[9] that outcrop there."

"So, how long have ya been here?" asked Sean.

"We've been here four weeks already and will return home in about two weeks. And what school are you with?" she asked.

"Ah, I am with *Cal State*.[10] We have heard so much about this wonderful place that we decided to do our camp here this summer. So far, it looks to be a wise decision, with lots of great projects within an hour."

"Well, if you need any advice," smiled Anna, "I'm sure my teaching partner and I would be glad to share our experiences. MSU has been coming here for at least 20 years, so it is very well established as a yearly camp."

"There appears to be plenty of time to get to know ya and ask lots of questions then. I just love yer southern accent, by the way," he said with a charming smile.

Anna immediately thought to herself, What accent?

Realizing that he was perhaps a bit too personal, he tried to change the subject and asked, "I imagine being from the Southland yer in some way involved in Petroleum Geology?"

"Well, your guess is close," she replied. "My graduate work involved deciphering petroleum well logs, but my first love has always been hard rock geology. Sadly, my graduate school was not strong in these areas."

Sean seemed genuinely impressed. "Well, we do have something in common. I hope ya will have a chance to visit Yellowstone Park before ya return home."

---

8   A range of volcanic mountains in southwest Texas on the way to the Big Bend area.

9   Rhyolites are the volcanic equivalent of granite. They form from lava flows above earth's surface and are light in color with a pinkish hue.

10   The use of Cal State in this story is fictional and is not meant to represent any faculty, students, or programs, past or present.

Anna smiled, "I have visited the park many times before with our students and always enjoy going back each year. The place that most intrigues me, though, is the banded igneous complex to the north of there, known as the *Stillwater Complex*.[11] I would love to visit that area. I've read about it for years, but we've never had the time in our camp schedules for any extra excursions."

"That's unfortunate," said Sean. "But I'll tell ya what; I am doing some fieldwork in Yellowstone Park, and I'll be back in September to check out some newly exposed areas in the newer caldera sequences. I have a friend working at the platinum mine in the Stillwater, and we could probably arrange for a mine tour if ya can get away for a couple of days. You would have to fly into Billings, though."

He surprised himself because he was not in the habit of inviting other geologists to join him in his fieldwork, much less someone he had just met ten minutes earlier. The invitation had been spontaneous, and he was not at all sorry he had made it.

"I'll have to think about it and try to get a few days off," Anna replied. "I'll definitely get back to you before we leave camp. I'm sure our paths will cross again, possibly in the *Beaverhead*." [12]

"I'd like that," said Sean, "but the Beaverhead is off-limits to my class for a couple of days until they get acclimatized. As I am sure ya know, 'twenty-something' students need some structure. Tomorrow morning, I will assemble them in a classroom and lecture them on the etiquette of fieldwork and how to comport themselves as visitors

---

11   The Stillwater Complex is an igneous banded series of platinum rich rocks. It is one of five rare complexes on the planet and is actively mined. It is located in the Beartooth Mountains which lie on the northern border of Yellowstone in Wyoming and Montana to the north. The place is used as a setting in the context of this story, but is not meant to depict any real events, past or present.

12   The Beaverhead is the fictional, local watering hole. It is in a hundred-year-old building and frequented by students, cowboys, and local folks. There is a dance floor, a jukebox, two pool tables, and numerous poker machines. It is a surprisingly congenial place, and every Saturday night there is a live band that usually plays country classics. It is loosely based on a real establishment called "The Metlen" in Dillon, MT.

to this small town. The learning curve in field geology is very steep, and I want to make sure they know what is required of them and how they should conduct themselves. I learned the hard way that it is essential to set down the rules at the very beginning rather than just respond to problems later, so no Beaverhead for them for a couple of days. I'm sure they think I'm unreasonable, but I do like to get off on the right foot."

Immediately, Sean recognized that he was lecturing an instructor from another camp, who had already had four weeks of experience and almost certainly did not need to be reminded by some know-it-all geologist from another school.

"I'm so sorry, Annie," he blurted out. "My mini-lecture was totally out of line, and ya should have told me to just keep quiet. Ya seemed interested, and I find ya easy to talk with. But again, I'm sorry."

Surprised that he called her Annie, she thought, *Annie? I haven't been called that since I was a little girl. My grandmother always called me that.*

Oddly though, it felt comfortable and natural for him to say "Annie." The way he said her name felt familiar and expected somehow. *How strange?* She thought.

"No need to apologize. I look forward to meeting you in the Beaverhead soon, and I'm sure our paths will cross in the cafeteria."

"I certainly hope so," said Sean, "… perhaps even this evening?"

Once again, Sean surprised himself, making a cafeteria date less than half an hour after meeting Anna. He thought, *What is going on here? Whatever it is, it just feels right.*

She was left standing in her room, feeling strangely excited. Despite being tired and hot, she felt unusually turned on by what had just happened. Being married, a mom, and a devout Catholic, the first thing she did was to cross herself and say, "Lord have mercy."

Anna closed the door and lay on the bed for a moment. Her thoughts went to her two boys, who were with their dad at his parent's ranch.

The youngest son was very nervous and often chewed his shirts when his mother would leave for extended periods. The older of the two boys was very outgoing and gregarious. He was a sweet boy who was a lot like his mom—forever seeing the bright side in all situations. Anna's husband *Robert*[13] was very strict with the boys, and without mom there to buffer, both children felt a little nervous and insecure.

Anna thought of her baby boy and how much she missed the little guy. She felt terrible pangs of guilt at these moments in her day but knew the money would make their lives better in the long term. The older son was very secure and had plenty of activities and friends, so Anna did not worry as much about him.

The worst part of doing summer field camp and summer field-mapping projects was having to be away from her boys. She missed their hugs and laughter. It was challenging to balance fieldwork, teaching, and family, but she was doing what she was trained and loved to do. To Anna, Earth was the most fascinating and dynamic planet in the solar system, and it was right there for her to explore and study.

Just as Anna felt she might cry, the voice of her family therapist played in her head: It will be good for your boys to be away from you for a while. When you return, you will all appreciate one another even more.

She soothed her guilt, collected her towels and toiletries, and felt a renewed motivation to be clean as she left to shower. If she didn't get cleaned up and over to the cafeteria, she would miss the evening meal. The camp had already paid for lodging and food, and Anna

---

13 Anna's husband, Robert Miller, father of her two sons. Robert is a fictional character and is not meant to represent any living person past or present.

was very frugal by nature. It would be wasteful and irresponsible to miss the meal.

Anna turned on the shower and didn't enter until the water reached the standard dorm temperature of 'slightly lukewarm.' The water felt unusually stimulating at the cooler temperature. She could feel it flowing over her face, her shoulders, her hair, down her back, over her buttocks. Her body felt uncomfortable, sexually anxious, almost to the point of being painful. As a scientist who used *natural family planning*,[14] she realized she must be near mid-cycle, and quickly forgave herself for having such lustful feelings.

Even though she had not really been keeping track of her cycle since she left for camp, she felt her feelings must result from some natural animal phenomenon. Feeling this level of arousal was new to her as she didn't remember feeling this strongly with her husband, much less a stranger.

As she dressed for the evening, she selected the only dress she had packed, and looked at herself with renewed skepticism in the mirror, which was only visible with the door of her room closed. She looked good—maybe too good? She left her room and noted the hand samples she had collected earlier. *I bet Sean would appreciate my treasures;* she thought. *I will stop by to talk to Adam,*[15] *too, and see if he knows Sean.* Perhaps she would find one of them in their room, and she could show off her amazing finds.

Meanwhile, Sean located his room at the end of the corridor.

Adam Darren, the head instructor from Anna's college—aka Dr. D., was a couple of doors down on the same floor.

---

14   A natural form of birth control which is sanctioned by the Catholic Church. The female keeps track of her cycle, including morning temperature, and the thickness of vaginal mucus throughout the month. The husband and wife agree to abstain from sex during the more fertile times of the reproductive cycle.

15   Douglas Adam Darin, Anna's fictional teaching partner from MSU, aka. Dr. D. Fictional character loosely based on a close friend and teaching partner but is not meant to be the actual person.

Sean's graduate teaching assistant, *Alex*,[16] was installed in the room opposite and had already unpacked his guitar and was gently strumming when Sean checked into his room.

"Where have you been, man?" Alex shouted across the hall.

"I just met this really cool chick in the dorm office," said Sean "and we're going to discuss field camp strategies at dinner tonight since her group already has four weeks under their belt."

"Strategies, eh? Okay, have fun." said Alex, sounding a little skeptical.

About an hour later, there was a quiet knock on Sean's open door. It was Anna, standing there looking good in a short dress.

She had showered, washed her hair, and put on a little makeup, using only some moisturizer, sunscreen, and a touch of mascara. Her hair was naturally curly, and her face was pear-shaped, like *Hedy Lamarr*,[17] or at least that is what an older friend had told her some years earlier... and those hazel eyes and freckles.

She had some objects in her hand. "I just wanted to show you some samples I collected in the *Ruby Range*."[18] Anna presented two excellent samples, one of black faceted tourmaline and the other of garnet.

Sean complimented her on her find, of which she was inordinately proud.

"If ya recall the exact localities, perhaps ya can show me on the map, so we can search a few weeks from now when my students are mapping there. Are ya off to the Beaverhead?" he asked cheerfully.

---

16   Alex, a PhD student working as Sean's Teaching Assistant at the summer field camp. A fictional character that doesn't represent any real person past or present.

17   Hedy Lamarr, an American/Australian film actress who was considered a rare beauty and talented performer of the 1930-1960s

18   Ruby Range of Montana is so-called because it contains gem-quality red garnets that had been mistaken for rubies by early prospectors. The range is present in southwest Montana. Garnets are red or green gemstones that occur naturally as dodecahedral crystals.

"I'm not certain yet," she replied with a smile and flirtatious tone. "I think I may wait a couple of days until I have better company."

"That's great," said Sean. "I hope our group is part of that better company."

"Oh, I'm sure of it," she laughed. "Have a great first day tomorrow."

Then she was gone.

"Awakening is the wondrous process of listening
to the call of the soul amidst the noise of life,
Turning inward and opening to… Light.
This is an invitation for you to rise above
the routine so that you can
experience the beauty of your awakening to time."
~unknown~

Chapter 2—Notorious Dr. D.

The cafeteria was in a building near the center of the small station and campus. As Anna left the dormitory, she could smell the aroma of meatloaf and potatoes — French fries in the air. She probably could have found the place blindfolded at this point because of her intense hunger and thirst. When she arrived at the cafeteria, she couldn't help but notice all the new students who had come from universities all over the country.

Wow! Our southern camp is outnumbered now!

The main dining hall was filled with college students wearing their newly purchased field mapping attire—backpacks, hand lenses, sunglasses, hats, bandanas, Tevas, hiking boots, clipboards, green earth-friendly water bottles, organic bug sprays—*Oh my! It looks like a world-class Lewis and Clarke or Patagonia outfitting store.*

Ben, one of Anna's younger students, shouted to her as she walked into the open room, "Look, Dr. Moore! Dr. D. is on his fifth root beer float!"

Across the room from her stood her teaching partner, Professor Adam Danis — "Dr. D." to the students, "Adam" to his close friends and mother. He was a small man with wild-looking gray hair, a cute button nose, and an impish look on his face most of the time. He was making one of his classic root beer floats.

Anna walked toward him and queried in an accusing tone, "So how many does that make?"

He looked at her as though his mother had caught him with his hand in the cookie jar and exclaimed, "Why, I don't know what you mean? I ate! I ate a lot!"

"The students say this is your tenth one," Anna lied in her best 'you're caught red-handed,' mom's voice.

He sang out with a defensive chuckling tone, "Why, ha-ha, what do you mean? This is my second only."

Anna nodded knowingly and moved to the end of the line to receive her tray and select her food. She collected her silverware and napkins and then proceeded on to the selection process. She wondered, *What to have? No meat, I hate meat. Mashed potatoes, green beans? Hmmm (yum)... protein! Yes, I need protein... a roll with butter? I still need protein, ah... cottage cheese and a chef salad with eggs; now we're talking...no dressing, it's fattening.*

The cafeteria worker motioned to a possible drink choice, and Anna responded, "No, I need two glasses, one for water and one for tea... thank you."

Anna found a table of her students and ate her fill as she watched Dr. D. making yet another root beer float!

"It's his tenth, Dr. Moore! I swear it is!" shouted Ben from across the room.

Dr. D., hearing Ben, shrugged his shoulders and turned his back to hide his dessert creation. He was notorious for his sweet tooth and his propensity for sneaking back to the vans while students were in the field, to steal their cookies from their lunch bags.

A sack lunch was prepared each day for the campers. The lunches usually had a sandwich, chips, an apple, orange, or banana, and two giant cookies. When students began the camp, they typically left their lunches in the van and returned at mid-day to seek refuge from the noonday sun. They ate their lunches and refilled their water bottles from the large containers stored on each van. Students were shocked and confused to find that each bag was missing one or both cookies—every single bag.

Who could the culprit possibly be? We know—Dr. D.

Anna now moved her attention from the antics of her teaching partner to listen to the conversations of the students as they sat discussing their trials and adventures of the day. She felt especially motherly and protective of the students, who seemed fragile emotionally, physically, and academically. One female student, who couldn't seem to find herself on an *aerial photo*[19] or a map, concerned Anna. *It is difficult to create a map of an area if you can't locate your position on the planet.*

Each day in the field, Anna made sure that she found each team of students, in pairs for security, to confirm they were well hydrated, not stepping on snakes or getting cactus spines through their boots, or becoming separated from others, lost, or wandering outside of the mapping area. She especially liked to find them and inspect their progress. She never gave them the answers, but skillfully led them Socratically to a logical conclusion. Anna was a gifted teacher and naturally nurtured all students, regardless of their age or level of skill.

After dinner, she walked back to her room and, after first making sure everything was prepared for the tasks of the following day, decided to escape to the Beaverhead for a few hours.

It was a critical time in the process for the students, who were summarizing their mapping projects. If she were in her room or nearby, the more insecure students would refuse to think for themselves and would seek her guidance. Students needed to use their own geologic sense to finish their maps and interpret the geologic information.

---

19   Field geologists use aerial photos, taken from a plane, to help them plan their field surveys and frequently map features on photos. These maps are Photogeologic Maps and are used in association with a field copy of a topo map.

Adam and Anna had agreed to make themselves scarce for the evening. This seemed to be the perfect time to get a beer and relax just a little.

Chapter 3—The Beaverhead

Summer evenings in this part of the Rockies were pleasant, with low humidity and gorgeous sunsets. Anna loved to walk past the well-groomed yards and quaint homes of the kind gentlefolk of the area. The town was filled with friendly people who waved and even struck up brief conversations with her as she passed. She had a delicate nature and would often engage the familiar faces with a big smile and a greeting...

"Hey, how are you doing this year?" Anna's southern accent was endearing to the locals. She often returned a friendly wave of recognition.

The town was nestled between two mountain ranges and provided the perfect locale for cool, dry evenings after scorching hot days.

The MSU camp preferred to arrive a month earlier than most of the other schools, to avoid the extreme heat conditions of the high desert mapping projects. Summer temps easily reached the hundreds in early July in this terrain. Their group overlapped with the other camps during the last few weeks of the field course.

After several weeks of staying in a rustic station, at a higher elevation with limited amenities, it was nice to stay in the dorms provided by the small college and field station. The dorm accommodations were perfect for the hotter temperatures of late June and early July.

The college had a scenic view of snow-capped peaks, and the town offered a pleasant, historical, and cultural experience for all who visited. The Beaverhead Saloon was only a few blocks from the dorms, and the walk included the opportunity to see architecture from the 1800s, with churches and bars on each corner. There were literally as many bars as churches.

Anna finally reached the main street which was lined with mom-and-pop businesses and was oriented east-west and parallel to the railroad tracks that passed through the town. One popular family bar, *"Grandpa's Place,"*[20] was known for being a source for good old Rocky Mountain family fun. It housed a full bar, pool tables and pinball machines, a coin-operated bucking horse for toddlers, and an expansive dining area where families could enjoy the famous western cuisine of buffalo, bear, and beef burgers, spaghetti, salads, and pizza. Grownups had a choice between pitchers of beer, longnecks, or tea, and the kids could have a pitcher of any soda pop they preferred.

She chuckled to herself as she passed, remembering the poor students who had been tricked into sampling the most famous burger in town, "The Burning Bear" burger, served only at Grandpa's Place. The burger consisted of locally hunted and butchered bear meat, with finely chopped jalapeños and onions kneaded into each colossal patty.

Anna didn't want to know which kind of bear. The entire idea of eating a bear made her very sad and nauseous. She was raised on a sustainable family farm where everything they needed was grown. Because of the butchering process, she rarely ever ate meat. Animals were people too, as far as she was concerned.

The first bite of the Burning Bear was typically excruciating and would easily make your eyes water. Drinking water, of course, would only make it worse. She particularly smiled at remembering

---

20   Fictional family bar based on the family bar in Dillon, MT, known as "Papa T's."

poor *Ben*[21] as he wept and panted for milk and crackers with his first try.

Dr. D., of course, laughed so hard he could barely stay in his chair.

Ah, Dr. D. was a mean one... he had done the same thing to her a few years prior, when she was a newly graduated Ph.D. student, working her first field camp assignment. He insisted that she had to try the burger as a rite of passage. No doubt, someone had tricked him, and so now he had to carry on the tradition, which was almost a hazing ritual for all new faculty and students to the camp.

Across the main street from Grandpa's Place was the old railroad station, now a museum where relics of mining, ranching, and hunting were kept for all as a reminder of the rich history of the area. Of interest was the famous, thirteen-foot-tall, stuffed Grizzly, standing upright, and a huge mountain lion, perched high above everyone.

Adam loved to take the new students in there and weave stories about how the areas they were mapping were full of such critters. Mountain lions, yes, but Grizzlies of that size were not as common in that part of the Rockies. Of greater danger was the mother moose with babies or rattlers just molting their skin. Any animal with a baby could be a potential threat.

Beyond the railroad tracks was an unpaved road, also oriented east-west. This dirt road ran directly in front of the "Beaverhead Saloon and Hotel," complete with hitching posts out front and horses tied, swishing their tails to shoo the flies. Large neon lights flickered and buzzed above the great swinging doors leading from the dirt street into the main hall.

Anna knew that the faculty would congregate in the booths and tables at the opposite end of the establishment, near the northeast

---

21   Ben, an undergraduate student attending the MSU field camp to finish his degree in geology. Fictional character that is not meant to represent any person past or present.

corner of the main room… as far away from the pool and poker tables as possible. This was a Friday night, so there would be cowboys playing poker or pool, and dancing.

Faculty and students from the geology camps would enter the swinging doors near the back to avoid any local entanglements. Some groups came in through the front doors, no matter who was in the bar. Anna preferred the back door to prevent the uncomfortable stares. She was timid, and the added attention felt awkward.

The dining tables and booths on that end of the great hall were oriented in such a way as to ensure unobstructed access to the dance floor, located directly below and in front of a western-style stage. Near the door was also a jukebox which offered selections of both kinds of music—country and western.

Anna could hear the noise of clinking glasses, people laughing and talking, and faint western music playing as she approached. She loved this area of the Rockies and its unique cultural experience. It was a piece of the "Old West," preserved for all to enjoy.

One of the greatest adventures for summer camp students was to go to a real saloon, complete with a very long bar with stools, swinging doors on both ends of the establishment, and horses tied up at wooden rails outside. The south doors of the saloon opened into an area which was oriented perpendicular to the doors and the long bar. This area was devoted to two poker tables with two pool tables alongside.

The view as one entered this great hall was very much like the ones seen in the TV westerns of the late 50s and early 60s, complete with the stairs leading up to the rooms for boarders. The tale told by the local historians was that the Beaverhead was a bordello and a saloon back in the 1800s. The only changes over time were the addition of a kitchen and remodeling of the upstairs to a long-term stay hotel for cowboys and weary travelers. There was also the distinct absence of an old-time upright piano, or dancing girls and barmaids dressed in fluffy dresses, complete with corsets and garters.

The modern barmaids wore tennis shoes, ponytails pulled through a baseball cap, jeans, and t-shirts. Several of them were missing teeth and carried jacketed knives attached to their leather belts.

Over her five years of teaching at the summer camps, Anna was very aware of the dangers associated with rowdy, drunken cowboys at a saloon, not to mention unruly, drunk students. She had experienced more than one scrape with cowboys and their girlfriends and had managed to rescue inebriated students from inevitable jail or bodily injury.

Quite a few students from other camps were not intimidated by the cowboy clientele and challenged them to a game of pool with ten dollars to go to the winner. The winner kept playing until he or she lost, at which point they would relinquish their right to the next game. The students won as often as they lost, and nobody got upset.

In Anna's camp, there had been a couple of students who ended up being attacked because they were flirting with the girlfriend of a cowboy. There was a notable incident in which Anna had to pretend to be the date of one of her drunken male students so that an angry cowboy would back off and re-sheath his knife.

Chivalry is not dead

Anna pushed through the swinging doors and entered the great hall where she spotted Adam sitting at a table with none other than "Sean" and several other men, who looked distinctly like geology professors.

He waved for her to come over and raised his arm to signal the barmaid that the table required another glass.

As she approached the table, two of the men stood up and greeted her. The ones who rose were clearly over the age of fifty—Adam and Sean. Those who remained seated looked more like graduate students or newly graduated professors.

She couldn't help but note that the older men had been taught to be gentlemen, and she was pleased to be treated like a lady, and a peer.

Adam made the introductions and Anna shook the hands of all, noting of course that Sean lingered for a moment before releasing her hand.

She had learned early on that men valued handshakes and made initial judgments based on the strength of the grip. She also knew that as a woman, she must present herself with high confidence to make up for the lack of strength in her handshake. Being an attractive woman meant that she also risked not being taken seriously. Women of her vintage were socialized to be sweet and kind and to know their place.

Anna worked hard to maintain her social grace and femininity while also gaining respect. This was accomplished by being assertive and intelligent, pushing the envelope, yet not stepping over an invisible line drawn by a male-dominated society and science profession. Male posturing was to be left to the men.

In some ways, she knew she had an advantage over most men. She was clearly female but could hold her own with any of the men intellectually. She could be sweet and gentle, which was her nature, yet also posture herself to do intellectual battle when needed. This was one reason Anna was so attractive to her colleagues. She was soft and smart, and her endearing qualities were especially appreciated by older professors, who were more sensitive to gender inequality.

Sean was especially attracted to these qualities in any woman, but especially in this one.

As Anna made polite conversation with the faculty seated near to her, she couldn't help but sense Sean's gaze. His attention was both exciting and intimidating.

She could see Sean and Adam talking, as she viewed them with her peripheral vision. She realized that even though Sean was talking to him; he was clearly looking beyond Adam and watching her. As Adam was speaking, Sean heard very little of the conversation. He occasionally replied, "Yep, yep…. ah… yes."

Sean couldn't take his eyes off the gentle southern beauty sitting down the table from him. He watched her as she lifted her longneck beer, still in the bottle, to her lips to drink.[22] He couldn't help but notice how she positioned her lips as she drank the beer. Not like a lady, but like a young man, complete with a polite, subdued belch.

What an amazing person, he thought. *She is adorable.*

The moment was broken when Sean heard Adam say, "and… there was Anna, helping the poor old cowboy as he tried to push his horse back through the swinging doors."

He laughed as he told the story of the day that "Moose," the cowboy, brought his horse "Skeeter" into the saloon. He then shouted down to Anna and laughed, "Hey Anna, you tell the story much better than me. Tell these guys about Moose and Skeeter."

Feeling a little put on the spot, Anna told the story and used her best impressions of the cowboy and the barmaid. Despite what Anna thought, she had a very distinct southern accent, which enhanced the comedy of the story. With all attention now on her, she began the tale.

"We were playing pool in the main hall, when this little old man, covered in dust from head to toe, his body shaped like a

---

22   It was considered customary for sophisticated persons to pour their beer into a glass, rather than drinking straight from a bottle. It was considered unladylike for a woman to drink from a bottle, vulgar in some social settings. Vulgar is defined in this case as unsophisticated, unrefined, lacking proper social graces.

question mark—no doubt because of years and years of riding a horse—walked through the swinging doors. He removed his hat as he came in, exposing his pale forehead, which had been protected by the brim of his cowboy hat. He was shuffling across the floor to the bar.

The barmaid shouts, 'Moose! I figured you'd be passing this way soon.'

To which he said, 'Rainier.' She gave him a longneck Rainier brand beer, and he took a lengthy swig before setting the bottle down.

To our surprise, a horse stuck his head and shoulders through the swinging doors, and Moose prompted him to come on in and join him at the bar.

'Come on, Skeeter'… sucking his teeth to make a tsk, tsk, tsk… sound, 'C'mon in'…

Skeeter walked into the main hall and right up to the bar.

The barmaid turned around and shouted, 'Damn it, Moose! I aint cleaning up no horseshit in here tonight! Skeeter! Out!!!'

'Ah, dadgummit, he just wants a drink too,' Moose says under his breath as he carries his brew and follows Skeeter toward the doors…"

Anna continued the story as everyone laughed…

"Skeeter makes it almost to the doors and then stops. I mean, he stops dead.

Moose was shoving on his haunches and telling him to move, but he wasn't moving.

So, I went over to help but refused to push from behind a horse. I pushed on the saddle, and we shoved Skeeter out of the swinging doors… with the barmaid, yelling behind us,

'Dammit, Moose! You can't take the beer outside with ya. It's agin the law!'

To which Moose shouted back, 'Just give me a dang minute!'

Moose sat the beer down on the wooden porch and tied Skeeter to the rail.

Skeeter then bent down and took the neck of the longneck beer, gripped it in his teeth, and upended the thing right there. Skeeter drank the rest of the beer and then dropped the bottle on the ground beside him—clink!"

Annie laughed at the memory. Her laughter was infectious. Once she started, people around her would have to laugh with her. It wasn't a choice.

"See, I told you she told it better than me," said Adam.

Everyone was so delighted by the story, including Anna, who had an enormous smile on her face at the re-telling. It was one of her favorite camp stories to share.

Adam excused himself, as he had already had at least two beers more than everyone, and her story had almost made him wet his pants.

As he and two others left, Sean scooted down into the vacant seat next to Anna, so he could be closer to the conversation between her and the junior faculty.

Anna was aware of Sean's smooth move but did not falter from offering sage advice on upcoming mapping projects, deliberately avoiding eye contact with him. The intensity of his presence was difficult to ignore, and she merely nodded, but was not listening to the conversations at the table.

She could not seem to take her attention off the man now so close to her. Even though his leg was at least four inches from hers, she could feel his presence, and part of her felt drawn to him. Her head felt full, and her ears were ringing. Always looking for a logical explanation for everything, Anna wondered if perhaps it was just the beer, or maybe she was dehydrated and just needed to drink more water. It was as though the rest of the activity in the room was at a standstill, and only she and Sean were present in that space, at that moment.

Shit, she thought, *I wonder if he can read my mind? Oh, Lord, I hope not. Focus, Anna, focus! Shake it off, girl.*

Adam returned and promptly sat in another chair, not even thinking twice about his own seat being taken.

After an hour had passed, a group of students entered the saloon through the side door. They were with a southeastern camp that had just rolled into town earlier that afternoon and were checking out the local attractions before getting started with their camp assignments.

As the students approached the bar and ordered drinks, Anna thought to herself, *Oh no. I did not expect to be babysitting another camp this evening. Where on earth is the faculty for this camp?*

She looked around the room and even out the large picture windows to the side street. She saw not a soul who looked like faculty. Anna, feeling a bit tired, turned to Dr. D., saying as she yawned, "I think I should get back to the dorm. We have a full day of grading tomorrow."

Sean chimed in, disappointed and surprised by her soon-to-be quick exit, "Are ya walking back alone? It's getting dark out there. I'm getting ready to head back too."

Before Anna could respond, she heard a voice from directly in front of her say, "Hey, wanna dance?"

Anna looked up to see a rather large, muscular man wearing suspenders. She thought to herself, *What on earth? Who dresses like that?*

She also noted that he had an unusually large mustache. It reminded her of the baseball player... *What's his name? Rollie Fingers?*

A bit flustered and confused by the two separate conversations and offers, she responded, "No thanks, I'm feeling spent. I think I'll be leaving soon."

The man, *Steve*,[23] stared for an uncomfortable second, as though he couldn't believe she would turn him down, and then walked across the dance floor to the bar where he leaned on the bar, ordered a beer, and continued to stare at her.

She was uncomfortable with his demeanor, and Adam whispered to her,

"That guy may be trouble. I saw him earlier today in the men's room at the dorm, and he seemed to be very rude to others. Maybe you shouldn't leave just yet."

Anna had known Adam long enough to know that he would not have mentioned being cautious if he were not legitimately concerned. He was an easy-going fellow and was generally relaxed and unflappable. The size and behavior of this man clearly concerned him.

Sean could see the concern and offered, "D., I will walk her back. He won't bother her."

Anna was not insulted by Sean's offer or that she was not involved in the decision exchange of two men who seemed concerned for her safety. Being raised in the South, she was used to chivalry and took it as a compliment, not an insult. It was expected and a sign of respect for a man to care about the safety of a woman in his company. She was flattered and shyly accepted his gracious offer.

Excited to be leaving with Anna, Sean excused himself to go to the men's room before beginning the walk back to the dorms.

While he was gone, Anna was feeling nervous, excited, and very, very guilty. Her feelings of attraction for this man, while she was still married, although separated from her husband, made her feel

---

23 Steve, a graduate student from a southeastern camp, who fancies himself a lady's man. Fictional character not meant to represent any real person living or dead.

confused and a little ashamed. *I should not be leaving with him,* she thought to herself.

She then turned to Adam and asked, "Why don't you just walk me home. I think I'd feel better about that."

"You aren't afraid of Sean, are you? I trust him. It will be okay. Besides, he's married," said Adam.

Whew, Anna thought innocently. *That means it will be easier to avoid this, this…. attraction I seem to have for this man. Wait a minute? I'm still married too, for the moment.*

She quickly turned to Adam and asked, "He knows I'm married too, doesn't he?"

"Don't know, he has never asked. But I'm sure it's nothing to dwell on," he said as he flashed his cute little sideways smile.

She could not honestly tell sometimes whether he was joking or being totally serious. Anna had always been very trusting and a little naïve when it came to such things. Her dad used to tease her the same way, and her trusting nature was one of her more endearing qualities.

Sean emerged from the men's room, and Anna rose to her feet to meet him. He politely pushed the saloon doors open for her and gave a nod back to his new friend, Dr. D. He also noted that the large strange man at the bar was looking in their direction. He thought to himself, *I sure hope he doesn't try anything stupid.*

The night air was crisp, and there was a smell of horses, dust, sage, and Grandpa's pizza in the air.

Anna thanked Sean for walking with her, and they were silent for a few moments.

As they crossed the railroad tracks, she could see the lights of a train far away in the distance, and thought, *It seems you can see forever.*

Sean noted the train lights too and commented, "Good thing we're leaving now. That train might have taken hours to pass."

By this time, it was quite cool, almost cold. Anna could feel the hair stand up on her bare arms and legs as they walked. Even though she could not see Sean, she felt his presence next to her and could hear him breathing as he walked.

Sean broke the silence and asked, "Did ya know that feller back there?"

Anna replied, "Who?"

"Ya know the one with the huge mustache."

"No, I did not," she responded indignantly. "Besides, I am a married woman."

"Oh, like that would matter to him?" said Sean with a chuckle.

"Well, it should," said Anna in her best self-righteous tone.

As they walked down the darkened streets, the stars became very clear—brilliant in fact. Anna looked up and exclaimed, "I love the night sky! I always wanted to be an astronomer."

At that moment, they both saw a fireball race across the sky in the distance, just to the southeast. "Wow!" Anna shouted excitedly and grabbed Sean's arm, "Did you see that?!"

Sean shouted back, "Yes, yes, I did. Wow, that doesn't happen every night now does it?"

The couple both stopped walking for a few seconds to take in the splendor of the celestial sight.

Anna realized she was touching him and quickly released her hold on his arm. It felt very comfortable, too comfortable, and she found herself wanting to put her arms around his waist and pull him close. She could feel her own heart beating faster. He was so close; she could smell him... not a body odor exactly—just an essence. It was very familiar, and she loved the scent.

She stepped away from him and became silent.

"What's wrong, Annie?" he asked.

"Oh, nothing," she said, "I'm just tired. I need a good night's sleep."

Still looking up at the sky, he said, "Yes, me too."

They walked the rest of the way in silence, as they both pondered the reality of their... "friendship?" Walking up the steps of the dorm, Sean opened the door for Anna. She thanked him once again and then exited down the hall to their left. Sean slowly strolled down the hallway to the right.

Chapter 4—Field Camp

The next day Adam and Anna sat at opposite ends of the dorm table in Adam's room, grading furiously. The objective was to finish by Sunday.

Adam had promised Sean that his team would spend some time going over the projects from MSU. Twenty-plus years of teaching in the same areas and refining the same materials would provide valuable insights. He was looking forward to sharing his experiences with another professor.

Anna was less thrilled because Sundays were her only day off. She knew, however, how it felt her first time as a teaching assistant and newbie. Her focus would be on helping Alex and avoiding uncomfortable entanglements with Sean.

She and her husband had separated before the camp started, and they hoped to reconcile on her return. Her attraction for Sean was strong, and he was married. In her mind, she had to place him inside a box she was not allowed to open.

As Anna sat back in her chair, stretching her arms high above her head, she yawned and let out a restrained primal scream, "Eeeeaaaa... Aggggh..."

"I beg your pardon," said Adam, looking over his bifocals at her in surprise.

"Oh, sorry, D. I guess I need another pot of coffee."

"Whatcha up to in here?" asked Alex as he stuck his head in the door.

Adam swung his chair around and offered, "Grading, wanna job?"

"I thought I heard someone say coffee." Alex was standing in the doorway with puppy dog eyes and holding a rather large mug in his hands.

"Ah well, guess I'll have to finish this by myself then," said D., hoping to get a response from Anna.

"Oh, you want MY coffee instead of his," said Anna. "His is too weak. You may as well be drinking brown water."

"That is not true!" said Adam indignantly. "You just want to grow hair on everyone's chest. I bet there's hair on your chest from drinking that stuff."

"Hah, and wouldn't you like to know?" teased Anna.

"Sorry D., I think I am gonna need Anna's special brew, as I haven't grown any hair on my chest as yet… ha ha."

Anna laughed and instantly felt guilty because she realized that Alex was probably sensitive about not having hair on his chest.

From the hallway, everyone could hear a stern, proper New Zealand accent, "All right. What's the meaning of this?"

Anna felt her heart speed up at the sound of Sean's voice.

Sean stepped into view, looking like he had just stepped out of a shower and forgot to dry off. "Did ya notice it's raining like hell out there?" he said as he focused his gaze on Anna. He tried to make eye contact, but she shyly looked away.

"Ah no," said D. "We closed the blinds. Besides, those storms are usually late afternoon and don't last very long."

"Lucky me," chuckled Sean, "I picked the perfect time to walk to the market, now didn't I? Annie, you were correct. This is a cool place."

"Yes, I love it here. I hope to one day retire here, I think," she said as she opened the shades to get a better look at the showers.

"You want a cup of coffee?" asked Alex. "D. says it will grow hair on your ass."

Anna chuckled as she placed five ample scoops of coffee into the filter.

"Let's see, one scoop for each of us ought to grow some hair."

D. scoffed. "Don't make enough for me. I want to sleep tonight, and I have plenty enough hair on my ass already. Thank you very much."

As the water heated, Anna felt Sean's gaze. She felt naked, exposed—like an animal trapped with no way to escape. Not frightened, but undoubtedly vulnerable. Thankfully, she could look out the window. This guy was a distraction, an anomaly in her life.

Sean felt awkward as Annie seemed to be less than engaging. *Perhaps she is just tired*, he thought... *or did I do something to offend her?*

"So, Sean?" asked D., "What do you think of that first mapping project?"

"It looks perfect for learning the basics," said Sean. "I'm really looking forward to getting out there and mapping it myself."

"I'm liking the second-week project, too. It looks better than the first."

"Oh, yes. The *Laramide* [24]structures out there are pretty straightforward," said D.

"Anna here mapped them all her first day out. She sat on the first ridge and mapped an entire valley with just a couple of photos and a topo map."

"Thanks, D.," said Anna. "It was pretty easy. I had a great remote sensing teacher as an undergraduate. He taught us how to map structures from satellite photos and stereo pairs to prepare for oil exploration jobs...so I had two semesters and lots of practice."

---

24   The Laramide Orogeny is a mountain building event that overprints most of the geologic features in the rocky mountain west. (Laramide) (Kelley & McCleary, 1960)

"Anna is also our undergraduate Structures prof.," said D.

"I'm sure she is a great asset to yer program," said Sean. "Any program would love to have her, I'd think. I know we would."

Sean had done it again, he barely knew Anna, and he was already trying to recruit her from MSU. He was honest, though. Their program would benefit greatly from more female instructors, especially those of Anna's caliber.

"Oh no, you don't!" said D. "We have her on contract, and you can't have her."

Anna felt her face flush in embarrassment as the two men showered her with praise. She was humble by nature, and the accolades felt out of place. She had once been told by her husband when they were first married, that he thought she suffered from *Imposter Syndrome*.[25] He said lots of things about what he thought was wrong with Anna, and she had become mostly habituated to his insults.

"So, Annie, if ya tire of D. here, Cal State might have a spot for ya," said Sean, ribbing Adam.

Anna was not impressed with the idea that she was only at MSU for or because of D. and would consider leaving for such a frivolous reason. She chose that school because it was near her husband and his family. Although grateful for the position and the opportunity, she sacrificed her personal career goals for the good of her children. They needed to be near family, and she didn't have much of a family. Robert's parents had always treated her like a daughter, and she was grateful for their love and support.

She watched the two professors as they discussed everything from fly-fishing to specific features present on the topo maps. Anna smiled to herself, *It is nice to see D. and Sean enjoying themselves.*

---

25 Imposter syndrome refers to a psychological phenomenon where a person achieves success but doesn't feel they were worthy of the success. There is a constant fear that others will discover the flaw. (Lavender, 2013)

They seemed to be rapidly becoming friends. *At least he's focusing on something other than me,* she thought, as she poured the coffee and served three mugs.

"Your first day, they will all see a snake," said Anna, speaking directly to Alex.

"It is inevitable in the Dinwoody.[26] You need to be ready to lecture them before they go out there about the do's and don'ts of first aid for snake bites."

"We have mentioned snakes and safety already, but yer right Annie, they will need a more focused lecture before going out there," said Sean, as he once again focused his gaze on Anna.

Alex looked a little bit concerned.

"Don't worry," said Anna, "They will be fine. Just remember that the snakes are more frightened of all of you than you are of them..."

"I'm not so sure about that," said Alex.

"Oh, didn't I tell ya?" said Sean, "Alex hates snakes."

"You might have picked the wrong profession then," smiled D.

"Oh, don't listen to them, Alex. Listen to me," said Anna, "You will be fine. Snakes let you know they are there, and you just slowly walk away. Easy, breezy."

D. and Sean looked at each other and smiled. There was a meeting of stinker minds at work, not unlike her boys when they were up to something.

"No sucking though," said D.

"Ya, no sucking," echoed Sean.

Annoyed by their intrusion, Anna continued... "Yes, no sucking the poison from the wound."

---

26 The Dinwoody Formation is Early Triassic (Scythian) in age. It is overlain conformably in many sections by the Thaynes Formation and often overlies the Phosphoria Formation. (Dinwoody) (Paull & Paull, 1993)

"Oh yes, I had heard this when I attended my field camp as an undergrad," said Alex. "I don't think anyone said what to actually do instead… or did they? Perhaps I didn't listen well enough?"

"Well," said Anna, *"You get them to calm down and sit still. Excitement causes the heart rate to increase, and the venom to circulate more quickly. Gently slow the blood flow between the wound and the heart."*[27]

Anna touched a spot-on Alex's calf. "If the bite is here, where it most likely would occur, you have to get between the heart and the wound. So, what would you do if the bite were… say here, for example?" asked Anna.

"Um, I'd press here?" He demonstrated by pushing on the artery above the bite.

"Yes, that would work, but how long will you be able to apply light pressure there?"

"Um, good point. What should I do then?" asked Alex.

"You can have someone apply pressure, or you can fashion a tourniquet with a shirt, bandana, sock, shoelace… but not too tight. If it is too restricting, the person might lose enough flow to their leg to have it amputated."

"Shit!" said Alex. "That would suck. I've had first aid and CPR training, but I don't remember it including a snake bite response. This is helpful."

"Yes," continued Anna, "… so the idea is to keep them calm and to slow the flow of the venom, especially to the heart. You do this until the chopper arrives. Running, walking, screaming, crying, etc., will only escalate the anxiety and circulate the venom more efficiently."

---

27   The author is not a medical professional. This advice is based on years of field medical training and should not be seen as a procedural method. Consult an emergency medical expert for more information.

"How does the chopper know to come if I am staying with the person and keeping them calm?"

"Good question," said Anna. "That's one reason they work as partners in the field. You leave them with their field partner or someone else, while you go to the van to radio for help. Your vans have CB radios, don't they?"

"Oh yes, duh. I knew that."

"Of course, you did. You just needed to talk it through. Now you know. The odds of having someone suffer a bite are minimal, especially when students are aware and know to watch for them. It will be just fine," said Anna.

Sean marveled at Annie's ability to calm Alex's nerves and instill confidence. She seemed to be a gifted mentor for others. He watched her carefully as she showed Alex how to make a tourniquet with her bandana and then encouraged him to practice the technique on her.

He couldn't help but note too that D. was also watching them. He looked particularly proud of his partner.

Sean wondered if D. was attracted to Annie too. His facial expression would suggest affection as well as pride. *Who could blame him? She's amazing,* thought Sean.

"They shouldn't ever get bit on the face," added Anna, "Tell the students to always step back and look under the edge of rock ledges before taking measurements. This is smarter than stooping over and then getting a surprise, like a bite on the hand or face."

"Wow, I never would have thought of that Anna," said Alex. "You sure know what you're doing."

"No, I just had to learn the hard way. I was on a rock unit in my first year and wasn't careful enough. When I approached a section where the rocks at eye level contained a bush, I didn't think to check the bush for a snake."

"Oh, my God! Did you get bit?"

"No, but darn close. The bush rattled, or rather, the rattler rattled in the bush, right in front of my face, and I leaped back to get away. The ledge I was standing on was only about a foot wide. I fell three feet down and back and landed on a sharp rock. My butt was bruised for the rest of the camp."

"Yes, I remember that," said D., "She is damned lucky it wasn't her head. She would have been dead. Instead, it was just a deep bruise, probably a bone bruise. It looked painful for sure."

"What? She allowed ya ta look?" asked Sean.

"Her? Nah, you wouldn't catch her naked in a Japanese bathhouse. Ha-ha. She's very modest in that respect."

"Ah, good to know, D.," snickered Sean. "We probably should cancel the skinny-dipping party we had planned later, huh Alex?"

Everyone laughed, except Anna. She didn't find the discussion too funny. Her prudish nature was a source of embarrassment. Growing up in a house with a grandfather who crept on her all the time made her seek to hide when changing clothes, bathing, and such. It was not something she shared widely, and it annoyed her that D. had noted it and then shared it with others.

Just before the pair left the room, Anna slipped a folder to Alex and whispered, "I will need this back, but you may use it for the first project. You'll need to be ahead of your students. I advise you to make your own map but have this one so you may confidently answer questions if you haven't already covered an area before your students."

"Thank you, Anna. I appreciate the leg up."

"Oh Anna," said Sean, "D. tells me ya know where a particular fossil is located in the second mapping area?"

"I sure do," responded Anna. "I wasn't the first to find it, but apparently I was the first to demand that other instructors know about it and help to protect it for future camps."

"Could ya locate it for me on the map, so I may go and find it too?"

"Certainly, I'd be more than happy," said Anna as she pulled out a folder containing her map of the area.

Anna was sitting on the second bunk with the camp's boxes of maps and materials. "It's in the *Jurassic Morrison Formation*[28] on this contour," she said, as she pointed on the map and lowered her head and shoulders over the map for a better look… "right there next to this fault zone."

Sean sat next to her on the bed so he could look at the map with her. He slid his shoulder and arm against hers as both moved in for a closer look.

She paused for a second and gulped. He smelled of fresh rain and his closeness felt…like…

"… and, you can't miss it…" she paused briefly… "if you get on this contour in the fault zone, here, and follow it to the northwest."

"I see," he said, turning his face toward her to look in her eyes. "That's awesome… Annie" … pause… "Thanks."

D. and Alex both noted their familiarity and glanced at each other in agreement.

"Uh, you guys have a great rest of your day, okay?" said D., hinting that they needed to leave so he could get back to grading.

"I guess we will see ya guys in the cafeteria tomorrow?"

"We'll be there," said D, standing up to see them out.

Sean stood in the doorway, while D. held the doorknob.

"Thank ya both… Annie."

She stood too, briefly, and awkwardly waved as he exited the room.

D. closed the door, "Well, that guy is a bit forward, isn't he?"

"Huh? What do you mean?"

---

28   The Jurassic Morrison Formation is widely known for the presence of vertebrate fossils, particularly dinosaur bones. (Morrison) (Zen, 1983)

"I mean, calling you Annie, and sitting on top of you like that. What the hell, Anna? He acts like he's been your friend for years. Doesn't that seem weird to you?"

Anna was looking out the window and not really listening to D. "Huh? What?"

"Never mind," he sighed as he sat back down to grade again.

The next day, everyone stayed close to the dorms. Anna did her laundry and offered to do Adam's as well. She couldn't help it. It was the mother in her, and Adam was an overgrown child who seemed to enjoy being mothered, especially by Anna.

While Anna sat in the laundry room reading, a couple of women from Sean's camp entered the room to get their laundry started.

"Are you a student here at the camp?" asked one girl.

Anna laughed, "No, I am a professor."

"Really?" asked the second girl.

"You look too young to be an instructor."

"Why, thank you," said Anna. "I'll take that compliment."

"What school are you from?" queried Anna.

"Oh, we are with the Cal State group."

"Really? So, you are starting your projects tomorrow then? How exciting for you. What's your instructor like?"

"Oh, he is so handsome, isn't he?" said the first girl.

"Oh, not that again," said the second girl. "He's really nothing special."

"Well, of course, you'd say that—you're married."

"Oh," said Anna. "You are married? Do you have any children?"

"No, my husband and I don't want children."

"Wow, I can't imagine my life without my boys," said Anna sadly.

"Wow! You don't look like you'd have kids either!"

Anna smiled and changed the subject, "How do you guys feel about beginning your project tomorrow?"

"Kind of scared here," said one girl.

"Me too. Just a little," said the other.

"Oh, my goodness, don't be scared," said Anna, "This is going to be an amazing experience. Just stay focused and know that hundreds of other geology students have walked those same ridges. You're going to have a terrific time."

For the next hour or so, the women got to know one another, and Anna offered to help them if needed, although without supplying answers. It was nice to talk to other women, and Anna felt inspired and hopeful by the number of women in the California contingent.

Chapter 5—The Field Experience

Please see the appendix for a section detailing the field experience.

Sean was excited to go to the first mapping project site. It was an area with sedimentary rocks that had been folded during a mountain-building event. The rock layers were stacked one on top of the other, making the folding and faulting obvious to the novice. It was a relatively easy first field experience and was needed to help build confidence.

[29]*Sedimentary terrain is the best for teaching basic mapping principles, like how to use the essential tools of the science. The locale also provided an opportunity for instruction in field safety when working in a high desert environment filled with rattlesnakes and cactus spines. The first project would provide a framework of knowledge for all projects to follow.*

Complex igneous and metamorphic[30] projects are more rugged to traverse and far more complicated to identify and map. These projects are at the end of the camp experience because they build on all other knowledge and skills.

Anna and Adam were traveling to a nearby ranch where metamorphic rocks were exposed.

---

29   Sedimentary terrain is an area of rocks that have been laid down in layers, one on top of the other, in a series of depositional sequences. The rocks are layered, like pancakes and are typically easy to differentiate from one another.

30   Igneous terrain includes volcanic and plutonic rocks which have formed from a molten state. These rocks intrude into other rock types from magma below the surface and also cover other rocks as lava flows on the surface. Metamorphic terrain can be any pre-existing rocks that have undergone change from heat and pressure.

It would be a more significant challenge for students to map because the linear features were less noticeable. Mapping trends and recognizing metamorphic minerals would present a higher level of geologic reasoning to put it all together.

Sean's students arrived at the first mapping project and were instructed in team safety, the use of basic field mapping tools, and about the types of snakes they would encounter. They learned proper behavior in dealing with high desert terrain, and the rules of etiquette when hiking on someone else's land.

Even though local ranchers were allowed to graze their cattle in the areas, the land belonged to the government, and permission was needed to enter BLM—Bureau of Land Management - areas.

The students traveled in teams of two for safety and began their trek into the unknown. Alex and Sean walked next to the students at first and then separated as the teams spread out.

As the week went on, there was little time for the new friends to interact. Their two camps were in different places, and they arrived and left at different times. They seemed to pass each other in the cafeteria and wearily in the hallways. The hotter days led to greater exhaustion and long hours with the students in the evenings.

Anna stayed up as long as the students were working, and she sometimes collapsed into the bed without showering or changing. She did change her socks each day, as taking care of her feet had always been a priority. Just as in the military, a field geologist's feet were essential to the mission.

On the last day of the week of mapping, Sean looked for a cool area to take a break and eat a bite. He preferred a shaded glen, but such locales were at a premium in this part of the Rocky Mountains. If he could find any shade which included a view of snow-capped peaks of a mountain range, so much the better.

As he sat there enjoying the banana from his lunch bag and a few sips of water from his water bottle, his thoughts were of Annie and the walk home on the first night they met. He also pondered his observations of her since they first met.

Sean had always admired mothers, and Annie's mothering nature conjured an image of the Madonna and Child, which was particularly inspiring to him. Annie was a Madonna in his eyes—an angelic being that mothered and cared for others.

He reflected on the one evening in the dorm common area, when he stood and watched her working with her students and his. She looked dirty and tired but stood or knelt next to each student with a question. Her face beamed with pride when students were able to gain clarity or confidence. Sean didn't even mind that she helped his students as well. He trusted her judgment. For whatever reason, he trusted her implicitly.

At this point in a mapping day, Sean would usually pull out his field journal and write a few personal notes of reflection, a tradition that he began long ago in his graduate years at *Otago University in New Zealand*.[31] On this morning, however, he couldn't stop thinking of her, of "Annie." He breathed in deeply and sighed, Ah Sean, she's... The words weren't needed. He closed his eyes and leaned against the cool shaded side of the rocks, thinking, I hope I see her again this evening at the Beaverhead. He knew that if reported tradition held, the camp faculty should be there that evening, as both camps were finishing a week-long project, and faculty needed to retreat for a beer and conversation.

After a long day in the field, Anna drove the hot, dry, dusty, and silent road back to campus. She could see all the exhausted students in the rear-view mirror, mouths hanging open, sleeping, and sprawling lifeless bodies across the seats.

---

31 University of Otago, New Zealand, was and still is one of the highest ranked universities in graduate studies in geology. The use of this college is fictional and is not meant to represent any faculty, students, or programs past or present.

Adam was in the very back with his boots sticking up above the back of the seat directly in front of him. The bench of the 1977 Ford, fifteen-passenger van, was the perfect length for his short stature. He was no doubt the one she heard snoring, as well.

A second van followed, driven by John,[32] the teaching assistant (T.A.). MSU's T.A. was a first-year grad student, so his duties included driving, security, minimal grading, and assisting as needed.

By comparison, Alex was a Ph.D. student and had duties more expected of a faculty member.

John was fondly referred to as "Big John" because there was a student who was also named John, an older man, who complained all the time and had disgusting personal habits. So, everyone differentiated the two by calling them *"Big John" and "Little John."*[33]

Big John often complained about having to drive the van with Little John, because Little John was continually releasing noxious gases. Older vehicles of this size lacked windows that rolled up and down, but instead pushed out and pulled in. The windows were usually fully extended, regardless of the outside temperatures, because of Little John's medical problem with flatulence.

This was also the reason that Adam rode in the van with Anna. He was grossed out by the guy and was free to sleep while MOM was at the wheel.

Anna had the pleasure of *Ben's*[34] company as he sat up front, navigating, which was his self-designated position. Ben was a senior

---

32   John, "Big John," is the MSU teaching assistant, TA. He was a first-year graduate student and his job was to drive and help out as directed. Fictional character, not representing any living person past or present.

33   Little John, an older undergraduate student with MSU and known for his excessive flatulence (farting). Fictional character loosely based on the author's experiences with young men and flatulence.

34   Ben, senior geology student at MSU who rode with Anna. Fictional character not mean to represent any person past or person.

and only needed this camp to finish his requirements. He adored Dr. Moore—Anna—and loved being her shotgun for the trips to and from the field. He also fancied himself to be the one who looked out for Dr. D., always carrying extra water for him in the field and fetching him a cup of coffee when on road trips.

Dr. D. didn't bring a backpack or water bottle to the field. He just wore a fanny pack for his keys and wallet. Students would always offer him water, so he never had to worry. He capitalized on his helpless persona to make sure he was taken care of.

Ben noted storm clouds closing in from the southwest and warned Dr. Moore that she had better get them out of the field before it hit.

In that part of the Rockies, afternoon thunderstorms—often violent—were an almost daily occurrence. In the high desert, a layer of fine clay accumulates on the surface of the dirt fields and roads in the mapping areas. This thin layer, when wet, becomes very slick and creates a hazard for skidding off the road or getting 'stuck in the mud,' with no escape until it dries.

They had been through a similar experience their first week of the camp when Anna was driving in slick muddy ruts trying to not get stuck. Even though it had rained, she had been successful, but not without drama and backseat driving from everyone in the van. If the stress of being told how to drive by a bunch of boys and men wasn't bad enough, she also had managed to run over a poor little chipmunk who had fallen into a rut in front of her.

Ben spotted the poor little thing just in time for Anna to see it scampering frantically and trying to climb the steep walls.

Terrified for his safety, she gently tapped the brakes to slow down enough to allow the little guy to escape. To Anna's horror, the van went into a slide, and the forward momentum took the van's front right tire right over the poor little thing. She was devastated and began to cry.

Everyone, including Ben, started shouting and laughing, making fun of Anna for deliberately murdering the poor little creature.

She did manage to get the van out of the field and onto pavement though before the storm cloud arrived to deliver an additional downpour.

Later, after all the students were off the van, Adam touched her arm and said sweetly, "Hey, I'm sorry about that. I know how much that must have upset you. It happened so fast; I'm sure he didn't suffer."

Anna was grateful for his tenderness and acknowledgment of her distress. He wasn't a complete jerk, but he enjoyed picking on her. His teasing was usually not directly in front of the students.

Jacob,[35] an older student in the camp, seemed to enjoy degrading the female professor. "How many will you hit today, teach?" he asked as he climbed onto the van each morning.

Adam would chuckle to himself when he heard Jacob tease Anna, to which she would shoot a disapproving glare in his general direction.

She forgave Adam though, for chuckling, as everyone did because he was just so darned cute.

Jacob, on the other hand…? Well, dealing with him required a level of professionalism that was sometimes difficult to muster.

Anna's reputation, as a 'murderer' of small creatures, did not end with the poor little chipmunk. Each morning on their drive from the camp area to the mapping areas, which usually meant leaving one dirt road to get on the highway and then exiting onto another dirt road; a vast community of high prairie gophers, smaller than prairie dogs, would line up alongside the route and stand facing the sun—east in the mornings and west in the afternoons.

---

35 Jacob, an older student in the camp and known for his acerbic responses and disrespect for women. Fictional character not meant to represent a specific person, living or dead.

From this lined-up position, with gophers on either side of the roadway, they would engage in an insane kamikaze game of "Gopher "*Red rover*",[36]... *will the gopher come over.*"

Hundreds of them would cross the road at the same time, running from the line facing the sun, to the opposite side to cheer on those crossing behind them.

Anna had no choice but to run over them. "Bump, bump, bump, bump, thud, crunch... bump..." Each one counted as points by the students. Both vans cheered, all the while accompanied by loud music, and laughing and shouting of the points accumulated. Thankfully, this morning ritual lasted for only the short time they traveled on the pavement.

The dirt roads presented different challenges, like washboard ribbing, grooves, and ruts, as well as the occasional snake. Anna could avoid the snakes. She would never go out of her way to kill any creature, not even a snake.

The experience of having to mow down gophers was upsetting to Anna, who had the year before put the van in a slide over a butterfly, a story that Adam enjoyed retelling repeatedly. Every so often, Ben would feel sorry for her, as she graciously endured the relentless teasing. "Hey guys, she grades your maps," he would say.

Anna just looked forward and tried to remain professional and professorial as she ignored their teasing. *MEN! BOYS!* She would think to herself. There were no females in Anna's van. She wondered to herself if a few more female, geology students wouldn't be a good thing for the program.

Even though most of the camp comprised males, there were two young women in the camp who came together from a school

---

36 Red Rover, Red Rover...a popular children's game in the 1930's where children form opposing lines, where one team holds hands or lock arms and asks the other team's members to one at a time try to break the line. If they are not successful, then they must join the line and continue to taunt the others to come one at a time.

in the Northeast. They always rode in Big John's van. Both seemed very shy and sat on the back bench together. Rumor had it they were both lesbians. In that time, though, there was a "mind your own business" unspoken rule in academia.

Anna didn't really care but had sort of wondered about them one day in the showers when she noted they liked to share a stall. Being a little naïve, Anna at first thought, *Oh look, they are trying to conserve water. That is environmentally efficient of them.* That was the first thought. The second one made her blush a little. *Oh well. To each her own.*

Sean and Anna's camp students spilled out of their vans at almost the same time that afternoon. Both camps looked tired, dirty, and in need of food and rest.

Anna spotted Sean standing inside the door of his camp's van. Being from New Zealand, he called the van a *truck*, which Anna found very interesting. She walked his way when Adam yelled to her and said, "Tell him we'll see him at the Beaverhead tonight." Anna nodded and continued to walk in Sean's direction.

He was wearing his field hat and looked like he had gotten some sun that week. Not burned, but he certainly looked darker than the first day she saw him. The deeper tan and dirt only accentuated his thigh and calf muscles.

As he closed the door, he saw Anna standing there with her field hat on and looking very dirty, hot, and darker too from the June sun.

"Annie?" he said excitedly. "Where did ya come from?"

She knew he was just joking and said, "Adam said to tell you we'd see you at the Beaverhead this evening. You are going?"

Sean leaned his head back on his shoulders and sighed in a teasing voice. "Oh, I guess so."

She couldn't see his eyes because he was wearing sunglasses, but she imagined his eyes were smiling.

After a momentary pause to finish collecting his things, he continued, "You bet. I wouldn't miss it after the week we've had. May I escort ya?"

Anna, to her surprise and with no reservation, said, "Sure, I'd love that."

"Be at yer door at 7:00 then. Okay, Annie?" he said as he walked in the direction of the cafeteria.

Anna was so excited to know he was going to be there, AND, feeling a little flustered that he was going to expect her to be ready at 7:00 p.m., skipped dinner to go straight to the shower before the students could drain all the warm water. She was giddy like a schoolgirl on her first date, singing on her way to and from the shower.

Sean had the same idea. He rushed through dinner and back to the dorm to also get clean and dapper for the evening. He was so excited to be with the prettiest geologist in town.

"Where are you going in such a hurry?" queried Alex, as he noted Sean's quickness to get his towel and toiletries.

"I am escorting the lovely Dr. Moore to the Beaverhead this evening," Sean said in a sing-song voice.

Alex laughed, "I'm headed there too, a little later."

"See ya there!" shouted Sean as he entered the shower room.

Chapter 6—The Dance

At precisely 7:00 p.m., Sean arrived and stood in the doorway, looking at her for a second before knocking to let her know he was there. He found himself charmed by the cute way she was spritzing herself. She was still primping and looking at herself in a hand mirror she had just then unpacked. It had taken her all of a month to pull it out of the bag.

Robert, Anna's husband, had always complimented her on being a low maintenance female and would have teased her about trying to improve on her appearance.

She didn't care. For the first time in her life, she felt pretty and desirable. It was such a new experience, and she loved it.

To Sean, Annie was beautiful just the way she was, tanned, slim, muscular... and her beautiful hazel-blue eyes.

She had gorgeous eyes. Her sweetness radiated from her face and everyone in the room knew she was a kind and generous person.

"Wow, you look nice," he said as he gently knocked on her door.

She looked shyly at the floor and was embarrassed that she had allowed herself to be so transparent in her vanity, "Oh, thank you." She quickly put the mirror out of sight and collected her ID and cash, which she skillfully slid discreetly into her cleavage.

Sean waited by the door, careful not to enter the room, ever mindful that Annie was a "Southern lady." He didn't know very many Southern women, but being a world traveler, he had learned over the years that there were different social norms for different regions of most countries, and the South seemed to have a different set of rules for gentlemen than the West Coast. He seemed to recall that if a woman was in her chamber alone, it was not proper to enter without being invited.

As Anna closed the door to her room, Sean held out the crook of his arm and said, with a decidedly Southern drawl, "Ya ready, gorgeous?"

To which she smiled widely and gladly accepted. She was charmed by his playful attempt at impersonating a Southern gentleman and looped her arm inside of his.

As they walked outside and down the steps of the dorm, some of Anna's students were sitting on the steps. They immediately started with the catcalls and whistling because they knew it would embarrass her.

"Who's your boyfriend, Anna?"

"Does your husband know?"

Sean chuckled, and Anna just ignored them.

As they walked away, Sean wondered if the teasing by her students would bother her. "Are ya okay? That didn't bother ya, did it?"

Anna nervously chuckled, "No, they tease me all the time about something."

At that moment, she didn't feel they were doing anything wrong. She was enjoying a pleasant walk with a new gentleman friend, and they were going to go have a beer after a long week of work. It felt nice to be treated like a lady. Anna wasn't aware of it yet, but she was smitten.

When they arrived at the saloon, Adam was already there, and had three empty longneck bottles in front of him. He hadn't even bothered to shower or have dinner. He saw them approaching and stood up to motion them to come to the table he had reserved—first come, first served, and he was first. They quickly approached and sat down as the barmaid brought frosted glasses and longnecks to the table.

Adam had ordered the drinks as he saw them walking toward the saloon from across the street.

Both Sean and Anna followed tradition and poured their cold ones into frozen mugs and moaned in delight as they quenched their thirst.

Anna lowered her mug and a mustache of froth remained. She giggled and quickly wiped it from her lip with the back of her hand, just as Adam handed her a napkin.

Sean found himself imagining his kissing her and removing it instead with his tongue. Her lips were so … soft and moist, despite the elements. He laughed at the scene of Alex standing up and reaching down the table to help her and wondered if Adam also wished he could have kissed her. *Wow, I may be jealous,* thought Sean. *She's a lady and I shouldn't be having such thoughts, Right? Oh Boy, I may be in trouble.*

As the evening progressed, other professors entered, and soon the saloon was full of chatter, music, pool balls clicking and bottles opening.

Adam had selected his favorite Patsy Cline album and was singing to himself.

Sean and Anna sat together, talking, and laughing and sharing stories of their week in the field with their students. It was such a wonderful evening, and Anna was feeling tipsy from drinking without having had dinner.

Sean walked to the bar and ordered some peanuts and more beer, while Anna excused herself to go to the ladies' room.

Being one of the few women in the place that evening, she was grateful that there was no wait. She swung open the stall door with a loud bang, not bothering to close it, and barely got her panties down in time. She started laughing softly... giggling to herself. She was truly having a great time.

As she walked past the long bar to return to her table, she felt an enormous hand grab her arm and pull her around. Before she had an opportunity to process what was happening, she was forced toward a large man's chest so quickly that she couldn't even see who he was.

He was very hard all over, and Anna felt her joy leave her, to be replaced by fear. *What on earth is going on?* She wondered.

The large man pulled her along like a rag doll to the dance floor, where she got the first glimpse of his face. It was that strange guy, Steve, from the other southern camp.

What is a student doing here? Don't they have projects due tomorrow too?

He seemed to be drunk and was trying to kiss her.

She put her elbows on his chest and blocked his kisses and looked at the table where she'd been sitting. Sean was not visible, and Adam was sneaking out the side door.

Panic suddenly came over her, so she began pushing with all her might against his chest.

He only pulled her tighter and took one of his huge hands and pulled her hips into his. She could feel what she assumed was his manhood, but he didn't seem to be turned on, thank goodness.

After what seemed like an eternity, Anna heard Sean's voice tell Steve that he was cutting in.

Steve seemed to just ignore Sean.

Anna was so scared. How on earth was she to get away from him? Should she scream? Would anyone hear her?

She then heard Sean say in an assertive tone, "Yer dancing with my date."

Steve reluctantly let her go, and Sean took over the dance. Anna was so relieved and was also humiliated by the entire experience.

"Why did ya allow him to treat ya that way?" asked Sean. He was surprised to see a woman who wouldn't deck a man for making such a move.

Shocked, Anna said, "What? I didn't let him do that."

Anna, however, was accustomed to having a male address the improper behavior of another man. It was expected that a man would step up and take care of that sort of situation.

Sean could feel her trembling and realized that the experience had genuinely frightened her. He thought to himself, *Surely; she has had to deal with this kind of stuff in the past... surely?* He had no idea that Anna had never had such an experience.

Being married since 20, she hadn't been in such situations before, at least not without her husband or another man to step in and take care of the interaction. She had faced down cowboys, intent on taking a female student home, and pretended to be the date of her students to diffuse a potential problem, but she had never had to defend herself before. Being a mama bear protecting her kids was a different dynamic than being sexually assaulted on a public dance floor.

Anna had never realized that she was attractive. Her husband had always told her she wasn't good enough—a mere "six" on a scale of one to ten. She knew she looked okay and cleaned up nicely, but it really wasn't until Sean that she felt pretty.

Even though Adam had left the saloon, his album was still playing.

Anna was now with Sean, which felt very safe and comfortable. Her anxiety and fear left as they moved together to the slow rhythm of the music. She started singing along, and Sean noted, "You have a nice voice."

Her face rested on his chest while she relaxed and placed her hands on his broad, muscular shoulders. Their bodies became closer as she moved her hands from his shoulders to around his torso.

For a few minutes, she needed to feel safe again, and being close to Sean took all her fear away. She was hugging him, and it felt right for them both. Her hips were gently against him, and she could feel him become harder.

Sean snickered slightly and pulled his pelvis away for a moment and said, "Oops."

Anna found herself smiling and giggling softly, "That's okay. It happens sometimes." She was trying to make light of it, so he wouldn't feel embarrassed. She assumed a gentleman like him would feel that way.

Meanwhile, Sean was understandably aroused as he felt Anna's slim, muscular body. As they swayed to the music, her breasts pushed into his chest and her hips fit perfectly into his. With her slender arm around his waist and her other hand in his, they were immersed in the safety of their mutual space. Neither wanted the dance—that moment—to end. This feeling was only slightly tempered by the intense, jealous stare of the guy Steve, who glared at them from the bar.

They walked home arm in arm in the same manner they had left.

Sean walked her to her dorm room door to make sure she was safely inside. He nervously said goodnight, also wishing he could stay.

Anna didn't want him to go, but it would not have been proper for him to stay. She shyly thanked him for a lovely evening and closed the door.

He walked in the opposite direction toward his dorm area but wished he could have held her all night long.

Anna fell against the door after it closed and sighed, "Oh my goodness, Lord. I think I'm in love."

She knew she would barely be able to sleep as her mind swirled. Praying the rosary always took her mind from trials and troubles of the world, bringing peace and the ability to sleep. So, she picked it up from the shelf over the desk and fell onto her bunk saying,

"Praise You, Lord for protecting me from that beastly man, and for the beautiful experience of being treated like a lady. Thank You too, Lord, for bringing this special man into my life. Please forgive me too for having carnal thoughts, Amen."

She continued to pray for God's guidance and forgiveness as a married woman, and especially for turning on a married man. How could what she felt be even remotely sinful? It seemed so right.

Sean lay in his bed and tried to sleep, but he found it very difficult to get the experience with Annie out of his mind. She seemed such an enigma to him. He could still smell the hint of jasmine from her hair, from where her head had rested on his chest. The scent of her body mixed with jasmine was absolutely intoxicating. Eventually, he was able to drift off as he replayed the music and the dance over and over in his head.

Chapter 7—Sexism in Science

Adam and Anna spent the next morning—a Saturday—in his dorm room, silently collecting student projects, which were all due no later than noon that day. The tension from the night before was clearly present between them, but neither mentioned the experience out loud.

Anna couldn't help but feel betrayed by her dear friend and teaching partner. How could he have left her like that? A man should have stepped in to protect her from the evil, pushy, Neanderthal student, especially when Adam acknowledged he was of problematic character. What a coward! Anna thought to herself. He ran the minute he saw trouble. She found herself questioning his loyalty and friendship.

Anna finished her part of the grading of the field notebooks and lay down on the twin bed on the opposite side of the dorm room, where she began reading a journal article about the Yellowstone volcanic complex. She was particularly interested in caldera sequences and the banded igneous complex, located some eighteen miles north as the crow flies, known as the Stillwater. Both places were intriguing to her, but she had only visited Yellowstone.

During the mid-term part of the field camp, she and Adam took students on trips through Yellowstone, the Tetons, and also to Glacier National Park, but they never seemed to have time for the mining district in the Beartooth Mountains. It was just too far out of their way.

When Anna was a little girl, she was fascinated by the eruptions of Kilauea in Hawaii. Her love of volcanoes led her to igneous and metamorphic rocks. Mineralogy quickly became one of her favorite classes because of the forensic nature of identifying them and determining the compositions and provenance of the rocks containing them. Even sedimentary rocks were more interesting when trying to discover the origins of the minerals making up the rocks.

Anna was limited in her graduate studies because the school's research focus was on petroleum exploration. She had always been interested in igneous petrology and geochemistry but was stuck with geophysics, which she loved, as well as petroleum geology and sedimentary petrology. If there were no professors with funding in these areas of interest, then she would have to find her own way to afford the research. This was not a possibility for someone without a Ph.D. at that given time.

Her mentor, Dr. Ronald J. Milner, had worked in the petroleum industry and had many contacts who were willing to provide all the data needed for a graduate student to use. A local company offered to have someone characterize a reservoir where all indicators pointed to prolific gas production, but the drilling had yielded mostly dry holes. It was an intriguing problem, and one that Anna found compelling.

It was a win-win for the company, the department, and for graduate students, who had to teach to earn their stipends, and still required research materials and funding.

Anna was an excellent student and enjoyed the teaching and research aspects of her studies, regardless of the area of focus. She produced an algorithm for determining the amount of clays in the subsurface units and could map the porosity vs. rock thickness and clay content.

Clays can fill pore spaces and keep them from filling with hydrocarbons—occlusion. [37]

Her research was pre-*GIS*[38] and included using layers of data, all overlain, to produce a final map which showed sand thickness, clay distribution, porosity, and structural features. Her process would help the company predict more efficiently where to drill. Before she graduated, she presented this method at a national conference for petroleum and sedimentary geologists.

The men who were present responded with, "So you mapped dirt?"

This was precisely the thing she had learned to battle as an undergrad and as a graduate student. She had developed a meaningful method for characterizing a reservoir with complex *diagenesis,*[39] which was the reason for the non-uniform nature of drilling results. If they could better predict porosity barriers, with respect to porous sands, they could select a site for drilling more efficiently.

While there were some men in the profession who valued female peers, there were far more who wanted to pinch a woman's butt and talk down to her. Women like Anna learned to roll with those comments and continue as though nothing had ever been said. She learned to pick her battles carefully.

Anna was a perpetual student of geology and continued to be a self-directed learner beyond her degrees. Teaching was one outlet that allowed her to continue to grow in knowledge and skills, particularly in igneous and metamorphic studies.

---

37 Occlusion of porosity can be from cementation by a wide variety of minerals or specifically from the mechanical infiltration of clays in sedimentary diagenetic processes. Diagenesis is the process that all sediments and rocks undergo from deposition to eventual uplift – exposure at the surface.

38 GIS, Geographic Information System, used to map, with the help of Global Positioning System (GPS), the exact position of features on the earth's surface.

39 All mechanical and geochemical changes that occur in a rock from deposition through uplift.

As she lay there on the extra bunk in D. 's room, reading an article about magma generation, production of ash eruptions, associated ash flows, and *ignimbrites*, [40]Adam looked in her direction and asked, "What has you so involved over there?"

"It's that journal article from Volcanology. The one I got in the mail before we left. I haven't had a chance to read it. It's talking about the geochemical correlation of the ignimbrites across the hotspot track. There is also a theory of magma generation... it's an excellent article."

Adam chuckled to himself, "Oh, really? Who's the author?"

"Um, S.M. Anderson," she responded. "I find the use of geochemical techniques in volcanic stratigraphy to be fascinating. There is so much we can discern about the evolution of magmas from minerals in the rhyolite flows. Wish I could go back to school and do some work with zircons."

"Yes, zircons are pretty good for telling us about the geochemistry of any rock that they end up in, I'd say, especially for determining provenance," said D.

"Oh yes," said Anna, "Zircons were a blessing for me when I was doing my Ph.D. research...I bet they will use the Pb isotopes too, to determine magma evolution."

"Ah, well, the guy to ask about that is your pal, Sean. That seems to be his area of expertise."

Adam sat across the room, clicking a pencil against his teeth as he read through a student's paper, smiling to himself.

Anna looked at him and asked, "What are you smiling about?"

He marked the report in front of him and turned the page without responding.

She wondered what he found so funny but continued to read. Her feet were away from the door, and she was positioned so that

---

40   Ignimbrites are igneous rock derived from fine, pyroclastic pieces of volcanic rock and ash, usually from pyroclastic flows

someone standing in the doorway could see clearly that she was reading a journal article. A few moments later, she sensed someone doing just that, standing in the doorway. She looked upside down at the open door. And who did she see?

Adam jumped to his feet and said, "Hi, there, what are you up to today?"

"Just taking a break from grading," said Sean.

Anna collected herself from the bed and laid the article upside down and open on the pillow, to not lose her place. She stood awkwardly while the two men talked. After a few moments of pleasantries, Sean pointed to Anna's journal and said, "Whatcha reading? Is that an article on Yellowstone?"

Surprised that he had noted her article, she picked it up and said, "Yes, I was just reading here about the correlation of ignimbrites along the hotspot track which begins in Idaho. I would love to do this kind of work. I've done a lot of correlation studies in sedimentary terrains and find *volcanic geochronology*[41] fascinating."

Adam interrupted, "Yes, that is all she has talked about. She has a thing for igneous rocks, especially ignimbrites."

Sean answered Adam, "Well, I do too. We seem to have that in common," as he looked at Anna, who was shyly looking away. Sean then asked Anna, "So who wrote the article? Do ya know the author?"

"S.M. Anderson?"

"So, ya know this S.M. Anderson, do ya?" Sean asked.

Adam giggled and went back to pecking his teeth with the pencil and grading.

---

41   Volcanic Geochronology is the science of determining the age and correlation of strata in volcanic terrain. The use of radioactive isotopes, paleomagnetism (the ancient alignment of metallic minerals with that of the earth's magnetic field), and specific stable isotope ratios of fluids found in inclusions within minerals within volcanic layers.

Anna responded to Sean's query, "No, I've never met him or her, but would love to one day, perhaps at a conference?"

Sean smiled and said, "Well, he's a good friend of mine, I might be able to arrange something."

D. giggled to himself as he continued to grade.

"Wow, that would be great," she said.

Sean then gladly regaled her on his knowledge of the geochemical methods being used in the correlation studies.

Anna was so impressed. *Wow! He is brilliant*, she thought.

After about half an hour of Yellowstone discussion, Sean turned to Adam and said, "Well, I need to get back to grading, I think… I just wanted to stop by and say hi."

Before leaving, he turned again to Anna and said, "Oh, but before I forget, what are ya doing this evening?"

Surprised that he asked her in front of Adam, she blurted out, "I think I'll be here grading, why?"

"There's a special event tonight that I'm sure you'd love to see. I could take ya?"

Anna was hesitant after what had happened the evening before. She didn't want him to think she was a loose woman or something. What exactly were his intentions? She felt oddly giddy and anxious by his invitation. After all, he saved her from that guy Steve.

She found she was attracted to the chivalrous acts of this very, very handsome knight from New Zealand. It was a great turn-on to have such an attractive and well-mannered man come to her aid. Should she go with him? She couldn't think about it right then and especially with Adam listening. What would he think of her?

She finally spoke and reluctantly declined. "I think I just need to get this grading done."

Sean and Adam exchanged glances and Adam chimed in, "Ah, go on Anna. I'll take care of it. You work very hard. It's okay to take a break."

"See there, Annie, you can go," smiled Sean. "It's settled then, I'll pick ya up at 8:00 p.m.?"

The two shook hands. His hand was rough, slender, large, and warm.

Anna felt like she was genuinely shaking hands with a friend. Not a new friend, but an old and dear friend. Even his scent seemed familiar. Uncomfortable with the new feelings, she blushed as he held their shake a few seconds longer.

After Sean left the room, Adam began giggling to himself.

Anna, feeling mildly annoyed with him, said, "What the heck are you giggling about? And, what was that all about? You know I'm married. You know he's married. Why would you even suggest that I go out with him?!"

Adam, feeling wounded by her chastisement, said, "I'm sure he has honorable intentions. He's a very nice fellow. I like Sean Michael Anderson."

He then picked up the article Anna had been reading and handed it to her. "You really don't know who he is, do you?"

Anna, confused, said, "Who are you talking about?" Then it hit her, "S.M. Anderson?!!! Is Sean...?!" Before Anna could clobber him with the journal, Adam laughed and ran out of the room. She was left standing there feeling stupid and dazed.

What the hell? Really?! No kidding? The guy she was dancing with last night was THE S.M. Anderson! Her Knight from New Zealand was THE S.M. ANDERSON? The man with the hard-on while they were dancing was the same guy who wrote the premier field guide on Yellowstone.

No, surely it can't be? Can it? Oh, Adam is really in trouble this time. Not only did he abandon me when Rollie Fingers was assaulting me on the dance floor, but he also knew who Sean was all along. Wait? They were both in on it!

She smiled and thought to herself; *They are a pair of stinkers—both.*

After a short time, Adam returned to his grading.

Anna ignored him and continued her work. She was clearly unhappy with him but had already moved on to focusing on the students, which was her way.

He knew she wouldn't stay upset for very long. She always forgave everyone and seemed to care about others more than herself. Her students came first. Everyone seemed to come first.

The afternoon of grading seemed to drag on, and Adam yawned loudly. He was clearly in need of his daily three to four p.m. nap. Each day he seemed to disappear through a secret door for at least an hour. Even in the field, he would appear to evaporate into thin air.

Anna was aware of this afternoon ritual and told him she needed a quick shower before she could continue with grading. She pretended to be tired to save him the embarrassment of having to announce that he needed a nap.

He seemed pleasantly shocked and gladly allowed her a break to take a much-needed shower.

Anna had a gift for being aware of the needs of others. Father William had once told her he felt she was an 'empath' and compared her to Counselor Troi on Star Trek. As she was a huge Star Trek fan, this was an excellent compliment for her to consider, although she didn't see herself that way at all. Instead, she realized that all moms are sensitive to the needs of others. It was clearly a mom-skill.

As she walked away, Anna imagined Adam gratefully grinning from ear to ear and feeling accomplished in his manipulation of that situation.

He too had noticed that she was empathetic, very dependable, fiercely loyal, and very predictable in her ability to forgive and to love unconditionally. It was one of the things that he secretly loved about her, but she would not learn of his feelings for her until much, much later.

Besides being pretty and intelligent, she had been socialized in the South, and could be secure when others were weak, yet gentle and loving when others needed her to be. It was part of the Southern conditioning of 'ladies,' and a passed down resilience from the women who preceded her. The conditioning included the finely-honed skill of allowing men to think they were in charge, while women were clearly the primary global thinkers and problem solvers.

Women problem-solved and then allowed the men to think it was their idea, and that they were in charge—both genders thinking they were manipulating the other, but the woman clearly, humbly, being the one who saw the big picture.

Her thoughts switched from Adam's need of a nap and her concern for her students, to processing her feelings from the night before. She remembered Sean—the touch, the scent, the music, the hug, his huge ... ahem. Anna knew she was falling in love with Sean. It scared her, and it felt amazing. She had never danced so intimately with a man before. This intimacy without sex was more enjoyable than actual sex had ever been.

Her husband Robert hated dancing and merely having intimacy without sex was not something he wanted. He wanted sex every day and would punish her emotionally if she could not comply.

Anna had to admit to herself in that moment of reflection, that she realized the reason she avoided this kind of contact with Robert was because she didn't want to have sex every time, he touched her, or she kissed him. His idea of foreplay was that there was no such thing. He often made Anna feel like an object used for his own pleasure, not a loving partner.

She had seen men have erections before, her husband, her sons— as babies, her grandfather... yes; he was a pervert. But she had never felt one in that situation before, where the male was spontaneously and overtly aroused by her, with her, in public!

Anna felt embarrassed for him as she assumed it was not something that he had intended. He was such a nice man, such a gentleman. Sigh... he filled her senses with a familiar intimacy. How could something so beautiful, pure, organic be considered unwholesome?

Chapter 8—An Adventure

Anna realized about an hour had passed, and she needed to get back to grading, especially if she was going out later. To her surprise, she had been walking for about two hours, and hadn't even noticed that the time was passing. In discovering she had been gone so long, she quickly took a shower and freshened up, to be truthful in her reason for leaving.

Feeling confident that she had given Adam ample time to rest. she entered the building and walked down the stairs to the men's side of the small dormitory wing. As she turned down the corridor to Adam's room, she could see that his door was wide open.

Anna heard voices as she approached. She could hear HIS voice, and to her surprise, he was talking to Adam. *Oh, my gosh!* She thought, *What am I going to do? I have to go in there and face them both. Damn!*

Anna took a couple of deep breaths and bravely walked to the open doorway and said in a teasing, yet accusatory tone, "What is the meaning of this? Aren't you two supposed to be grading?"

They both looked in her direction and smiled and laughed.

Adam announced with his teasing chuckle, "Sean here just dropped by to rub in the fact that he is finished with his grading for today. I assured him WE would be finished in time for his surprise this evening, which is soon."

"Hi Annie," said Sean, "ready to go see something I bet you've never seen before?"

Adam excused himself and left to the men's room, leaving Sean and Anna alone in awkward silence.

Sean spoke nervously and low, where others couldn't hear, "I'm sorry if I offended ya last evening. I didn't mean for that to happen. It just did. Give me a chance to make it up to ya. I have something very, very special to show ya. I guarantee it won't take too long and it will be worth the effort."

Anna, feeling appreciative of his apology and realizing he was a gentleman, gladly accepted.

Sean extended his hand and said, "Friends, then?" to which she replied with a nervous smile and extended her hand. "Friends." Sean nodded in agreement and seemed content that he had made amends.

Adam returned, and Sean announced that he would take Annie on an adventure, but that he promised to have her back for grading tomorrow.

With a look of surprise on his face, Adam faced Anna, grinned, and said, "This okay with you?" to which she replied, "He's piqued my curiosity. I'd like to see whatever it is he is talking about. Is that okay with you?"

He winked, smiled, and said, "You two have fun."

"See ya around 8:00?"

"Sure, I'll be ready."

Anna and Adam continued grading in silence for the rest of the late afternoon. Looking up at the analog clock on the wall, D. asked in a teasing voice, "Hey, it's getting late, you'd better go get ready for your date." He was clearly trying to get a reaction from her.

"Are you trying to get rid of me?" she asked.

"I think we need a break and you have a hot date." Once again, trying to get a reaction from her. Anna gave him a disapproving glare, and he giggled.

Sean appeared in the doorway fifteen minutes early, "Ya ready to go?"

"Can't wait," replied Annie, and the two walked alone down the dark corridor and out into the cold, dry, desert summer air.

As they exited the building, Sean exclaimed, "Isn't it wonderful Annie?"

Anna thought indignantly to herself, *Annie? I wonder why he calls me Annie. My name is Anna. A N N A!*

They walked to his car, and he opened the passenger door for her.

She thought, *Wow; I wish more men were like this one. In fact, I wish my husband were like him. Sigh...*

They got in, and Sean drove out of the parking lot.

Anna queried, "Where exactly are we going?"

"You'll see, you'll see," he responded in a flirtatious tone.

Anna couldn't help but feel nervous as they passed through the lights of town and drove north out of the city. She thought to herself, *Oh my gosh! I don't really know this guy! He could pretend to be friendly, so he can rape and murder me! What an idiot I am! Oh, please, Lord, don't let him hurt me.*

Anna became very still and strangely quiet as she allowed her inability to trust men to creep into her mind.

Sean seemed to notice her fear and said, "Aw Annie, there is absolutely nothing to fear from me, I assure ya I just want to be yer friend."

It was almost as if he could read her mind. She nervously replied, obviously not being entirely truthful, "Oh, there's no problem, really. I am just curious what could be out here in the middle of nowhere, that's all."

He replied again, "You'll see. It's really cool."

She was very curious now and began rummaging through her mind, trying to determine what on earth he had to show her. *Prairie dogs singing to the moon? Wait, there's no moon. Darn, it can't be that. Is he playing a joke on me? Perhaps like "snipe hunting"*[42] *in the south? I just can't imagine.*

After about a half hour, Sean turned left and drove down a dirt road. He was whistling. Anna thought, Why is he whistling? I'm getting upset at this game he's playing. She really hated not being in control of yet another situation with a man.

The car stopped in front of a gate, and Sean turned the engine off. It was pitch black outside. What on earth? Anna thought.

He got out of the car, jumped, and slid onto the hood, and reclined against the windshield, just like Steve McQueen or Fonzie of Happy Days. He was a cool dude.

Anna could see his silhouette, barely, through the glass and was left speechless. She then heard him say, "Hey Annie, come on out here with me. It's fantastic!"

Anna reluctantly got out of the car and reached her hands for the right-hand side of the hood. She couldn't see a thing! She couldn't even see him now. As her throat closed in fear, she heard his voice through the darkness, "Up here with me."

He reached out his hands and ran them down her shoulders, arms, and finally to her sides. He gave her a lift, and she was up on the car's hood next to him.

"Don't be nervous," he said. "Just lean back, relax, and look up."

She leaned back onto the glass and looked up to the sky. She heard him ask, "What do ya see?"

Anna couldn't believe her eyes. It looked like sheets hanging in the sky. She asked excitedly, "What is that? Is that....is that...?"

Before she could say it, Sean spoke, "It's the aurora! See, I told ya it would be terrific!"

---

42   Newcomers to a community in the south, or young men trying to gain their manhood, are duped into hunting for a fictitious creature known as a snipe. It is a ruse, or a joke often played on the naïve.

She looked in amazement and giggled. "Oh, my gosh! I've never seen the aurora before. It is so beautiful! How did you know?"

"I have friends in high places. Naw, really, I know folks who do this kind of thing for a living, and they told me. I knew you'd like it. D. told me you had never seen it before."

Anna responded in shock, "He knew this was what you wanted to do?"

Sean laughed out loud, dodging her punch and with his tongue surely in his cheek as he said. "Yup, he did."

They had done it to her again! She had been fooled twice by these two. She was pissed but still amused, because she had a great sense of humor and could see the fun in their collaboration.

It was Adam's character to be engaged in these types of things. She had to smile to herself as she imagined him smugly chuckling to himself back at the college.

As they sat there, marveling at the night sky, the two began talking and sharing about their families back home.

Sean told of his wife, *Sophia*.[43] He spoke of how they met when he was doing post-doc work at Cambridge University. She was a language arts major of Italian descent. She spent many summers in Italy with her aunts, uncles, and cousins, who still lived in the old country. She spoke fluent Italian, and this seemed to be the one thing they both had in common. They both loved the sound of the romance languages and frequently spoke to each other in such a fashion. He spoke of her with great love and admiration and clearly adored her.

Sophia was a talented, beautiful woman, who had given up her hopes and dreams to be his wife and the mother of his children. She was Mrs. Dr. S.M. Anderson. He and their children had been her entire life. She had her artwork and poetry and spent many

---

43   Sophia Adriana Marcotte Anderson, the Italian born wife of Sean and mother of their two daughters. Fictional character and not meant to represent any real person, living or dead.

hours pouring herself into the canvas, imagining that she was *Michelangelo* or perhaps *Faustina Maratti*.[44]

Sophia was a godly woman, who could have done much, much more with her life, and he spoke of his regret at her not being able to do more. He encouraged her to be more independent, but she was pleased with her life as it was.

Their special relationship was clearly not because of anything lacking with Sean's marriage. He obviously adored his wife and didn't seem unhappy with her. Understanding this made their attraction even more confusing.

Annie spoke of her children and her guilt at having to leave them. She spoke of her husband Robert, who was a brilliant architect and described the first time they met and fell in love. They were both at a party, and she was singing and playing her guitar. He fell in love with her natural beauty and talent, and she fell in love with his deep blue eyes and his beautiful smile.

She also spoke of her admiration for his intellect and about his desire for them to grow as separate individuals. He even wanted an open relationship, which Anna could not and would not agree to do.

Despite the fundamental differences in the couple, he was the primary motivator and inspiration for her ability to pursue her own dream in the sciences. He knew she was insecure and was usually her own worst enemy. She was clearly grateful to him and definitely loved her children.

Sean wondered how Robert could ever encourage her to have an open relationship. He couldn't imagine sharing his Sophia with other men.

Anna did not share with Sean about her separation from her husband and how they were struggling to find a way back to

---

44 Michelangelo was an Italian renaissance sculptor and the artist who painted the Sistine Chapel. Faustina Maratti was an Italian Baroque poet and painter.

reconciliation. That part was very embarrassing to her. She saw it as a failing and didn't feel comfortable sharing her struggle with her new friend.

Chapter 9—The Great Volcano Escape

The two talked until dawn, not even realizing that the night had gone. They spoke of religion and their beliefs about everything, including how the Stillwater Complex was formed and about the magmatic evolution at Yellowstone.

Sean realized that Annie had a love of volcanoes and recounted an experience he once had with a Peruvian volcano, while he was doing post-doc work at Cambridge University. He and his research team were almost killed in the eruption. Anna had always dreamed of seeing an eruption and was very interested in hearing his account, especially how they all managed to escape.

At that time, years before St. Helen's, the evolution of volcanology as a science, the ability to forecast the timing of volcanic events was elusive. The use of sequence volcanic stratigraphy, age dating and mapping of the distribution of past flows, geochemical analysis of gasses, magmas, and rocks, as well as the frequency and distribution of shallow seismic events, gave volcanologists the 'best guess' that the science could afford, but it was still not good enough.

Sean's interest was in a central Andean volcanic complex. His research was focused on the evolution of magmas and the production of ignimbrites.

Ignimbrites have minerals present that could yield information about the geochemistry of the magma that erupted to form the ash-flow deposits on the flanks of the volcano. Each flow give a geochemical snapshot of the magma at the time of the eruption.

Sean quickly became an expert in continental subduction[45] and subsequent volcanism in the Andes. He also became an international expert in the production of ignimbrites.

Annie knew that his current research in Yellowstone did, in fact, focus on the evolution of those magmas and the ignimbrites, as she had read the article written by him on the Yellowstone sequences. She was very awestruck as she encouraged him to share his story of the "great volcano escape."

How many geologists can say that they narrowly escaped an eruption? thought Annie to herself.

"Ya see, we had traveled to the central Andes and had been on the volcano for about a week, sampling gases, fluids, and rocks, of course. It was certainly pre-Mt. St. Helens, and as a rule, volcanoes are unpredictable anyway, but particularly at that time. Shallow seismic events were a frequent occurrence, so they were barely distinguishable one from the other…"

Annie interjected, "So you had become habituated to the seismicity? That's not good."

"Perhaps," Sean said in a questioning manner, tilting his head to one side as he tried to recall if he specifically noted a preceding seismic event.

Annie was sitting straight up on the hood of the car by now, with her legs crossed in a variation of the lotus position, leaning forward and hanging on his every word.

"Anyway, I was asleep in the tent that evening and heard it begin to rain, only it didn't sound like rain. It was a weird sound, but ya can certainly recognize rain falling, now can't ya? I had left the canopy off so I could see the night sky. When I heard the rain,

---

45 Subduction is a tectonic process where a lithospheric (upper most part of the mantle, which includes the crust of the earth) plate converges with another plate and the resulting collision results in one plate moving beneath the other. This is usually if they are of differing densities, such as when a continental lithosphere plate overrides an oceanic lithosphere plate during a collision.

I thought, 'Shit, that will make things messy for sure,' so I exited the tent to put the canopy on. To my surprise, it WAS NOT RAIN falling, it was big, fat pieces of ash!"

"Oh, my goodness!" said Annie, "What did you do?"

"Well, I yelled for everyone to get the HECK out of there, that's what I did!" said Sean excitedly. "I looked up and saw the gray cloud directly above in the atmosphere and knew it was just a matter of minutes before the ash column from the vertical blast might come straight down on us and flow down the slopes."[46]

"Jesus!" shouted Annie.

"Well," continued Sean, "We grabbed as much as possible and ran like hell downslope to the truck. We dropped stuff all over the place on the way, and then threw what was left in the back. It seemed like the truck was miles away. None of us had boots on, so it was a full-tit, adrenaline-fueled slather[47] down that slope. After we got to the jeep, I managed to get the keys out of my pocket... thankfully, I had put them in my shorts just in case and drove like hell downslope.

"It was extremely rough, rugged, still dark, and very dangerous.... we bounced all over the place, running over rocks, bushes, sliding through loose gravel, and at one point almost rolling the truck, as we could see the erupting plume spreading out. It was enormous, gorgeous, terrifying overhead. I'm not a praying sort, but I was sure hoping the blast had enough energy to keep it going up until we could get the hell out of there. We knew the flow would soon follow us down the slope and had very little time to escape before being overcome."

Sean paused for a reflective second, a dramatic pause, and then continued his story.

---

46   Column collapse isn't a given, but it is always prudent to expect a pyroclastic flow and exit quickly.

47   New Zealand phrase, "full tit" and "slather" for a chaotic, frantic run with no organization.

"We were barely in front of the flow, seriously.

Martha,[48] one of the grad students, kept screaming, 'Drive faster! It's coming!'

Dougie,[49] the other grad student, kept yelling, 'FUCK! FUCK! FUCK!'

So, even though I couldn't see anything going on behind us, I knew our lives depended on me going fast and not rolling the truck.

I must tell ya, that experience scared the shit out of me. We made it somehow.

The locals said we looked like 'gente fantasma - ghost people' because we were covered with thick gray ash.

Thankfully, we had bandanas to tie over our faces. It was a hell of a mess for sure. That eruption killed lots of animals, and tragically, a few people sleeping in a nearby village. The ash is suffocating, rich in silica. It gets in the lungs and turns to a cement of sorts. Humans can cover their faces and can somewhat filter the larger pieces, but the poor animals…sigh…poor buggars didn't stand a chance."

Annie was silent for a few seconds and then said, "That's an amazing story, Sean. Terrifying. So, you didn't feel the initial seismic event or the shock wave from the vertical blast?"

"No, just the ash falling. We were too high up to not be in danger, although we hadn't made it to the crater yet. We were still mapping strata and collecting samples lower on the slopes and would eventually have made it up there in the next week… so, we got the heck out of there, thankfully."

"Were you able to go back to your campsite?" asked Annie.

---

48   Martha Marie Zepeda, a first year PhD student collecting samples for her dissertation research, fluent in Spanish. A fictional character and not meant to represent any real person living or dead.

49   Doug Rodriguez, "Dougie," a first-year master's student who spoke fluent Spanish and was hoping to begin his research that would continue into a PhD. Fictional character not meant to represent any real person, past or present.

"Oh no, absolutely not. It was completely lost in the pyroclastic flow. If we had stayed, we would have been killed."

Annie placed her hand over her heart and could feel her own anxiety at the thought of him being killed, anyone being killed.

"Yeah, that was too close for comfort," said Sean.

"Thank God you woke up," said Annie.

"Well, thank goodness I heard it in time. The others hadn't heard it at all."

"So, did you go back and finish your work?" asked Annie.

"We did what we were able to. It was just too dangerous for us to get as close as we needed to collect samples. That beast was too unstable. Reluctantly, we had to leave with whatever was stowed in the truck. We couldn't afford to come back until the following summer, and then we were only allowed in with the local team. We had collected quite a bit of data before it blew and had surprisingly good luck with the samples we collected."

Annie could see his face coming into view with the rising sun and saw that he was not telling her a huge story, but that he did, in fact, feel lucky to have made it out alive.

As the sun continued to rise over the field, the little gophers began to scamper from one hole to the next and to face the sun in their usual fashion.

Sean picked up dirt clods and chunked them at the little critters.

Anna was quick to chastise him for trying to hurt them. "Sean, stop that! That is mean."

"Are ya kidding me, Annie?" he exclaimed indignantly. "They are filthy little creatures that eat each other."

"But they are still God's creatures!"

"They are still God's creatures..." repeated Sean in a mocking tone.

"Why are you so mean, Sean? "

Pained by her tone, he apologized. "Oh, I'm sorry, Annie. Sometimes I'm a real asshole."

"Why do you call me, Annie?" she asked, "My name is Anna."

"Because Annie is cute, just like you."

She smiled at him and said, "We'd best be getting back before Adam sends out the cavalry."

"Shit, it is morning, isn't it? I had a great time talking to ya, ANNIE."

She laughed and replied, "Me too."

As they drove back to town, they were both silent.

Annie was tired but didn't feel like sleeping. Sean felt the same way. He parked at the side of the building where no students would see, and they both went their separate ways to the morning meal.

Walking into the dining hall, Anna could see Adam standing in front of the juice dispenser. He looked like he was trying to decide how many glasses he could fit on his tray.

She quickly got into the breakfast line before he could see her. She got her granola cereal, fruit, bacon, and coffee and sat down at the table across from him.

He had managed to carry his biscuits, gravy, bacon, eggs, three glasses of milk, two glasses of orange juice and one coffee without spilling the entire tray.

Anna was very careful to avoid eye contact with the faculty or students that had witnessed the embarrassing event from two nights earlier. She could still feel the social sting of being treated like that in front of everyone.

Adam looked up, wiping gravy from his chin, and said in a fatherly tone, "Well, when did you make it in?"

Anna found herself blushing and wanting to tell a bald-faced lie. Instead, she replied, "Late."

He just chuckled, to which she asked, "What is so funny?"

"Oh, nothing, should something be funny?" he answered. "Snicker, snicker."

Anna said boldly and proudly, "It was the aurora borealis, Adam."

He hated being called Adam, so he quickly dropped the subject and went back for seconds of everything.

Dr. D. was a thin man, in his early fifties, and stood about five feet, five inches tall. He didn't seem capable of gaining weight, no matter how much he ate. Some believed his secret was eating whatever he desired at least once a day.

Adam was a well-published expert in structural geology and tectonic frameworks. Although he was very well-known and had trained many brilliant students and new faculty--Anna as well--he was also a very humble man, with a quick and a facile mind. He possessed the impish demeanor of a happy hobbit, or perhaps an elf.

It was no wonder that he ran away instead of defending his friend the other night. Anna found herself quickly forgiving this cute little guy. She realized that her expectations of him had been unrealistic. It was just not in his nature to deal with conflicts of any kind. His talent was manipulating others into fighting his battles for him.

By mid-morning, Anna was feeling the weariness of not sleeping the night before. Seeing how tired she was, Adam offered to have her go sleep while he finished the grading. She was touched by his generosity but declined. Just as they were finishing the final totals for the grades, Sean appeared at the doorway. He looked like he had been sleeping all day long, and like a cat that had captured a canary.

Anna felt her heart skip a beat when she saw his salt-and-pepper beard and gentle smiling eyes.

Excitedly, Adam blurted, "I heard you had a late night at the aurora. Where did you end up seeing it?"

Sean chuckled, "Out at Old Potter's Gulch Road."

Anna looked shocked because she hadn't even noted the exact spot, they had been parked all evening. How could she have missed Old Potter's Gulch Road? That was the first mapping project of the six-week course for everyone! *Wow, what a strange experience this has been,* she thought to herself.

Chapter 10—Old Friends

After exchanging polite conversation with Adam, Sean spoke directly to Anna. "Do ya wanna get out of here and do something with me?"

Anna looked at Adam as if to ask permission to go.

He responded, "Go ahead, I can finish these totals."

She was so excited she could hardly contain her enthusiasm. She couldn't believe how excited she felt inside about spending more time with her new "old" friend.

As they walked to his car, Anna seemed more relaxed with Sean and asked, "What did you have in mind?"

"You'll see."

Anna was not having any more of this "you'll see" stuff and said, "Oh no, not that again! For real, what are we doing?"

"We'll know when I figure it out...ha-ha."

He didn't have a clue! He just wanted to do something, anything with his "Annie."

Driving down the main street of the small town, his mind was racing to try to find an idea that would be proper and something friends would do. He was very aware now of Annie's devout Catholic faith and her desire to live a holy and grace-filled life. He respected and even admired her for this type of commitment and moral ethics, even if he didn't have any specific religious beliefs of his own. He admittedly admired this quality about both Sophia and Annie. She was like Sophia; both were smart, beautiful ladies, and both loved God.

Sean did not know precisely why he was so drawn to Annie, but he shared the familiar feeling that she also felt. Like they were old friends and that they were somehow cosmically connected.

What to do? Dammit, what to do? Sean thought to himself. He did not want to do anything to offend his new friend. Just as he thought they might have to do something where everyone and anyone could see and interrupt, he drove around the last curve of town and saw the Mountain Sky Movie Theatre.

He shouted, "I've got it! I've got it!" ...pause...turning toward Annie, smiling, "Let's watch a movie!"

Annie responded, excitedly, "That sounds great. I haven't seen a movie since before my youngest son was born!"

The decision was unanimous. They were going to see the only movie showing. It didn't matter what movie; they were just going to be there together.

When they pulled into the parking lot and saw the poster, "The Last Waltz" with "The Band" they looked at each other in surprise and said simultaneously, "I love The Band!"

Sean quickly got out and ran around the car to open her door. He then jogged ahead to open the theatre door as well. After they entered the lobby, he extended the crook of his arm and she casually looped her arm in his. He proceeded to buy the movie tickets, as well as the popcorn and drinks, but paused briefly before ordering to see if Annie had an opinion.

"Don't ya know what ya want? "he asked.

"I really don't care, whatever you think will be just fine."

He opted to get one large popcorn and two small drinks and was struck by Annie's unwillingness to order for herself.

She was very accustomed to men buying everything, date or otherwise. It was considered a sign of respect for a man to pay instead of allowing a lady to do so. This was expected of any gentleman.

Sean was not socialized in the South and found it peculiar for a woman to be so submissive, so indecisive. Women from his part of the country would punch you if you opened doors for them or offered to pay for anything. He was baffled, but just went with the flow of things. *Southern customs it is,* he thought to himself. *I think I like it.*

The couple entered the main hall, and Annie followed Sean to his preferred spot in the theatre. They both sat down, and their arms touched. He could feel her small, well-defined muscles, and she could feel his strength pressing against her.

Annie felt her heart pound and became acutely aware that she was feeling turned on. The smell of this man was making her feel... um... *Oh boy.*

Each time she reached for popcorn; Sean could feel her press her soft left breast against his forearm. Her essence, "Annie, with a hint of jasmine," was intoxicating.

He was no longer confused about his connection with her. It was not just a fluke that they met and had this strange connection. His attraction for her was not only her intellect, the cute way she drank a beer, her adorable Southern accent, or her jasmine scent; it was primal.

Sean wanted to have his way with her right there in the theatre, in front of everyone. The musical performances only enhanced his emotional responses and he wished he could stand up and dance with her in the aisles.

Annie tried to watch the movie and focus on the characters instead of her own sexually heightened state. She had learned early on how to squelch the sins of the flesh. Usually just imagining Jesus watching was enough to shame her out of any impure thoughts as a teen. No Jesus this time, it was full-on Sean and Annie, and it was intense. Thankfully, the music seemed to engage her enough to take her mind off the sensations for a little while.

Sean tried to do the same, but his situation was a little bit more difficult to diffuse.

After the popcorn was gone and the drinks were empty, he and Annie sat arm to arm, touching but not really touching...together but not together... Not just like old friends, but as lovers. It was familiar and very sensual and sensuous.

She imagined their auras pulsing to the point of having everyone noticing them. Surely, everyone else sensed it too. When she looked around, everyone seemed to be watching the film. It was just her imagination, obviously. The metaphysical tension was palpable.

At one point in the movie, Sean's hand brushed her knee, and he felt her shudder in response. The next time, his hand landed on her knee, and he did not move his hand. Sean wondered if she would be offended. He knew it was not proper, but he just couldn't help himself.

Her knee was so beautiful. Her thighs and calves were so muscular and well defined. They were just as he had anticipated... remembered? It was as though he had touched them many times before and had memorized every inch.

Just when he thought he should move his hand or risk losing Annie's respect for him, she reached down and put her hand on top of his.

She too felt it familiar to have him touching her, and for her to take his hand. Her hand looked tiny and perhaps a little bony compared to his. He turned his hand over, and their fingers entwined. She did not resist or shyly pull away. Sean then gently brought their hands over to his lap, where the two sat comfortably, as a couple, enjoying the rest of the movie.

Sean was not accustomed to feeling emotional to the point of tears, but in this movie, sharing intimacy with Annie, he couldn't restrain himself.

Annie looked over at him after hearing him sniff and could see tears running down his cheeks. He was not sobbing or making any outward expression of his deep feelings, but he could not stop the tears. She then looked back at the movie and the song that was playing and wondered if he had perhaps been hurt by a former love in his life.

There was clearly more to this man than just his masculine and academic prowess. He seemed to be sensitive.

Annie did not see it as a weakness, but instead a very attractive quality. She was now totally in love with this man. She felt like she was in an unbelievable dream.

When the movie ended, they stood up and walked to the car. It was dark by now. Both were tired and subdued but clearly not ready to say goodnight to each other.

After they were in the car, Sean began, "Annie, I'm so sorry for being so forward. I don't know what it is. There is something between us, I can't explain... I can't put it into words... I just can't help...," the tears began to flow.

Annie reached up and wiped his tears from his cheek with the back of her delicate hand. "I know, I feel it too. Strangely, I feel like I know you. Your touch, your smell, everything screams out that you and I are...."

"Lovers, soulmates...together forever," he said.

"Yes. What is this all about, Sean? You and I are both married. This is not okay, yet it feels soooo right."

He responded, "I know," as he kissed her hand, then her forehead, then her closed eyes, and let out a sigh of resignation.

"Is that why you are crying?"

"Ah, nah, dear. I've just never felt like this before...ever...in my entire life." He said, as he slapped his thigh with anger at his inability to get a hold of his emotions.

They sat together in silence, looking deeply into each other's eyes.

She could see that he adored her.

After the long silence, Annie looked loving and reassuringly into his eyes and said, "We both have a long week of mapping with our students. We'd best get some sleep."

Sean nodded in agreement. He drove back to the parking lot behind the dorm, where they sat together, holding hands for several minutes. They did not want this moment to end.

Reluctantly, Sean walked Annie to her room. It was nearly 11:00 p.m. by now, and it seemed proper to make sure she made it home safely.

They embraced in front of her open door and felt as though they were whole and exactly where they were supposed to be--together. The thought of breaking their embrace felt painful, like they were being torn in two.

Annie pulled away suddenly, though, when she heard a door open down the hallway. She turned away from Sean and went into her room and quickly closed the door without looking back at him. She locked the door and lay on the cold tile floor. It felt so good against her incredibly warm body. The starkness of it took away her intense feelings of painful separation and lust.

Tears began to roll down her face as she was overwhelmed with emotion. She prayed softly to herself, *Lord have mercy, Christ have mercy, Lord have mercy.*

She went on and recited the chaplet of divine mercy and finally found peace again in her soul, as tears of pain began to wane. She felt as if part of her had been pulled away. She was naked and alone with her soul open for Jesus, Mary, Joseph, all saints, and most of all, God to see. "Lord forgive me, a sinner. I love you, my Lord, with all my heart and my soul. Please have pity on me and forgive me for my impure thoughts and actions. In Jesus' name, I pray, Amen."

Sean stood at Annie's door for a few seconds, not really wanting to leave. He wondered if he should knock and imagined her standing on the other side, willing him to return to her. She would open the door, and they would then be able to be together, perhaps just lying together and feeling each other's heartbeat.

As he began to take steps back toward her door, one of Annie's students entered the hallway on her way to her room for the evening. Sean suddenly felt like it was not proper for him to be standing in a woman's dorm hallway with female students walking by.

The awkwardness of the moment and the weariness he felt, from the lack of sleep that day and the night before, reminded him that he had a full day of mapping with his students the next day. He hesitantly walked down the hall and away from his "Annie." He felt melancholy too, as the distance between them increased.

As he lay on his bed to finally go to sleep, he thought to himself, *Goodnight Annie. Sleep well.*

Chapter 11—Are we there yet?

The final week of mapping was there for Anna's camp. Sean's camp was entering their second week.

They had briefly seen each other across the cafeteria that next morning and both of their faces lit up. It honestly didn't take much for both Anna's and Sean's students to notice that there was a special connection between the two. Some of the students whispered and smiled.

Adam couldn't help but note the "lover's glance" as they smiled at one another from across the room. He leaned over to Anna and whispered, "You two friends now?"

Anna didn't hear Adam, even though she was sitting right next to him. He looked down at his plate, not sure what to say next. She then realized that she hadn't responded to him and said, "Oh, gosh, I'm sorry, what were you saying?"

He replied, "You two seem to be pretty good friends these days."

She looked at him sweetly and said, "D., he's a very nice man. Even you told me that. Remember?"

"Yes, I suppose he is," said Adam in a disappointed tone. "Just be careful, okay? I wouldn't want to see you get hurt. And besides, he has a big butt."

Anna laughed and whispered, "D.?! What are you doing looking at other guy's butts?!" She then smiled at Adam and thought it was sweet that he was worried about her.

He felt protective of Anna because she seemed a little naive and sensitive. There had been more than one time that he wanted to punch Robert in the nose for the way he mistreated her in public.

Anna viewed Adam as her friend and mentor, more like a big brother. She had no idea that he was jealous of Sean, and how he really felt about her.

As everyone was finishing up and heading toward the trucks, Sean stopped briefly at the table where Anna and Adam were sitting and said, "The last week, huh? Stay safe up there, Annie. Enjoy the *Frazier Batholith*."[50]

She flashed a big smile because she couldn't wait.

Adam chimed in to warn Sean about the "dead cow formation" that had been particularly nasty the second week for their camp in the *Comer River* deranged fold and thrust mapping area.[51] "It looked like it was just about to explode when we left it a few weeks ago. So, it may not be too much trouble this week. Just thought I'd warn you," said D.

Sean nodded knowingly saying, "Yes, there is usually at least one every summer in that area, I've been told," winking at Annie.

She shuddered just remembering her first-time mapping in that area and not noticing a dead cow until she was right on top of it. *Yuck*, she thought.

The Mondavi field camp students and faculty wearily climbed into the vans and headed to their final mapping project of the camp in the Frazier Mountain mining district. This project was an hour's drive from the field station-campus and would prove to be very challenging to everyone, physically and mentally.

---

50   The Frazier Batholith and mining district is a fictional location based on the many places visited by the author.

51   The Comer River is a fictional area based on the Big Hole River area of Montana.

The slope angles for the hiker were from 30 to 45 degrees, which made upslope movement strenuous, not to mention the nearly 3,000-foot elevation change.

After what felt like more than an hour's drive, the vans stopped, and the students all piled out and prepared to take everything with them into the field. There was no returning to the vehicles for water or food here. This area was steep, with substantial elevation changes. It would not be wise to have students going up and down numerous times.

Adam began his ascent up the steep, crumbling slope of loose *meta-sedimentary*[52] materials, with several campers in tow. He was like a mountain goat and would always be one of the first to hike up from the road, some 1,200 feet straight up, to get to the mapping area.

Once to the mapping area, the elevation began at just under 7,000 feet and rose to 9,500 feet.

D. was first to climb to the highest contour on most projects and did so to give himself a good view of the entire class below. He could also identify the students who seemed to be struggling. Adam genuinely cared about their safety and their learning, but just had a different way of expressing his concerns.

Big John was strategically placed in the middle of the pack, and Anna was bringing up the rear, like a mother bear watching over her cubs. Adam felt relieved when he could finally see her appear, usually following or leading the most vulnerable students.

In this area, there was always a chance of a rattlesnake encounter, especially near the top of the mountain, where weathered rocks

---

52   Metasedimentary refers to metamorphosed sedimentary rocks and soils. They are the result of a magmatic intrusion which baked the surrounding rocks and sediment. This process is called contact metamorphism where the original rocks and soils were subjected to high heat in the subsurface.

allowed for prime nesting. The locals were very good about sharing information with camp faculty about the cycle of the local snakes.

Adam felt that the snakes were probably just waking up and moving around at that elevation and was more than a little concerned about safety. If rattlers have molted, they are blind and strike at almost everything that moves. Baby rattlers, in particular, are highly venomous. A snake with a rattler can warn someone walking near them. This is best for both the snake and the hiker.

Anna, having a strong connection to animals, seemed to know that the snakes meant her no harm. She usually spoke to them as she walked away from them in one direction, while they slithered in the opposite direction.

The campers had already received a safety lecture and had been exposed to rattlesnakes and bull snakes in the high desert sedimentary terrain of their first two mapping projects. They quickly learned about how to safely navigate the habitat of the snake, and that rattlers didn't want anything to do with them, really. If they just walked away, the rattler would go their own way. They only strike if they feel threatened or trapped. In this area, there was no evidence of a recent molt, so just being aware would probably be enough.

As Dr. D. would say, "This is their home, and we are walking through their living room. Be mindful of them and the kinds of places they may be resting or hiding and approach those areas with caution. Always expect a snake to be underneath a rock. If you don't hear a rattle when you approach, then it's probably safe to take the strike and dip of the strata, but that is no guarantee, so always look and listen."

Even though the students were experienced now, the wildlife in this area could result in a deadly encounter if the students and staff became complacent. Adam was always a little nervous for the students at Frazier Mountain because it was an elk reserve and was not just home to lots of rattlesnakes. Some years the ground literally crawled. The area was also the natural habitat for mountain lions, and bears, particularly grizzly bears, who enjoy feeding on the elk.

To reduce the risk for campers and faculty, the mapping time for each day started around 9:30 a.m. and ended by 5:00 p.m. This gave everyone ample time to cover ground, while predators stayed out of the heat of the day. The most dangerous time was when the sun began to go down, from dusk until nightfall and in the predawn hours.

The outcrops of the Frazier Mountain mining district offered a diverse array of igneous, sedimentary, and metasedimentary rocks. Igneous intrusions produce contact metamorphic zones where molten magma melts and bakes pre-existing rock. This process guarantees a rich variety of igneous rock compositions and textures to challenge a student to apply classroom learning in the field. Hydrothermal mineralization too provided a rich array of accessory minerals and microstructures. The classification of igneous rocks depends on the ability to approximate the percentage and distribution of minerals present in each rock.

In this project, the student is challenged to determine the minerals in the rocks and classify each by the abundance of minerals like quartz and feldspar.

The greatest challenge for a novice is to distinguish the different types of igneous rocks from one another in the field. Classroom laboratories usually do not have every rock one might see in nature, but if the students have learned how to identify minerals in rocks and determine textures and general compositions, they have a pretty good chance of at least getting close to understanding the types of rocks present in an area. This knowledge, coupled with an understanding of plutonism,[53] helps the student to discuss the overall regional geology and how this area of exposures fits into that story.

---

53 Plutonism is the process where molten rock material, magma, crystallizes and solidifies into igneous rock beneath the surface of the earth.

The outcrops in the mapping area were particularly far apart and gave the students a workout in how to map igneous outcrops as well as a test of their physical endurance. Unlike the sedimentary terrain of their earlier mapping experience, there were no stacked layers of rocks, which stretched on laterally, and were easily mapped along contour intervals. One could comfortably sit on a high contour and map an entire valley of sedimentary rocks, including folded and faulted structures, on a stereo photo.

The outcrops at Frazier Mountain were sparse, and each one was slightly different from the others. The last two projects of the camp were indeed the most challenging, as the students had to map rocks that had either been changed significantly – metamorphosed -- or had crystallized under the surface from a magma. Each area offered a wide variety of mineral assemblages.

Anna particularly loved this project because she loved igneous geology. She especially liked to take the students through an old railroad cut, which exposed the remnants of a magma chamber that had long since cooled and crystallized. It was like walking through a *pluton*[54] and was especially exciting for Anna to share with others.

Even Adam got excited when she enthusiastically pointed out specific composition changes, zoning in minerals, and other structures present from the cooling of the magma. As a junior faculty, Anna taught many of the undergraduate courses taken by the students now using that knowledge in the field. Adam had hand-selected Anna as a field methods instructor because of her broad background in geology and her love of teaching.

The campers ascended the mountain with Dr. D., while Anna lagged behind to make sure that all students made it up the steep terrain to the beginning of the mapping area.

---

54   A pluton is a large igneous intrusive structure, where the rock crystallized from a magmatic intrusion beneath the surface. Over time the pluton is exposed at the surface as surface rocks and soils are removed through weathering and erosion.

Jacob and Little John were bringing up the rear, while all the younger students were well ahead of everyone, except for Dr. D, who was always ahead without exception.

Little John, in particular, was having difficulty with the steep terrain. "Man, we'll never catch up. We may as well just sit this one out."

Anna was behind them, patiently following, and heard their conversation.

"Yeah, those kids are already to the top with Dr. D., and we're still trying to make it up to the mapping area," said Jacob.

The students clearly felt that they were doomed.

Looking back and realizing that Anna was behind them, Jacob quipped, "Hey teach, can't you keep up with Dr. D?"

"Oh sure. I just make sure that all of you make it up the hill." She instantly felt guilty for making such a comment, as both Little John and Jacob were older students, with a little bit more weight to carry than others. They were already feeling challenged, and Anna needed to be sensitive to their struggle.

Jacob stopped and looked back at Anna and said, "Hey, I don't need you to babysit me," and motioned for her to move on ahead of him.

Anna just smiled and said, "It is okay, you know."

"What's that, Dr. Moore?" asked Little John.

She now had Jacob's attention as she imparted words of wisdom to the two older students in the camp, "It's okay to take your time walking the mapping area. It seems like the kids are ahead, but they are missing a lot of cool stuff on their way up. If you guys are smart, you'll take your time and map as you go. It may take you longer, but your map will be more complete. Being fast or being the first doesn't always mean that the map is better, or the information is correct."

Little John's body language relaxed as her words helped him to feel better about moving so much slower than the other students.

"Just remember these simple rules," she said, "Don't lose elevation unless you have to, and if you feel lost, use your Brunton compass to triangulate your position using landmarks, and don't forget to check the drainage on your map. If all else fails and you are truly lost, follow the drainage until you find the road below. There is a road that circles this mountain, and you will be found. Okay?"

"Okay, Dr. Moore," said Little John in a grateful tone.

Anna nodded to them and walked ahead to the first significant outcrop of the mapping area. It looked like a huge boulder that was sticking up above the ground. The other students had missed it on their race to the top. She found a section of the rock that was relatively free of *lichens*,[55] and she perched herself so she would not be missed.

The rock was a classic *quartz monzonite*,[56] but many of the students would mistake it for a granite or granodiorite, given the amount of quartz and feldspar that was present in the rock. It was a perfect example of how they should not judge a rock by general color or appearance only. It is easy to be fooled if you do not use the classification techniques taught in igneous and metamorphic rocks class. They would have to estimate the percent of minerals in the rock to make a firm classification.

She sat patiently and watched Jacob and Little John struggle up the slope. When they reached her and the outcrop, she asked them

---

55 Lichens are a combination of two organisms that work in tandem, fungi and algae. They preferentially colonize and attach themselves to feldspar and other minerals in igneous rocks. They grow on rocks, trees, logs, the ground. The fungi provide protection and decompose other organisms, while algae provides the breakdown of minerals constituents for consumption and photosynthesis. Lichens are a big part of the weathering, breakdown chemically, of igneous rocks at the surface.

56 Quartz Monzonite is a rock classified by less quartz and equal parts of feldspars. Granites crystallize at a lower temperature and have the same basic minerals as the monzonite or granodiorite, but with less quartz. They look similar in the field in terms of color because of the presence of feldspar minerals in the rocks. Each, however, crystallizes out of a melt at different temperatures, so they have varying degrees of low temperature, vs intermediate temperature mineral crystallization.

to take out their maps. She showed them exactly where they were on the map, and directed their attention to a few landmarks, which would help them to stay in the mapping area.

As they began to continue up the slope, she said, "Hey, isn't this an outcrop I'm sitting on?"

Little John turned around and walked back to her position. He began his inspection and note-taking.

Jacob stood in place ahead of them and said, "Obviously, it is a granodiorite."

Anna responded, "I don't know, tell me the percentage of minerals you see present? You need to write these in your field notebook. After that, make a sketch too, and note your initial assessment of this rock, based on the minerals present and the abundance of those minerals. Place a number in your notebook and a corresponding point on your map. If needed, you may also take a small sample with you for later inspection. A tiny dot of whiteout and a sharpie works nicely, too, for marking your outcrop for sampling. Put the same number that is on your map and in your notebook on your sample, though. Then you will be able to double-check yourself when you get back to the dorms."

"Hey, that's pretty smart, Dr. Moore," said Little John. "What if we gather our samples on the way back down--we won't have to carry them up the hill then, right?"

"That might seem more efficient, but you might forget, too," advised Anna.

"I won't need samples," remarked Jacob confidently.

She waited for them to make their assessments and sketches and to put a corresponding number on their map for the outcrop, which matched their field book entry. "What type of weathering do you see up there at the top where Dr. D. is standing, guys?" she asked.

"I see a Dr. D. Formation and a Ben Formation kissing the backside of the D. Formation..." said Jacob.

Little John and Anna both chuckled at that observation.

Little John then answered, "It looks like igneous weathering."

"Duh," said Jacob. "This is just an igneous project, after all. What other kinds of weathering would you expect?"

"But does this type of weathering have a name and what does it typically mean in terms of the type of rock being weathered?" asked Anna. "Is there another name?"

"Spheroidal!" answered Little John excitedly. "IT'S SPHEROIDAL WEATHERING!"

Anna nodded proudly and then moved on ahead to the next outcrop that they would need to find and identify on their journey to the top. The slope up the mountain was covered in tall grass, at least waist deep. Anna often followed the path of the elk in the dewy grass in the mornings. Deer and elk typically choose a serpentine trail of least resistance.

Chapter 12—SAFETY FIRST

After making sure that Little John and Jacob were on the right track up the hill and had done an excellent job on the second outcrop, Anna decided to take a short water and snack break. She had a suspicion it might also be the last time she would be able to "take a leak" in private. She followed a gentle path of laid down grass that led to a grove of trees and rocks. In the center was a large opening with an oasis of large stones. They were perfect for sitting and admiring a vista of peaks visible in the distance.

Anna found the best spot and took off her backpack. She breathed in the mountain air, scented with cedar and spruce, and thought to herself, *Thank you, God, for this beautiful moment.*

She unscrewed the cap of her metal water bottle and took a long, refreshing swig. *Water tastes so good from an aluminum water bottle,* she thought. *So much better than those nasty plastic ones.*

She opened her pack and pulled out the brown paper sack lunch that the college field station program had prepared for the campers. Hers was a vegetarian lunch bag, complete with the classic sandwich of two slices of white bread and a couple of cheese slices in between. Included in the lunch bag was also an apple and two large oatmeal raisin cookies. *Ah, this is excellent,* she thought.

Anna pulled the slices of American cheese from between the bread slices and then tossed one of the slices about ten feet away. To her surprise, a large rodent-type varmint, probably a *marmot,*[57]

---

57 Marmots look like large squirrels, with the same cute expressions as they timidly eat. They live in the crags in rocks, especially those at higher elevations in mountain ranges.

scampered from behind the rocks, grabbed the slice of bread and quickly disappeared. She laughed and said, "Well, I'm glad you could use that, my little friend."

The cheese slices were tasty, and she decided to save the apple and one of the cookies for lunch. Just as she was beginning to put her lunch back into the backpack, she noticed what looked like a mother *chipmunk*[58] and a baby chipmunk on some rocks nearby. She squinted her eyes… "Well hi there, what are you guys doing?"

After a second or two, she saw what looked like the baby jumping up and down excitedly on the back of the mother. She squinted a little harder, and suddenly the activity became clear and she said, "Oh my, I had no idea. Sorry, you guys."

After the morning respite and embarrassing the two chipmunks mating, she decided she had better urinate before leaving the cover of the trees. She was sure that everyone at the top of the mountain would see her pee if she waited until later.

Anna wore a full torso leotard under her field shorts, which allowed her to pull her shorts down without having to expose her naked behind in the field. Having students all around, she did not want to embarrass herself or any of her students with a fully exposed hiney. She removed her belt that carried her Brunton compass, camera, and hammer, and then removed her field hat. After looking around carefully, she quickly pulled her pants down and pulled the leotard to one side.

As she squatted there in a vulnerable position, she could see legs in the trees in front of her. Not just four legs and one animal, but many legs of all different lengths. She froze her movement and just watched the legs as they began to emerge from the low-hanging evergreen branches in front of her. They ran swiftly past and were moving so fast that she could feel a breeze from their movement.

---

58   Chipmunks are a small version of the squirrel and have a less bushy tail. They are tiny compared to the marmot.

Anna had squatted to pee in front of a herd of elk that was now running past her. It was an amazing sight, and, of course, her camera was too far away to grab.

A magnificent male elk appeared and stood on a rock in front of her as his herd raced by. He was enormous with his rack held high, and he snorted in her direction.

She had heard that you shouldn't look any animal in the eye if they were frightened. She looked at the ground in front of her and began to pray out loud, "Oh Lord, please don't let me die here with my shorts around my knees."

Her voice began to shake as she did what came naturally to her in times of trouble, "Our Father, who art in heaven…" Anna closed her eyes as she prayed. She heard the male elk snort loudly and move in her direction. She felt sure he was going to kill her, and she braced herself for the impact.

He walked right up to her and snorted.

She could feel his breath on her face. It smelled a lot like a cow's breath, fresh grass, and grains. He blew his breath all over her once more, and she then felt his body move past her. His hooves hit the rocks behind her and became quieter with distance.

She was scared and frozen in the squatting position. Her legs were trembling, and she was not able to stand up. When she realized she was not going to die, she tried to stand, but instead fell over backward and lay there, with her pants still down.

What an awesome, terrifying experience, she thought. *This one will go in the long list of camp stories for sure. No, wait, no one should ever know about thi*s, Anna laughed to herself. She could not let anyone know that she did not practice what she preached. She could hear her own words in her head, *don't go anywhere by yourself in this area. It could prove deadly.*

"What an idiot!" Anna laughed out loud. After she caught her breath, she rolled over onto her knees and stood up, pulling her shorts up at the same time.

She looked down at her boots and chuckled to herself, "But hey, Dad will be proud to know that I didn't pee in my boots." Her dad had given her a book titled "How Not to Piss in Your Boots" when she graduated with her B.S. in Geology years earlier.

Anna exited the wooded area and began her long trek to the top of the mountain where everyone would be gathering for lunch. Her legs still felt somewhat shaky from her terrifying adventure below.

She could see *Ben, Jeff, Jenny, and Mary*[59] tossing a Frisbee at the top. *Seriously? They have a Frisbee up there with all the rattlesnakes. Idiots*, she thought. *Oh well, at least they are not complaining.*

It took her about half an hour to reach the group.

Adam was sitting in the shade and eating a cookie.

Anna wondered sarcastically to herself, *I wonder who gave up their cookie for poor Dr. D?*

"Well, how are they doing?" asked Anna as she found a rock, safe from cactus needles and snakes, and sat next to Adam.

"Well, Ben thinks he knows what is going on. Jenny and Mary made it to the top. Jenny is pretty sure they must have missed something. Little John and Jacob are still struggling up the hill. *Jeff and Brad*[60] want to snowboard instead…. you know, the usual," he said with a little chuckle. "Perhaps we need to spread out and assume strategic positions on outcrops so that they can get enough info to start piecing this together,"

"That's a great idea," said Anna, noting Big John's nod of agreement as well.

---

59   Ben was introduced earlier. Jeff is a senior geology major from Seattle, WA. Jenny and Mary, are the lesbian couple from the NE. All are fictional characters that are not based on any real persons past or present

60   Jeff and Brad are senior geology majors from Seattle. Fictional characters not based on any person past or present.

Just as Anna and Big John agreed, there was a terrifying shriek from the direction of the Frisbee players. All three of the instructors stood up and ran toward Jeff, who was screaming and leaping laterally across the rocks,

"Fuck, I'm bit! Fuck, I'm bit!"

Anna felt like she might have a heart attack as she saw that Jeff had on only Tevas and was now falling all over the place. Would they be able to catch him if he was bitten? It was like in a Chemistry lab, and someone is on fire. You must tackle them with the fire blanket because they will run instead of 'stop, drop and roll.'

After Adam managed to catch him, it became clear that Jeff had only heard a rattle at the same time he felt a cactus spine enter the side of his foot. He assumed he was bitten.

Everyone had a laugh at Jeff's expense, and then they all went back to mapping. Poor Jeff had cactus needles in his calves and feet, though.

"This is going to slow you down a bit," said Anna, as she carefully helped Jeff remove one of the needles from his big toe. She handed him her tweezers and at one point, her pliers. He painfully removed each spine, and she followed with a dab of alcohol from her tiny med kit.

"Son of a BITCH!" he screamed as he yanked each spine free.

Anna then gave the Frisbee group a scolding mother's stare, which they surely understood. They had scared the hell out of her, and that kind of nonsense would cease.

The week moved quickly with more drama on Wednesday, when a thunderstorm with nickel-sized hail and cloud to ground lightning moved over the area. Anna told the students near her to get on the ground and to use their clipboards or backpacks to shield their heads.

Jacob, of course, was going to stand and stare the storm down, until a bolt of lightning hit a tree on a ridge below him. He then decided he'd better get down too.

Anna sighed in frustration as some of the students continued to gawk at the storm instead of following her instructions. She didn't care how silly it looked, she knew that lightning killed more people each year than any snake, mountain lion or grizzly.

Hail was always a risk as well. Some pieces could get to the size of baseballs and would require unearthing a rock. The rock might also have snakes or bugs beneath. It was not easy to lift a rock above the head to protect the brain and upper body, but it was better than having a cracked skull and broken bones.

Anna pulled her body into a sitting fetal position and placed her clipboard over her hat, holding it from below with her fingers. She hoped her demonstration would help someone else. The rocks were too large for lifting above the head up there, and there would surely be some bruised folks from this pelting.

She recalled one-time years ago when she was in the field with students and they were hit by quarter-sized hail that left bruises on her breasts, shoulders, and buttocks. These were deep painful bruises too. Being able to lift a rock was preferable to simply using a clipboard or a backpack, which only helped if the hail was up to nickel size. It was particularly difficult to hold a clipboard above the head without exposing the fingers, which could easily be busted. The rock posed a similar problem, but if it wasn't a terribly heavy rock, it was a matter of balancing the stone with your head and hands from underneath.

Thursday turned out to be even more exciting with Adam finding a deer carcass in the same clearing where Anna had been on Monday. This find was compounded by Ben's and Jeff's discovery of bear claw marks thirteen feet up on a tree at the top of the mountain, where there had not been any the day before.

Anna was more than ready to get everyone off the mountain before dusk that evening, and they still had one more day to be there. *Thank goodness for the hot days.* The bears would surely be sleeping somewhere during the heat of the day.

Adam reported the kill and bear claw marks to the local forest service and Elk reserve staff, so they would be aware of a predator in the area.

That final day of mapping, the forest service members were also in the field to investigate, which made Anna feel better about the students being there too.

The MSU faculty made sure that every team of students knew where they needed to spend their time collecting information. The idea was to get up there and get back to the trucks early at four instead of five o'clock.

Little John and Jacob had done an admirable job despite Jacob's snarky manner.

Mary obviously copied Jenny's map, they had the same wrong mapped points.

Ben's and Jeff's maps were sloppy but reasonably correct.

All in all, the students were doing fine. June had ended, and the students were feeling exhausted and ready to be getting home.

This project should be a fun one to grade, thought Anna. She was not looking forward to the grueling session for her and D. This was going to be a marathon to get all the projects graded and get all kids packed up and ready for the return trip.

Four o'clock rolled around, and everyone was at the vans, except for Jacob and Little John. The campers were anxious to get back to have dinner at the dorm and there they were, sitting and waiting on the guy who farts all the time, and the jerk who had to be his partner.

Adam asked Anna if she would consider going back up with him for a look. She instructed the students to stay put and to call for help if they weren't back to the vans by 6:15 pm.

Ben pleaded with Dr. D. to let him go instead of Anna, but this was clearly a mission for the pros. They didn't need another student on the mountain to compound their worry.

Big John was in charge, and everyone knew the drill. They were concerned for Little John and Jacob, but they were also now worried about Dr. D. and Dr. Moore. *What if the bear that left the claw marks the day before had eaten Jacob, and Little John got lost? What if the bear gets Dr. D. and Dr. Moore?*

D. and Anna scrambled up the twelve hundred feet back to the mapping area and used Anna's binoculars to scan for the students. There was no sign of the two fellows. Reluctantly, they slid back down to call for help.

Adam was worried sick. He had never lost a student during his twenty years of teaching this course. The nearest radiophone was at a small diner-gas station about two miles down the main road. They quietly rode to the diner and left their lost students behind with the sun going down. It felt like death in the vans.

When the vans stopped, no one was to get out. Only Adam went in to borrow the phone and call the authorities. After about two minutes, he emerged from the establishment and waved for everyone to come on inside.

The two missing students had gotten lost and were picked up by a truck and brought to the station just half an hour earlier. Apparently, they had done what Anna told them to do when they became hopelessly lost.

Everyone was relieved and thoroughly pissed because they had all missed dinner at the dorm. The group was starving, so Anna suggested a stop at the pizza place on the way into town.

Adam agreed, so the vans traveled to the pizza barn.

Big John's van got their first and they all jumped out and quickly found two large tables inside to seat their large group.

Little John and Jacob were the last ones to enter the pizza place.

Dr. D. spoke up as though he was finishing a conversation with someone, "Well, yes, I do believe that they told me they would provide pizza for everyone this evening."

The duo looked like deer in the headlights, and Dr. D laughed. "No kidding, aren't you guys buying?"

All the other students and Anna were cheering, "Pizza! Pizza! Pizza!"

Jacob pulled his pockets inside out to demonstrate his lack of funds.

Little John just looked like he wasn't sure if he was being teased or not.

After a few moments, Dr. D. announced, "I was just teasing, Anna is buying the pizza."

Anna, being the sweetheart that she was, prepared to gladly buy the pizza.

When the bill came, though, Adam took it to the front and paid the entire amount. That was his intention all along. He just loved watching everyone squirm. When the vans returned to the dorm, they wearily left and drudged inside to shower and relax before finishing their projects.

Dr. D. granted an extension until Saturday at 6:00 p.m. so that everyone would have time to rest and then complete their work the next day.

Chapter 13—Convergence

Anna entered the dorm and walked to her room. As she opened the door, she heard Sean's voice behind her. "Wow! Where have you guys been?"

She was so glad to see him that she put her arms around his waist without thinking about how filthy she was from a day in the field and how inappropriate it might appear if a student were to see.

"It was a hell of a day," she said. "A hell of a week. We almost lost a couple of people today. They got lost, and we couldn't find them."

"Shit, but ya did find them?

"We did." Anna said reassuringly, "They had gotten lost and walked down to the road below the mapping area. We found them at the Polar Bear Diner down the road."

"Good, that has to be one of an instructor's greatest fears."

She agreed and then invited him into her room. They sat there for about half an hour laughing and sharing stories of their week in the field. It felt so good to just sit, talk, and laugh.

"Do ya wanna go to the Beaverhead this evening?" he asked.

She looked at him wearily and said, "I would love to, but I desperately need a shower first."

"It's okay, Annie. I can wait for you."

She collected her things and went to the shower.

While sitting in Annie's room, Sean couldn't help but notice the picture of her sons that sat on the table next to her bunk. *Cute kids. The youngest one looks just like her. It must be difficult to leave them for this long.*

He then noticed her rosary beads and picked them up to look at them. They didn't look particularly special, but they did look worn like they had been used more than once. They were tan beads made of olive wood with a Benedictine cross hanging from the circle of beads.

Sean wondered, *What do these markings mean on the cross? Ah well, Annie. It means something to you.*

He tried to imagine her praying with them and smiled at the thought of her kneeling in prayer. It reminded him of his wife, Sophia. Both women had a strong spiritual connection to a creator, and he admired both of them for their unyielding faith.

Annie had shared with Sean how she had wanted to join a convent at age fifteen and how her parents refused. She was forced to date boys, but never truly lost her calling to serve God.

After she married and had children, she was drawn back to the church and to her original spiritual journey.

Her husband Robert saw her need for a spiritual life as a sign of weakness and often joked at how she would no doubt join a convent one day when he dumped her.

Sean set the beads back on the shelf as Annie entered the room. She was all washed, dried, and smelled like jasmine. She was wearing a clean pair of shorts and a cute Spanish frock with embroidered flowers on the neckline and sleeves.

Sean stared at her for a moment and thought, *She is so pretty.*

Annie noted his stare and said, "What are you looking at? She naturally assumed that he had noticed something out of place and quickly checked herself to make sure she was in order.

"Just you," he said as he rose and put his arms around her.

They stood there and hugged for a few moments until Annie heard a door open into the hallway. She pulled away suddenly as she realized how it would look to students to see their professors--married professors--embracing like lovers.

It was Sean's older student named *Alison*,[61] who had a room across the hall from Annie. She and Annie had become friends over the past weeks and struck up conversations in the laundry and the bathroom. Alison paused for a moment, smiled, and asked,

"Are you guys going to the Beaverhead?"

"We sure are," said Annie with a big smile. "Are you going too?"

"No, but you kids have a good time. See you tomorrow."

Sean was a little surprised at their familiarity and wondered if they had been talking about him. *Good Lord*, he thought. *I hope my students don't all find out about Annie and me.* Sean prided himself on his professionalism with his students and didn't want to lose their respect.

Annie noted his reticence and assured him that Alison had not mentioned him as they walked down the hallway and on toward the Beaverhead.

As they entered the darkness, Annie felt Sean's hand near hers, and they both reached and held hands. It was spontaneous.

The night air was so cool and crisp. She felt invigorated by the evening air and the walk with Sean and didn't want to ever let him go.

As they entered the light of the streets, they continued to hold hands. At this point, neither one of them cared what others thought. They were together, and that was all that mattered.

When they reached the Main Street of bars and restaurants, Annie suggested that they go somewhere other than the Beaverhead, so they could talk and hear one another. She just wanted to be with Sean and only Sean.

---

61 Alison was an older Earth Science major from California who was taking summer field camp to fulfill her geology requirements for teaching. She is a fictional character loosely based on a friend of the author, now deceased.

Sean agreed and figured that he knew the reason why she wasn't keen on the Beaverhead. He too did not really want to have any negative encounters and didn't care where they went as long as he was with Annie.

They walked past the swinging doors, past the Cowboy's Wash Laundromat and back around the blocks, until they eventually ended up at Grandpa's Place. They sat in a corner booth and talked about their favorite actors, whose pictures were hanging on the walls,

"I can't believe you guys are leaving on Monday." Said Sean sadly. It didn't seem possible that they could have just found each other and now must be separated.

"Yes, but I must admit to being excited about seeing my boys again. I miss them so much."

"That must be difficult for ya to leave them to do this kind of work."

"Yes, it is. I don't look forward to seeing their dad again though."

She finally admitted to Sean that her marriage was ending and even though Robert had moved out and they were separated, she had still been hoping to reconcile for the sake of the children.

Now that she had experienced such a spontaneous and fulfilling intimacy with a man, it was clear what would make her happy, and it was not sex without intimacy. The intimacy that she shared with Sean, without sex, was far better than any sexual encounter she'd had before. She was in love with him and she knew he was in love with her too. They didn't have to say the words, they felt it. Their connection, their love, was much more than words or sex.

In Annie's mind, this was what love was really supposed to feel like. This is what God had intended for a loving, nurturing relationship. It should be filled with respect for the dignity of each partner, and not just nonstop sexual intercourse to gratify a partner.

"At least you are separated and having issues in yer marriage, Annie. What the hell is my excuse," he said, as he looked down at the watch Sophia had given him for his birthday.

"I'm so sorry, Sean," said Annie. "I feel guilty for …whatever this is."

"Oh, goodness, No! I love this…whatever this is. It's friendship. It's more. I just don't know… I just don't know. It scares the hell out of me, and it's also the best thing that I've ever felt. Ya know what I mean?"

"Yes, I think I do."

"Ah well," said Sean, "Let's not waste our time trying to figure it all out then. Let's just enjoy the time we have, okay, love?"

They sat, talked, and drank beer for what seemed like a very short time. To their surprise,

Grandpa's was getting ready to close. The couple walked back to the dorm, not arm in arm but with their arms around each other's waist.

Annie wondered aloud, "Will I ever see you again?"

"Oh yes. Of that, I am certain."

She choked back tears and tightened her grip around his waist. "What we have is so special, Sean."

"It's a once in a lifetime kind of experience," he replied.

They walked silently for the rest of the way back to the dorms. They both had a long day or two coming up, and both agreed that they wanted to see each other again before she was to leave.

The couple stopped in front of her door. Sean looked around to make sure they were alone and then leaned down to kiss Annie sweetly on the cheek and then lifted the back of her hand to his lips.

She put her arms around his neck and gently pulled him down where she could sweetly and tenderly kiss his cheek and nose. They held hands for a moment or two considering each other's eyes and then finally released their fingers.

For Annie, it was yet another night of lying alone in her bed and thinking of Sean instead of her husband, wondering what God's plan was for this experience. *Was it a sign that she could truly be loved and that what she had with Robert was not what God intended?* She would have to ask Fr. Steven and the sisters on her return.

For Sean, it was another evening of being alone in his bunk thinking of Annie. *How could they legitimately see each other again?* He did not want this to be the end, either. They were more than friends. If nothing else, they would remain old-new friends.

Chapter 14—It is Final

Annie skipped breakfast the next morning and was in Dr. D's room bright and early to begin accepting student projects. She did this so that Adam could take care of the servicing of the vans and getting things ready for the return trip.

Ben was first, of course, and sat for several minutes talking to Dr. Moore about the return trip. "I can't wait to camp at Devil's Tower!" he said. "Apparently, they are showing 'Close Encounters' every single night this summer."

Annie was so amused and charmed by his enthusiasm. She thought, *Students like Ben are such a breath of fresh air.*

"See you later this evening at the Beaverhead, Dr. Moore," chortled Ben, as he left through the open door. "Hope you don't have to work too late on these projects."

The next student to come was Jacob, who looked disappointed to find Annie instead of Adam. "When will Dr. D. get back?" he asked. "I have questions for him."

Annie didn't take it personally and suggested that Dr. D. would return in about two hours. "Do you need a little more time, Jacob?" she asked.

He looked surprised at her question, and sheepishly asked, "Yes, is that a possibility?"

"Absolutely. Everyone works at different rates. What is important is for you to finish the project. It is also important for you to do a good job and to have learned something in the process. I'm sure that Dr. D. would approve."

Jacob half-smiled appreciatively and exited the room.

Anna felt a personal satisfaction at being able to help him. She thought to herself, *It is students like Jacob who challenge us, but they are also the ones who make teaching worthwhile, especially when they can be transformed in some way.* She silently praised God for her ability to help him.

Adam returned and told Anna to feel free to go get some lunch if she'd like.

Anna asked, "Do you want me to bring you anything?"

She already knew the answer, as she wasn't hungry and knew all too well that he hadn't had time to stop and get lunch. He knew that if he gave her the free time to get lunch, she would provide sustenance for them both.

"Sure," said Adam. "Whatever you're having."

"Ok then," she said, "I'll bring you your favorite, a jalapeno burger with fries...and a vanilla shake, is it?"

His face lit up with childish anticipation and nodded that he wanted exactly what she had suggested. *He is so predictable,* thought Anna, as she smiled to herself and set out on her journey to the "Burger Barn" down the street.

She walked out into the afternoon dry heat, humming to herself. She was happy and had a skip in her step as she gleefully greeted the fellows in the gas station and then the woman with the very large (fat!) cat.

The smell of burgers and fries filled the air as she approached Adam's favorite diner. She could also see Alison and two other students from Sean's school. Alison motioned for Anna to join them.

"You're awfully happy today. I wonder if a special someone is to blame?" She asked in a teasing voice.

"I'm always happy," said Anna, "Haven't you noticed?"

Alison looked her in the eyes and said, "I see it in your face. You're in love."

"I am just happy," Anna said, "You know how I am?"

"Sure, sure," Alison teased. "Maybe you're not, but I'm pretty sure he is. The way he looks at you…? Lady...believe me."

After about half an hour, Anna returned with Adam's favorite food, and they worked into the evening to finish grading. Anna heard music coming from down the hall and wondered who was playing the guitar. She noted that Sean's door was open, but he was absent. She stuck her head in Alex's room to see who was playing music.

"Annie!" said Sean excitedly, "Come on in and enjoy the music."

Alex stopped playing and stood for a moment to get a beer from the cooler. "What's your poison?" he queried.

"Ooooooh, I'll take a *Moose Drool!*"[62] said Annie excitedly, as she perused the choices available.

Alex was playing a *Bill Staines*[63] song. Annie loved his music and began harmonizing, *"There was a time gone by … Simple love was the love I knew...now once again, I remember you..."*

Sean and Annie had no idea how prophetic those lyrics would one day be for them. As Annie sang, Sean was so pleased. He had heard her sing along to the jukebox but was amazed at how gorgeous her authentic voice seemed to be.

Alex was pleased, too, and asked, "Do you play?"

"Oh yes, I play all the time," said Anna.

Alex handed her his guitar, and she began to play.

"Will you sing us a song?" he asked.

---

62 Popular brown ale brewed in Missoula, MT at the "Big Sky Brewing Company." Annie's favorite beer.

63 An American, popular folk song writer and artist and was one of Annie's favorites. See the bibliography for a complete citation.

Annie nodded and began singing a folk ballad. As she played and sang, she closed her eyes. Sean wanted so much to get up and kiss her eyelids. She sang like an angel, and her voice had a very haunting nature to it; naturally beautiful, just like her. There was a hint of Joan Baez, mixed with Nancy Griffith and of course, Mary Black.

Feeling weary from the day of work, Annie thanked Alex for his hospitality, and Sean followed her into the hall. "So, tomorrow's yer last day?" he asked in a disappointed tone.

Annie choked back tears as she quietly said, "Yes, afraid so." Her eyes were so sad as she looked at him.

Sean leaned toward her and whispered in her ear, "I could stop by later if ya want."

She nodded and responded quietly, "I will leave my door unlocked," and left to go to her room.

Heart and Soul

"Do you think that you have a choice in loving someone?
The answer will always be no.
Your soul picks who you love, and your heart seals the deal.
How little a choice we have over such things
when your heart knows what it wants,
and your soul knows when it's real."
N.R. Hart, "Heart and Soul."

Annie went to her room and lay down on her bunk. She wasn't sure what would happen but knew she wanted to be with Sean. She laid there, wondering if Sean would be able to get away from the gathering downstairs. As her eyes began to close, she heard her doorknob turn. Her heart leaped in her chest, and she sat up on the bed.

It was Sean. He entered the room and closed the door.

Annie stood up, put her arms around him, and leaned toward the door to lock it behind him. The couple stood there together, just as they had during their dance.

Sean leaned down and kissed her gently on her cheek. She put her arms around his neck and pulled his face toward hers, and they kissed.

Annie began running her hands under his shirt and touching his muscular chest and back. He shuddered and together they removed his shirt. She sat on the bunk, pulling him with her.

Sean whispered, "I'm so scared."

"Me, too."

Sean removed Annie's shirt and began to kiss her face and neck while cradling her firm, yet soft breasts in his hands.

Annie could feel he was aroused, and she gasped at the size of his... his... She kicked off her shorts as Sean lowered his to the floor.

With no fumbling or hesitation, their two bodies merged. Sean was deep inside of her, and she gasped as she felt his powerful hips and thighs push gently into hers.

Sean began to moan loudly, saying, "Annie, Annie, ahhh!"

After a few moments of oscillating slowly in and out of her body, his exclamation of pleasure began to escalate into a high-pitched crescendo of passion.

Annie placed her hand over his mouth and said, "Shhh, shhh..." and then couldn't contain her own vocalization of intense pleasure.

The joining was not fast or frenzied, but instead slow and controlled to maximize the motion, penetration, and pleasure.

Annie had never had a lover who focused so much of his primal energy on watching their two bodies move together and screaming with pleasure at each movement.

Sean pushed himself up with his arms so that he could watch Annie. With his chest up, he looked down to see their bodies beautifully coupled. "It's so beautiful, Annie," he whispered.

He could see all of her body as he made love to her. Her breasts were full, and her nipples were erect. He watched her face as they moved together and touched her nipples with his fingers. With each complete cycle of penetration, he could feel them become harder and harder.

Annie panted with each movement and wanted to scream as she felt him swell even more inside of her. Just as she thought she was going to explode with pleasure, she opened her eyes to see Sean lean his head back and scream as he began to climax inside of her.

To her astonishment, she felt her own release with him. She had never done that before with anyone. The couple screamed out in pleasure together as Sean slowly continued to move to allow both he and Annie to experience the full measure of joy.

Unexpectedly, Annie could feel wave after wave of orgasms as Sean slowly moved. She continued to move and put her arms around him and pulled him down on top of her. They lay there together with Annie's thighs trembling from his hips pressing into hers.

Sean was much bigger than her and she felt every ounce of his muscles on top of her. Sensing this, Sean moved to lie beside her. As he rolled, she did not release her embrace, and she continued to roll over on top of him and sat astride his hips.

He reached up and caressed her breasts once more. Annie began to moan and move again, "Ooooooh," and he was erect again inside of her, and they were one once more.

She wanted to scream as she experienced yet another orgasm from the penetration.

As he cupped her breasts, he forced himself to lie still as Annie moved. She was now in control and began to shake her head from side to side and gasp in release as she had the most significant and prolonged orgasm of her life. She felt like she had been running a race. Her throat was sore and dry.

As Sean felt her nipples harden and then release with her orgasm, he couldn't help but climax with her.

Annie continued to gasp for air and shudder with pleasure, Sean thought, *My God Annie, could there be anything more beautiful?*

The couple lay there together for hours; one body, one spirit, making love repeatedly. It was like nothing they had ever truly experienced before, or at least for Annie it was the first time she had realized that she could even have multiple orgasms.

Sean and Annie lay there like spoons in a drawer, exhausted from making love repeatedly.

Annie woke to Sean's beautiful smiling eyes, as he had been watching her as she slept.

She looked at his face and stroked his beard, "Good morning, love," she whispered softly.

"Morning," he said quietly. "I'd probably better go, Annie. The sun will be up soon."

Annie pulled him close and would probably have pleasured him for hours, except for the fact that she had to go to the bathroom-- badly. He no doubt felt the same. She hated for him to go but knew it would be difficult to not be seen by the students if he did not go soon.

She lay there watching him dress. His body was so strong and smooth. He was very tall, tan, and oh the muscles of his legs. They were so well defined. *Oooh...He is …. sigh...so sexy, and his butt... was not big,* she thought indignantly. *What on earth was D. talking about?* As he pulled his shorts on, she wanted to wrap her legs around him. Annie thought that he was the most beautiful form she had ever set eyes on.

After making sure he was completely dressed, he blew her a kiss as he slowly opened the door, looked both ways, and ran.

She was left alone, aching for him. Annie was in love. She was not hungry but knew she could find coffee in Adam's room, and he would surely be up waiting on his slacking partner by now. As she showered, Annie couldn't believe how incredibly sore her thighs felt. She almost hated to wash his scent away. His smell made her feel safe and relaxed. She wrapped her towel around her and began to brush her teeth.

Alison entered the bathroom, smiled big, and said, "Wow, was that you last night?"

Anna blushed and said, "Oh my gosh, don't tell me."

Alison started laughing and said, "I went to see who was dying. The auras swirling from beneath your door was a hell of a show. It was beautiful, lady. Simply beautiful."

"Oh, my goodness," gasped Annie. "I hope others didn't notice."

"Oh, no one missed that light show. It was like fireworks on the 4th of July in that room. See, I told you he was crazy about you."

Sean quickly returned to his room and managed to avoid being seen by Adam, who had his door open and coffee brewing down the hall. He felt totally knackered from the extreme physical activity of the night before. He thought to himself, *Sean, that was a hell of a thing. Wow! My God, Catholic girls are really ... they are just wonderful.*

As he leaned forward into the shower, he could hear someone enter the area behind him. He turned around to see Adam brushing his teeth. He felt for a moment like Anna's dad had just entered the bathroom, but of course, they were about the same age, so that was ridiculous. Sean knew that Adam felt protective of her and probably secretly was a little jealous of their special connection. *Who wouldn't love Annie?* he thought.

The two men nodded to one another as Sean left the shower to get dressed. "Hey, I have coffee in the room if you have a mug.," said Adam. "Come on down and get some."

"Ok, sure," said Sean, but deep down inside, Adam was the last person he wanted to talk to that morning.

Even though Sean was not a Catholic, he was confident that the entire dorm knew he had enjoyed a night of passionate lovemaking with the prettiest lady in the camp. Annie was the one that should be feeling Catholic guilt, not Sean.

Annie entered Adam's room, and he immediately queried, "What were you up to last night? I thought I heard you singing down the hall. That was you. Right?"

"Oh yes, replied Annie, avoiding eye contact to hide her guilty conscience and quickly added, "Yes, and I went right to bed too."

Adam stopped and looked at her for a long moment, "You went directly to bed, did you?" He asked, in an accusing tone as if he knew something that she didn't.

Just as Anna was about to have to engage in the sin of either telling a lie or admitting a night of unbridled, sinful passion, Alex walked up to the door and said, "Is that coffee I smell?"

Thank God for Alex, thought Annie. She heaved a huge sigh of relief at not having to answer the question. She was a horrible liar and had always been told she was too honest about everything.

Adam at once became a gracious host and showed Alex his stash of sweeteners and creamer in his top left drawer. Soon several people were in the room getting coffee.

Anna found herself making at least two more pots as D's idea of coffee was a little bit of coffee in a lot of water. She was an expert at making a bold blend of coffee using just about any brand.

Sean was noticeably absent from the coffee line, and Annie wondered if he was sleeping. She knew she was exhausted and would have a stressful day and figured he must feel the same way.

Campers were beginning to file out of the dorms with their laundry and were making plans for this 4th of July holiday, while faculty members worked to finish grading in time to also enjoy the day. There was a discussion of taking a van to a neighboring town for a good old-fashioned Rocky Mountain Rodeo. Others were interested in playing pool or poker at the local establishments.

It was Sunday, so some students were finding their way to local churches. Anna knew there would be a Mass at noon, so she would have to work until 11:45 and then walk to the church a few blocks away. She wondered if there would be time for her to attend Mass.

"D., do you think we'll be finished in time for me to go to Mass today?"

"Oh, sure." He said, "I wonder if they have confessions on Sunday?"

Anna, shocked, asked in an indignant tone, "Why would you think I need to go to confession on a Sunday?"

"Well, you didn't go yesterday like you usually do, so I just assumed you might need to today. Why, did you do something you need to feel guilty about?" he teased.

Anna felt her face get very hot as she blushed at his question and stood there speechless.

"Hey, I was just kidding, okay?" said D. "We will get this done in time."

"I'm just tired," she said, to which he replied, "Well, we both need a good night tonight for that long drive tomorrow."

Anna's heart sank, and she felt so sad at the thought of having to leave Sean the next day. She excused herself for a moment and walked to the bathroom on the floor above them. After a few moments of tears, she composed herself, washed her face, and returned to finish her job.

Chapter 15—Heaven Can WAIT

The church bells from St. Anne's began to ring in the distance, and Adam and Anna were still grading. He looked over at Anna, who looked very tired as she was slogging through one of the reports… "Isn't that the church bells calling you Catholics to supper?"

Anna looked at him with a half-smile and said, "Yes, I guess I should go? I will be back in an hour, and then you can take a break, how does that sound?"

This was satisfactory with Adam, who intended to take a nap anyway while she went to church. "Go enjoy your church, "he said, as he waved her out of the room. "I will see you in an hour."

Anna walked down the sidewalk to the church and was pleased that she had not missed the opening song. Apparently, the bells toll about ten minutes before Mass, so that everyone has time to make it to the church.

As she approached the steps to the church, she could hear the congregation singing one of her favorite songs, "We Are His People, The Flock of the Lord."

Anna loved that song. Nothing gave her more pleasure than to attend Mass and sing. She was tired but felt joyful as she sang. She found a spot on the very back pew against the wall.

The church was late 1800s and early 1900s architecture, no doubt copied from European churches. It featured the long narrow main room filled with pews on either side of a central aisle, which led up another set of steps to the altar, positioned in the center of the top platform. Behind the altar was a wooden cross of contemporary design with what looked like a lovingly hand-crafted *corpus*[64] hanging with clearly detailed nails in the hands and feet, a crown of thorns and the familiar wounds of Christ. Directly below the corpus was a traditional-looking *tabernacle*,[65] and flanking the altar were the statues of Joseph and Mary -- the Holy Family.

The readings for the day dealt with the mercy of God and how nothing keeps God's love from us, except our own choices. In the book of Matthew, Jesus is commissioning His disciples to go forth and spread the word of God. As part of the instructions to them, He discussed the conditions for discipleship and eternal life. [66]

> Matthew 10: "37 Whoever loves father or mother more than me is not worthy of me, and whoever loves son or daughter more than me is not worthy of me; 38 and whoever does not take up his cross [67] and follow after me is not worthy of me. 39 Whoever finds his life will lose it, and whoever loses his life for my sake will find it..."

The priest emphasized these readings and the message of God wanting all to seek him and to love him by choice, not because one felt they had no choice.

There is always free will and when a person chooses to sin-- chooses earthly treasures instead of heavenly ones--then God is truly sad because the choice was freely made to not make a relationship with God a priority.

Anna reflected on this and pondered her options in life. Had she genuinely put God first in her own life? She felt compelled to

---

64   Corpus is Latin for body – a dead human form. In this case, the corpus is that of Jesus Christ.

65   The Catholic Tabernacle is a portable sanctuary which houses the body of Christ. Some are lined with gold. It is considered a holy lodging of the Lord.

66   Holy Bible, Matthew 10: 37-42.

67   ...as disciples of the Lord, we are asked to die for our own sins, so that we may be reborn with Christ. We must share in his passion and death, so that we too may rise to eternal life through Him and with Him.

ask God, *Is my cross to bear, a loveless, abusive marriage or loving a married man, or is it both? Why did You put Sean in my life, Lord, if You didn't want me to find true love, true happiness? Am I genuinely glorifying You in my relationship with Robert? What do You want of me, Lord? Where do You want me to serve You? Come Lord and strengthen and guide me, so that I may choose to take up my cross and follow You, to truly serve You in my life. Amen.*

On her knees before God, Anna watched as the priest held up the host for consecration and said, "Take this, all of you, and eat it, for this is my body, which will be given up for you."

Anna fixed her gaze on the body of Christ, and spoke aloud, "My Lord and my God."

"Take this all of you and drink from it, for this is the chalice of my blood, the blood of the new and eternal covenant, which will be poured out for you and for many for the forgiveness of sins. Do this in memory of me."

Again, with her gaze fixed on the consecrated chalice holding the blood of Christ, she responded, "My Lord and my God."

Anna had freely and with great faith proclaimed the divinity of Christ and her recognition of His grace presence in the Eucharist. This bread and wine were, in fact, the very same that Jesus broke and shared with His disciples at the Jewish *Seder*[68] meal at Passover.

At that very moment, she realized that even though Jesus loved her and called her to His feast, she was in a state of mortal sin. Even though she felt that her relationship with Robert was not a sacramental union, she had to consider that Sean's might be. She had just committed adultery, which is one of the big ten. *"Thou shalt not commit adultery."*

---

68   Jewish service on the first nights of Passover. Jesus was a Jew and the last supper with his disciples is in fact a Jewish Seder meal because it was the religious observance of God's Passover of the first born of Israel.

She had taken a vow before God and His church to love her husband and to be with him, forsaking all others, until death. Sean had obviously taken a similar vow. Any sexual relationship outside of marriage would be considered a sin.

As a Catholic, she could not in good conscience, approach the communal sacrament while in a state of mortal sin. To do so was in itself a sin.

Anna felt such a tremendous sense of guilt and unworthiness. Tears welled up in her eyes as she sat in the back. She watched as everyone lined up and moved forward to receive the body and blood of Christ; to become temples of the Lord; to be filled with grace; to share in grace received. There she sat feeling sinful and sorrowful, not worthy to touch the body and blood of Christ; genuinely separated from God.

The very definition of sin is *"willful separation from God."*

Even still, Anna felt the grace presence of the Lord as she quietly knelt and prayed. She knew she was being purified simply by sitting in the presence of the eucharist, the body of Christ, but she still felt the sting of separation, her willful separation from God.

If she were not willing to put God before Sean, she would not be able to participate fully as a part of the body of Christ. She was left feeling so sad. Not only was she separated from God, but also tomorrow she would be separated from her soul mate, her once-in-a-lifetime love, Sean.

Anna prayed quietly, *God, how can such a love be so wrong? Why is this love wrong, and the experience I have with Robert considered, right? One love brings me joy and self-respect, while the other leaves me feeling degraded and worthless. Please, Lord, forgive me my sins and my human weakness, and forgive Sean. Please don't allow my selfishness to harm his eternal soul too. In Jesus' name, I pray. Amen.*

Anna joined in on the closing hymn, "... *Lead me, Lord, by the light of truth...*"

What a beautiful song and message? thought Anna. She was the first to walk down the steps of the church to shake the priest's hand and thank him for his excellent homily. As she walked away, she felt the love of God within her. She knew that God loved her regardless of her feelings at that moment.

He was always waiting with open arms to heal the broken and to recover the lost sheep. God was with her and loved her. This reality would sustain her in the weeks, months, and even years to come.

When she returned to Adam's room, she found him lying on his bunk, gently snoring. She smiled and thought about sneaking in and tickling him while he was vulnerable. He was like an overgrown child in so many ways and triggered the mother in all women he encountered. He was a little boy who needed their help...so sweet, so cute, so helpless...ah...and he played on those instincts better than anyone else Anna knew.

She decided to let him sleep a little longer and walked on past his room down the corridor to Sean's door, which was open. She shyly looked around the corner to find him and Alex working on projects.

Alex noticed Anna first and said, "Hi there!"

Sean nervously stood up and said, "Oh, hi there!"

"Sorry, D. is snoring, and I saw your door open. Thought maybe I'd catch you guys snoring too," she said with a big smile and a chuckle.

"Not here." Said Alex, " We are working hard so we can go watch fireworks later this evening."

"Are ya going to the fireworks?" asked Sean. "Yer welcome to come with us."

Alex looked a little bit surprised that Sean had so enthusiastically invited Annie to join them. He didn't mind, but clearly had been noticing a vibe of attraction from Sean toward Annie.

She responded, "Oh, I'd love that. I hope D. and I will be finished by then."

Again, Alex was smiling at the schoolboy behavior of Sean when talking to Annie. He knew Sean as a formidable intellectual and a genuinely nice guy as well, who seemed to be reduced to a nervous and giddy schoolboy when Annie was in the room.

Sean nervously responded, "Okay then, Annie. I'll come to check on you two when we get ready to go."

Alex was sure he could sense a change in Annie's demeanor as well, like a maiden on her first date. *Ha-ha…they are just too funny,* thought Alex.

Annie smiled and said, "You bet," as she turned on her toe and almost skipped down the hallway to Dr. D.'s room.

For Annie, all thoughts of separating herself from God were gone. She was happier than she'd ever been before in her entire life and how could that be if God wasn't part of this cosmic equation, which included Annie and Sean as variables.

Chapter 16—Fireworks

Anna returned to find D. awake and running his fingers through his hair. "Oh, you are finally up," she chirped."

"Yes," he said, "You must have had a good Mass. You seem very happy."

"I always love Mass," she said, "Oh, and Sean and Alex invited us to join them for fireworks this evening as well."

"Well, of course, they did," said Adam with a sarcastic tone. "I'm sure they invited you, and you have invited me...hmm?"

Anna looked guilty and said, "Well yes, but I assumed they meant you too."

He just laughed and began to pour another cup of coffee. "I'm sure they will miss you," he said as he picked up a project and continued to grade.

The fireworks would not begin until about a half-hour after dark, so when the clock turned to 8:00 p.m. Anna looked over at Adam and said, "Hey?"

Before she could say another word, he motioned to the door and said, "Go, freshen up. I'm sure your boyfriend will be here soon enough."

Anna gave him a look like, "You are kidding, right?"

He then said, "Just go. See you soon."

"You are coming too, aren't you?" she said with sadness in her voice.

"Maybe, we'll see. Now just get."

Anna gladly left to go get her dress she had washed and hung up. As she entered her room, she saw her bunk with the sheets entirely off and on the floor and was reminded of the goings-on from the night before, a firework display of the cosmic kind.

Wow! Annie, what the hell? She thought to herself as she picked up her clothes from the floor and gathered her mostly wet towel to go rinse off the day's sweat.

Sean and Alex both walked together down to Dr. D. 's room, where he was sitting and still grading.

"Ya are coming with us, D.?" Said Sean.

"Sure you want me to?" asked D.

Surprised at D.'s candor, Alex chimed in, "Yes, it's going to be fun. We'll have beer too."

Anna then walked into the room, and all three men stopped to give her a once over. She was glowing, absolutely glowing.

Adam found himself feeling very attracted to her in a way he hadn't allowed himself before.

Alex thought to himself, *Hubba, Hubba, Sean. You lucky dog.*

Sean and Annie smiled at each other, and everyone else in the room disappeared for what seemed like an eternity, but just for a few seconds. Anna broke her trance and said cheerfully, "So where do we find these fireworks? Who's driving?"

Alex, clearly the only one who had done his homework, said, "Oh, we will walk there from here and then on to the Beaverhead for a goodbye send-off to you guys. Sound okay?"

Everyone nodded in agreement as Adam gathered his things and followed them out of the dorm room.

The group of friends and colleagues walked out into the dusk of the day to see one of the most beautiful mountain sunsets of the summer camp. It was simply stunning, with oranges, pinks, light blues, and *crepuscular rays*[69]--also known as God's rays--that streamed through the broken *stratocumulus clouds*[70] on the horizon.

Anna looked up and excitedly directed everyone's attention to a cloud with a "silver lining." "Can you believe it, guys? An actual silver lining! I've seen everything now; the aurora, a fireball and now a silver lining."

They all smiled at Anna's infectious enthusiasm. She was simply a delight.

"Does it get any better than this?" she asked.

"Not for you, Anna," said D. in a teasing voice, with a satisfied smile on his face.

The sun was slowly going down, and everyone seemed to be walking in the same general direction. Apparently, the entire community knew what was going on, and this heightened Anna's pleasure at realizing that it was a big deal. She loved fireworks.

As they approached an area with people with lawn chairs, blankets, etc., Anna suddenly acknowledged that they hadn't thought to bring anything to sit on. The thought of sitting in a bush-hogged field wasn't very appealing, so she would stand. The ranger station was sponsoring a controlled display to make sure that the station and small town would not burn down if things went awry.

Anna noted a set of playground equipment nearby and asked, "You guys want to go sit on the swings? It might be less buggy than the field."

"Excellent suggestion, Annie," said Sean.

---

69   Sunbeams that usually occur at sunset. Rays that appear to begin when the Sun is below the horizon. Also known as God rays.

70   Clouds that are usually low hanging on the horizon and not high up in the atmosphere.

Adam felt a twinge of annoyance at his calling her Annie. He was clearly jealous of their friendship and couldn't wait to leave the next day to get her away from this *"slick git"*[71] with an accent.

Alex and D. both decided to stay and stand in the field. Anna and Sean walked over to the swings and sat down.

Sean didn't quite fit in his tiny swing seat, so he stood behind Annie and offered to give her a push, "Annie? wanna swing?"

"Sure, I haven't done that since I was a little girl," she giggled.

Annie could feel the air move through her hair as it lifted her hair back, away from her face. She had on a short little dress, and the breeze blew up her skirt and enveloped her thighs. The experience was so fun and sensuous.

Sean loved watching her lean back and enjoy each forward oscillation; being with Annie made him feel like a kid again. Her love of life was so infectious.

How could anyone be this happy? How could WE be this happy? he thought.

For the couple, everything else was outside of their combined space. They were together, and someone with the ability to see auras, like Alison, would clearly see the intertwined spiritual connection, and it was beautiful.

As Alison said, "swirling, brilliant energy...truly beautiful to watch." According to her, Sean and Anna had their own fireworks the night before, and those were every bit as awe-inspiring as the ones set off during big celebrations.

As the fireworks began, Annie and Sean abandoned their own activity and walked over to be with the others. Alison and a couple of other students were also standing with Alex. Everyone looked up and enjoyed the celebration.

---

71   A pejorative, in this case implying that the person was a charmer but of questionable ethics.

Alison asked Anna, "Hey, I wonder if this noise is bothering the wildlife?"

Anna responded, "Gosh, I hope not. However, I don't see how they could not notice it. Thankfully it will only last about fifteen minutes."

The air was filled with the smell of sulfur, freshly mown hay, and dust. Anna was glad for the ability to sense so much of the world around her. She would never forget this night with her friends, and especially with her Sean.

"Well, let's get to the Beaverhead!" said Alex.

"I'm buying," said Sean.

Annie and Adam were both smiling and glad to be sharing a brew with their new friends and colleagues.

As usual, the place was packed, but Adam was able to find a booth. He was so lucky in that manner. Annie slid in next to him and then Sean, followed by Alex, then Allison and two other students in chairs that were pulled up. There they were, drinking the night away, laughing and enjoying each other's company.

Adam got up and went to the jukebox.

Annie shouted over the crowd noise to Sean, "There he goes. I'm sure he will select *Patsy Cline*." [72]

Sean chuckled, "I certainly hope so. I want one last dance before ya go."

Annie smiled and looked at his eyes, which were glistening in the lights of the saloon. He was the most handsome man she had ever seen.

Alex and Alison glanced at one another and smiled as they both noted that the couple was in their own little space once more.

Adam sat down and began to sing when the song "Walking After Midnight" came on. Sean and Annie asked to get out of their

---

72   Dr. D's favorite country vocalist. She was an award-winning singer and songwriter of the 1950s.

spot in the center of the booth. Sean took her hand and led her to the dance floor. This time, he really was with her, and she really was his date!

They began to dance a slow two-step. Annie was so impressed that he knew the southern dance form. She laughed and followed his lead as he pulled her around and slid around the dance floor.

They looked like two Olympic skaters, only slower. Annie's dress pulled up slightly in the back as Sean put his arm around her for a twirl.

Adam was mesmerized and wished it was him dancing instead of Sean. After all, he had taught Anna how to two-step years ago.

Alison had a wide smile on her face as she watched her new friend and her favorite professor have a wonderful time simply enjoying each other. *It is so romantic,* she thought.

Sean put both of his hands on Annie's hips as he pushed her through the dance. At the end of the dance, they moved together, chest to chest, hips to hips and then the music changed to a slower song, Patsy Cline's, "Crazy, …I'm crazy for loving you…"

As they moved slowly together, there was no space between them. Annie put her head on his chest and didn't mind who might be watching. She didn't even notice Steve at the bar looking disgusted that Sean was with her instead of him.

Sean glanced over at the booth where Alex and others were seated and wondered what they might be thinking, but like Annie, he really didn't care at this point. He was with her, and that was all that mattered. He held one of her hands, in the classic two-step fashion, and the warmth of her body on his and her face on his chest felt so comfortable and loving.

The song changed again, and it was a faster song. Sean took Annie's hand in his and put one hand on her hip to push her to the traditional two-step distance and began to dance once again. "She's in Love With the Boy, "came on. Annie started singing loudly, *"She's in love with the boy."*

Sean, feeling a little bit tipsy began to sing too, *"He's in love with the girl."* Ha-ha.

They were both laughing as they sang and danced. Alex, Alison, and even Adam were all laughing too.

Annie could not remember having a better time in her life. She was so in love with this wonderful man and did not want to ever let him go.

The dance ended, and the couple came over to sit down.

"Wow, you guys are great together!" Alison shouted excitedly.

"Who knew Sean could dance like a Southerner?" said Annie as she looked at Sean's big smile.

"Hey, we two-step in New Zealand too, ya know," said Sean.

Adam chimed in with a laugh saying, "Hey, I taught her everything I know, and that's not much."

Alex ordered another round of longnecks, and the group sat there for another half hour or so. It was getting late when Adam finally leaned over to Annie and suggested, "We might better call it a night. We've got a long drive tomorrow."

She agreed and yelled to Sean, "We need to go. We've got a long drive."

Everyone nodded in agreement as they stood up to shake hands and give hugs and well wishes.

Sean and Annie gazed at each other for a few moments, and he knew she would leave her door unlocked again for him. She didn't have to say it.

Alison thought to herself, *Oh boy, I bet there will be more fireworks this evening for sure.*

Chapter 17—Long Trip Home

Anna, Big John, and Dr. D. met at the trailers and hitched one of them to each of the vans. Anna had roused all campers at 6:00 a.m., and they would soon be arriving with their bags for loading. Big John loaded his van and trailer, and Adam and Anna loaded theirs as well. Everyone was somber and seemed tired, not excited, as they prepared for the return trip.

All thermoses were filled with Adam's brew, and they were ready. It took another hour for the last of the students to arrive with their belongings.

Anna and Big John then had the pleasure of collecting room keys and checking the rooms before departure.

Jacob had "accidentally" taken a pillow, which had to be returned, but the others seemed set and ready to roll by 8:30 a.m.

Alison, Anna's new friend, came walking from the dorm holding an envelope. The envelope had Alison's mailing address-- this was pre-internet.

"Anna, I want us to stay in touch, okay? I just really love you." she said with tears in her eyes.

"Me too, Allison," said Anna, as she hugged her tightly and joked through tears that there was no stamp on the envelope.

"Have you seen Sean yet?"

"Not yet, but he said…" and Annie saw him leaning against the doorway to the dorm, eating grapes.

He had been watching the two women as they said goodbye. Earlier that morning when he left her room, he had promised that he would not miss sending her off. Annie looked at him, and he began to walk over to her van. Everyone was loaded and ready to go.

Adam intercepted. Sean shook his hand and wished him a good "rest of camp," and Sean wished him a safe journey home.

Annie nervously took her place in the driver's seat while the two men talked. She wasn't sure how they were supposed to say goodbye. Just when Annie was sure she wouldn't get to hug him again, he came around to her door of the van, reached up and helped her down from her driver's seat, right into his arms. Her feet barely touched the ground as he embraced and kissed her passionately in front of everyone.

The students on the vans erupted with cheers, making all kinds of noise at the sight of Anna being kissed by Sean.

He put her hat on her head, lowered his sunglasses so she could see his eyes, and told her, "This is not goodbye. I will see ya in September, and we will go to Yellowstone and the Stillwater together. I promise."

She smiled and laughed through tears. She waved goodbye as she looked back to see him standing next to Alison as the vans pulled away.

"Wow! Dr. Moore. I'm speechless," said Ben, astounded at what he'd just witnessed.

Anna turned to him and said, "Me too."

"You know, I think he likes you," said Ben.

"Apparently so," said D., indignantly.

Anna didn't address any other questions or comments about Dr. Anderson and herself. It was just a kiss. But that was all she could think about for the ten-hour drive to Devil's Tower Wyoming. Ben did his best to make light conversation, but Anna was quiet and somber.

Adam found himself strangely in a position where he had to engage in the light banter with Ben instead of Anna. At one point he crawled into the back seat on top of pillows and blankets and slept for several hours because he just couldn't keep up.

"Dr. Moore? Is it true that Devil's Tower is haunted? I read an account of ghost Indians running through the place at night."

Anna had to chuckle and respond to that one. "Ben, I have no idea, but it would definitely make for an interesting night of camping, don't you think?"

She was so grateful for Ben, who had managed to get her out of her slump. For Ben's sake, she hoped that Devil's Tower was everything he was anticipating: "*Close Encounters of the Third Kind*,"[73] and "Ghost Indians" haunting the place. She also hoped that he would care about the geology as they hiked the trail the next morning as planned.

Anna was particularly thankful for Ben on this extended trip. He didn't doze off once. He kept looking at the map, reading articles, and even changing the radio channel when the station would become too weak to hear--no XM or FM in the older vans. He was a perfect navigator and so cheerful about everything, unlike Jacob, who kept saying, "Why don't we skip this attraction and just push on home?"

Big John could see the other students roll their eyes each time Jacob repeated his complaint. He was no doubt thinking the same thing, but knew the students needed to see this geologic feature, as it was about halfway home and a perfect spot to camp. It was also a twenty-year tradition to make it the last stop of the camp. Therefore, Jacob would just have to get over it.

The caravan reached the campsite at dark, and Dr. D. checked in with the campground office. Everyone climbed off the vans and opened the trailers to begin the setup of tents for the evening.

---

73   A popular sci-fi movie directed by Steven Spielberg that came out in winter of 1977.

Anna didn't want to pitch a tent, so her spot was on the first bench of her van. She would get more restful sleep and have more time and energy to devote to getting campers loaded and, on the vehicles, the next morning.

Dr. D. always pitched his tent, and he could do it in two minutes flat. The students timed him.

Anna chuckled as she remembered the first night of camping together on the high plains of Colorado. In the middle of May, it was not unusual to have severe thunderstorms with large hail, damaging winds, and tornadoes. The students were all beginners and were learning what to do and not do. Everyone was settled into their brand-new tents, and as usual, she opted to sleep on the van seat. Adam established his record for the fastest time of tent set up, and things were getting quiet for the evening.

It was warm and more humid than usual for the high plains, with thunderclouds developing to the west. Anna was keenly aware of the cloud structures, having grown up in the 'tornado alley' of the south-central U.S. She knew they might be in for some bad weather, so she warned all the students to make sure their tents were securely fastened and pegged into the ground.

She also carried an extra bag of supplies to help students who were not prepared. In addition, it was suggested that they place rocks, backpacks--anything with weight--in the corners of their tents to keep them from blowing away.

When Anna finally lay down to sleep for the night, she couldn't help but watch the lightning show in the high tops of the *mesocyclone*[74] to the west. It was beautiful. She lay awake, watching it for a few hours.

---

74   A mesocyclone is a large, rotating air mass within a convective storm.

As the storm approached, students began to leave their tents and come to her van. Big John was asleep in his van, and he had visitors as well.

Anna reassured them that the storm seemed to be tracking to the north of them as it moved in the classic southwest to northeast fashion. She warned that they would probably experience some rain, hail, and high winds, and that they would probably be safer in their tents. In the back of her mind, she knew that a direct hit from a tornado would make the vans a dangerous place to be. She didn't want to frighten them though, so she just watched the storm closely and allowed them to seek shelter with her. She would lead them to the cinder block bathrooms if things got too dicey.

The wind picked up and began hitting the camp in gusts with horizontal rain. The van was rocking back and forth, and the students watched in horror as tents started to come loose and blow away. Some tents collapsed but stayed in their place, presumably because they listened to the advice of the instructors. Everyone seemed to be in a van, except for one person, Dr. D.

"Oh, my God! Dr. D. is going to die! Should we go get him?" yelled Ben.

Anna reassured them that he was probably dead asleep and would not want them to bother him. "He is never bothered by storms, you guys. He will be okay," as they watched his tent be blown to one side violently with a slapping motion.

On one side--*windward*[75]--of the canvas, at the bottom, was a form that was clearly Dr. D's body, with other objects at his feet and head. The wind was blowing the top of his tent to the other side--*leeward*[76]--of the canvas with a violent, "whappa, whappa" motion. He was fast asleep and couldn't care less. Anna marveled at his ability to just sleep through such an extreme event.

---

75   Windward – the side facing the wind
76   Leeward – the side sheltered from the wind

The next morning, Anna and Big John helped the students to find most of their tents and other belongings. Their first night of camping had been a learning experience for sure.

After several camp setups and breakdowns, the students became pros at the process. This group was now well-seasoned and didn't need much help to be efficient.

Anna felt a sense of pride in her students, as they were able to successfully pitch their tents through the rest of the camp experience.

The only exception was the stop in *Glacier National Park*[77], during the mid-class tour. Students were too afraid of bears to pitch tents.

Dr. D. insisted that all of the faculty put up their tents so that students would be encouraged to do so as well. As the three stood around the campfire, quietly drinking a beer, and freezing in a slow, cold rain, it became painfully clear that none of the students were getting their tents out.

Adam broke the uncomfortable silence and said, "I guess the bear lady scared them."

Big John agreed, "Yep, it should be interesting to see how they all sleep in there together."

Anna wondered out loud, "Don't they know that the bears in Glacier have can openers?'

D. responded, "I don't like this. There is a greater probability of one of us being eaten if there are only three tents instead of thirty-five."

The three stood there together quietly, miserably, watching the students interact on the vans.

---

77   Glacier National Park is an area in extreme northern Montana that borders Alberta, Canada. It was designated a park in the early 1900's because it featured active glaciation, as well as depositional and erosional features associated with alpine glaciation.

On Anna's van, they could observe Ben, sitting in the driver's seat, listening to the radio, and drumming his fingers to the music, while other students played cards or read books.

In Big John's van, they could see the two girls sitting in the back seat cuddled up together, others reading, playing games. Then suddenly all the windows pushed out and doors flew open. Everyone began exiting the van covering their noses and mouths and were coughing and cursing. It was clear that Little John had had a gaseous emission because people were hitting him with objects.

Adam took a swig of beer and said, "That man has a medical problem."

Big John replied, "They must really be afraid of bears to sleep in there with that."

They continued to drink their beers as they watched the show. Yes, Anna would not soon forget this group of interesting students.

With the camp at Devil's Tower set up, Anna noted that Ben was excitedly seated and waiting for the show to begin. She saw Adam at the payphone across the campus and walked his way, figuring he was letting his wife know their ETA for the next day.

After he exited, she went inside and pulled out the number for Sean's room at the campus. She had only three dollars in quarters but was able to catch him and hear his voice again. He was glad to hear from her and to know they had safely arrived at their evening destination.

As time was running out, Annie heard Sean say, "I love ya, Annie." Just as the time was ending, Annie managed to say, "I love you too." It felt oddly satisfying to be able to at least talk to him for a minute or two.

As she walked back toward the campsite, Ben shouted, "Dr. Moore! It's about to start!"

Anna smiled and decided to go watch the movie with Ben. He had been such a good sport and navigator that day. It gave her great pleasure to share that experience with him on their last night as teacher and student. She had never seen the movie, "Close Encounters of the Third Kind," so it was a pleasant way to end a very tiring day.

The next morning, they loaded up and drove up to the tower[78], where everyone made the hike up to see the igneous rocks exposed. It was a sweltering day, and Jacob chose to stay with the van. The rest of the group took pictures and gathered the tourist information and geology handouts.

Then it was off on another day of nonstop driving until they all reached home again.

---

78   Devil's Tower is an ancient magmatic intrusion that has been exposed through erosion. As the magma cooled it formed polygonal columns. It stands as a butte above the Wyoming plains, but is clearly igneous.

Chapter 18—Home Again

Driving south and into the heat and humidity felt unbearable in the old vans that had no A/C. All windows were down or pushed out. The wind whipped through the vehicles as the dirt of the road settled on their faces and belongings. The music was blaring on full volume, and Anna found it difficult to stay awake at times.

Adam relieved her at one point, and he too had difficulty staying awake. Big John seemed to be doing okay. He flashed his lights to stop only twice, and that was for students to visit the restroom.

Thankfully, there were late evening rain showers along the trip route to help cool things down for the remainder of the drive. The closer they got to home; the less Anna looked forward to dealing with the reality which faced her.

Each time the group stopped; the instructions were to be back at the vans in 10 minutes. When the doors opened, the students would exit and spread like the four winds. Some would get soft drinks, others used the restroom, and still others would try their hand at scratch-off lottery tickets.

The faculty would usually sit patiently waiting for up to half an hour for all students to return. Jacob was often the last one to return to the vans. Little John suggested that the caravan leave him behind at one of the stops.

Eventually, everyone arrived safely at MSU and wearily unloaded the trailers and vans. The students hugged Adam, Anna, and Big John, thanking them for a wonderful camp.

Anna couldn't help but feel sad to see them all go. Even though they were exhausted, the instructors remained until all students had been collected by their friends and families.

Now it was time for her to refocus attention on her boys and their lives going forward. She couldn't wait to see them again. It would probably be the following day, as they were with their dad at their grandparent's home.

The boy's grandparents lived on an expansive, cattle ranch where they primarily raised *Black Angus*.[79] There were so many things to keep young boys preoccupied. There were cows to milk, fences to mend, horses to ride, lots of interesting farm animals, hay baling, gardens to hoe--it was just an excellent place for young boys to learn about becoming "real men."

She enjoyed visiting the ranch herself, as it felt like home to her more than her home with Robert and the boys.

Their grandfather--*Bob Miller*[80]--was one of the nicest men Anna had ever met. He adored Anna and often spoke to her about how to deal with the many moods of his son.

Her mother-in-law was a beautiful woman--*Betty Miller*[81]--who had given up a career in nursing to be a stay-at-home ranch wife. She was a great mother and an excellent cook, and she often worked side by side with her husband in the fields.

Anna was so inspired by Betty, especially her superior intellect and ability to be the best at everything. She excelled in county fair competitions, taking first prize in baking, chili, canning, jellies, and jams, and showing her farm animals.

---

79 Angus cattle are a small, common breed of beef cattle that are raised on the high and low plains of North America. They are a popular brand for their meat.

80 Robert Allan Miller, Anna's father in law. Fictional character and not meant to represent any particular person living or deceased.

81 Betty Marie Miller, Anna's mother in law. Fictional character and not meant to represent any particular person living or deceased.

She seemed to be the perfect wife, and she too loved Anna, at times taking Anna's side when Robert would make her cry. It was clearly a woman thing, where they knew they must take care of each other. For this, Anna was always grateful. Her in-laws were simply the best. She knew too that they also hoped for a reconciliation between her and Robert.

The next day, Anna phoned the ranch and spoke to her boys. They were so excited that she was home. "When are you coming to get us, Mommy? Gran says you can come to stay here with us if you want and play games."

She assured them that she would be out later that same day. Gran came to the phone and encouraged her to pack a bag and stay with them for a few days. Anna reluctantly accepted the gracious offer, but she would have to do a few chores first.

She unpacked her bags and began to do laundry. As she put her clothes in the washing machine, she couldn't help but smell the essence that she shared with Sean. Part of her did not want to wash her sheets or blankets. She stood there, holding her pillowcase, and began to cry. "Oh, God, I do miss him."

While the laundry washed, Anna curled up on the couch and took a short nap. She was remembering her time with Sean and wishing she could be back in the Rockies, in his arms. She had tried to call him, but he was no doubt in the field with his students.

Later, she put her clothes in the dryer and stepped into the shower. She was beyond nasty from two days of camping and driving in the heat, humidity, and open windows of the road. As she lathered her body, she felt every curve, remembering how sexy and beautiful she had felt with Sean. If he had been there at that moment, she would have made passionate love to him. She imagined soaping his body, rubbing his muscular shoulders, chest, and *oh my...* She had to stop those thoughts!

Speaking out loud, she said a prayer, "Oh Lord, help me to focus on what I need to do, here and now. Take care of Sean and his students, please keep them safe. Let him know that I love him. Amen."

She was so exhausted but needed to go see her boys. Her hope too was to avoid having to see Robert, as she was not exactly sure what to say about their status. She needed time to process her own feelings about him, and now Sean too.

Robert had moved out in the spring semester before Anna went to teach the camp, and it was understood that they needed couple's therapy before he could return to their home with her and the boys. Robert was a brilliant man, but he was also an arrogant bully. He had a temper problem, especially when he drank too much.

Anna had fallen in love with his good looks and his intellect but soon discovered that he had a good guy/bad guy persona that was difficult to ignore. Even though she loved the good guy very much, she could not live with the raging bully side, who kept her off balance all the time. She particularly didn't like the way he lost his temper with their boys. At times, she would find herself in between him and the boys, and the recipient of his physical wrath.

The emotional ugliness, however, was the most damaging to Anna herself, and that is the part she asked to break from. Robert clearly loved his boys and was not a horrible father, except for his propensity for losing his temper and raging at them.

Robert had decided to go live with his parents for a while. He assumed that Anna would miss him terribly and beg him to return. To his surprise, she was empowered by friends at the church and others to stand up to him.

The plan was to have Robert live with his parents until Anna returned, with the hope that the separation would allow them both time to reflect on how much they loved and needed each other. The couple would then be in a better position to seek counseling and work toward a stable reconciliation.

In Robert's mind, though, Anna was the one with the problem. He didn't have any issues except her unwillingness to conform to his idea of who she should be. Robert saw her as a bright lady who needed to complete her college degree. Her success was also his success. His ego would not allow him to settle for someone with only a high school diploma. He genuinely wanted to see her emerge from her cocoon and become a brilliant butterfly. It was for this reason that he was supportive of her in her education and pushed her to continue to pursue her dreams intellectually. He was in love with her simple beauty but was most attracted to her intelligence. He never told her, but he was in awe of her ability to solve complex problems, usually in her head.

Robert tolerated her *palliative*[82] need for the Catholic Church if it kept her happy and allowed him to be in control. It was like a giant wart on her shoulder or backside. He could look past it for the most part, if he had access to the rest of the package.

It was when Anna began to grow spiritually and emotionally, from a frightened little girl to a self-assured woman, that he felt she was changing too much and too fast. She was outgrowing him. All changes were okay with him if he was in control of the changes, or so this is what Anna's therapist had told her.

Before going to teach the camp, Anna had gotten on her knees and begged him to please seek counseling for himself and with her. As a Catholic, she desired to love her husband and to work through their issues and to hopefully find a Christ-centered resolution.

---

82 Palliative refers to reducing pain without addressing the reason for the pain. In the case of the dying person, there is no cure, but the patient may be kept pain free and comfortable. In this case, Robert uses it is a pejorative (expressing contempt) implying that religion is used to make people feel better but doesn't change their underlying deficiencies.

His comment to her was, "You are the one with a problem; *you* go to a counselor."

This was hurtful and frustrating for Anna, as she had been going to counseling for some time with her boys and with priests through the church. She had been working on her issues, which she freely acknowledged. Without Robert accepting that he too had problems, there was not much more Anna could do except continue to pray and maintain her own personal growth, which she had hoped would include reconciliation with him.

The closer Anna became to Jesus and the church, the more Robert hated the church. In his mind, she was cheating on him with every priest--and Jesus Himself for that matter. All he knew was that he was losing his sweet, innocent, trusting Anna. Instead of growing with her, he *invalidated*[83] her progress in her spiritual life and perceived it as a direct threat to his dominance in their relationship.

As Anna drove the hour it took to reach the ranch, her thoughts were with Sean and how much she missed him. *I will try to call him later to let him know I made it home safely.*

Anna found herself feeling a little heartsick about the life she and Robert had shared and built together, as she passed the fence posts and fields of beautiful horses and healthy cattle. The Miller family was her family, and she loved them and the ranch.

Anna used her maiden name for her professional career, but she was considered a Miller. She was part of something much bigger than she was, and she was the matriarch of her part of the Miller legacy. She had delivered sons, which made them heirs to the 200-year-old Miller family heritage. In some ways, it probably felt much like a large clan, where the women were expected to give up

---

83   In this case, invalidation involves a lack of empathy and the refusal to acknowledge the valid ideas or concerns of another.

their own desires to serve in the role of wife, mother, and partner to the man of the family.

Even though Robert was progressive and encouraged his wife to seek degrees and to teach as a college professor, it was not seen by everyone as a positive in terms of supporting a lifelong Miller partnership. Anna's academics did not fit into the perceived historical role of wives of the Miller clan.

Anna turned down the long gravel driveway to the ranch house and could see her mother-in-law and sons standing on the porch watching for her. The boys vaulted off the porch of the large, two-story, southern plantation home and began to run down the long rock walkway toward her car. She jumped out and was tackled to the ground by both boys, who sat on her and laid on her in the grass as she tickled them and laughed. Anna looked over at her mother-in-law, Betty, who was smiling from ear to ear at the reunion of mother and children.

"Anna, you look like you have been through it. You have lost more weight," she said in a gentle, accusing tone. "Come on in and let's have coffee and pie. The boys helped me to bake them this morning."

"Mom, Mom, Mom, Mom," both boys speaking at the same time, "Mine is better, we have to try mine first!"

Anna knew this meant that she would have to eat at least part of two different kinds of pies, or there would be hell to pay.

"Robert will be out later this evening. I think he has missed you."

Anna nodded and tried to appear positive about the prospect of seeing him again, but instead felt a massive pang of guilt, for she had not missed him at all.

"We've had some great times these last eight weeks, but it is so good to have you back again," Betty said as she put her arm around Anna's waist and walked with her to the kitchen area.

"Did you have any difficulties this summer?" she asked, as Anna usually had camp stories to tell when she came home. Sometimes it was horses in the saloon or cowboys with girlfriends who had no front teeth, etc. Betty and Bob both enjoyed hearing about the adventures of the summer geology field camp.

The boys climbed on Anna and shared their adventures of the past few weeks, both telling of how much fun they had. Anna looked at her mother-in-law and lovingly mouthed, "Thank you," as the boys seemed beside themselves with information and joy. Anna could not thank her and Bob enough for taking care of the boys and Robert in her absence. She knew too that Robert had been there helping his dad.

Robert had grown up on that ranch, and it was expected that he would help when he could. His dad had funded the college degrees of all the Miller children and a few of the grandchildren as well. If the truth were known, he had also helped Robert to pay bills while Anna finished her degrees. They were a family that was very close-knit and part of a sustainable farming and ranching tradition. Anna and Robert had both grown up in hard-working, family farm-ranch environments.

As the day turned into a late afternoon, Betty made tea and asked Anna if she wanted to play a game of dominos before beginning dinner. Anna was weary but loved playing any game with her mother-in-law. She was a formidable opponent for all who played games, and dearly loved challenging Anna as well.

Betty treated Anna as a daughter, not just a daughter-in-law. She was clearly family and was very loved. Even though Anna had parents of her own, she always felt like she belonged to Bob and Betty too. She was doubly blessed.

As usual, Betty was stomping Anna in the game when the boys ran out of the front room again to greet their dad in the driveway. Anna's heart stopped as she realized it was indeed Robert. He would sense that something was amiss. She was an open book for most people but especially for Robert.

He also knew exactly how to charm her and to make her forget the ugly experiences where he degraded her and made her feel inadequate. The nice guy was hard to resist. He would take advantage of her forgiving nature, just to have the bad guy take over and do irreparable harm.

Betty sensed the fear and tension in Anna and met her son at the front door. Anna could hear her suggest that they go to the kitchen for coffee and pie, for which Anna was very grateful. After about ten minutes of conversation in the kitchen, Anna walked down the long hall, and bravely faced Robert. She took a deep breath and appeared.

"Hi, Robert," she said with a smile.

He stood up and gave her a huge hug and a kiss on her cheek. He tried to kiss her on the mouth, but she had turned her cheek toward him instead.

"It's about time you came home, don't you think?" he said, smiling. "The boys have really missed you and so have I. We've all been here working, while you've been hiking and camping in the mountains."

Betty chimed in, "Now Robert, you know it's a job. It just happens to be in a beautiful place with interesting experiences."

Anna nodded in agreement with Betty and was grateful for her blocking of the negative.

"Are you staying for a couple of days too, Robert, or are you going fishing again this weekend?" asked his mother.

"Well, I don't know," he said as he looked at Anna. "I guess it depends."

"Of course, you will," said Betty cheerfully. "Let's go decide what to have for dinner."

"Anna, why don't you take a nap while we get things settled."

Anna nodded gratefully and climbed the broad, majestic staircase to the guest room provided for her at the top. It felt like she was in "Gone with the Wind" when she visited the ranch, or perhaps "The Big Valley." The boys followed her up the stairs, and they too lay down with Anna for a nap.

Anna was so grateful for their hugs and their love, but it was a little bit warm for all three of them in the one bed. She stripped off the blanket, and they all lay on top of the sheets. The ceiling fan was on high, and the large ranch windows were open with a stiff southern breeze blowing through. It was just perfect for an afternoon nap. It felt like home. Anna was indeed happy to be home with the Miller family. It was just Robert she didn't feel comfortable or at home with.

Anna slept very hard and woke to the smell of BBQ. *Yum.* She loved that smell.

She and the boys came downstairs to help, but everything was already set up. Robert was helping his mother with the tablecloth, and they had set out all the plates, utensils, and napkins on the long bar, which was lined with goodies on the opposite end. Dinner would be in half an hour, and everyone would be there. Betty was a pro at doing these things on the fly.

Anna asked, "Is there anything I can do, Betty?"

"No, just go get the kids and you cleaned up for dinner. We've got it all under control here."

Anna wearily led the boys to the washroom, and they all got their own washcloth for washing faces, necks, and hands. Ah, it felt so good to be home, but she looked in the mirror at her tired and gaunt face. The light, the joy she had experienced in the Rockies, had faded. She missed Sean. She missed the mountains. She missed her eight weeks of freedom. *Sigh.*

Dinner had turned into a Miller family gathering with everyone showing up. It was a grand party, complete with coolers of beer, boxes of wine, plenty of food, family, friends, ranch workers, and several games all going on at once.

In the game room, there was a rowdy game of pool, and kids of all sizes playing ping-pong. Robert and his brothers-in-law were playing darts, and Bob and Betty were engineering a card game.

Anna knew she would be pulled into the card game. She was terrible at darts, found ping pong tedious, and didn't care for pool, as it sometimes led to people getting angry. She particularly didn't want to deal with *men* getting mad at her for beating them. She was quite good at pool. Cards--where she played as either Betty's or Bob's partner--was delightful for her, and safe. She was so grateful for her mother-in-law's insight into keeping her and Robert from having to speak to one another in a private setting.

Betty, no doubt, engineered the entire gathering so that she could enjoy them both without having to deal with Robert picking a fight with Anna. She was a brilliant and caring woman. She probably knew deep down inside that Robert and Anna should have never married one another. She realized that they were intellectually compatible, but Anna was entirely too sensitive emotionally, and had low self-esteem. That made for a very dysfunctional relationship with her son, who didn't seem to have the ability to keep from being acerbic and mean-spirited more than he needed to be when dealing with someone as fragile as Anna. She loved them both and loved their children, but knew it was probably just a matter of time before Anna was brave or unhappy enough to end the marriage.

They played cards for several hours, with Anna and Betty beating everyone who joined them. They were an unstoppable duo when it came to counting cards and interpreting each other's hands based on how they each played.

Betty had trained Anna well at the fine art of "the tell." God help Anna, though if she missed a signal. They continued playing well into the evening.

The boys both fell asleep with little *Ben*[84] asleep on Anna's chest. He was astride his mother's waist with his head on her shoulder and chest. At one point, everyone laughed when Anna noted a long string of drool dripping from his mouth to her leg.

Bobby was asleep sitting in a chair, holding his [85]favorite transforming toy. He was a big boy and would battle sleep until the very last moment.

Anna knew from experience that the party would go on into the night, so she excused herself, took the boys, and tucked them into her bed. She gladly had them with her in her room. It felt so nice to have their little bodies next to hers again.

As she lay there between them, she heard the door open to her room.

It was Robert. He tiptoed in and stood at the end of the bed, looking at them.

She pretended to be asleep and hoped he would kiss the boys and just go. He did not. Instead, he crawled on top of her and lay down with his full weight. She couldn't breathe, and he smelled of alcohol.

The boys stirred, and Anna said, "Robert, please, don't. The boys."

He backed off the bed, taking her with him. He was a much larger person than Anna, and she had no choice but to go with him. She kept pleading as she whispered, "No, Robert. No. Please just let me sleep."

He didn't say a word as he carried her against her will and took her through the side door and out onto the porch. She continued to quietly plead with him as she pushed on his shoulders to push

---

84   Ben, Benjamin David Miller, is the younger of Anna's two sons. Fictional character and not
       meant to represent any particular person living or deceased.
85   Bobby, Robert William Miller, is the older of Anna's two sons. Fictional character and not
       meant to represent any particular person living or deceased.

him away. She did not want the boys to wake up and see their dad being mean to their mom.

He ignored her pleas and angrily flipped her forward and pushed with all his might as he bent her over a chair and held her tightly.

She was in a nightgown with loose-fitting underwear, which did not stop Robert as he unzipped his pants and forced himself inside of her. As he raped her, she cried as silently as possible as her body trembled against the chair back. She did not want her children or other family members to know what Robert was doing to her. Her face was pushed into the seat of the chair in front of her, where she had difficulty breathing, although she would never dare to scream out. With each thrust of his hips, she swallowed back her tears and her desire to scream.

When he was finished, he left her lying over the chair, sobbing softly.

As she tried to stand, the chair fell over backward onto her shins and feet, scraping them painfully as it fell. At that moment, she hated him so much. It was not in her nature to hate anyone, but at this moment, she hated him.

Instead of a sweet aroma, as she experienced with Sean, their shared essence had a damp and dank aroma...musky, with a darker tone. She could feel his semen flowing down her thighs and began to gag and throw up in her mouth at the smell of their combined fluids. Anna had always had a keen sensitivity to smells and sounds. It was part of why she enjoyed life so much and felt the pain of others so profoundly. She was what her grandmother would call a "sensitive." She experienced everything with heightened awareness--nature, God, everything.

The entire experience was so traumatic for her. The smell and sensations were utterly disgusting as she stumbled to the toilet and began to throw up her dinner. Robert made her sick to her stomach. After she finished gagging, she showered, changed her clothing, and returned to her bed and lay between the boys, where she cried herself to sleep, thinking of Sean. How could she tell Sean about this? How could she ever tell anyone about this?[86]

"God, surely this is not what You intended marriage to be. Please help me, Lord. I want to understand," she prayed through her tears.

The next morning, Anna came downstairs. Betty had coffee on, and breakfast started.

"Are you hungry, Anna? Grab a cup and a plate."

Anna grabbed a cup, poured coffee, and began to quietly cry. She gently wiped the tears from her face, but Betty noted them just the same. She wanted to tell Betty everything, about Robert, about Sean, but she couldn't share any of those things with her. She loved Betty and cared about what she thought of her.

Betty dropped everything, came to hug Anna, and whispered, "Was he mean to you again?"

Anna couldn't speak, she just quietly cried.

Betty sat her down and told her to just relax. "I will get you a plate. It's going to be okay."

Anna just sat with tears now rolling down her cheeks as she trembled with emotions. Betty handed her a box of tissues and said lovingly, "Better go wash your face and put on a smile for your boys, okay?"

Anna nodded in agreement and set off for the washroom to freshen up.

When she returned to the kitchen, she found Robert drinking coffee and hugging the boys. He looked up at her and smiled as though nothing had happened the night before. He felt no remorse, no empathy. How could he be so happy?

---

86 This scene between a wife and husband is not meant to depict any specific event or experience past or present, but is perhaps often an experience for women, the world over, who live in societies that see women as property and lacking personal dignity.

Her stomach knotted, and she ran back to the washroom to vomit.

This time Robert followed her and came in directly behind her, keeping her from shutting the door. As she vomited, he lovingly rubbed her shoulders and said, "I've missed you so much."

When Anna was able to regain her composure and cease gagging, she turned and sat on the side of the tub, looking at him. "Robert, I can't go on like this. I love you. I love the boys, but I can't be married to you anymore. Last night? That was...," she continued in tears.

Robert gently touched her shoulders and said, "Ah, you don't mean that. You are just tired. Besides, you know you like it rough. Right?"

"No Robert, that was not okay." She continued in tears, "I have decided that I just don't want to do this anymore."

"Do what?" asked Robert in a mocking tone.

"Be married. I just can't do this anymore. I am so sorry."

"Who would want you other than me, Anna? Seriously? You need me," said Robert softly laughing in disbelief.

Anna looked at him through tears, not believing what he was saying to her and said indignantly, "Believe it or not, there are people who find me attractive."

"Sure, there are," said Robert sarcastically.

"No really," she continued, "I met someone this summer who thought I was special. I know that I can be loved by someone else."

Robert laughed aloud this time and said, "What? You met someone else? You are a liar. There is no one else."

"Yes, there is Robert. I love him, and he loves me," said Anna tearfully.

"Was it any good, though?" Asked Robert in a joking voice.

Anna just cried and began having dry heaves again.

Robert then said, "Hey honey, like I've told you before, you can have sex with as many guys as you'd like, as long as you save some for me. I don't intend to divorce you."

Anna washed her face as he put his arms around her from behind and rubbed his hard penis against her buttocks. He had told her once that it turned him on to think that other men wanted her too.

As she reached to get a towel to dry her face, he tried to pull her shorts down. At this moment in time, Anna was brave enough to say to herself, *No more!* She raised her voice for the first time and yelled, "I need to go see the boys. Please just leave me alone."

Robert released his hold on her as she pulled the bathroom door open and exited, leaving the door open behind her. He laughed at her as she walked away from him down the hallway and shouted, "Welcome home, honey."

Anna entered the kitchen and sat down. Betty looked at her and said quietly, "Everything okay?"

"No," answered Anna, "but you and I can talk later, okay?"

Betty acknowledged, and they could both hear Robert slam out of the front door.

Anna jumped with the slamming of the door. Her nerves were so raw, and it was clear--she was more than sad, she also looked angry. Anna never seemed angry with anyone, so Betty knew this was a serious break.

When she looked at Betty and shook her head "No," it was clear to Betty that Anna was indicating there was no hope for their marriage.

Betty was very saddened by this, but she did understand that her son was his own worst enemy.

Chapter 19—Till Death Do Us Part

Later that evening, Anna spoke to Robert's parents. She tearfully admitted to them that she believed their differences were irreconcilable.

Bob, Sr. held Anna's hand, saying, "We love you, Anna. You know that. You and the boys are very important to us. You do what you feel you must do, but just know that we will not take sides. Okay?"

Betty agreed with her husband as she reiterated, "We love you, and you will always be family."

This assurance gave her great comfort, but it didn't ease the intense sadness and embarrassment that Anna felt at having failed to reconcile with Robert. Anna had experienced true love. She did not have to settle for being raped or mocked in a relationship. Love could be romantic, beautiful, and respectful of the dignity of both persons, as one. What she had experienced with Sean was what she had only read about. She never dreamed it was real or that she was deserving of such a love. That kind of love was exactly what she believed God wanted for her, and she would not settle for less ever again.

After the visit with the Millers, Anna gathered her boys and headed home to begin preparing for their school, her own classes at the college, and to seek guidance from the church on her separation. She would focus on her children and on getting ready to teach classes at the college. As she unpacked the boys and herself and began to settle in for the evening, the phone rang. Anna's heart jumped into her throat as she rushed to beat her oldest son Bobby to the phone. She didn't want him answering, just in case it was Sean.

Bobby won the race and properly answered, saying, "Miller residence. Who may I say is speaking?" He was so cute and so mannerly. She couldn't be mad at him and was very proud of his phone etiquette.

"Okay, Mom? It's someone named Michael Anderson."

Anna stopped for a moment, confused by the name, and then it dawned on her that Sean was using his middle name. Smart fellow.

"Yes, my mom is here. Just a moment please," said Bobby, as he covered the phone receiver and whispered, "It's a man with an accent, Mom. Do you want to speak to him?"

"Yes, I will speak to him," said Anna in a very proper manner and with a very big smile on her face.

"Hello, this is Anna. How may I help you?"

As she spoke, she waved Bobby to his room, excusing him from his "Man of the House" job of answering the phone.

"Hello?" she said again.

"Wow, he was quite proper, wasn't he?" said Sean.

"Yes, he was," said Annie, out of breath from her excitement at hearing Sean's voice once more. All her troubles melted away, replaced by smiling and laughing as she and Sean spoke.

"Do ya still want to join me in Yellowstone?" he asked in a kidding voice.

"Of course," she giggled.

She was so excited that he was already planning to do his fieldwork in Yellowstone, and a special visit to the Stillwater Platinum Mine.

Just as when they were physically together, there was nothing but them in their bubble of space. Each time he called she would feel elated for hours after they hung up. "Thank you, Lord, for this love that You've sent to me. Please, forgive any aspect of it that is not for Your glory," she prayed to herself as she praised God for Sean in her life.

It was decided that Robert and Anna would remain separated for the time being. Anna kept her appointments with her therapist and counselors through the Catholic Church. In each meeting, it became clear that her marriage to Robert was not sacramental and was indeed destructive to both Anna and Robert.

Robert's being an atheist wasn't the primary problem, as he willingly allowed his family to be active in the Catholic Church and even attended church for important sacraments requiring both parents. He was very accepting of the Catholic Church and traditions.

The problem was with his inability to admit that he had an anger management issue. The fact that he was hyper-sexual, had anger issues, and refused to accept any responsibility for his behavior, contributed to the separation perceived by Anna in their marriage. His physical and psychological abuse was another issue that Anna did not wish to address unless she absolutely had no choice.

Even when filling out the annulment questionnaire for the church, she refused to share the intimate details of Robert forcing himself on her without her consent. The entire experience was so degrading for her, and she was embarrassed by her inability to control any aspect of the interaction.

Her spiritual advisor, *Fr. William*,[87] had met with her on many occasions and knew that Anna did not feel loved or respected in their sexual relationship. This time Anna confided in him that she had met Sean and that this was the first time she had ever felt pretty and special.

"I love him, Father, desperately...Has God ordained this? Is Sean in my life so that I may know true love?" asked Anna.

---

87   Father William is Anna's spiritual advisor. Fictional character not based on any real person past or present.

"No girl," answered Father, "You and Sean have shared something very special, but God would not ordain an adulterous act. He is married. You are married. It is adultery."

Anna began to sob. "But I love him, Father. He is tender, loving, and he loves me without reservation. I've never been loved like that before."

Father William was very loving and said, "Yes, it is special, and certainly you deserve to be loved in this manner. I can think of no one more deserving of the love you describe. What Robert does is not what God intended, but you deserve better than either of these men are able to provide. You must pray, dear, and ask for God's guidance. You must work on getting yourself right with God first, and then all else will fall into place for you. If you want to end your marriage to Robert--which I recommend--then the church will do what we can to help you. Your relationship with Sean will only hurt you in the end, because he is married. You must consider this. You deserve to be loved by a man who is free to love you, and you him."

Anna tearfully responded, "I'll never love anyone the way I love Sean, Father. My heart is with this man and will be forever."

It was clear to both Fr. William and Anna that she could not make a reasonable confession and vow to "go and sin no more." She was in love, deeply in love, with a married man. She would willfully remain separated from the sacraments until she could walk away from Sean.

In the weeks to follow, the church gave Anna the names of attorneys who were parishioners and specialized in Family Law. She filed for a formal separation as she moved on with her own life and immersed herself in teaching and being a single parent.

Robert came to visit several times a week and became a better dad in some respects, because he did not have the stress of dealing with the family dynamic of two hyperactive boys.

Anna and Robert began to speak to each other as friends again, and Anna even considered that they might share the custody of their children.

However, that would soon change, when Robert started dating a woman who was determined to cultivate seeds of discontent and hatred.

Sadly, their divorce would be ugly, and Anna's affair would become a major issue used against her in court proceedings. She was clearly a harlot and not fit to be the mother of Robert Miller's children. The fact that their dad was sleeping with another woman didn't really matter in the broad scheme of things. He was driven into another woman's arms because his wife had broken his heart by cheating on him. It was all so very unfair to Anna, who had really tried to be a good wife and mother.

The sting of the insults was only tempered by the loving phone calls to and from Sean. He became her strength to fight for freedom from a loveless marriage. She did not entertain fantasies of Sean leaving his wife and rescuing her, though. She was very rooted in the reality that Sean was married and loved his wife and his family. What they had was special, and she was willing to live without him physically in her life if he loved her, and they could share their special relationship.

In her mind, she did not have to have sex with him to be in love with him. They shared more than sex. It was an intimate friendship, which transcended just physical touch. She felt fulfilled by their connection, which included their shared love of music, geology, laughter … it was a healthy, loving relationship on so many levels and explosive physically when they were together.

Chapter 20—Together Again

"Mommy?" asked Ben, "Why do you always have to go somewhere? I don't like it when you leave."

As he rubbed his little eyes, Anna's heart sank, "Oh baby, I'm going to be gone for only a few days, I will be back before you know it. And besides, Gran is looking forward to you staying with her for a few days."

"She will bring us cool rocks, Ben!" interrupted Bobby excitedly. "Our Mom is the coolest mom ever!"

Anna smiled through tears as she hugged her little men and reassured them both. "You two take care of each other, okay? And I promise to bring you cool rocks."

"Where are you going again, Mommy?"

"I'm going to the Yellowstone volcano, sweetie."

Ben put his hand over his mouth and gasped fearfully, "Is it going to blow up?"

"Of course not, Ben. Do you think our mom is stupid enough to go into an active volcano?"

Anna laughed out loud as she hugged them both and said, "No, it's not going to blow up for a while. It's been at least 640,000 years since the last huge eruption, and at least 170,000 years since the last smaller eruption, so I think Mommy is safe."

"And that's a very long time!" said Bobby in a sing-song voice. "Just think, we aren't even twelve yet and even Mommy isn't thousands of years old."

Little did Bobby know, but his mother had indeed hiked into active volcanoes before. Perhaps she was more stupid than even she realized. *Ha-ha!*

Anna had made plans to have her classes covered and had purchased her round-trip ticket to Billings. She was beyond excited to be able to see Sean again, and to see Yellowstone through the eyes of a volcanologist, who was more than just a little bit interested in the science.

When she filled out her leave form for the college, she honestly wrote that she was taking "personal days," but listed those as geology field trips. Anna had difficulty ever being dishonest, but she felt she had represented her absence in the best way possible. She had the blessings of her chairman and her mother-in-law, and that was all the validation she needed to engage in personal and professional development activities which took her away from her children.

Robert had also given his blessing, which helped Anna to feel better about leaving the boys. Even though they were not together, she still loved the man that she fell in love with and married. He was the father of her children and would always have a place in her heart, regardless of how he treated her. The man she loved was a different man with his children. The good Robert, the man who was a great dad and a funny person, was still dear to her. Sean, however, had the rest of her heart, and that was not about to change.

Adam gave Anna a ride to the airport and quizzed her about her field trips. "Who is leading this field trip? How many are going? Be sure to take lots of pics for a presentation to the department when you return, especially of the Stillwater Complex."

He had assumed that it was a group of people, and Anna did not correct him. She felt bad about the omission, but she treasured her close friendship with him and didn't want him to feel anxious for her in the least. She did not want him to know that she was going to be alone with Sean. He was already jealous that Sean was even going to have anything to do with the field trip.

"Be careful, Anna. You've been through a lot lately, and you may be vulnerable," he advised in a fatherly manner. "Have fun with the geology but be careful with Sean. Remember he's a married man, okay?"

In a choked-up voice, Anna said, "Oh, I am painfully aware of that Adam. Thank you for your friendship. I really appreciate everything that you and *Pam*[88] do for others."

He dropped her at the terminal and said, "It is my pleasure, Anna. You take care and have fun."

Anna suffered from terrible anxiety when it came to flying, but this trip she didn't even worry about it. She was so excited to be seeing Sean again that she completely forgot about how terrifying the takeoff and landings could be, that is until the last plane she boarded was approaching the runway in Billings. She had no idea that it was going to land on top of a mesa. *Shit! Shit!* She thought to herself, as the plane seemed to be landing *on the TOP OF A Mountain.* If that wasn't bad enough, the plane didn't seem to ever stop. *Is it going to stop or fly off the other end? What the hell?* she thought, as she gripped the armrests on either side of her. *Who puts a landing strip on THE TOP OF A MESA?* she screamed inside her head.

After the plane safely landed, she continued to shake for a few minutes as she departed the flight. The flight attendant was cheerfully greeting everyone as they exited, and Anna nervously commented to her, "I was scared to death."

The pilot came out of the cockpit at that moment. Anna was somehow on the last seat on the plane, and he said with a huge smile on his face, "Oh, you mean the runway? That was fun."

---

88 Pam, Pamela Deloris Danis is Dr. D's wife. Fictional character and not meant to represent any particular person living or deceased.

"Of course, you'd like that, wouldn't you?" Anna said, laughing.

Anna could talk to anyone, anywhere, anytime. It was in her nature to be quiet and to enjoy being alone, but she did enjoy talking to strangers, more than friends sometimes, as friends always ask too many personal questions. She had a genuine interest in other people though, and there were really no strangers in her life, just new and passing friends.

She exited the plane, Sean had given her instructions earlier to go to the parking lot, and he would be waiting. Annie traveled light and made her way through the small airport carrying her backpack and fanny pack, which contained her ID, a prayer card, pics of her boys, and limited funds.

As she exited the building, she could see Sean leaning against his car. He looked so handsome and incredibly sexy, posed calmly against the hood, wearing his sunglasses and field hat. He looked relaxed, but he was giddy with anticipation at seeing his Annie once again.

Sean watched eagerly for her to exit the doors, and then there she was. Wearing her boots, jeans, large grey sweatshirt, and smiling with that big infectious smile of hers, with her long, curly chestnut hair blowing away from her face, under her favorite field hat. The two waved, and Annie walked to him as she dropped her bag.

She fell into him as she put her arms around his waist, and he pulled her head to his chest and pulled her entire body into his.

They both held each other and continued to lean against his car for a few minutes.

Annie breathed in deeply and was instantly calmed by the smell of his body. She was home again and felt safe... whole again.

Sean had acquired a hotel room for them for the night. They skipped dinner and went straight to the room where they made passionate love most of the night.

"Darling, darling, darling," Sean chanted as he felt himself slip effortlessly into Annie repeatedly. It felt like a silk glove, which fit him perfectly. He gently cupped her breasts in his hands with each penetrating motion. He loved to feel her nipples harden as she became more and more aroused. With each movement, he could feel her squeeze him tighter and tighter inside of her.

Annie grabbed the head of the bed frame and lifted her hips into the air as Sean moved deeper and deeper. She held that position, as she climaxed repeatedly, moving her hips upward with each shudder, and moving her head from side to side with each release.

Sean watched her beautiful form as she moved. As a scientist, he was fascinated at the response of her nipples to repeated heightened sexual tension. The observation turned him on, but also served as clear evidence that they indeed had something special.

Annie simply was one of the most responsive lovers he'd ever had, and just like in her personality, nothing was hidden. She was honest in her physical expressions as much as her emotions. She truly enjoyed being with him, and he loved sharing that experience with her.

He tried to focus just on her, as he wanted her to enjoy it as much as possible. In Sean's mind, it was the most beautiful experience in the world, watching their bodies move together and seeing the intense physical pleasure of his partner.

For Annie, these were mind-blowing first-time experiences, which left her head spinning. She would climax first, which never happened in her past sex life, and then would experience the full measure of his pleasure, which included filling her completely in a gradual manner, rather than all at once. The first penetration was always full and extremely pleasurable, but the continued fullness coupled with her own involuntary contractions, produced an orgasm for them both, usually at the same time.

She loved to watch him, watch them together. The connection between them was simply beyond joy. It was a mind, body, soul.... a complete spiritual connection. The pleasure for them both was transcendent.

They considered each other's eyes as they moved together. It was so loving, not just sex for the sake of sex, but two people completely and totally in love with one another.

The next morning, they had breakfast, and Sean shared the plan for their Yellowstone visit, which was work for him. It was strictly against the rules to collect rocks in the park, but he had a special research permit granting him permission to collect samples as he mapped the distribution of flows to the north and east of the primary caldera. Their transect would be across sections of the Rhyolite Plateau to the northeast, which is overlain by the more recent flows.

Annie had always been interested in sequence volcanic stratigraphy and was interested in perhaps correlation of incomplete sequences. For her this was an amazing opportunity to learn from Sean in his area of expertise.

Sean had been trained in petrology and geochemistry in addition to volcanology in his undergraduate and graduate studies in New Zealand. He later engaged in post-doc research at Cambridge University, where he became an expert in the Central Andean Volcanic Zone in the Andes, where there are thick continental crust and abundant calderas.

His driving ambition was to test hypotheses he had proposed for magma generation in the crust and to use detailed field observations to decipher the fundamental processes involved in the production of the enormous ash eruptions and associated ash flows and ignimbrites. If these cycles were repeated, they would pose an existential threat to human civilization. These super eruptions, e.g., the 600ka eruption at Yellowstone is an order of magnitude larger than the largest known historical eruption.

Annie's undergraduate and graduate work had been in characterizing oil and gas reservoirs in the subsurface, using geophysical and petrochemical methods. She was trained in geophysics, as well as sedimentary and carbonate petrology (Petroleum Geology). She enjoyed her work with mineralogy in provenance analysis, using cores from wells drilled in the target areas.

Her postdoctoral research was in the paleo reconstruction of the New Madrid seismic zone's tectonic framework. Her focus was on using stratigraphic and structural sequencing to help predict future risk for civilian populations in the rift zone. She was also a very good field geologist and was adept at collecting detailed information in the field, so she would be a good field partner for Sean, regardless of their two different areas of expertise.

Chapter 21—Yellowstone

Sean and Annie set up their tent in a campsite located about a mile from Sean's research area. Their camp was nestled on the edge of a Douglas fir forest with a view of the *Absaroka Mountains*[89] in the distance, across a high meadow, which dipped gently downslope into a stream valley containing a pristine graded stream below.

As Annie relaxed into her chair, she felt so happy. The air was cool, fresh, crisp, and filled with the scent of fir trees, and wood smoke. It was so quiet; she could hear the stream flowing some distance below them.

The late afternoon scene was made even more enjoyable by the view of Sean unpacking his camp cooking equipment and cheerfully preparing to cook one of his favorite dehydrated *REI*[90] camp meals, Chicken Linguini.

Annie couldn't help but smile as she watched him proudly show off his brand-new propane stove and his meal packets.

"Hey Annie, check out this feature! It allows the stove to light automatically without a match! I got this stove for a bargain price too," he said in his thick New Zealand accent.

"Do you need some help?" she asked from the comfort of her chair.

"No, ya just sit there. I have this," he said proudly.

Annie giggled to herself and quietly praised God for the beauty of the earth and the opportunity to be with Sean.

---

89   Absaroka Mountains, mountain group to the northeast of the Yellowstone caldera in Wyoming.

90   Recreational Equipment, Inc. – A store that sells gear for outdoor activities.

After dinner, they made sure that everything was cleaned and stored safely away from the tent. In Yellowstone, it is important to have nothing in or near your tent that would smell of food. Any scented items, including detergents, perfumes, lotions, and film canisters for photography, would be enticing to the keen sense of smell of bears and small rodents.

The sun was highlighting the Absarokas and the dewy grass of the meadow, as the sun began to set. Everything was getting very dark, except for firelight from their camp and other camps in the surrounding area.

Annie smiled to herself at the sound of children's voices in the distance as they giggled and laughed. She couldn't help but think of her boys, who were at home with their grandparents.

As dusk gave way to the night, the stars popped out one by one until there was a dark blanket of the sky with brilliant star patterns. It was easy to see how the Egyptians could have thought that the goddess *Nut*[91] was wearing a star-studded gown as she arched herself over her mate Geb of the earth below. The Milky Way was also clearly visible as they faced looking to the northeast. Annie had always loved the night sky and spent many hours as a young girl lying in her bed watching the cosmic parade each night before she fell asleep.

This experience, as she and Sean sat quietly holding hands and looking at the stars, almost seemed like a dream come true. She breathed deeply and noticed her breath as she exhaled softly and could see the faint condensation mist as it left her lips. Taking a sip of her beer, she thought to herself, *This must be how being alive feels.*

She looked over at Sean and noticed he too seemed very relaxed and she couldn't tell if he was awake or had drifted off to sleep.

---

91   Goddess Nut, Egyptian Mythology, arched over her partner Geb and wore a dress filled with stars. She is said to give birth to the Sun each morning (Billing, 2003)

"Sean," she said in a whisper, "Are you asleep?"

"No, it is just so nice, isn't it?"

"Yes, love," said Annie, "I don't think it gets any better than this, does it?"

Sean looked at her and smiled as he leaned over to her and pulled her face to his. He cradled the back of her head in his strong hand and sweetly kissed her on the lips. He sat back in his chair and replied, "No, I don't think it could."

After they finished their beers, Annie asked reluctantly, "Should we try to get some sleep? It's going to be a long hike tomorrow."

"Oh yes, we have at least two miles to cover," said Sean excitedly.

After they stowed all items away, they stripped off their clothing, down to their undergarments, and Sean took a bag with their clothing to a tree downslope from their tents and raised it high off the ground, securing the cord to a spike in the ground.

Meanwhile, Annie entered the tent and began to nest for the evening. She zipped their sleeping bags together to form one large bag, placed their pillows at the open end and tossed a blanket over it all. When she finished, she lay on top of the blanket and gazed at the stars directly above the tent. The canopy was not on the tent yet, and the stars could be clearly seen through the mesh opening above.

After a few minutes of peaceful reflection, she could hear the footsteps of someone running up the slope and toward their camp. She wondered what on earth was happening and sat up to exit the tent for a look. Just as she began to stick her head out of the tent, Sean lunged into the tent, grabbing her as he entered, laying them both flat out across the newly made bedding.

They both fell headlong, lengthwise, into the tent laughing, almost pushing out the side of the tent on the opposite side. Annie had always been a little jumpy, and his abrupt behavior was both frightening and funny.

After tickling and kissing her, Sean sat up to get a sip of water and to take his medications. As he leaned forward, he farted loudly, to which Annie responded, "Sean Michael Anderson! That was gross!"

She began laughing as he too chuckled at the absurdity of the moment. She was laughing so hard at him that she too could not keep from emitting a tiny little toot as well. Sean quickly responded to that insult with, "Well, Annie Moore, that too was gross!" To that they both continued to laugh and pass gas.

"Sean, we may have to open the flaps," said Annie. "I'd hate for the bears to come and investigate the strange odors in our tent." They both continued to laugh as they lay there next to one another, looking up at the night sky.

Sean continued to make Annie laugh as he recounted fond memories of when he was a young lad camping for the first time with his classmates in New Zealand. Sean told of his experiences with his best friend in college at Otago University, *Jim Donovan*, [92]who Annie would soon meet on their trip to the Stillwater.

Jim had spent many years as the senior geologist with *Rustenburg Mining Company*, [93]which extracted Pb and Pd ores from the Bushveld Complex in South Africa.

To Sean's surprise and joy, Jim had recently been hired by the Stillwater Mining Company as a consultant. He now lived in Red Lodge, MT and drove into the mine each day.

Jim contacted Sean and suggested that they meet while Sean was doing his fall field research. Sean seized on this opportunity to be able to show Annie the complex as well as have her meet his

---

92   Jim Donovan, one of Sean's closest friends from college. He works at the Stillwater Mine in Montana. Fictional character and not meant to represent any particular person living or deceased.

93   Jim is a fictionalized character not meant to represent anyone from the company https://www.mining-technology.com/projects/marikana-platinum-mine-rustenburg-south-africa/, which is used in a fictional sense for this storyline.

oldest and dearest friend. Apparently, Jim and Sean were involved in all kinds of shenanigans as undergraduate geology students.

Chapter 22—The Moehou Man

Sean told one story where the duo engaged a fellow student, a Saudi national, during his own Senior Field Methods course in New Zealand.

"The guy, '*Omar*,'[94] was just so rude and entitled," began Sean, "His father was a Saudi oilman and wanted his son to have a degree in geology, so he sent him to college, and he managed to pass all of his classes. He was now at our field camp because it 'fit into his schedule.' All he needed was this course for his dad to accept him as a working member of his company. Well, this *bloke*[95] smoked cigarettes nonstop and left his lit butts lying in the field. Ya could always tell where he'd been because he left them like breadcrumbs along the trail.

One evening, we were camping in a field near Swinburn Volcanic Complex in the *Waipiata Volcanic Field*[96] area. We pitched our tents in an area near the flows, which would allow us to peg. We had outcrops of basalt lava flows on all sides of us. The wind never stopped blowing..." he vocalized the haunting, howling noise to demonstrate the ferocity of the environment. "The sides of our tents were oscillating in and out, a sort of breathing motion," he was sitting upright now and demonstrating a billowing effect with his arms and hands.

---

94 Omar was a Saudi student attending the Summer Field Methods Course in New Zealand. Fictional character and not meant to represent any particular person living or deceased.

95 A bloke is an informal British term for a man, a guy.

96 Kaulfuss, Uwe & Nemeth, Karoly & White, James. (2012). Field Guide Miocene subaerial to subaqueous monogenetic volcanism in Otago, New Zealand.

"It was really, really difficult to sleep with all of the wind," he said, as he lay back down with his hands over his heart, staring up at the ceiling of the tent and recalling the rest of his story.

"Omar was very nervous and couldn't sleep. His tent mates were rude to him and picked on him because of his constant *whinging*[97] and the 'in and out' of the tent movement to smoke. He was a real *drongo*[98] who just wanted to stand outside for half the evening smoking. This behavior practically *drove his tent mates around the bend.*[99]

Jim was friends with *Ed*,[100] who was one of the guys sharing a tent with Omar. So, together we hatched a plan to try to get Omar to stay in the tent at night."

Annie was now sitting up and looking at Sean very intently, very curious as to what this plan would involve, and feeling a little bit sorry for poor Omar.

"You guys didn't hurt him, or anything did you?" she asked in a concerned voice.

"Oh no," said Sean, "we would never intentionally hurt anyone. It was all done in fun, okay?...

So anyway...on this night, Jim had collected coats and gloves from two other guys in the camp, and I helped him to squeeze into four sets of coats, pants, and gloves. Jim looked scary for sure in the dark.

Meanwhile, earlier in the evening during dinner, Ed proceeded to tell the story of the *Moehau Man*, which is a New Zealand version

---

97 British term for "whining"

98 Drongo is a kiwi (nonindigenous peoples of New Zealand) term that means idiot.

99 A phrase used in New Zealand to describe driving people crazy.

100 Ed Smart is Sean and Jim's classmate from Otago and became the main geologist at the Hawaiian Volcano Observatory Fictional character and not meant to represent any particular person living or deceased. The use of the HVO is fictional in this story and is not meant to represent the park or any personnel associated with the park in the past or present.

of the Yeti or Bigfoot. Only the locals knew that the Moehau Man was not indigenous to this part of *New Zealand*.[101]

"Everyone seemed intrigued by his story because they knew he was a local kid, a *Maori,*[102] and if he was concerned, the story must have some merit. Some of his classmates were concerned when he mentioned that his only fear of camping in that vicinity was from the stories that the locals told about the Moehau Man, who was said to have the scream of a woman and typically carried off grown men, who would never be seen alive again."

Annie began to chuckle, "You didn't?"

To which Sean replied in a serious tone, "Oh no, I didn't, but Jim did." he laughed. He seemed very amused at the memory of the ruse.

"So, what happened?" pressed Annie.

"Well," said Sean, "Jim snuck out while Omar was still in his tent and hid behind a nearby outcrop. After I heard Omar pass by my tent..."

Annie interrupted, "Wait, how did you know for sure it was Omar when the wind was blowing?"

"Good question," said Sean, "...he didn't pick up his feet, and he slid his feet along as though he were wearing flip-flops, so it was easy to distinguish his passing from someone else."

"Oh," said Annie, "Please continue."

"...Anyway, I stepped out of our tent and walked toward Omar, who was smoking and cursing. Ya couldn't hear a darn thing really, at least not voices. I motioned to him in polite greeting. He offered me a smoke, and I declined. We then both stood there for a few

---

101　Moehau Man is a Maori (indigenous peoples of New Zealand) myth about a creature analogous to the Yeti or Bigfoot.

102　Indigenous Polynesian people of the mainland of New Zealand. Kiwi are white people who came later.

minutes with the wind blowing us so hard that we had to turn our backs to it to stay warm.

"A few minutes later, Ed emerged from their tent and came to stand with us. Ed had a thermos of warm tea, and we all shared a sip.

Ed yelled, 'Aren't you afraid to stand out here alone?'

'No!' yelled Omar, 'I'm not afraid of silly camp stories.'

Omar didn't realize it, but Ed and I were there to make sure that he didn't try to kill Jim when he showed up to scare him."

"So, what happened?" asked Annie excitedly.

"After a bit, Ed and I began to walk back, and when we got near the tents, we turned around to wave to Omar. When we did, we saw Jim creeping slowly from behind an outcrop, looking very menacing. We both pointed behind Omar and acted worried.

Omar just waved back at us, not realizing that we were pointing at something behind him.

We then began to wave our arms and run toward him.

Omar became frightened of us and turned around to run away. He must a thought that we wanted to kick his arse or something," Sean said, laughing, "When Omar turned around to run, Jim grabbed him!"

"Oh no!" laughed Annie, covering her mouth.

"Omar dropped his g**damned *durrie*[103] and screamed bloody murder. He took off running *full tit* away from all of us toward the outcrops from where Jim had appeared. He, Omar, fell over a few rocks and rolled down a rubbly flow, not as sharp and painful as an *a'a*,[104] but not soft either.

"We all ran after him to see that he was okay, including Jim, who still looked like a ferocious Bigfoot creature. As we approached,

---

103   New Zealand term for rolled cigarette.

104   A'a flow is a rubbly, slow moving basaltic lava flow that has sharp edges during quick cooling at the surface.

with Jim closing in behind us, poor Omar screamed again, got up, and ran toward the tents shrieking over the wind. By this time, EVERYONE had emerged from their tents to see what the matter was."

"Was everyone in on this?" asked Annie laughing in a scolding tone.

"No, ha-ha! No, ya see, everyone else saw Jim running behind Ed and me, and they began running in the opposite direction as well. It was now a *full tit, open slather.*[105]

"We then knew that WE were in terrible trouble because it was dark, we were in a volcanic field, and even our instructors were terrified and running away from the Moehau Man, who was stumbling, falling, groaning and yelling behind us all."

Annie and Sean lay there howling at the thought of the entire camp running in their *skivvies*[106] and falling all over volcanic rocks trying to escape Bigfoot.

"Was everyone okay?" asked Annie as she caught her breath.

"No, not really," he said with an uncontrollable laugh. "We were all skinned up and in need of ointment and Band-aids--everyone but Jim, who was well padded. He did have a busted nose though from Omar's punching him to get away."

"So, did you guys get in trouble?" asked Annie naively.

"Oh, yes!" said Sean chuckling. "We were given quite a talking-to for sure. Although I'm sure our instructors no doubt thought it was pretty funny too, after all of the night terror subsided."

"Wow, I can't wait to meet this 'Jim' character," said Annie.

"Me neither," said Sean.

As the evening merged into the early morning, Annie continued to lay there watching him smile and laugh as he told story after story. She loved to listen to his stories; it was almost like hearing

---

105 Kiwi phrase meaning 'running, free for all.'
106 underwear

an audiobook, as each experience was described in detail and with such clarity that she could almost feel as though she were there with him in time.

She too shared her memories of geology field trips in graduate school with her very colorful professors, but nothing brought her more joy than watching Sean laughing at his own stories as he reminisced.

Occasionally, he would stop talking and turn his head to look at her, saying, "Are ya awake, Annie?"

She was so quiet and so enthralled that she didn't speak, she just listened. Annie would respond, "Oh, I'm just enjoying your stories, Sean. You are such a great storyteller."

"I suppose having years and years of experience leads one to have a few stories to share, don't ya think?" he said as he turned over toward her and hugged her tightly.

They kissed tenderly and held each other. He gently kissed her closed eyelids as she ran her fingers down his side, to his broad shoulders, and then over his back. Their bodies were so close and so exposed, and it was so nice to have this moment of intimacy without sex. They were together, comfortable, and would fall asleep in each other's arms.

As Sean held her closely, he spoke to her softly, pulling his head back so that he could see her face, "I love ya, Annie. I really, really do."

Annie closed her eyes and felt tears welling up, as she put her arms around his neck and pulled him closer and said, "I love you too. Thank you for this."

"For what?" asked Sean, "Loving ya? How could I not?"

Annie sighed and fell asleep with her face, nestled in his chest. Her head was under his chin, and they lay there facing each other, embracing as they slept.

Chapter 23—Ignimbrites

Annie slept so soundly that she didn't even notice when Sean got up to go get their coffee and breakfast started. As she woke up, she could smell coffee and ... *Is that bacon?* She thought to herself, *Oh my goodness, I overslept!*

She sat up and saw that her clothes were at her feet, where Sean had obviously retrieved them from their perch downslope. She quickly got dressed and exited the tent.

"G'day, Sleeping Beauty," he said in a teasing voice, "How did ya sleep?"

"I'm so sorry, Sean. I meant to get up earlier."

Sean stopped what he was doing, stood up straight and tall, and said, "Now Annie, remember what I said before about ya apologizing all the time? Ya have nothing to apologize for with me, so please stop it. I am so glad ya had a good night's sleep."

She smiled shyly, he gathered her in his arms, and they embraced. He kissed her neck, her face, the back of her hand and finally her lips. She pulled away, laughing, "Oh no... Morning breath ... better not kiss me before breakfast and definitely not before coffee."

Sean laughed and swatted her behind as she walked away, "It doesn't bother me. I just enjoy kissing ya."

She walked upslope into the grove of fir trees behind their campsite. Annie could hear birds chirping loudly and the sound of children playing far in the distance. There were so many birds of all different kinds it was difficult to distinguish them one from another. She couldn't help but notice a three-toed woodpecker that was pecking on a dead tree. He noted Annie's approach, stopped pecking for a moment, and looked in her direction.

"Hi there, little guy," she said. "My dad would have loved you."

Also, thinking to herself, *Dad, you would be so proud that I recognized the white bars on his dorsal side and could identify him without counting his toes.*

As she continued, she was able to identify a few jays and heard the soft repetitious warbling of a mountain bluebird. The mountain bluebird was one of her favorite high forest birds, with his cute little powder blue wings. She couldn't see him, but could hear his morning song, "Chirp chirpilla, chirp, chirp, chirpilla, chirp chirpilla."

She tried to call back, but her song just didn't quite match. Her dad could have called to him, for sure. *I wish you were here, Daddy.* Annie thought sadly, *You could help me to identify the rest of these sounds for sure.*

Annie's father *Paul*[107] had passed away a few years earlier from lung cancer. He was a thin, handsome man of Scots-Irish descent and was an accomplished biologist and conservationist. As a little girl, she used to accompany him to the field as he did field surveys of ecosystems, and even stood by his side in demonstrations against lumber companies that were decimating the deciduous forests of the Southeast.

Some of Annie's fondest memories were from her field excursions with her dad. They shared a love of nature, and both enjoyed escaping the stressful home environment--both doing anything to avoid conflict, and both sharing a deep love of science and nature.

Annie enjoyed the farm life and the work, but her dad would prefer to be anywhere but slaving away milking cows or harvesting crops.

---

107   Charles Paul Moore, Annie's father. Fictional character and not meant to represent any particular person living or deceased.

Annie's mother *Moira*[108] was a beautiful athletic lady and was the family bookkeeper and farm manager. She was the backbone of their family and the one who balanced the budget and paid the bills, often complaining about the waste of money and time invested in fishing trips, field excursions and nature photography. To her, it invested little in the family and didn't help their family to maintain or sustain the farm where they all worked and lived.

Moira had grown up during the Depression and was not able to leave the farm life which sustained her parents, grandparents, and now her own family. She ran the family business, while Annie's dad was an academic. Even though he was a conservationist and loved the farm, he never wanted to be a farmer. Together they made things work, but Annie's mother was never truly happy. They both shared a love of nature, but Moira was much more grounded and willing to focus her efforts on the day-to-day business of sustainability for their family.

Moira was the child of Irish immigrant parents who had traveled west from New York and took advantage of the *Homestead Act of 1862.*[109] She was an intelligent woman who had not had the opportunities afforded her husband, who had served in World War II, and was able to attend college after the military.

They had met at a soda shop one day, and it was love at first sight. He continued his studies and teaching, while Annie's mother worked on the farm with her aging parents and raised their children. She clearly resented his reluctance and inability to work the farm but loved him for his kindness, sensitivity, and comedic sense of humor.

---

108   Moira Amelia Finnegan, Annie's mother, Fictional character and not meant to represent any particular person living or deceased.

109   "a special act of Congress (1862) that made public lands in the West available to settlers without payment, usually in lots of 160 acres, to be used as farms." https://www.dictionary.com/browse/homestead-act

He was an extremely fun person to be with, and he adored Annie's mother. He was considered lazy by her grandparents because he was not a farmer. His father-in-law, also a child of immigrants, often insulted him for being an egghead. Annie could relate because she too was ridiculed for spending more time with her encyclopedia set than her farm chores.

Paul often stayed away from the farm to avoid negative comments and any conflict. It just wasn't in his nature to fight. Annie was very much like her dad in temperament, and she too avoided conflict if at all possible.

Annie eventually found a perfect spot to relieve herself, where she was certain she would not be visible to the other campers, especially the children. As with all things, Annie loved all the sounds and smells of the forest, including the aroma of her own urine as it blended with the forest floor organics. It was sweet, and she marveled at the gentle cloud of steam that rose upward as it hit the frosty forest floor.

She paused in the squatting position to observe the eddy's in the cloud that was formed. Things of this nature were fascinating to her. Everything about nature was intriguing and worthy of a moment of observation and reflection. Eventually she learned to keep those observations to herself if she didn't want others to tease her, especially those in her family. They loved Annie but considered her special in a weird way--everyone but her dad.

Paul and Annie seemed to share this intense desire to know and understand everything that they experienced.

After what seemed like a very short time to Annie, she walked back downslope to the campsite where Sean had dished up their breakfast and was already eating his and sipping coffee.

"Ya must have gone a long way off. I was beginning to wonder if I needed to send out a search party," he said jokingly.

"I just wanted to make sure the children the next campsite over didn't get to see a full moon rising this morning," she laughed.

He had no idea why she had taken so long. That would be her little secret, especially the flow patterns she saw in her urine cloud. Annie chuckled to herself as she was amused by her own nerdiness.

It was going to be a nice day for fieldwork, and she was looking forward to hiking with Sean and learning from him as they collected samples and mapped outcrops. Her field research experience was mostly in soft rock sedimentary geology, and she wasn't sure exactly how to go about collecting fresh pristine samples in igneous settings.

Even though there were sedimentary rocks and deposits in the area, it was the volcanics that Sean was most interested in sampling. It would be nice to be able to find any outcrops, which also included strata from earlier eruptive events.

Igneous rocks are generally much harder to break because they form from a molten state (liquid at high temperatures) and tend to be relatively high in silica, which makes them very hard--hence the designation "hard rock" vs. "soft rock" geology.

Sean was a hard rock pro and would teach her how to collect and reduce the rock samples to hand sample size. Each sample needs to be shaped for the maximum surface area and the least weight to have to carry. She knew she would be carrying at least twenty to thirty pounds of hand samples back to camp by the end of the day and was grateful to be with someone experienced in the collection process.

They traveled to their *transect* area[110] and exited the vehicle. As they hiked the trail, which was off the designated path, Annie talked nervously because she was quite afraid of meeting a grizzly.

---

110   Transect refers to the linear path that the field geologists follow as they map features.

She knew that if they made enough noise, theoretically the bears would hear them and would go the other direction.

Sean seemed to be in his element, exuding confidence, and focused on the task at hand. He had hiked in Chile and Peru, in the high Andes, and in New Zealand, so he was like a mountain goat. This terrain was nothing for an athlete of his training. He had traversed areas that Annie could only dream of one day experiencing. She eventually relaxed and began to just follow his lead, forgetting about her fear of anything.

Sean was a natural and gifted teacher, even with another geologist and professor like Annie. He was also very aware of Annie's desire to learn as much as possible from him, so he gladly pointed out the different textures and minerals present in both rhyolite flows and volcanic tuffs in the area.

Although most of the rhyolites in the caldera were uniform in composition, the units Sean was looking at exhibited zoning in *phenocrysts,* [111] which would hopefully help to determine the evolution of the magma which produced the different flows. Perhaps the crystalline mush had formed previously, and the zoning would show that there were two or more different magmatic phases?

Annie was particularly excited by the *basal units.*[112] They were sedimentary but appeared to have been 'cooked' by the intense heat of the volcanic flow immediately above. As she knocked some of the baked meta-sedimentary rock loose, she tried to imagine the intensity of the flow and the heat that welded this soft rock into a harder rock material than the original.

She broke a piece of volcanic tuff and began to trim it to hand sample size.

As she hammered away at the edges, Sean came and asked, "Want me ta show ya how to 'smallen' that rock?"

---

111 larger mineral grains within a fine-grained rock
112 A rock layer visible at the base of a sequence of exposed rocks.

She stopped and looked at him, "Smallen?"

"Ya, that is the highly technical term that I use to describe the process," he snickered.

Annie lowered her sunglasses so that he could see her eyes and gave him a "You're kidding me?" look.

"Yesh, shweetheart," he said with his best Sean Connery, Scottish accent.

Annie laughed out loud and said, "Sure, please do show me how to 'smallen' a rock… I'm going to have to remember that one."

"Well, ya see, ya take the sample in yer hand like so…"

Annie noted how big and strong his hands were as he continued to demonstrate the time-honored method, "…and ya set up a rhythmic tapping, like so."

To her amazement, he was gently tapping the rock so that the hammer was bouncing, hitting, and recoiling, in what she recognized as "harmonic motion." He was using harmonic resonance to break the rock.

Sean continued, "Ya see, ya don't have to hit the rocks hard to break them down. Ya just simply hold them in yer hand and tap them in this fashion until they break apart on the edges. See?"

Annie couldn't help but show her amazement at the ease at which Sean broke each rock into a hand sample. She couldn't wait to try it for herself and picked up a broken piece from the ground.

Sean watched her work on the rock in her thin hand and hated to tell her that the sample she picked up probably wouldn't work. She would clearly need a little bit of practice to master the skill of reducing an igneous rock to hand sample, but she was getting the hang of it. He hated to interrupt her, but he had to let her know that all sides of the sample had to be fresh and lacking any surface weathering.

"That's very good," he said. "Yer gettin the hang of it, BUT, if ya want a pristine sample, ya need ta select ones like this," as he picked up the perfect sample and showed her how fresh the surfaces were.

Annie wasn't offended and was impressed that he had not made fun of her. She was beginning to see why his field students admired him so much. He was never insulting and was very patient and kind in his instructions. The mark of a truly gifted teacher is one who celebrates the student's successes and progress, even if it is not perfection.

Annie and Sean hiked for another day, collected the needed samples for Sean's research, and would now break camp and travel to the Stillwater Mining Area in the Beartooth mountains to their North. She was so excited to be going, especially now that she knew more about Jim, who was going to give them a personal tour of the area.

Jim and Sean seemed to be very close friends, and she couldn't wait to meet someone who was such a huge part of Sean's early life.

Chapter 24—The Stillwater Valley

Sean woke up with Annie's head resting partly on his chest and shoulder. He had lain on his back and apparently snored during the night because his throat felt dry and sore. The dry night air contributed to his extreme thirst.

Annie's elbow was on his waist with her arm draped upward and her hand over his heart. He could smell her hair, which was scented by the wood smoke of the previous nights of camping in Yellowstone. Even though they both could use a dip in the river to clean up, they were very comfortable with their own animal essence, which was not offensive at all to either one of them.

Sean stroked her arm, her hair, and placed his hand on hers, over his heart. He was memorizing every curve, every shape, every texture, and never wanted to forget any of it.

He recalled looking up at her the night before, as he held her breasts and watched her experience extreme pleasure. "Annie, you are so beautiful," he said as he moved his large hands over her hips and the small of her back to feel her muscles as she moved on top of him.

His hands moved down her legs to her knees, to her ankles, then back to cradle her waist and hips. Her skin was so soft and smooth, and he wanted to touch every part of her and feel her warmth and excitement. Yes, he thought, Annie was beautiful, but he knew the entire experience was beyond description.

She then opened her eyes and looked up into his smiling, loving eyes. Time seemed to stand still as they regarded one another.

He had been leaning on his elbow and watching her as she slept. She looked so innocent and kind of silly with a tiny bit of drool leaking from the corner of her mouth. He brushed her hair from her face, to behind her ear, so he could look more closely at her cute freckled nose. He smiled as he remembered her telling him that her grandfather told her that each freckle was where an angel had kissed her. He thought to himself, amused, *You've certainly been kissed a lot by the angels, my dear.*

"Good morning love," she said, as she reached up and touched his beard. "What are you doing?"

Sean smiled sweetly and stroked her cheek, "Watching ya drool on yourself...ha-ha. No, just counting the number of times you've been kissed by angels," he said as he kissed her on the cheek.

She reached up and stroked his forehead, feeling the lines at the corner of his smiling eyes.

He had a very soft, yet rugged face, which showed the many years of being in the elements. His beard was neatly trimmed and had a blend of black, brown, red, and white. Sean kept it short, clean, and surprisingly soft.

Robert also had a beard, but his was rough and sometimes felt like needles.

Sean's beard gave his face a very strong, handsome appearance.

Annie thought to herself, *Could I love him any more than I do right now?* And with that thought, she became emotional.

Sean had no idea what his love meant to her, not really. He knew that her husband was a jerk and that she was lucky to be rid of him, but she had not shared many details. It was just too painful, he assumed.

When he saw her tears, he wiped them away, saying, "What's wrong, Annie?"

"Nothing," she said as she smiled through the tears and pulled him close to her. "I'm just so happy. That's all."

She had not told him much about how she was degraded by men before him. He just knew that he loved her and that she loved him too.

They were committed to enjoying the experience without questioning it too much. It was complicated by their being in marriages with other people, but that didn't seem to dim their affection for one another.

Her tears were tears of both pain and thankfulness. Sean's love seemed like a dream, too good to be true. Deep down inside, she had learned through bitter experience not to trust in love and in dreams; they rarely came true and almost always ended with a sword through her heart. While she was certain of his love and trusted him very much, there was a part of her that never felt good enough, and always felt unworthy of true love.

After lying there for a while together, they both rose and exited the tent into the morning sun that was filtering through the trees. The *Stillwater River*[113] could be heard roaring nearby as they both walked in different directions.

Sean had been there with his students on more than one occasion, but this was Annie's first time. It had been dusk when they set up their tent the night before, so she was not aware of the exquisite beauty of the valley and especially the river.

There was a light early morning fog hanging gently in the air above the river.

As Annie approached the river, she couldn't help but notice that the sound of the river blocked out all sounds of nature nearby. Even the singing of birds was barely audible as well as her own voice as she spoke aloud, "Praise you for this beautiful experience, Lord."

It was a powerful yet soothing sound, and the cold air excited all her senses as it moved over her body. The air was filled with

---

113 Mountain river, with headwaters in the Beartooth Plateau on the Wyoming/Montana border.

the smells of evergreen, moss, other organics, and the mist of a mountain stream. She was falling in love with this special place, and it would become one of the few places where she could escape to find healing, peace, love, and the presence of God. The *Stillwater Valley*[114] would become the key to experiencing her own rebirth and redemption.

Sean could see Annie in the distance, looking up at the Flatirons[115] on the front slopes which framed the valley entrance. He was so happy for her as he knew how much she had longed to visit this place. *I am so glad I could be the one to bring her here,* he thought proudly.

As she approached the tent, he decided to stand there and watch her. She seemed to be lost in her own thoughts and didn't even see him. It was just as well, as he was enjoying the experience of watching her take it all in.

He had walked to the car to collect his bar of 'Ivory soap,' toothbrush and towel. Just as in Yellowstone, it was not wise to have anything in or near the tent.

The "Beartooth" mountains were not exactly named for the shape of the peaks from a distance, but instead for the bears that called the area home. The plateau where part of the banded igneous complex was exposed was only 18 miles north (as the crow flies) from Yellowstone. In the fall of the year, the bears would be making their way back to the mountain meadows and wooded caves for hibernation in the winter.

"Ya want ta join me for a dip in the river?" he asked as she neared the tent.

---

114 Stream valley, cut by the Stillwater River, which gently meanders as a graded stream on the valley floor below.

115 Geologic formations created by the differential erosion of folded and uplifted rocks in a mountain belt. On the flanks of the folds, the rocks weather to produce features that look like irons standing up on an ironing board, against the flanks of the tilted materials.

Annie looked up in surprise and said, "Are you crazy!? It's too cold!" as she pulled her arms into her oversized gray sweatshirt.

"Ok, suit yourself," he said as he walked toward the river.

As Annie watched him walk away, she decided to follow him after all. She reached into her bag, grabbed her own towel, and ran to join him. *This could be fun,* she thought to herself. *Painful, but fun*, she mused. She touched his arm, and he turned and smiled, and yelled over the roar of the river, "Glad ya could join me. Let's find the perfect spot. Don't want ta get washed downstream!"

She nodded and followed him as he led her to one of his favorite spots in the river. There was a relatively shallow tidal pool crotch-deep for Annie, but thigh-deep for Sean, where the water swirled gently but didn't jet downstream.

He turned to her and shouted, "This is it! Perfect."

She watched in disbelief as he stripped off all his clothes and waded into the ice-cold water. She found herself screaming on his behalf and laughing as he proceeded to reach down and splash the icy meltwater on his privates, up under his arms and eventually over his head and face. He had a single bar of ivory soap, and he used it to wash his hair, his beard, his …. everything, and then tossed it to her and shouted, "Yer turn."

She managed to catch it and laid it on a nearby rock as she took off her shoes and jeans--while camping, she rarely wore undergarments.

"Hurry up. It's freezing in here!" he laughed and continued to rinse himself.

She took everything off but her sweatshirt. She was not convinced that she could withstand the temperature at all. Also, even though Sean had seen every part of her naked, she was still very prudish about being totally naked in front of anyone, even Sean.

He made fun of her as she refused to take off her sweatshirt and laughed loudly as she screamed and entered the water. He reached out his hand and helped to pull her into the deeper part of the pool. When she got close to him, he grabbed the bottom of her sweatshirt and raised it quickly, up over her head. Even though she resisted just a little, he was stronger and managed to pull it off without getting it completely wet.

She stood there like a shy Catholic schoolgirl with one arm cradling and covering her exposed breasts and the other hand covering her nether region.

Sean gave her sweatshirt a long toss and proceeded to cup his huge hands and pour water over her body.

At first, she screamed, and it was very painful, but eventually, it felt very nice as he took the bar of soap from her and began to lather her entire body. His hands were so strong and warm as he rubbed soap over her. Having him massage every inch of her body was very exciting as well as relaxing.

They both laughed as she pulled herself to him and began rubbing his body with hers to get him soapy too. It was so much fun--more fun than any festival ride she could ever remember being on as a teen.

They splashed each other with water and eventually rinsed the soap off and left the pool to get dry. Neither one of them bothered to put their clothes back on. They collected their clothing in their arms, slipped on their shoes and ran back to the tent, where they entered and climbed back into the now cold sleeping bags.

Annie's lips were blue, and she and Sean cuddled together, rubbing each other's bodies to get warm. Sean climbed on top of Annie to use his body to warm hers and found himself warming up enough to slip gently inside of her. Annie gasped as Sean began to move. They both enjoyed the waves of pleasure, as they held nothing back against the roar of the Stillwater River.

This time Annie focused totally on Sean's pleasure as she kissed his chest and concentrated her energy on feeling his every movement inside of her. She embraced him with her arms and legs, as he laid his weight on her and held her head firmly with both hands. With this, he allowed himself to experience his own intense sexual joy

Annie wrapped her arms around his back and shoulders and pulled him closer to her, so she could feel the tension and release of his entire body, not just within her. She was so happy that she could sense every wave of his pleasure from head to toe. For the first time in her life, she wanted to bring pleasure to a man, rather than just be "taken" by a man and wait for him to finish. This was "making love."

Sean fell asleep on top of her, but she didn't mind. He was heavy, but she wanted to feel his body as he completely relaxed. She didn't want them to end, not yet. It was now late morning, and Sean rolled over and apologized to Annie for crushing her.

"It's okay, dear," she said as she kissed him. "I loved every minute of it. Are you hungry?" He nodded.

"You lie here," she said, "I'm going to the car to get some things. Okay?" She got up, dressed, and walked downslope to his car, which was parked about a sixteenth of a mile away.

They had relaxed most of the morning, and they would need to get up to the mine for the tour by the afternoon.

She elected to pass on the stove and trying to cook anything, instead collecting the protein breakfast bars and cans of espresso that Sean had so expertly planned for their wilderness experience. Annie entered the tent with their breakfast-lunch and was surprised when she discovered he was NOT THERE!

Where the heck is, he? She looked in every direction and didn't see him anywhere. Scanning the trees and rocks, she hoped to see his shape somewhere, but nothing. She even turned around to look down the trail toward the car, and still he was not to be seen. Feeling frightened, she began to panic. She turned around again and began to shout his name, and he grabbed her.

"Boo!" he said loudly, as he began to tickle her from behind.

She screamed and turned around in his arms. "Sean Michael Anderson!" she said scolding, as she slapped his shoulders.

He laughed loudly as he picked her up off the ground, kissing her neck and placing his face in between her breasts as he pushed his head under her sweatshirt.

"You scared the hell out of me!" she shouted.

He then lowered her slightly, so he could move his head out of her sweatshirt and kissed her passionately on the lips.

"Uh oh," he said, "We'd better stop this, or we will never see Jim today."

Annie laughed to herself and said, "You started it."

"Oh," he groaned as Annie wrapped her legs around him. He lifted her up higher and unzipped his pants as he carried her back into the tent and laid her on the ground. She removed her jeans but left her sweatshirt on, as he once more made love to her. She removed his shirt, he removed her sweatshirt, and they were once again totally naked and immersed in making love.

They made love until their bodies were too weak to continue, leaving the protein bars and espresso drinks unopened in the corner of the tent. Neither one knew exactly what time it was, but they didn't care.

Jim might have to wait, thought Sean, as he drifted off to sleep.

Sometime later, Sean opened his eyes to see the faint amber glow of the tent. Annie was asleep and snoring, but the sound was barely audible over the roar of the river. It was so cold, and he wondered how long they had both been sleeping.

He was very thirsty and began to feel around for his water bottle amongst the scattered clothing and sleeping bags. As he moved his hand under the clothing, he felt one of the unopened cans of espresso that Annie had brought earlier. That was not what he wanted now, so he carefully placed it in the corner of the tent and began to organize the debris around him. He managed to find both protein bars and feasted on one of them, while still searching for his water bottle.

Eventually, he found Annie's bottle and decided it would be quite okay to drink her water, and he would share his with her after she woke. He felt his watch and picked it up, squinting, because he wasn't sure where his glasses were, either. Noting the time of 2:00 a.m., he couldn't believe that they had managed to miss the afternoon and the evening of the day before. He wasn't even sure what day of the week it was anymore.

Annie stirred and rolled over with her back towards Sean.

Sean noticed her shudder at the cold of her exposed back and pulled himself to her, pulling the sleeping bag and blanket over his shoulder as he drew his body closer to hold and warm her. He put his arm around her and moved his fingers and hand to rest between her breasts so that he could feel the beating of her heart.

The space between her breasts was so warm. Her shoulder was so soft to his lips as he gently kissed her from shoulder to the top of her head. She moved her hips slightly to fit snugly in the space that was still separating them. As she moved her hips, she felt herself become aroused at the presence of Sean behind her. With this motion, she noted he too was becoming aroused.

Sean moved his arm, placed it under the bend of Annie's knee, and raised her leg as he again slipped inside of her. They moved together and somehow found the energy to once more experience great joy. Annie had yet another first-time lovemaking experience, and Sean seemed to have finally depleted all energy he had for lovemaking.

He rolled over onto his back, with one arm across his forehead and the other one across his stomach, and exhaled loudly, saying,

"That's it. I have nothing more. I couldn't possibly do anything more."

Annie was also lying on her back, breathless and physically weak, thinking the exact same thing, as she too assumed the same posture. She weakly rolled up on her elbow and looked at him. "Oh, I see how it is...pause... I guess the honeymoon is over now?"

Sean moved his arm from his forehead, turned his head to look at her in shock and said, "Are ya kidding me?" in indignant disbelief. "Jeez, lady. What the hell do ya want?" he said, laughing. They both lay there exhausted, laughing.

The joy of making love with Sean seemed to erase all her other previous negative experiences. He was her one and only lover, and that is how it would be for the rest of her life. She had been with two men, but never had she been able to sense their needs so naturally and feel so adored and special in the process.

Annie got up and stepped outside the tent. She normally took a bottle of water with her to help cleanse herself, but this time, she enjoyed feeling the moistness and smelling the scent of their lovemaking. Her only concern was that a bear might also find it interesting. She wiped her feet in the forest flooring and re-entered the tent. She knelt next to Sean and watched him as he slept.

She found herself wanting to kiss him but knew he must be exhausted. She pulled her sweatshirt over her naked body and pulled the end of the sleeping bag over her legs and feet, as she found the protein bar and the emptied package of the other bar. She nibbled her bar and sipped what was left of her water as she sat there, watching him sleep for what seemed like hours.

Annie was quite used to waking mid-morning and using that time to speak to God. The rest of the day was so hectic with children, driving, classes, etc. This was a special time that she focused her prayers and listened in her heart and soul.

Her rosary was in her bag in the car, but she did not need her rosary for prayer. She had 10 fingers, knuckles, and toes. When in the field, Annie rarely was able to attend Mass, but she always tried to find time for prayer, especially the rosary.

She wasn't sure of the day, so she decided to meditate on the sorrowful mysteries of Jesus' passion and death. As she asked for peace in their troubled world, safety for her children, conversion of the hearts of all who hate instead of love; her special prayer this morning was for the special love that she shared with Sean. Annie whispered, "Lord, please protect us from all physical harm, forgive us our human failings, and let the love I have for and share with Sean somehow bring You glory, Amen."

She had reconciled herself to being separated from God in the sacraments of the church, but did not feel unworthy of God's love, mercy, and forgiveness--especially the joy. Nothing this special and beautiful could be possible without God's love. The presence of God was the reason she felt joy. Without God, she would feel guilt and shame, which was not the case at all.

Chapter 25—The Field Trip

Later that morning, they both rose again and dressed for a day of hiking and exploration of the igneous-banded series of the Stillwater Complex. Sean used a payphone and called Jim, and they planned for a meeting. They decided that touring the mine would take too much time and energy, so the field trip would just be of the different banded layers of the reef, which were easily accessed on foot and by road.

When they arrived at the post office building in the small town below the mine, Jim was waiting for them. Jim was darker in complexion than Sean and was noticeably shorter in stature. He was stocky and wearing a black and green vest over a t-shirt and blue jean shorts. His legs were very muscular and tanned, and he wore the classic sock and boot combination expected of a field geologist. On his head was a white ball cap with "NY" on the front, and had a very large, ragged-looking pouch hanging over his heart. Inside was a very large hand lens. He wasn't wearing a coat and appeared to be very comfortable with the cool temps of the day.

Annie slowly got out of the car, allowing the two men to greet one another first.

Jim shouted to Sean, *"Kia ora mate!"*[116] as he briskly walked to meet Sean.

The two men shook hands, followed by a manly hug, which included the traditional Maori hongi nose press. At first, Annie

---

116   Maori greeting for a friend

thought the two men were kissing, which seemed rather awkward, but then she noted they were simply pressing their noses together.

Sean then turned and introduced her, "This is Annie Moore. She is the geology professor from the south that I was telling ya about. She is a close friend of mine and has been helping me gather samples in Yellowstone."

Jim smiled widely and seemed to genuinely assume that they were just friends at the very least. "Any friend of Sean's is a friend of mine," he said excitedly, with a very distinct New Zealand accent.

Annie was relieved, as she didn't want to embarrass Sean.

Jim then pulled her closer to him and briefly pushed his nose on hers.

She thought for a second, *oh no, is he going to kiss me?* But then she remembered that he had touched noses with Sean, so she didn't resist the close contact.

Sean laughed at the look on Annie's confused face as Jim had really thrown her off with his greeting.

"*She'll be right,*" [117]said Sean as he hugged Jim again and both men continued to laugh and walk together.

The interaction between Sean and Jim left Annie feeling like she had missed something, but oh well, the two men seemed to be happy and she knew she was outside of that special relationship. It was quite comfortable, as she remembered Sean's stories of the two as young mates and enjoyed watching their interactions. They were comical together.

She couldn't help but feel a little awkward, though, when Jim asked Sean how Sophia was, and if Annie had been one of his many former students.

Sean had mentored many great geologists and saw to it that each one had every opportunity to have a good job when they graduated.

---

117 "She'll be right" is a Kiwi phrase meaning that everything will be ok.

To Jim, it made perfect sense to assume that she had perhaps been one of the many students that he trained over the years.

Annie did wonder, *How many female students does he bring up here?* She felt her special love might somehow be diminished by the existence of others. Those fears went away immediately when Sean smiled at her, and she could see in his eyes that he adored her and was proud for his best friend to meet her. He was with her and only her at this moment in time, and it was obvious.

Her insecurities had always been an issue, but she had spent quite some time actively working on changing those negative thoughts. Trusting in Sean's love for her helped her in her reprogramming.

She simply nodded at Jim when he asked about her and followed Sean's lead in terms of explaining their friendship.

The trio got into Jim's all-wheel-drive Subaru Outback, which was packed full of camping equipment and field supplies. Annie gladly took a seat in the back so that Sean, who had much longer legs, could sit comfortably up front with Jim. She couldn't help but note the musty smell of a car that obviously hadn't been cleaned out in some time.

"Wow Jim, you have lots of hammers back here," noted Annie. "I'm not sure I've ever seen so many different ones before."

"Oh, those are just ones that I have collected. You'd be amazed at how many people leave their hammers on outcrops," he said chuckling. "Pick one out that you'd like, Annie. It will be my special gift to ya on yer first trip to the Stillwater."

"Really?" asked Annie dubiously, as she wasn't sure if he was kidding with her or not. She had always had trouble telling when someone was teasing her, and this guy? She had heard about his sense of humor.

"YES!" both men said in unison, laughing.

"Well, okay, then," said Annie. "I like this baby sledge."

"Excellent choice!" shouted Jim over the laboring engine as it pulled a steep grade.

Wow, thought Annie, *I will treasure this.*

"It looks like it's been used more than once. What an honor. Thanks, Jim."

Being in the back of the vehicle also gave her a unique perspective and vantage point for watching the interactions of these men who were like brothers. She felt so blessed to be able to be part of such an interesting interaction. Sean had included her in an aspect of his life, and this made her very happy. There were many layers to Sean, and this was a side of him she had not had the opportunity to observe before. To see his love for someone else was a gift, and it gave her a measure for comparison for his interactions with her. Apparently, she and Jim were both very special to him.

The windows were down in the vehicle, and Annie couldn't hear their conversation clearly, but she did enjoy the smell of the dust from the gravel road and the dry breeze that was blowing through. It filled her senses, and she removed her hat so she could feel the sun on her face as the breeze blew her hair back.

She glanced forward and caught Jim looking back at her in the rear-view mirror. Annie flashed him a shy smile when he winked at her. Jim seemed to be a very sweet man with a great sense of humor. She wondered if he was trying to flirt with her and blushed at the thought, hoping that Jim couldn't see her color change.

The road was not very steep but was rugged and bumpy. Along the route, there were multiple road cuts which were excellent for showing the different facets of the banded igneous rocks leading up to the mine.

There had been a long and rich history of mining in that area. The layered expression of the deposits and faulting of the strata in the area allowed for relative ease in exploiting the mineral resources present. Both iron and chromium were available and had been mined previously to make steel. The current mining operation was to extract platinum for catalytic converters and was in full production at that time.

To a geologist like Annie, whose experience had been mostly in sedimentary geology, the strata looked like sedimentary rocks that had been tilted due to tectonic uplift or faulting. Upon closer inspection, they were bands of *cumulate*[118] minerals and metals -platinum group elements, held together mostly by a complex silicate mush, that had settled out of magma. The crystal settling could have been due either to gravity settling or density differentiation, within a magma chamber. The magma chamber apparently had also received periodic injections of new melt material, which added new minerals to the mix. (Knappen & Moulton, 1931) (Stillwater Complex trip. 2016, August 25).

The layers that were particularly fascinating to Annie were the crystalline greyish-blue layers, which were predominantly composed of the mineral *plagioclase feldspar,*[119] in particular, Labradorite - calcium, aluminum silicate, with a small percentage of *ferromagnesian*[120] minerals. These rocks, which are made up entirely of this specific mineral assemblage, are known as *Anorthosites.*[121]

---

118   The Stillwater suite of rocks is characterized by the presence of cumulate minerals, as the geochemical processes were unique to the region. The layered effect was the result of magmatic processes which allowed for gravity settling and density differentiation with the injection of each new cycles of new magma, (Phinney)

119   Plagioclase Feldspar is a mineral found in igneous rocks. It is a Ca or Na aluminosilicate mineral with two planes of atomic weakness and is readily identified in high and low temperature crystallization. In hand samples they appear as tiny rectangles within the matrix of the rock. Minerals themselves frequently have striations or grooves which help to determine the Ca to Na content of the intrusive rocks formed.

120   Ferromagnesian minerals are the dark minerals present in igneous rocks made up of Ca, Mg, and Fe.

121   Anorthosites are igneous rocks made up almost entirely of the mineral plagioclase feldspar. The feldspar is Ca rich – meaning it crystallized from a high temperature melt, and also has minor amounts of ferromagnesian minerals. The minerals tend to have a grey to blue hue in appearance.

Annie had not actually seen an Anorthosite before, so this was an exciting day for her. She was particularly enthused to be collecting samples to bring back for her Igneous and Metamorphic undergraduate class.

Plagioclase feldspar had been one of Annie's favorite minerals since her own undergraduate days. She always remembered it--and later taught it--as the "groovy" mineral. It has what appears to be visible grooves or "striations," much like you'd find on a vinyl record.

While most minerals present in igneous rocks - in particular - are only stable and crystallize out of a melt at specific temperatures and pressures, this group of complex silicate minerals seem to also do this, but crystallize along a spectrum of temperatures, containing varying amounts of specific elements in the chemical composition. [122]

The higher temperature ones are rich in calcium (Ca), like Anorthite, and the lower temperature ones are rich in sodium (Na), Albite. Each one of the different minerals along this spectrum is considered plagioclase feldspar in terms of chemical and crystal structure, but with varying amounts of Ca and Na. Each one exhibits different colors, varying from grays, blues, and greens, with some of iridescent and of gem quality when polished.

The continuous series contains an array of unique minerals, all very close to each other in composition, but each one crystallizing out of the melt at different temperatures and pressures. In this way, plagioclase feldspars are very good indicators, along with other minerals, of the composition of the original magma where the minerals were formed.

---

122 Continuous series is associated with Bowen's reaction series in igneous rocks where there are two paths of crystallization within the same cooling theoretical melt. In the continuous series, the mineral type is the same with only varying amounts of minerals associated with temperature of crystallization – stabilization- Plagioclase Feldspar crystallizes out of the melt in a continuous series with a basic aluminosilicate structure with varying amounts of silica, Na, and Ca, stable at specific temperatures and pressures.

Annie's absolute favorite of the series was the one known as "Labradorite," which displays a spectacular iridescent play of colors and is considered gem quality.

One specific physical characteristic, which each plagioclase feldspar exhibits in both hand specimen and optically in thin section, is the "striations," which are visible in the tiny rectangular faces of the minerals. Of particular fascination is that the amount of Ca or Na may be determined based on the inclination of these grooves when viewed optically in thin sections (microscopically).

Anorthosites became important to Annie in her undergraduate education when she realized that the rocks on the moon, which allowed it to shine so brightly, were also considered Anorthosites.

As a child, she lay awake many nights, looking up at the moon, studying the features, and wondering why some areas were dark and others were so bright. Later in her teen years, when she had built her own telescope, she began to look at the surface features, imagining what it would be like to walk there.

She remembered vividly when Neil Armstrong walked on the moon. Her parents did not own a TV, but her grandparents had a black and white in their living space. It was one of the most exciting experiences of her entire life.

NASA reported that the rocks were "*igneous*" rocks.

Her love for astronomy had also become a love of geology, because both Earth and the Moon had igneous rocks. The dark ones were *basalts*, not unlike the ones she had read about in Hawaii, and that made up the ocean floor. The ones that reflected light so brilliantly were determined to be mostly Anorthosites.

This experience laid the groundwork for her to enter geology as a career. Her fascination with the planet Earth, the Moon, and the solar system led her to want to know more about the planet on which she lived.

As she stood there touching the crystalline, gray-blue rock, which was in tilted bands in the outcrop in front of her, she imagined what the rocks on the moon must look like too. She thought to herself, *I wonder if the grains are bigger in the Anorthosites on the moon? Perhaps smaller?*

She touched them with the awe of a child and smiled big at Jim and Sean as she asked, "These are the same as the ones on the moon?"

Jim said to this, "Not exactly, Annie, but pretty darn close." Apparently, he was the expert on these rocks, and Annie felt so privileged to be able to learn from him about their origin, formation, and chemistry.

Sean was smiling on the outside and inside as he watched Annie have an experience of a lifetime. She truly did have the faith and curiosity of a child, and it was a joy to behold. At the end of the day, Annie was in love with the Stillwater Valley, the banded series of igneous rocks, and the Stillwater River.

Jim insisted on being a gracious host, and he asked Annie and Sean to join him for a meal and spirits at the small bar in the valley below. The bar was also a diner and had wonderful burgers as well as beer and a jukebox. The three sat and talked for hours, enjoying each other's company.

Jim asked Annie, "So, what exactly is yer interest in the Stillwater?" thinking she was perhaps interested in a research project.

"Oh, I teach a summer field methods course, and I've been trying to get a field trip to the area for at least five years. We never seem to have time. We always hit Yellowstone and then on to other volcanics. This place just always seems to be out of the way for our midterm tour. Sean was teaching a summer course too, and he told me about this opportunity to get to see it for myself. I gladly found the time to come check it out. Thank you so much. Just seeing the Anorthosites was worth the plane ride, which landed on a MESA!"

Both Sean and Jim looked at each other and laughed. They knew exactly what she was talking about, having probably wondered the same things, too, when they first landed.

At one point, Jim selected a few tunes on the jukebox. The tunes were mostly classic rock, but when a Patsy Cline song began to play, Annie and Sean looked at each other and Sean motioned for her to join him on the dance floor. The couple danced while Jim looked on in amazement at how good they seemed to be at dancing together.

"Wow you guys have obviously danced together before, haven't ya? What was that dance ya were doing anyway?" asked Jim.

"Oh, that's a Texas two-step," said Annie, laughing proudly.

Sean interrupted, placing his hand over his heart and feigning indignation, "No, madam. The two-step is indigenous to New Zealand. What's with this Texas stuff anyway."

"I don't believe I've ever seen that before here," said Jim, "And definitely not in New Zealand!"

"Annie can teach ya, Jim," offered Sean. "She's a really good dancer."

"I'm sure she is," said Jim in an accusing manner, obviously directed at Sean.

Annie looked at Jim and Sean and said, "Well, okay then, let's go," motioning to Jim to join her on the dance floor.

Sean was amused as he watched Annie try to dance with Jim, who was noticeably shorter, placed his face on her boobs, and looked up at Annie like an infant, jokingly, for Sean's benefit.

Annie didn't mind this, as he did seem to be having difficulty standing, and she was having to "lead." At one point, Jim tried to spin her, and she almost fell over.

He grabbed hold of her to steady her, and his left hand landed on her behind. Annie shoved him gently to the proper two-step distance, looking at Sean, who was laughing.

Jim had drunk a few beers and was feeling spatially challenged--he was falling over his own feet and Annie's. "I'm sorry, Annie, dear." he said in a slur, "I am just so bloody pisssed."

"It's okay, Jim," said Annie, "there's no need to be upset. It takes some getting used to." She kept patiently trying to help him, but he just couldn't seem to be able to control his legs and feet.

Sean was having such a good time watching Annie and his good friend as he laughed at them both.

Finally, Jim stumbled back to his chair and said to Sean, "I'm just too pissed, old boy. I just can't do it."

Annie wondered why he was pissed and felt a little bit guilty that she hadn't been able to help him learn how to do the dance.

Jim excused himself to go to the men's room, and Annie apologized to Sean, "I'm so sorry. I didn't mean to make him mad, and what's with the hands everywhere?"

"Oh, that's just Jim, Annie. He's not mad, and he always dances like that. He's just too drunk to stand up."

"But he said he was pissed. I don't understand," said Annie.

Sean laughed loudly and said, "Oh, he's from New Zealand and schooled in Britain. A Brit is "pissed" when they are drunk."

"Oh!?" said Annie, feeling a little bit stupid that she didn't know that at her age, but also relieved that it wasn't her fault.

When Jim returned from the men's room, Annie had made sure that they each had a hot cup of coffee to help them all sober up a bit.

Sean excused himself, and left Annie and Jim alone. Annie leaned over and said innocently to Jim, "I'm so sorry that I wasn't able to help you learn the dance steps."

Jim then placed his hand on her right thigh and moved it up to her crotch area, saying. "Ah, that's okay, doll. It's just fun to be here with ya."

Annie was mortified. She looked him squarely in the eye and said sternly, "Jim, do you think I'm a slut?" as she stood up angrily and moved to another chair across the table. Even though Annie had lived with sexual harassment her entire life--and especially in her chosen field-- she was still surprised and offended when an experience was so overtly degrading to her personally.

This time, Annie felt empowered. She had found the courage to walk away from a marriage where she felt degraded. Experiencing Sean's love and respect for her had led to an increase in self-confidence. She was finally able to stand up for herself, instead of just waiting for a man to take care of it for her. She didn't realize it, but if Sean had known what had happened, he would have been very proud of her.

Sean returned at that moment, and Jim didn't say anything more. He had been wounded by his own behavior and by Annie's rejection.

Sean could tell that something was different and said, "Well, Jim. It's been great. Annie here must catch a plane tomorrow evening, so we'd probably better get some rest."

"Where are ya two staying?" asked Jim.

"Oh, we are up at the site just below the first *crag*,[123] near the bend in the river." The three friends continued to talk for a while longer.

Annie was quiet, while Sean and Jim continued to talk about the mining business.

---

123 A rugged cliff or opening on a steep mountain face.

Jim had sobered up some and looked across the table at Annie, "Hey, you'll be right then?" he asked. "It has sure been nice ta meet ya. I'm sorry if I offended ya. I was just having fun."

Annie felt genuinely relieved that he had acknowledged his misbehavior and said, with a forgiving smile, "No worries Jim. Likewise."

Sean drove Jim's car back to the post office, where Annie and Sean gathered their things, said their goodbyes, and thanked Jim for such a great time.

"I hope he will be okay," said Annie to Sean.

"Oh, he doesn't have too far ta go. He'll be right. Besides, he's had some time ta sober up."

As they drove back to the campsite, Sean looked over at Annie, noting her silence, and asked, "Well, what did ya think?"

"I love the Stillwater," said Annie.

"No, I meant bout old Jim Boy!" he laughed.

"Oh, Jim...pause...He seems very nice and so smart. He also seems different when he drinks...all hands."

"Oh yes, I should have warned ya about Jim," said Sean, giggling to himself. "He fancies himself a lady's man, and he can be a little forward at times."

"A little forward?" retorted Annie.

Sean could sense that Annie wasn't impressed with his behavior, and then he said, "I'm sorry if he offended ya. He's just Jim."

"Well, he was awfully drunk, Sean. The drink brings out the worst in some people. I'll give him the benefit of the doubt. Except for being drunk, he was funny, and I enjoyed watching you two have a great time. You two are clearly lifelong friends."

They went back to their campsite and spent one more night on the river. On this night, they both lay together talking, laughing, and enjoying the sound of the river once more.

"Sean?" asked Annie, "Do you love me?"

"Why do ya ask that? Of course, I love ya. Silly girl," he said as he laid his head back down. "Annie, ya really do need ta work on yer self-esteem, ya know that?"

He then whispered in a comforting voice, "Ya have absolutely nothing to worry about," as he pulled her head onto his shoulder and she put her arm around his chest.

"You and Jim sure seemed to have a great time today," said Annie, changing the subject.

"Yes, he made those undergrad days bearable and fun...ya know all the shenanigans."

"Oh, so that explains it," she said in an accusing tone.

"What?" said Sean.

"Your desire to scare me all the time," said Annie.

"Yes, that is quite fun, isn't it?" he asked in a matter of fact tone and laughing, as he moved just out of her reach.

A tickling wrestling match commenced, with screaming and clobbering of each other with pillows. Annie started giggling uncontrollably and became too weak to continue. She hadn't had that much fun since she was a little girl.

"Sean, I love you," she said, laughing uncontrollably.

Together their laughs were infectious. They could continue laughing with each other almost as much as they could continue having sex.

After they settled down and lay quietly together, Annie said, "I don't want to leave tomorrow. Can't we just camp here for the rest of our lives?"

Sean rolled over to face her and pushed up on his elbow, "No sweetie. I wish we could, too, but we just can't."

She knew they couldn't, but being Annie, she had to articulate her feelings. They kissed passionately, and Annie laid her head on his shoulder as he lay on his back. They fell asleep holding each other.

The next morning, they got up and broke their camp. Both focused and worked like pros to separate and pack things into Sean's car. They had to make their way back to Billings that day, where Annie would catch her plane in the evening.

As they left the river and the valley, Sean stopped the car, so they could take in the full view of the entire valley. It had been dark when they arrived, and he wanted Annie to see it with him one last time. The couple stood together, embracing, and listening to the now gentler, more graded section of the river, as they said goodbye to this special place for them both.

As they said goodbye at the airport, Annie tearfully asked, "When will I see you again?"

He pulled his sunglasses down as he had the last day of camp and said, "This is not goodbye. We will see each other again soon. I promise."

She tearfully walked away to check in for her flight and could not contain the tears. She was so sad at having to leave him and return to her failed marriage and impending divorce. She knew she had responsibilities at home, not just to her children, but also to her students. *I will never forget this time together, especially the Stillwater Valley, the Anorthosite, Jim, and the roaring river.*

Sean too fought back the tears, as he watched Annie walk away. He was comforted only in knowing that he would make good on his promise to see her again.

Chapter 26—To have or have not

Annie and Sean went back to their separate lives, calling each other almost every day. They had a two-hour time difference, but that didn't matter. Annie knew when he would be in his office each day, and they agreed to a specific time frame. It was the highlight of both of their days to get to talk to one another. Hearing Sean's voice was one of the few things that kept Annie going each day.

The divorce was particularly ugly and trying but knowing that Sean loved her and supported her emotionally was of great comfort.

Because they were both academics and attended the same conferences, they were able to justify being in the same place and time at least once or twice a year. It was not always easy for them to plan to meet one another, as they would both have to have a legitimate reason for attending a conference in the same city. Usually, funding would not be easy to receive unless a faculty was presenting a paper, or mentoring students who were presenting papers. Finding funding to attend was an ethical issue for both, as they would not attend just to be with one another. They chose only conferences where they both had an academic reason for attending in the first place.

Annie had some difficulty with the private portion of such funding. She was a single parent who was shouldering the expense of her family while waiting on child support from a nasty and lengthy divorce process.

Sean helped her as much as he could, but his situation was a little more difficult, since he shared his life with someone else who might become aware of his activities. He wasn't separated or going through a divorce. He, in fact, loved his wife too, and would not intentionally hurt her.

At times, Annie felt on her own in their relationship, but she continued to love him despite the loneliness and the one-sided aspect.

At the end of the fall semester, Annie, and Sean both had abstracts to present papers at a national conference in San Diego. This was going to be the first time they were together since they left each other at the Billings airport.

As promised, Sean arranged for a hotel room, and he and Annie paid for their own registration and travel expenses. Sean sent Annie the detailed itinerary with his hotel reservation information a few weeks before their departure, and she provided hers as well. They were both excited about getting to see each other again, but the conference was also a great opportunity for professional development for both, as academics.

Annie signed up for a pre-conference field trip and would arrive two days before Sean. The field trip included hiking in the desert of Southern California and looking at debris flows and volcanic stratigraphy. After Yellowstone, she was determined to go on as many field trips as possible that included sequence volcanic stratigraphy.

She boarded the Greyhound bus provided by the conference and saw that she was one of only two women in a group of at least thirty. Even though this was not unusual, her field trip became very interesting, socially, when they arrived at the hotel where the field trip was based.

Hotel rooms were assigned by the field trip leaders, who had rooms reserved for everyone enrolled in the limited-space excursion.

Annie met in the hotel lobby with the other field trip attendees and checked in, receiving her badge with her name and a printed field trip guide. Her name badge said "S.A. Moore." She didn't mind that her name wasn't spelled out, as it made sense to not take up the entire badge for such a thing.

When her last name was called to get her room key and to meet her roommate or mates for the next two days, she was surprised to find that she had been partnered up with a gentleman from the Northern Territory. He was a diamond specialist who had grown up in England and was quite intrigued at the prospect of sharing his room with a female colleague.

He reached out his hand and said in a very cheerful thick British accent, "*Peter Ward*[124] here. Looks like we are going to be roommates."

Annie replied, "I'm not too sure about that. We'd better see if there's been a mistake," as she walked to the counter to have them check the list.

Peter followed Annie, hoping that there hadn't been a mistake, as he was quite excited to be able to share his room with such an attractive female geology professor.

There was no mistake--Annie and Peter had been assigned, accidentally, to the same room. She turned to Peter saying, "I don't mean any disrespect or insult to you, but I don't think it would be proper for me to share a room with a male professor. I am going through a nasty divorce, and it wouldn't look right."

As she said it, she realized how ridiculous it sounded, because she was planning to spend at least three days with Sean after the field trip. But that rooming would not be a matter of public record, so it was going to be okay. This was a matter of public record, so

---

124 Peter Wayne Ward, diamond specialist and field trip participant from the Northern Territory of N. America. Fictional character and not meant to represent any particular person living or deceased.

she convinced herself it was appropriate to insist on having her own room, or perhaps sharing with the other woman on the trip. Peter agreed with her and was now more than willing to see if he could assist in solving the problem.

As it turned out, the other woman was sharing a room with her husband, so Annie would have to have her own private room if she didn't share a room with Peter.

When Peter learned this, he spoke up and said, "I'll be glad to pay for her room. She's got a bit of a problem with a matter of public record, and I would rather make sure she has her own room."

Annie was so grateful for his offer but insisted that she needed to not have to pay for a room, since it was clearly a mistake.

Peter then offered, "Okay, why don't you give her the room that is reserved for both of us and I will pay for my own room. I'm perfectly okay with doing that."

The hotel and the field trip coordinator agreed to this solution to the problem, and Annie was granted her own room.

"I am really not comfortable with you having to pay for a separate room. I am so sorry about that," she said sadly.

"Well I would like to have shared a room with such a lovely lady, but when you spoke of your dilemma, it made sense. I'm not offended or bothered at all. May I at least buy you dinner?"

Annie looked at his extended hand and said gratefully, "I would love to. Thank you for being such a gentleman," and she shook her new friend's hand.

At dinner that evening, she learned that Peter had a Ph.D. from the University of Alberta in Canada, and his area of specialty was in fact diamonds now, but his graduate research area had been in economic deposits of igneous complexes. He had spent time in the Bushveld Complex in South Africa and was very intrigued by her visit to the Stillwater complex. He even knew of Sean's friend, Jim, who was an authority on Banded Igneous Complexes.

"How on earth did you end up being a diamond specialist in Canada, Peter, if you were into igneous petrology and geochemistry in the Bushveld?"

"Well, you see, while I was in Alberta, I played in a Celtic group. When I had to move to South Africa for mining exploration work, I continued to play for my own enjoyment. Eventually, I met other people from Europe and other places, who worked in SA, who also shared a love for that kind of music. We formed a band.... well, to make a long story short, we traveled to a Celtic music competition in Toronto, of all places, and I met a beautiful young woman named *Maggie Malloy*. [125] I fell in love and had to make her my wife. The Northern Territory geological survey needed an economic geologist and a diamond specialist. So, I got the job and was trained to be their diamond specialist. The rest is history."

"What an incredible story, Peter but does Maggie know that you go around sharing hotel rooms with female geologists?" Annie asked with a huge smile on her face.

"Ah, you got me there, didn't ya?" said Peter. "Well, she probably wouldn't have known about it, would she?" he said, kidding.

Annie laughed and said, "Oh...I am so telling her when I meet her!"

It was the beginning of a long and wonderful friendship for Annie and Peter. At the end of their field trip, he promised to write to Annie and to have her come to the Northern Territory for a field trip to show her diamonds and other economic deposits of interest. Also included was Celtic music and meeting his lovely bride Maggie.

Annie promised to take him up on the offer. She was genuinely going to look forward to meeting this famous Maggie in person.

---

125 "Maggie," Margaret Mary Malloy, Peter Ward's wife. Fictional character and not meant to represent any particular person living or deceased.

Chapter 27—San Diego

Annie rode the bus back to the San Diego convention center, and then walked several blocks to the hotel that Sean had reserved for himself.

She knew he wouldn't be in until later in the evening, so she approached the front desk and said, "Hi, I am supposed to be meeting my boyfriend here a little later. Sean Anderson? He reserved a room for us, and he isn't due in until after 6 p.m. I would really love to get cleaned up and be there when he gets in. Is that doable?"

The very nice young man at the desk looked at Annie's honest-looking face and her dusty field attire and said, "What's his name again?"

Annie pulled out the reservation information that Sean had mailed her earlier and showed him the reservation.

The young man smiled big, winked, and said, "Oh, I know what you are doing. You want to surprise him, don't you?"

Annie grinned big and whispered, "Is that okay?"

"Oh, it sure is. He's a lucky guy, I'd say," he said as he handed her the key to the room.

She thanked him profusely and entered the elevator to go to the room.

It was a very interesting older hotel, and the room was very cozy. It felt like she might have been in a 1940s movie, maybe with Humphrey Bogart. Annie entered the room and took a long, luxurious shower. She was hungry and very tired, but she was so excited to be seeing Sean again that she just lay on the bed and fell asleep.

Later that evening, she heard someone at the hotel room door. She was startled and began looking for a shirt because she wasn't completely sure it would be Sean that early, and she was NAKED!

Sean opened the door and was surprised to see her. "Shit, ya scared me, Annie!" I thought I had the wrong room." He closed the door, and they immediately embraced one another and began kissing. "Oh God, ya feel great," said Sean.

She put her arms around him and breathed in his scent. He didn't wear deodorant, and she loved the smell of his body. He smelled like home to her, and the rest of the world could stop now that they were together again.

Annie removed his blazer and helped him unbutton his shirt. She kissed and rubbed his chest as he unzipped his pants and began to lower them. He didn't even bother to remove his shoes. Annie laid back on the edge of the bed and pulled Sean down on top of her and inside of her before he could finish undressing.

Sean lifted himself up in almost a *planking* posture so that he could see their bodies together as Annie moved up to him repeatedly.

He said, "Look, Annie, look. It's so beautiful."

She grabbed his shoulders and lifted herself up, so she could also see, and when she did, she experienced an unexpected orgasm. Her entire pelvis spasmed and released. Leaning her head back, but still holding his shoulders, she screamed as Sean kissed her neck and moved down her body to kiss her breasts and her nipples as she continued to shudder.

As she lay there recovering from such an intense experience, Sean removed the rest of his clothes, his shoes, and his socks and moved her from the edge to the center of the bed, so his legs would not be dangling. He slowly began kissing her ankles, her inner thighs, her stomach, her breasts, her nipples, and her neck and then began kissing her passionately on the mouth.

As they kissed, she put her legs around his hips and moved her body up to meet his as he effortlessly moved inside of her. They made passionate love for hours and hours. They did not leave the room for what felt like days. Thankfully, they both had presentations later in the week, so they weren't missed much at the conference just yet.

Sean and Annie were very hungry but continued to have orgasm after orgasm together. At one point, Sean breathlessly proclaimed, "Annie, there is simply nothing left."

They both laughed and lay together for hours. Eventually, they both got up, showered, and made it down to the lobby, where the young man who had given Annie the key was grinning like a Cheshire cat.

"Wow, this is the first we've seen of you two," he said, winking at Annie.

Annie blushed like a bride who had just been on her honeymoon.

Sean put his arm around her, and they walked out together to the street. They walked for a while and stopped at a sidewalk cafe for dinner and drinks.

They both attended the conference, where they went their separate ways as academics, but met each other each day for lunch and then later for dinner.

On the last day of the conference, they decided to go to the famous San Diego Zoo. Annie had never seen it, and Sean gladly paid for them to go, as he hadn't been in a few years himself.

The two felt like children again, seeing all the exotic and wide varieties of animals present. It was such a pleasant day, and Annie loved being able to hold Sean's hand as they walked together through the expansive zoo campus.

As a child growing up on the farm, Annie had always been the "Ellie May" of the family, making friends with all the animals and getting into serious trouble with everyone.

"You can't make friends with the pigs, Annie," her grandfather would say. "They are supposed to be slaughtered. If you make them all pets, how are we supposed to eat them?"

She hated the entire process of slaughtering the animals and usually cried because she felt their pain. It was such a traumatic experience for her that she refused to eat any animals. She became a vegetarian and lived as one for most of her adult life.

Of the zoo animals, Annie liked the penguins the best. She could have stood and watched them for hours as they swam and interacted with one another.

Sean and Annie both felt sadness when visiting the primates.

"Can ya imagine spending yer entire life in a cage?" asked Sean, as he and a male gorilla regarded one another through the glass.

Annie stood and watched a mother chimpanzee as she held her baby to her breast and ate a piece of fruit. She related to this mother, as she had also nursed her babies.

"Oh, your baby is so precious," she said to the mother monkey, making eye contact with her and smiling. "You are such a good mother too," she continued. "I'm so sorry that you have to be in there." She walked away and suggested that they visit some other part of the zoo.

As before, they both went their separate ways and continued with their separate lives, still loving each other despite the miles between them and the lack of physical contact for long periods of time.

Chapter 28—Spring Break

Spring semester classes began, and Sean and Annie were once again actively teaching, doing research, and planning for their separate spring break field trips and upcoming summer field camp and field research ventures. The couple talked to each other at least every other day and maintained a close friendship and collegial interactions with fellow geologists.

Anna was teaching Igneous and Metamorphic Rocks, Spring Break Field Trip Class, and Introduction to Physical Geology.

Sean was teaching *Volcanology and Petrology*[126] courses as well as mentoring Ph.D. students in research projects. (Rao, 2014)

Anna and Adam were actively planning for the next summer's field course as well as the spring break field trip to the Big Bend area of Texas. Each year the spring break field trip course rotated through areas of geologic interest and was open to upper-level undergraduate as well as graduate-level students in the geosciences. Faculty rotated as well, depending on their areas of expertise. This year, it was Darin and Moore, who were the lucky ones for the spring break planning and class offerings.

Sean was joining a friend of his from New Zealand on a field trip to the volcano observatory in Hawaii. This trip was a huge draw in terms of enrollment in his spring Volcanology class, which was taught every two years. It quickly became a standing rib for him

---

126 Petrology is a branch of geology that studies rocks and the conditions under which they form. It includes environments of formation, geochemistry and includes microscopic examination of minerals and cements within the rock.

to tease Annie about his trips to exotic places, while she was stuck in Texas.

She wished she could have found a way to go with him, not just because she loved him but also because of their shared love of volcanics. The thought too, had crossed her mind about having him join her on a field trip.

It would have been stressful, she thought. *Having him along on a trip with my colleagues and students would have stressed us both. I would not have been able to spend as much quality time with him as I would like…. sigh… Also, how would we share the same tent without others talking about it….and the noise we would make, to boot? Oh, my goodness, it would not be a good thing at all.*

She was consoled in knowing that it would not have been professional for either of them to do such a thing and reconciled herself to their separate spring break field trips and summer camps. Maybe they could go to Hawaii together one day for a legitimate geology experience, or perhaps New Zealand? Yes, she would just have to dream about those times in the future and not dwell on the missed opportunities of the present.

As Anna packed for her trip, the phone rang. She managed to reach the phone before her son Ben, who also tried to see himself as the man of the house and often competed with Robert.

"Hello," she said.

"Hello Annie, I'm glad it was ya this time," said Sean in a relieved voice. "I'm at school and getting ready to go to the airport to fly to a volcanic island with 30 students. Wish me luck?"

Annie laughingly asked, "Don't you mean you are flying to an island paradise with 30 students, and I should be jealous?"

"No, No," he said, "We will only be on the paradise island long enough to catch a connecting flight to Hilo, where the wind never stops blowing, and it smells of sulfur most of the time."

"Oh yeah, yeah. You poor thing," she said in a mocking voice. Well, I just finished packing my things, and I get to take 20 kids through the entire *Paleozoic*[127] and keep them from freezing to death and falling off cliffs and out of rafts along the Rio Grande River. Let's trade, okay?"

"Ha-ha… No way!" he said. "I love the smell of sulfur, and besides, I get seasick in a boat….and isn't the Rio Grande just a tiny little *crick*[128] in that area anyway?"

"Sure, you do, and it's a raft, and there is whitewater for Pete's sake," said Annie, doubting his sincerity and honesty.

"Well, I've got ta go, sweetie," said Sean. "I miss ya."

"I miss you too, love," said Annie. "Be safe, and remember that I love you, okay?"

"Same here," said Sean…. silence…. Oops, I mean, I love ya too."

"You'd better," she said. We'll talk next Friday?"

"Yes, next Friday, I promise," said Sean, as he hung up the phone.

Times are a-changing?

Anna met the students at the vans, where their roommates or parents dropped all the field trip kids. Sleeping bags, blankets, winter coats, backpacks, hammers and …. everything but the kitchen sink was lying on the ground around the trailers and vans.

Ben and Robert were there waiting with Grandma Miller to see her off for spring break. As usual, it hurt to leave them, but she had to go be a mom to grown children and hope they learn something in the process. She also enjoyed working with Adam again. He was

---

127 The Paleozoic Era is the geologic time frame from the Precambrian through the Permian. Ranging from 540 my to 66 my.

128 "Crick" is a pronunciation of the work "Creek" in some areas of the US, particularly in the NW Region.

an outstanding geologist and a good friend. They made an excellent teaching team.

Dr. D. and John, the T.A. from field camp, showed up together with John carrying D.'s camping equipment, as well as his own. Dr. D. had his arms filled with essentials for the trip. He had Halloween-sized bags of peanut M&Ms, miniature Snickers bars, a thermos of his special brew, and his favorite pillow for sleeping in the van.

Anna had the file folders with lists of students, their medical release forms, and the fee waivers needed to enter and exit all the national and state parks along the way. She had already put her camping equipment in the trailer and van and carefully placed the folders of information in the front door pocket, so she went to sit with her boys and mother-in-law while everyone loaded.

Ben and Robert were both big boys, and she could barely hold them both on her lap at the same time, but she managed. While soaking up the love of her boys, she watched the group dynamics at play.

She couldn't help but notice that the only females on the trip were clustered together giggling and primping in the mirrors of the van, while the guys loaded everything on the vans and trailers. Anna felt a little bit disgusted at the way the girls didn't seem to take any responsibility beyond placing their pillows and backpacks in and under the seat that they all had predetermined to be their special bench for the trip. In some ways, Dr. D. reminded her of these gals who referred to themselves as the *geobabes*.[129]

Ugh, thought Anna as she spoke aloud and rolled her eyes, "I think I'm going to be sick."

---

129 Fictional term generated by fictional female geology characters meant to distinguish them from other women in geology. It was the late 70s early 80s and women were seeing figures in pop culture who were celebrating their femininity, and perhaps exploring their newly found place in a male dominated culture—a culture that seemed to value women based on their superficial aesthetic value, rather than their academic prowess.

"You don't see yourself in them?" asked Betty in a joking manner.

"Absolutely not!"

"Well, remember dear that this field didn't always attract young ladies. You must be a role model for them," she said with a warm smile.

Anna knew she was right, but it still made her want to be sick. Thank goodness for Betty, who was a friend and not just the grandmother to her children--such a wise woman.

Women geologists of Anna's vintage and older had not had an easy time as females trying to compete and be taken seriously in the math and sciences. They were subjected to sexism, misogyny, and sexual harassment--not by everyone, but by too many. Older men who worked in the industry pinched behinds and winked with inappropriate nudges that were connected to veiled language regarding sex.

"You know, I could probably do you a few favors in terms of your career... (wink, wink) ... if you know what I mean?"

Anna felt helpless to defend herself, so she simply ignored the gestures and pretended as if she were too dumb to understand the advances. Her memories of events included "We all know you are here for the men, right?" and "...Besides, you are just too pretty and sweet to be doing this kind of work."

It was all so infuriating, but Anna had never felt like she had any choice but to take it, if she wanted to succeed. Most of the advances were behind closed doors or were made in a subtle manner so others would not notice. If others saw, they just ignored it as well because it was such normalized behavior...a sort of action of endearment or a compliment in some men's minds.

Anna's being married offered some protection for her, but it did not stop the harassment, which began long before she had married. As a small child and into her teen years, men in her life would touch her inappropriately and expose her to uncomfortable situations meant to encourage arousal. These men included her grandfather, an uncle, an older cousin's husband, and the old man down the road who would ask her if she wanted to ride on the motorcycle with him, just to name a few.

Even her first real job as a laboratory tech in high school exposed her to the advances of an older man who used his position to intimidate and touch her without permission. He would put his arm around her shoulder while she washed the laboratory dishes and suggested she needed to learn about sex from someone older and more experienced. She simply played dumb so that she wouldn't lose her job, but he eventually got tired of her rejecting him and fired her anyway.

She was too ashamed to tell anyone about any of the previous encounters. As with many women and young girls, she was not to blame but felt that something had to be horribly wrong with her to cause them to do such things. It must somehow be her fault.

She had admired other women who were older than her in the field of geology, like *Katia Krafft*,[130] whose partner and husband had afforded her opportunities as an equal partner in the field of volcanology. There were other women, too, who had a certain machismo about them and were able to "grow what they needed" to compete with the men.

Anna had always been too shy, and her self-esteem was too low to do any real battle in terms of posturing herself physically with men. Her strength was in her ability to work very hard to achieve academically. Her grades were earned and not dependent on her having to buffet the advances of men.

---

130 Katia and Maurice Krafft were French volcanologists committed to cataloguing all of the different types of volcanoes of the world and in particular the most dangerous of flows known as the pyroclastic flow – 'nuee ardente.' Both were tragically killed in a pyroclastic flow in 1991 at Mt. Unzen, Japan.

She was smart and pretty, so she was given opportunities that others were not. Anna didn't just excel academically but also developed great interpersonal instincts and used this intuition to know when to keep her mouth shut and to roll with the punches.

To navigate in the ocean of sharks, she adapted and adjusted as needed to accommodate the needs of any man and some women. Avoiding sexual entanglements was somewhat easier because she was married, but she still suffered many indignities.

It honestly seemed a little unfair that she had to subdue her own femininity and endure such treatment in her years of growth, to now see that women in geology could somehow be allowed to be geobabes, with what seemed like lower expectations academically as well. *How was that okay?*

It was now time to go over the rosters and get down the road, so Anna hugged her boys and Betty one last time.

"You be safe out there. You hear?" said Betty as she hugged Anna tightly. "Don't worry about your boys. I've got that covered."

"Thank you so much," Anna said with tears welling up in her eyes. She was so grateful to Betty for her loving support, as a single mom and as a professional.

Betty could have hated Anna, but instead felt the need to help her achieve the goals in her life that Betty was not afforded. In some ways, she was envious, and in other ways, she was living vicariously through her brave, intelligent, and beautiful daughter-in-law.

Anna lifted herself up into the driver's seat of her van and handed the clipboard with everyone's name on a list to her new co-pilot and navigator for this field trip, John Michael Schaeffer, "*Mikey*"[131] for short.

"Now listen up, folks," he yelled over the chatter. "Dr. Moore wants me to take roll ... Samuel Collum, Bryan Easterling,

---

131 "Mikey" John Michael Schaeffer, graduate student from Florida and Anna's co-pilot for the trip. A fictional character not meant to represent a real person in the past or present.

Daniel Giles, Jeffrey Grubbs…. All are present and accounted for, Dr. Moore."

"Thank you, Mikey. Please take this other folder and clipboard back to John and leave it with him for their van."

"Ok," said Mikey excitedly.

"I appreciate your willingness to step up and be helpful," said Anna as she put their folder in the front bin of the van.

Mikey was a graduate student from Florida, who was hoping to get the job of field camp T.A. for the upcoming summer. To volunteer to help on this trip and to do a good job meant he would have a foot in the door. He also knew that Anna was a bigger pushover than Dr. D.

Dr. Darin had the pleasure of the *geobabes* on his van. They all thought he was so "cute and adorable." Anna was happy that they liked him more than her because she wasn't sure she could stomach the giggles and flirting from female geology majors for the two-day drive to the Big Bend of Texas.

What's the world coming to, she thought, *All those years of no women, just the guys and me and now geobabes. Are you kidding me?*

She knew she was probably being too judgmental and should celebrate women -- even silly girls -- who were interested in planet earth. She just would have to keep an open mind and try her hardest to be fair and kind, strong and feminine, professional, and a good role model….

Oh, who am I kidding? she thought. *I just need to be me and let them be them and accept that it takes all kinds, right? Sigh…Lord give me strength.*

Everyone was loaded and accounted for, so the class began their journey.

The first stop for the evening was to be in *Yellow Rocks Canyon*.[132] It was in an area where there had been a *failed rift* and subsequent volcanism. The rocks forming the bluffs of the canyon were capped with sandstone units, which were heavily cemented with clay minerals.

Oxidation[133] of the iron in the clays is what gave the rocks a red and yellow appearance -iron oxides, *limonite* -yellow or tan, and *hematite*- reddish-brown. Yellow tan was the dominant weathering color, so the canyon was named "Yellow Rocks."

A graded stream flowed through the valley and had carved the sedimentary rocks that formed the cliffs. The volcanics were nearby but were not present in the canyon where the field trip group would be camping. The group would visit those on the following morning.

The camp faculty set up their tents and assisted the novices with their setup for the evening. Anna left the geobabes to the men and carried around her bag of tricks to help those who were not as prepared.

A little later, Adam approached Anna and said, "Uh, the girls brought sleeping bags, but no pads. What do we do?"

What he meant was, "the girls forgot the pads that they needed for their sleeping bags and do you have any extras, so they don't suffer tonight?"

Anna looked at him and said, "Really, D.?"

He looked worried about the poor little things, so she relented and said, "I have some extra blankets they could use. If they fold them into rectangles and place them under their sleeping bags, that might help."

---

132 Fictional canyon loosely based on Red Rocks Canyon in Oklahoma and the failed Oklahoma Rift Zone.

133 Oxidation is a chemical reaction of the minerals in rocks and soils with oxygen in the air. It is also known as chemical weathering. This process changes the mineral composition to include oxygen. Oxidation of Iron is what gives a rusty nail the rust and reddish color.

Adam smiled a big smile and said, "I knew you'd have a solution. Thank you."

He collected the extra blankets and proudly took them to the girls to help them set up for camping that night.

Anna could hear them in the distance as he approached, "Dr. D.! You're our hero! Giggle, giggle, inaudible...giggle, giggle..."

Ugh, thought Anna, *things sure are changing. I do hope the blankets help, though.*

She cared about them even though their behavior annoyed her.

Chapter 29—Never a Dull Moment

After an eventful evening of a campfire, a few hot dogs, beers for those old enough to drink, and laughter, the campers settled in for the evening.

Anna entered her tent and gladly removed her boots and stretched out inside her sleeping bag. As she lay there staring at the darkness around her, she couldn't help but think of Sean and imagine that he was probably still navigating airports and traveling to his destination. She missed him. Camping just didn't feel the same. Her sleeping bag smelled like *them*, too.

"I'm not going to cry," she said. "I know I will see him in July."

She placed her backpack behind her and leaned her back against it. This gave her the feeling of not being completely alone in her tent.

Brrr.... she shuddered at the cold of the evening. It was a damp cold that chilled one to the bone. Even though it was spring, it was still winter at night in most of the higher elevations. Her thoughts went to the girls who had not brought pads to place between their sleeping bags and the ground. She hoped they had folded the blankets properly and placed them correctly to avoid the cold. Without a pad between the bag and the ground, the warmth of the body would be transferred to the cold sleeping bag and the ground beneath. It would be miserable for anyone who was sensitive to the cold. It wouldn't be okay to have sick kids for the week, either.

Anna said her prayers as she thought of Robert, Betty, Ben, Bobby, and of course, Sean and his students. She drifted off to sleep, trying not to dwell on all the things that were beyond her control.

After everyone had been asleep for several hours, the stillness of the night was disrupted by the sound of someone snoring loudly, and engines racing in the distance.

I guess it is teenagers out on a Friday night, thought Anna. I *hope they all stay safe.* The zipper on her tent began to jiggle and to unzip.

She sat up on her elbows and reached for her flashlight and can of wasp spray, "Who the hell is it?" she shouted in a threatening manner, with her finger on the cap of her can ready to blind a possible rapist or murderer.

"It's just me!" shouted D., who had managed to get the zipper stuck in his haste to enter her tent.

"Oh, uh, just a minute," she said as she stood to help unzip the tent.

"Do you hear those engines?" he asked.

"Yes," she said as she stuck her head outside of the tent. "What's going on?"

"It's a bunch of drunk kids, and they are racing around here in the dark. I'm afraid they will run over us if they aren't careful."

"Oh, right," she said as she wiped her weary eyes.

"What should we do?" he asked.

"Let's walk down the road here and be ready to engage them if they come into our area," said Annie.

"And just how will we stop them?" asked D.

"Uh, let's get in a van and drive that way. I'll grab my baseball bat too," she said confidently.

"Uh, okay, I'll get my rock hammer." Said D.

Anna, Mikey, and D., along with John, climbed into a van and drove to block the road. The four exited the van and stood in front with the headlights beaming in the direction of the engines. Each was armed with a flashlight. Annie had her bat, D. had his rock hammer, Mikey had a skateboard, and John had a small tree branch. Weren't they a sight at 3:30 a.m. if someone came their way?

"What the heck will you do with that thing?" asked John as he pointed to Mikey's skateboard. "Ride off to get help?"

"More than you can with a stupid tree limb," answered Mikey, as he lifted the skateboard into a defensive posture, much like a Klingon might do with a *Bat'leth*,[134] and assumed a battle stance with knees bent slightly and hips squarely above his feet spread to a distance to best receive force from an aggressor.

Anna chuckled to herself at the sight of these two guys readying for battle, while Dr. D. assumed the same defensive posture with his tiny little soft rock hammer.

The four could see headlights in the distance traveling in semi-circular patterns, which no doubt indicated that the drivers were cutting figure eights in the campsite grass in that area.

When the headlights began to break and come their way, they all positioned themselves in front of the van. Anna on the left, D. safely in the center, Mikey next to Anna, and John was on the right side.

To their fear and amazement, a motorcycle sped past on John's side and raced toward the stream and their group's campsite. Another bike sped past on Anna's side, almost hitting her as she spread herself onto the van door.

One of the trucks heading their way skidded to a stop a few feet from D. and quickly reversed course, spraying dust and gravel in all directions as they raced backward in the opposite direction.

Meanwhile, students were exiting their tents and yelling as the motorcycles skillfully rounded each tent, throwing up dust and

---

134 Klingon weapon of choice. Shaped like a bladed crescent. see bibliography for complete reference

ripping up grass. It was like watching a horse and rider in a barrel race at the county rodeo. Students ran in all directions, and the three instructors were terrified that a student would be injured.

Anna was particularly concerned for Mikey, who was a student volunteer. She took off in a dead run after Mikey and the speeding motorcycles, followed closely by John and Dr. D. Even though they were surprisingly quick, no one could get close enough for a good swing. Anna directed her flashlight on one of the riders, and within the broad cone of the dispersed light, she could see students fleeing and getting on top of picnic tables and into the second van. It was quite an exciting free-for-all.

D. ran back to the van blocking the road and turned it around to shine the headlights on the camp.

The geobabes apparently did not leave their tents and simply sat in their tents screaming in horror as the motorcycle circled them several times. If it hadn't been such a serious event, Anna might have laughed, but instead, she felt compelled to run to their defense.

She and Mikey stood between the rider and the geobabe's tent on one side, while John stood on the other side, but the rider made a broad circle around them all before racing off toward the van parked in the way.

They watched as the cycle sped past the van on the driver's side past Dr. D, who was forced to take a headfirst dive into the bushes on that side too. John quickly ran into the bushes behind him and lifted him.

D. was clearly shaken up and covered in dust and pieces of vegetation but seemed to have escaped injury.

John and D. got into the van and drove quickly toward the entrance of the campgrounds. Anna assumed it was to call authorities, so she went around to each group of students making sure that everyone was okay.

One group began making coffee because they weren't going back to sleep.

The geobabes were huddled in their tent, crying.

Anna could hear them and asked if she could enter. They couldn't hear her, and when she began to unzip their tent, they started screaming again. She began to speak calmly, "Ladies, it's Dr. Moore. Ladies…. ladies…. shhhhhh….," now whispering. "It's Dr. Moore. I'm coming in Okay?"

"Huh? Oh sure," said one of the girls.

Anna entered their tent and said very calmly, "Ladies, the cyclists are gone. It's okay now. Are you alright? Is anyone hurt?"

"What the fuck was that?" cried *Sarah*,[135] an undergrad from D.'s Sedimentary Rocks class.

"Yes. Who the heck was that?" yelled another.

"Are they coming back? Shit, I'm afraid they will come back!"

"It's okay, ladies. Dr. Danis and John went to inform the authorities. I'm certain they aren't coming back. They did what they came to do, and that was to terrorize us. So just calm yourselves and try not to worry. It's truly going to be okay."

"Oh, okay. Thank you, Dr. Moore."

"Yes, Thank you so much."

"I'm still scared," said one, still weeping.

Annie left their tent and approached the young men who had made coffee.

"Dr. Moore? Want a cup of coffee?"

"Do I!" she said as she reached and gladly received the cup. "Thank you, guys. Wow, that was something now wasn't it?"

---

135 Sarah, One of the geobabes. An undergraduate in Dr. Ds Sedimentary Rocks class. Fictional Character…

"You bet," said *Dan*.[136] "What the heck was that all about anyway?"

"Well, I guess it was a group of kids just trying to scare people. I'd say they succeeded," said Anna, sipping coffee.

"I think so," said Dan. "Is Dr. D. gonna call the cops?"

"Yes, I assume that he is doing that right now. I think the drama is over for the evening."

John Michael – Mikey -- approached from the darkness, asking, "Dr. Moore, is field camp this exciting?"

Anna laughed, "No, it's exciting in different ways, though. It's always an adventure when taking students on camping field trips."

At daybreak, Anna saw the van headlights returning to their area. D. and John wearily exited the van and announced that the cops had arrested the guys and would be out to collect a statement before we could leave.

"Is everyone okay?" asked D. "Were there any injuries? Was any property damaged?"

"No, just rattled nerves," answered Anna.

"Good," he said with a sigh of relief. "Then this statement shouldn't take very long."

The sheriff's deputy came, and Dr. Darin gave the statement, and now they were off for the *Permian Reef*[137] of the Guadalupe Mountains, Carlsbad Caverns in NM, and on to Big Bend.

I hope that Sean isn't having this much excitement, Annie thought to herself. She imagined students falling through active lava tubes and worse.

---

136 Dan Giles, an undergraduate student in Dr. Moore's Structural Geology class. Fictional Character named after a deceased friend of the author. Dan was a great geologist and a close personal friend.

137 The Permian Period is a geologic period at the top of the Paleozoic Era. It is known for having large benthonic, one celled organism (Foraminifera/fusulinid). The end of the Permian period (66mya) is marked by a mass extinction where over 90% of life on the planet was extinguished.

Chapter 30—Hawaiian Volcano Observatory

Meanwhile, Sean was wearily waiting for a connecting flight to Hilo to take his group of 30 students to meet his friend *Ed*,[138] who was working at the Hawaiian Volcano Observatory (HVO) in Hawaii.

Dr. Edward Smart was also from New Zealand via Britain and had done his undergraduate work with Jim and Sean. He was the same Ed who had to share a tent with Omar at their field camp. It seems that most of the young talent that came out of that program had in fact gone into hard rock, volcanology, and/or economic geology.

Ed had been at the HVO for about 10 years and loved having scheduled field trips of graduate students and especially old friends like Sean.

The HVO is located on the rim of Kilauea Volcano's summit caldera. Kilauea and the other active Hawaiian volcanoes are ideal natural laboratories for researching the workings of volcanoes, and for the budding geologist to explore the technologies used in monitoring active volcanoes. (Nakata, et al., 1998)

For Sean's class, it also offered a first-hand look at the formation and ongoing deposition of flows for application in the study of sequence volcanic stratigraphy.

One of the aspects of Ed's job at the observatory was, in fact, the tracking and mapping of all flows on the island as well as the

---

138 "Ed," Dr. Edward Smart. Sean and Jim's friend from the Otago University days. Fictional character that is not meant to represent any professional associated with the HVO in Hawaii. The HVO is used as a fictional experience, loosely based on the field experiences of the author.

evolution of the magmas generating the flows. For a geologist like Ed, it was nothing to walk on three-minute flows – three minutes to go from molten to solid enough for standing - to teach graduate students how to collect fresh samples.

Ed was much thinner and less muscular than Jim, but still taller than Jim in stature. He had long, stringy gray hair, which he kept braided most of the time, with a noticeable bald spot on the back of his head. He usually wore a ball cap, but when he removed it inside, the actual color of his skin was much pinker, freckled, and lighter, than the deeply tanned exposed parts. His skin was rough and dry, and his lips kept a constant glisten from the frequent application of Vaseline to diminish the painful cracking that would inevitably occur from excess exposure to wind, sun, and the '*vlog*,'[139] the fog from the volcanoes.

Another of the main things that Ed monitored on the island was the *aerosols,* as they are a primary source of pollution from volcanoes and affect human populations, as well as contribute to the atmosphere.

Sean enjoyed being in the field with his students, particularly when he could share his love of volcanoes. He loved all aspects of the field of volcanology but was interested in the evolution of magmas over time. The generation of magmatic volatiles – gases -- was exciting to him. Even though his research focus involved continental crust, the Hawaiian Island Observatory was a perfect place to introduce volcanology students to the overall basics of volcano monitoring, as well as to discuss the environmental aspects of human populations living near volcanoes.

Some of the topics covered in their 7-day field experience included learning about a variety of monitoring methods:

---

139   Vlog is a term used by locals and volcanologists for the 'fog' that develops from volcanoes.

Ground deformation, Seismology, Physical Volcanology, and Gas Geochemistry.

One of the things that Sean required of his students was a journal of their experiences. There were prompts for writing, which included a personal reflection on what was learned. He had learned from a professor and graduate mentor of his at Otago University, the utility of writing the human feelings and experiences of fieldwork.

The reflections were a challenge at first, but Sean soon learned what *Professor Oswald*,[140] his master's degree advisor, had no doubt learned from his own mentor of years ago. There was more to geology than just collecting data. It was an experience of the human senses and allowed for introspection and contemplation of life as well.

Dr. George Willard Oswald, now deceased, was trained as a field geologist in the UK and had studied at Cambridge. His field experience was extensive, and his published works were required reading for anyone interested in doing research in the Taupo Volcanic Zone of New Zealand. He had written many articles on the volcanic and structural evolution of the zone and was an expert in silicic magmas of the region.

Sean expanded on his research, and under his direction, became an expert in his own right regarding the calderas of the Taupo Volcanic Zone.

While Dr. Oswald's students were working with him in the field, he required them to record data, not just in a field notebook, but to also expand upon the data collection by keeping a "diary-journal" of their personal experiences as well.

Through this practice, Sean had discovered that he had a gift for writing and frequently wrote of his experiences and those of

---

140 Sean's graduate mentor at Otago University, New Zealand. Professor George Willard Oswald is a fictional character and does not represent any faculty past or present at the college.

others. He would later in life find that his journals would be easily transformed into a memoir and would provide a timely recording of the evolution of volcanology as a science as well.

After meeting Annie, Sean began to write about his feelings for her. He sent her letters from field camp after she left and after each of their trips together but did not always express his deepest feelings and experiences that were written in his private journal. Those experiences were reserved for him only.

Annie loved his style of writing, which was vivid and very descriptive. She found that she could easily visualize the experiences that he shared. It was as if she were walking on mountain trails with him and could see the sunsets he described, even the smell of dust and sulfur, and feel the heat of the day in the field. Through his writing, he would share a part of himself with her.

She looked forward to opening his hand-written letters, which were elegant with beautiful flowing lines of script. His penmanship had a flare of sophistication, and his vocabulary was never ordinary or crude. He was clearly a scholar and a gentleman. This rugged man of the field had a flair for prose, and the written expression was eloquent. It was a dimension of Sean that Annie enjoyed immensely and never anticipated.

While sitting at the campsite that first evening on the rim of Kilauea, Sean used his headlamp to write in his journal. His thoughts went to Annie, and he began to write as though he were writing to her, without mentioning her name. He wanted to share this experience with her and wished she could have been there too.

"You would love it here, despite the air being filled with the smell of sulfur and methane this evening. The night is so completely black that one can hardly distinguish the constellations in the night sky. Along the horizon in the distance, I can see the faint red glow of the lava that is most certainly flowing on its journey to the sea. There is also the sound of drumming and chanting in the distance, which is presumably the famous "Night Marchers" down in the lava fields below the main crater. Legend tells of ancient spirits of warriors, who march in the evenings, especially at the full and new moon phases, to protect sacred spaces. Ed says it is locals who are making offerings to *Pele*[141] and have nothing to do with ancient spirits. Who knows for sure? I just know it is a beautiful sight, and the sound of drumming for Pele only adds to the allure of this unique experience. One wonders how many times throughout earth's history, that man has sensed this."

Anyone reading his journal entries would be able to see through his eyes, the eyes of a geologist and a man deeply in touch with nature itself. From this trip on, Sean's journal entries were written in the form of a story as he shared his experiences with Annie, some of which he included in his letters to her.

The journal entries were far more descriptive and complete than those shared in his letters, with the recounting in his letters becoming more of a summary of journal highlights. Nonetheless, Sean was not only a skilled field geologist and gifted teacher, he was also a writer with the ability to draw the reader into the field experience.

The next morning, the students, faculty, and guide all hiked to places where the students could actively and safely see volcanic features, like lava lakes, craters and to see *pahoehoe*[142] and *a'a*[143] lava flows as they form.

The first stop was the Kilauea Iki, and it was a perfect crater for observing 'real-time' formation of a *lava lake*.

The most exciting part of the journey for the students was hiking to an active flow field on the East Rift Zone below Pu'u O'o

---

141 Pele' is the goddess of volcanoes and fire

142 Pahoehoe lava flows are formed from fluid lavas with low viscosity. They have a ropey texture and are relatively smooth deposits after they cool and harden.

143 A'a lava flows move more slowly than pahoehoe and are characterized by very sharp, blocky flows.

on Kilauea.[144] Everyone had already watched the volcano safety films and passed their quizzes on the mainland, so there should be no major surprises for the group. All had their thick boots, hats, and lots of water.

As they walked across a vast older field of basaltic glass, *lava tubes,*[145] a'a, and pahoehoe features, they could see the convective currents rising above the black expanse far in front of them. Sean and Ed both pointed out the convective air above the *breakout flows*[146] in the distance and advised the students to proceed cautiously once they reached the area. They were careful to follow Ed and Sean to avoid any missteps.

Finding active flows was a little intimidating for the novice, as you could feel the intense heat of the air and see the eerie red glow of the lava beneath their boots. It was scorching, and the smell was anything but romantic, but what an experience for students who were studying volcanology!

Sean was giddy as they approached the molten, glistening, metallic gray flows with a fiery glow at the *toe.*

The students carefully walked across lava flows and identified *lava crusts, lava toes, and inflation processes,* as well as 'active breakout' features and lava flows. It was so exciting for everyone to finally see the moving lava.

One girl named *Emily*[147] wouldn't stop yelling, "Oh my gosh, that is real fucking lava!" while her classmates tried to videotape the experience for their class video journal project.

---

144 See map in the appendix

145 Lava tubes are the empty spaces left beneath a hardened surface where lava once flowed in streams.

146 New flows break through the toes - terminal margins - of existing flows to advance beyond the end of the first flow - breakouts

147 Emily, one of Sean's more problematic and colorful students of Volcanology. Fictional character and not meant to represent any particular person living or deceased.

Bryan,[148] one of the students doing the filming, said to Em, "Hey, we are trying to film here, will you please shut up!?"

Everyone laughed, and she limited her enthusiasm (or at least the language) after that point. It was a bit difficult at that time (pre-cell phone cameras) to videotape. The battery life was usually only a couple of hours, and Bryan kept having to start over whenever Emily would yell. He didn't want to have to spend vast amounts of time trying to edit the film when they returned. They only needed about 15 minutes in total.

Ed and Sean demonstrated sampling techniques for the class as students took photos and videotaped.

Pahoehoe "toes" fill *crevasses*, overlap one another and seem to be able to form quickly just beyond the end of the ropey surface of the flow. Some toes even demonstrated roping, as they began to cool and flow at the same time.

The students were then given a chance to try the techniques as well.

"Who's up?" said Sean cheerfully as he wiped sweat from his brow.

Emily bravely stepped forward, took the hammer from Ed, and began to inch her way forward toward the newly forming toe of an overlapping flow. As she got close enough for the hammer to touch the red-hot tip of the toe, she began to yell, "Shit, shit, shit! That is so hot!" She held the hammer in her gloved hand, quickly got a tiny sample of the lava, and backed away.

"It's pretty hot fer sure," said Sean as he chuckled at her holding the hammer like it had red hot poop on it and putting it in Ed's can of water.

Bryan just filmed it and didn't say a word about Emily's cursing. He was so intrigued by the entire process that he wasn't too worried

---

148 Bryan, Volcanology student who is filming their field experience. Fictional character and not meant to represent any particular person living or deceased.

about her language. Every student who wanted to try was given a chance to sample, while Sean and Ed carefully watched the flows to make sure everyone was safe.

The group hiked back across the black, glassy basaltic sea and returned to camp. They were hungry, tired, and dirty, but each felt accomplished in their quest for flowing lava and the opportunity to document and videotape the sampling process in real-time.

Ed and Sean sat in their chairs outside of their tent and talked about old times in college and the current state of the world.

"Ed, so ya seem very happy here. Is there a girlfriend, perhaps?" asked Sean.

"Oh, I don't have time for dating Sean. Pele is my mistress, and she keeps me pretty busy," said Ed laughing.

"I know what ya mean," said Sean in a serious voice, meaning, he really did know what he meant about being kept busy by love.

Ed just imagined that he was making conversation and never dreamed that Sean had two women in his life that he loved. That would be too much for any man, he supposed.

Sean found himself feeling a little bit sorry for Ed that he had never found someone. At the same time, he was jealous of Ed's freedom to do exactly as he wanted. Sean didn't resent his wife and family or Annie's love, but he did dislike the complexity of having to juggle the demands of all, including his teaching, research, and mentoring of students. It was a lot for any person to manage, and Sean was deeply engaged in all of them.

The next day they were going to visit Green Sand Beach to learn about a unique *hydrovolcanic*[149] feature which resembles a *Tuff Ring*[150] but lacks a *central vent* that is usually associated with the landform.

---

149 Hydrovolcanic – magma and water interact.
150 A tuff ring is a landform associated with hydro-volcanism

This volcanic feature was more likely formed as it flowed into the sea. When the lava reached the water, it sprayed, fragmented, and splattered in all directions, forming what is commonly referred to as a *littoral cone*, which lacks the classic central vent of the tuff ring. It produces thick ashfall deposits, which produce a volcanic tuff with a few fine phenocrysts within the matrix. In this case the minerals *olivine* (green) and *pyroxene (black and green)* [151] weather out of the deposits to produce the green sand of the beach.

As a side attraction for this unique feature, the tiny cove is a favorite spot for swimming among geology field students and tourists on the island.

---

151   High temperature minerals that are associated with mafic and ultramafic magmas and lava flows. Olivine forms green silicate crystals and pyroxenes can be green, black, brown…a variety of colors depending on the composition of the parent magma and the crystallization temperatures and pressures.

Chapter 31—Big Bend

Anna opened her eyes to the sound of loud snoring. Disoriented, she blinked and noted the fog on the bottom part of her glasses. *Where am I? Where are the boys?*

Just as panic began to set in, she looked around and was quickly reminded that she was camping. *Oh, that's right, they are with Betty and Bob.*

But where am I? Is Sean here? Oh yes, I'm in Texas. She then relaxed and took in the view of the campsite.

The bright moon illuminated the hillslope across the river. Burros appeared to be grazing as they slowly moved along different contours. With her head and shoulders propped on her backpack, Anna was in a perfect position to view the desert floor beneath them. The camp was situated up-slope from the Rio Grande River on a sand-covered terrace.

It was mid-March in the Big Bend of Texas and even though the desert was warm during the day, the nights could get uncomfortably cold, especially for a camper missing a sleeping pad. The entire geology field trip group had to pack lightly for their river float, so novice campers brought a sleeping bag and their backpacks, which didn't always have room for a bulky pad.

An older student in the group, *Edward Stone,*[152] had been banished from the rest of the camp the previous night because of his challenges with breathing. The first night of camping had been

---

152   Edward Stone, an older student on the field trip, who snored loudly. Fictional character and not meant to represent any particular person living or deceased.

so eventful and tiring that his condition did not come to everyone's attention until the second night when he was dubbed the *Snore Master 1000*. [153]

Dr. D. liked to camp at public campsites every other night to make sure that the beginning campers would have access to a shower. Nothing is worse than being in a van with no air conditioning and the smells of fifteen stinking feet and bodies.

The Carlsbad Caverns campsite included clean showers, premier campsites with excellent grass padding, a convenience store, and security. It also included, as neighbor campers, families, retirees, church groups, students, and motorcycle pods.

Edward turned in early that evening and proceeded to create an embarrassing spectacle. He sounded like a wounded animal, in between moments of snorting and explosive farting. The snoring enraged other campers who began honking their car horns and yelling obscenities.

Some people exited their tents and went to their vehicles to distance themselves from the noise. If MSU hadn't had such a large group at the site, they certainly would have been sent on their way.

Dr. D. was mortified. Being an older gentleman, he was somewhat of a prude.

Anna and John were both impressed at Edward's ability to sleep through it all.

"How do you suppose he sleeps through this?" asked Anna.

"Beats me," said John.

"Pretty disgusting if you ask me," said D.

With a snort, followed by muffled, juicy sounding, hrumpf, Anna wondered too if he might need a change of underwear in the morning.

---

153 Nickname given to Ed because of his annoying sleeping habits.

Eventually, the campers were able to ignore the disruption. Some laughed loudly every time Ed farted, which made Anna feel embarrassed for him. Dr. D. just shook his head and walked away, leaving Anna and Big John to mitigate the social disaster.

The next day the camp traveled to the Rio Grande River to begin the first leg of their three-day river journey through the canyons.

The float trip included a raft tour through the sedimentary sequences of the ancient Rio Grande Rift. This particular area was known for its spectacular views and whitewater rafting excitement. The stillness in between rough waters allowed for relaxing, sunbathing, and storytelling.

Whoever was in D.'s raft would no doubt hear his stories of legendary trip experiences, myths, and well-spun lies. He was very well known for his ability to capture the attention of all near him when he began his long tales.

Each raft held six to eight people with backpacks and duffels. One raft carried the geology essentials, which included water, food, cooking supplies, AND a rather large cooler of beer. Only the very best rafters were allowed on the "beer raft."

Anna was one of the more experienced rafters, so she had the pleasure of being on the raft with Dr. D, who was a seasoned rafter and the self-appointed captain of his vessel.

Anna watched the geobabes load into their raft with the exquisitely chiseled river guide captain. He was nicely tanned, wore a ball cap, and had sunglasses.

"Now, he is easy on the eyes," she whispered to D.

"Humph…. of course." groused Adam.

Upon noting that the girls were wearing bikinis underneath their safety vests, she shouted sage advice, "Hey, you ladies need to wear clothing over your legs and arms. The sun will burn you quickly, especially on the river."

"Oh, we know," shouted *Alice*,[154] the younger of the three.

"We are wearing sunscreen. We want to get some sun. Giggle, giggle, giggle…"

Anna shot a look at the river guide as though to warn him to please keep an eye on these ladies. They were in his care now, and he was responsible.

David,[155] the guide for *Beyond Fun Adventures*,[156] nodded in acknowledgment. She couldn't see his eyes because of his sunglasses, but she knew he was aware of his added responsibilities.

Anna was experienced with field trips and the unique experience of camping with a diverse range of preparedness. As a mother, not just a professor, she carried extra essential supplies, particularly feminine hygiene products for the rare female student, as well as insect repellent, sunscreen, and first aid supplies for insect bites, nausea, diarrhea, headaches, and the common sunburn. For Anna, it was like planning a large family vacation where anything could go wrong.

The field trip group met their rafting guides and entered the rafts. The river was gently flowing, and the temperature was mild. A gentle breeze was blowing and kept everyone cool, despite the direct sunlight.

Anna knew that the beautiful day should not be taken for granted. She had been careless before and knew the consequences of not covering her body from head to toe. She wore her broad granny style hat, with a drawstring to make sure it wouldn't blow off of her head, a long-sleeved white shirt, bandana around her neck, and jeans to cover her legs and calves. Some of the students

---

154 Alice, the youngest of the geobabes. Fictional character and not meant to represent any particular person living or deceased.

155 David, the chiseled river guide for the geobabes. Fictional character and not meant to represent any particular person living or deceased.

156 Fictional rafting company. Not based on any particular rafting company in the past or present.

wondered about appropriate attire on the river, and Anna told them to use sunscreen, wear a hat, and cover their bodies.

"Dr. Moore aren't you going to be too hot?" asked one of the students, amused at her attempts to cover her entire body.

"I'd rather be a little warm than to be sunburned," she confidently retorted.

Dr. D. and John dressed similarly, with Dr. D. donning his khaki African safari hat and John an Astros ball cap.

Each team dutifully wore their life vests, if nothing else, and began practicing their rafting techniques when the water was deep enough. Each team had to learn the commands of the raft boat guides and also how to respond as a team. A lack of practice and expertise might result in the dumping of an entire raft into white water rapids.

The guides were serious about safety but were also very cheerful and seemed to enjoy their jobs.

The anticipation of white water was exciting and difficult to imagine on such a smooth day on the river. The sky was filled with fluffy clouds that seemed to move leisurely across the sky. Birds fluttered down to the water's surface and back up again, as they collected insects that floated on the surface of the water. Turtles were out sunning themselves on the dead logs extending out over the river and also on rocks on the bank.

Anna leaned back slightly and rested her weight on her arms and allowed her face and neck to absorb the sun.

Dr. D. looked over at her and smiled. "Could it get any better than this?"

"Nope," she replied, "Thank you, God, for this glorious day."

As their rafts moved effortlessly downstream with the flow of the river, some students napped, others played cards or took pictures, and the lucky ones got to hear Dr. D. tell his stories and jokes. Anna enjoyed listening to the conversations.

Dr. D. was a skilled storyteller. He had a deadpan expression, and each story-joke he told was delivered with a serious tone, leaving the listener wondering if it was indeed a sharing of essential facts or experiences or if there would be a punchline eventually.

"Is that true, Dr. D?" asked one of the students.

Anna chuckled to herself, as she hadn't really been listening.

"Oh yes," laughed Dr. D..... "It's totally accurate. There have been UFO sightings in the Davis Mountains for years...."

She had known him long enough to know he was totally pulling their legs.

The rafting caravan pulled one by one up to an extended point bar deposit and began carrying all supplies from the rafts to a position upslope from the river to set up camp for the evening. A couple of large plastic buckets were placed in a small grove surrounded on three sides by a berm with bushes.

The area was in a low spot facing the river and was a natural barrier between the campsite and the more private space for human waste collection. It didn't, however, keep the other rafters from being able to see all as they passed by on their way downstream to other sites.

As an undergraduate student, Anna had been embarrassed while relieving herself on a similar river trip. *Each toilet bucket has a thick plastic bag lining with a snap-on toilet lid to hold the liner bag in place.* She had always been prudish about her body and was very careful to quickly lower her pants and sit on the toilet before anyone could see her. To her dismay and extreme embarrassment, an entire raft of young men saw her and began hooting and hollering. There she sat in all her glory, perched on the plastic throne, exposed for the world to see.

As a female faculty, she didn't want her students to get a glimpse of her naked. She knew that she would take a flashlight and go later on in the evening.

One by one, the campers visited the nature bathroom and washed up for the sack lunch dinner provided for their evening meal. Thankfully, the wind was blowing in such a way as to keep the smell away from the campers.

The first night on the river, Dr. D. suggested that Ed move down onto a large outcrop near the river to keep campers from wanting to kill him in his sleep.

Ed gladly complied and was not bothered by the proximity to wildlife. He was a veteran and had endured much worse while serving in the military some years earlier.

Sadly, the acoustics in a river and canyon setting was not conducive to the muting of sound. The sound of his snoring was amplified and echoed through the canyons. Even the burros across the river joined in as they engaged in a nocturnal conversation of snorts, farts, and bellows.

Earlier that evening, Anna had nestled into her sleeping bag with her entire body covered from the elements. She zipped the bag tight and brought the top section closed over her head and face, leaving only her eyes, nose, and glasses exposed. Her sleeping bag was one that she had bought as a graduate student, and it kept her warm in temperatures well below freezing. It also had thick layering and offered comfort despite not having a pad beneath her. Apparently, she had dozed off quickly after getting comfortable, having gotten little sleep the previous night.

As she looked out across the sea of students and faculty, who were laying out on tarps like burritos on a baking sheet, she could see the tiny condensation clouds of breath leaving their mouths and noses. The symphony of snores was actually rather soothing--and funny.

Scorpions skittering across the white sand was a sight to behold. The smaller ones were trailing the larger ones with their little tails curled in the classic stinger positions, ready to do battle if needed.

Anna was both fascinated and creeped out by the sight against the glistening sand.

Thankfully, she did not see any rock rattlers, which was her greatest fear and the primary reason she had her head and shoulders elevated above the ground. The quiet of the desert was very sensuous, and one could hardly ignore any of the features, including the sound of the ripples in the river below.

Edward, the burros, the river, the hills, the sand, the critters, fellow campers, the night sky, the cold ground, the warm sleeping bag, her own breath, the fog on her glasses--she now needed to pee... it was all awe-inspiring and also very funny.

Anna chuckled, "Imagine that? Isn't it magnificent?"

She marveled at the night sky. Even with the moon rising, she could still see a few bright stars and constellations.

I wonder which constellations should be visible here at this time of year? she thought to herself, as she turned her eyes to the west and stretched her neck to view to the north, looking for Orion and Sirius. *If I see Sirius, then that bright star just over there might be Canopus.*

Wow, that is a bright star? Perhaps it is Jupiter?

Anna was disappointed that she hadn't thought to review the star charts before the trip. Stargazing was one of her favorite pastimes. If the moon weren't almost full, she could easily have found key night sky markers and would have been able to identify the stellar performers.

She was fully awake now and taking in all of the experience, especially grateful for the warmth and solitude of her sleeping bag. Nothing was getting into her bag with her unless it could get past her mouth and eye opening. In her imagination, she would quickly unzip her bag and shoo any uninvited desert wanderers. Barring an invasion, the bag would not be unzipped until morning, not even to go to the bathroom.

The next morning, Anna could see Dr. D. returning from the berm near the river with a few twigs of dried wood. She wondered if he would use it to start a fire or if there was some other specific reason for the particular debris gathered.

"Hello down there!"

"Oh, hi, Anna. Want to help me make coffee?"

"Do I?"

The students had built a fire the evening before, and the dead coals were in the center of a carefully crafted circle of stones. The stone hearth had been made long ago and was presumably used by other campers as well, as it also had a separate, heavily weathered metal stand for holding pots.

Dr. D. scattered the coals with a long stick and assembled a small pile in the center.

Big John walked up as the smoke began to rise and offered pieces of paper trash from a bag to help with the coffee fire. Together they managed to boil water for instant coffee, oatmeal, etc.

The rafting tour provided one meal a day, and that was in the evenings. The rest of the food consisted of camp snacks, fruits, nuts, chips, and of course, beer after a long day's journey. The float trip leaders provided sack lunches for the previous evening meal and promised a huge feast the second night on the river tour.

After everyone packed up their beer and trash, the tour embarked on the second day of rafting. This day would require all to use the rafting training they had received at the beginning of the trip. White water was between them and the second night on the river. The supply rafts would need to make the arduous journey safely if the campers were all to enjoy a feast and beer that evening.

Anna attended to the needs of the students with sunburns from the day before. The geobabes had gladly exposed most of their bodies to the solar rays the day before and were now red as lobsters. She passed out aloe cream, as bottles of vinegar were too heavy to pack along and advised them to wear hats and long-sleeved shirts and pants for the days' travel. Sadly, this was the same advice she gave the day before, but... *Alas, youth--they must learn the hard way,* she thought.

Chapter 32—Sunburns and Luaus

Sean may have been in a different part of the world, but he experienced similar difficulties with novice hikers and campers.

After two days of walking flows and examining volcanic features and processes, several of the students donned tropical sunburns, which were very painful. At the latitude of the Big Island, and especially near the vernal equinox, the sun's rays were very direct, and the UV exposure was quite high. A volcanic cocktail of volcanic gases, direct sun rays, and humidity, fair-haired people, with sensitive skin, were very susceptible to miserable burns and irritation.

Being extremely fair in complexion, Emily was particularly unhappy as her burn quickly formed blisters. Her eyes were swollen, and her lips were cracked. "Fuck this shit!" she screamed as she stood sobbing in an icy shower.

"Hang in there lady," said her tent mate, *Rachel*.[157] "The cold will take the heat out of the burns, I promise."

"I hate Hawaii!" Emily screamed. "I hate volcanoes!"

Her torment was so loud that the other campers could hear her.

"Is Em ok?" asked Sean, as Rachel exited the shower area.

"Oh, she will be. She is just miserable at the moment. I've given her some aloe to put on the burns after she showers. I'm sure she will be good as new soon."

---

157   Rachel, PhD student in volcanology. One of the Teaching Assistants, T.A., for this trip. One male and one female. Rachel was assigned Emily. All fictional characters and not meant to represent any particular persons living or deceased.

"Ah geez, I sure hope so," said Sean, feeling very bad for Em, especially with her screaming that she hated volcanoes.

"She'll be right, mate. The luau should cheer them all up tonight. You'll see," reassured Ed.

"Fuck! Fuck! Fuck!" could be heard by all in the breakfast area, and everyone giggled at the unique way that Emily always expressed herself. It didn't seem to matter if it was good things or bad things, they all ended up including an expletive or two to express her joy, fear, rage, excitement....

The rest of the day was filled with mini presentations assigned to small groups during the semester. Each team had researched a different geologic area of the volcanoes that were visited on their trip. Students selected their own area of interest and were responsible for providing an overview for the rest of their classmates. They were grouped according to their shared interest in a volcanic area. A strict rubric was given, and they were left to make their own decisions about the distribution of labor for the project.

The camp area had a crude meeting hall with chalk and cork boards hanging on the walls, benches and long tables lined up for observers, as well as electricity, and an overhead projector for old fashioned lectures with overhead sheets. A sizable stand-up screen was also provided as well as an ancient projector, and even a slide carousel if needed. It wasn't state of the art, but it was all a geologist required for a presentation.

Before leaving on the field trip, Sean had carefully compiled his student's written research articles into a field guide for the trip. Team research assignments had allowed the students to be engaged in their own learning experiences and to realize ownership in the course content to be learned.

After a day of scholarly presentations, grading, and class discussions, the group was ready to travel to a nearby resort for a luau with traditional roasted pig, tropical dishes, drinks, and the famous Polynesian fire and hula dancers. No Hawaiian visit, geology or otherwise, would be complete without a traditional luau experience.

Everyone showered and put on clean shirts and shorts. They knew the place was going to be a little bit upscale from their camping experience, so they even wore their clean flip flops, and clean socks for their boots.

Sean and Ed stood at the bus stop and patiently waited on all of the "kids" to emerge from their tents...one by one, spit, and polished.

"Hey, they clean up nice, mate," said Ed.

"Ya, most folks can get things right if free food and drink are at stake," said Sean grinning.

Emily emerged with Rachel and walked in a stilted fashion toward the line of students waiting. She looked like a robot with her arms out from her sides and her knees flexed outward so that her thighs would not touch too closely. Her hair was up in a neat bun, her lips glistened from ointment, and her skin glowed in a rose tone through the white cream slathered over her entire body.

"Ah, geez," said Sean, as he watched her walk toward them. "How is she going to sit down on the ground, mate?"

"Oh, she will figure it out. No worries, Sean. She's a big girl," said Ed

Even Ed's reassurance didn't make Sean feel any better. He was concerned about one of his favorite students. Being a dad of daughters back home, he had a special place in his heart for his female students.

"You right there, Em?" asked Ed as Em approached.

"Fuck NO! Do I look alright?" she announced loudly. "I'm a fucking leper."

Sean cringed at her use of such foul language, especially in front of Ed.

Her fellow students laughed at the bold statement of the obvious.

"Em, it will be better tomorrow," said Sean, "The first couple of days is the worst."

"Yes, Emily. He's right," said Rachel.

Emily looked down, resigned to her misery, and nodded that she would be okay, but then thrust her shoulders back and held her head high as she announced loudly, "I am IMPERVIOUS!"

Her classmates all cheered, laughed, and clapped. "That's right, Em!" "You got this!"

Ed leaned over to Sean and whispered, "See there. I told you she'd be right."

After what seemed like a long drive, the bus arrived at the Majestic Kalua Kia Hotel and Resort.[158]

"Classy, man!"

"Damn. Are you sure this is the right place?" asked Scott,[159] sniffing his armpits.

"Fuck yes!" yelled Emily from the back of the bus.

Everyone laughed and exited the bus and couldn't help but notice the ocean view from the hotel breezeway. There was a relaxing wind blowing, and the endless ocean stretching out away from them, complete with a rising moon, was a sight to behold. The sun was setting behind them, but the colors of the sky and clouds behind the palm trees were breathtaking.

Sean thought to himself, *Ah sorry Annie, this may well be paradise after all.*

"Sure wish you were here too…" he sighed to himself.

---

158 Fictional hotel based on hotels found in Waikiki. Not intended to represent any current or past establishments.

159 Scott, an undergraduate upperclassman in Sean's volcanology class. Fictional character and not meant to represent any particular person living or deceased.

"Who ya talking to, mate?" asked Ed, "Your girlfriend? Ha-ha!"

"Ah, nah...nobody," he said as he looked sadly at the view. "Let's go eat some pork."

The students filed in and took their seats on the ground at their designated tables as performers on the stage sang classic Hawaiian lounge songs. Very relaxing, but definitely different than the music the students were accustomed to hearing.

Emily groaned and whimpered as she assumed an Indian style position on the ground in front of the table next to her friend Rachel.

All enjoyed the experience, which included ocean breezes, fire and hula dancers, and a very dramatic *haka*[160]to end the show. To the student's surprise many of the people in the crowd, including Dr. Anderson and Dr. Smart, also engaged.

A luau was a must for any Hawaiian experience. Seeing a haka up close and personal with your instructors participating was an experience to remember for sure.

Sean and Ed were pleased to be part of giving this experience to the volcanology students. Many would probably never have this experience again. Feeling the ocean breezes with a hint of sulfur, the sand of black and green beaches, and watching lava flows entering the sea would be stories to tell their future students and grandchildren.

160　Haka is a Maori ceremonial dance.

Chapter 33—Texas and Aliens

After a long day of roadside geology stops in the Marathon and Davis Mountain areas, the weary caravan stopped at *Delano's*,[161] a famous burger drive-in near Fort Davis, Texas. "That will be nineteen Texas Burgers with cheese, one chicken burger without cheese, and three cheese sandwiches with nothing on them. Oh yes and fries all around, lots of salt," said Dr. D., as he pulled out his wallet.

"Yes, and let's have twenty ice cold Pepsis too," he added.

He was treating everyone to his favorite meal in all of Texas, the Texas Burger, Fries, and ice-cold *Pepsi*.[162] Everyone else had Coke products. D. loved Pepsi, and if he was buying, everyone was getting Pepsi, except the geobabes."

Annie walked up next to D. and asked, "Do we need to get three ice glasses of water for the girls, too?"

"It's a mystery to me how they can stuff themselves with organic chips and beer but are not allowed to drink soda pops or eat beef and cheese," D. said, as he looked over his sunglasses which were on the end of his nose.

They both smiled at one another and chuckled, as Annie stepped up to add the additional drinks to the order.

---

161 A fictitious diner based on the variety of diners that dot the rural landscapes in Texas.

162 Pepsi cola is a carbonated beverage distributed in the US, that is popular in Montana, but not in all southern locales. It is Dr. Ds favorite drink.

As the sun began to set on the *Fort Davis Area*,[163] the caravan pulled into the campgrounds. It was dark, but the campgrounds were well cared for, and there were very nice circular areas with covered camping around a central pole.

"There is electricity!" shouted *Amy*,[164] one of the geobabes.

"Eeeeee! And showers too!" they screamed.

Annie laughed to herself as she listened to all of the conversations and voices in the darkness. She truly loved hearing their interactions.

"Did you see that?"

"Oh no, you guys! No way?" said another voice in the distance, followed by raucous scuffles and muffled laughter.

They sounded happy and relaxed, which was quite a change from the previous nights which had involved snoring and public disruptions, diarrhea, and sunburns from first-time experiences.

"Yes, this was going to be a nice, quiet evening," smiled Annie to herself as she lay on her back on the picnic bench and looked up at the amazing star-filled sky.

It was clear. Lights were out at 10:00 pm because of the nightly star party which was held in the nearby amphitheater area. A park ranger led a viewing each night during the year for visitors who were interested in the natural open sky, naked-eye observatory.

Annie didn't go to the amphitheater--she had been many times before and was enjoying her own celestial canopy.

Even though there were several miles and time zones between them, she imagined that Sean was looking up at the same stars and wondered if he was thinking of her -- them. She couldn't wait until Friday, so she could hear his voice once more.

---

163 A fictional camp set in the Davis Mountain area of southwest Texas. It is not meant to depict any particular camping area, present or past.

164 Amy, the oldest of the geobabes. Fictional character and not meant to represent any particular person living or deceased.

Annie fell asleep on top of the tabletop and began to snore gently. The dew from the night air accumulated on her face and hair. She woke up several times, feeling very cold and damp, but didn't want to move around much at that hour of the evening, for fear of waking others. Besides, what was a little bit of cool and damp when the stars were so brilliant? Even the sound of loud snoring in the distance did not interfere with the moment.

Pulling her bare arms through the sleeves of her sweatshirt and curling into a fetal position, she allowed herself to go back to sleep. With her knees also pulled up under her, she looked like a gray blob, perhaps a large bag left unattended?

Sometime later, Annie woke to the sound of urine flowing onto the ground near her. She lay still and wondered who on earth was up and relieving themselves. It was surely one of the guys, as the sound would indicate that the fluid was falling from some distance above the ground. The person sneezed loudly and farted at the same time.

"Oops," she heard the voice say.

"He" then turned and walked in the other direction.

Ewww, thought Annie. *That smells.*

Feeling a little grossed out, she decided to get up and wander to the van and find her place on the front bench. As she unfolded her body from the sweatshirt, someone began to scream and run away. It sounded like a woman.

Startled by the sudden scream, Annie also shouted, "Jesus, Mary, and Joseph! What the hell is going on?"

Apparently, one of the male students had wandered down to go pee in the middle of the night and had not seen Annie laying on the tabletop in a ball. When she moved, he was startled by the sight and began to scream.

Much like Sean's story of the Moehau Man, Annie had unintentionally become an alien waiting to abduct one of the students who had heard the story of alien abductions in that part of Texas.

Annie ran toward the screaming and collided with Dr. D. Both of them recognized the other and held onto each other in the dark as they continued. By this time, others were awake, and either cussing or voicing concern. After their first night camping, they weren't shocked by anything.

To Annie's surprise, it was Mikey. He was describing seeing a gray being rising up out of a spaceship. She didn't have the heart to embarrass him in front of everyone, so she calmly said,

"Oh, I bet that was that tent bag that I left down on the tabletop. It was flapping in the breeze earlier this evening. That was probably what you saw."

"No, this thing was skinny, pale, and was very tall when it stood up. It looked like it had come out of a cocoon or something."

"Well, I'm not going back to sleep," said one of the geobabes.

"I'll go check it out," said Dan, "I've got my knife on me."

"NO! Dr. Moore and I will check it out!" said D. "You guys go back to sleep."

Anna and Adam walked downslope away from the campsite. D. had a flashlight and was illuminating the way.

"I'm sorry, D.," said Anna.

"Why, you aren't an alien, are you?" he asked.

"Weeellll, kind of…" she said chuckling.

The light stopped. D turned the light on her face and said, "What!?"

She smiled and motioned for him to put the light down, "I fell asleep on the tabletop and I guess Mikey wandered down that direction to go to the bathroom."

"What?" asked D. "Are you kidding me? How the heck did he get an alien from you sleeping on a picnic table?"

Anna laughed and explained, "I was curled up inside my sweatshirt, so …. I guess he saw me uncurl and stand up on the bench. It apparently startled him."

"Hahahahaha…." D. doubled over in laughter.

"Shhhhhh," said Anna. I don't want the others to know. It might embarrass him, and I know he wants to do field camp this summer."

"Well, we'll see about that," laughed D.

***

Both field trips, Hawaii, and South Texas, offered undergraduate and graduate students unique hands-on field experiences in sedimentary and volcanic terrains.

Annie and Sean had many things in common. Their mutual love of the field of geology, teaching, and volcanoes connected them uniquely across space and time. No matter where they were in their individual journeys in life, their shared love of geology, astronomy, and music never left them lacking the ability to share their ideas. The intellectual connection raised their relationship to another level beyond just the physical and spiritual. They were intellectually stimulating to one another other as well.

Chapter 34—The Plateau
Old Friends

That following summer, Annie accepted a field geologist position, which was personally offered by Jim for his mining company. The job involved as much as six weeks of mapping, laboratory, and report writing in the summer months. She would have to give up teaching part of the field methods course but saw the project as an opportunity for professional development.

Teaching a field methods course was one thing but working as a field geologist in the industry would give her a renewed perspective and experience to share with her students.

The exploration company that owned the mine had areas that they wanted explored for future production. Jim invited both Sean and Annie to join him in this *project*, of which he was the project manager. [165]

Annie was a little bit dubious about being the only female in the group, but this was the reality of working in field geology during this time in history.

Sean had to teach at least two weeks of the field methods course for his school, and then he would join them for the rest of the survey project. His goal was to help Jim, legitimately be with Annie, and to collect the Stillwater Suite for his Igneous-Metamorphic Petrology class.

---

165 This survey project is a fictitious project that takes place in an area that has been mapped extensively over the past 100 years. It is not meant to depict past, or present projects and the personnel are fictional characters and have no association with current mining or geology projects in the area.

The suite of rocks from one of only five banded igneous complexes on the planet was a premier addition to any geology department display case, as well as the addition of a variety of cumulus minerals and rock types that are unique to such a locale.

Annie had the very same goal and was very excited to be able to collect her suite with two of the finest petrologists in the business.

Two suites for educational purposes would be easily obtained.

Jim promised to facilitate that endeavor by mailing the samples to each school. He would claim the cost as an educational outreach budget item attached to the contracted amount for their survey work.

Sean promised to make sure that Jim behaved himself too, so she was set to make good money over the summer and bring home a prize suite as well.

As a single mom, she needed extra pay. In Texas at that time, divorce was not immediate. It took eighteen months, and Annie had little to no child support until a settlement could be met in court.

With the help of Jim and Sean, an exploration team was assembled to map the area to the north of the complex. This area was not included in the original survey of the distribution of platinum group elements and structural geology.

The leader of the field mapping team was a well-seasoned economic field geologist from South America, *Stanley "Stinky" Walton*.[166] Stinky was also an old buddy of Jim's from his South America mining days. They had mapped economic deposits in South Africa, the Peruvian Andes, the Arctic north, Greenland, and New Zealand together.

Jim was very confident in Stinky's ability to lead the field mapping team. He even boasted of once being with Stinky when

---

166 Fictional character, Stanley "Stinky" Walton, field geologist and one of Sean, Jim, and Ed's friends from their mapping days. He is British, probably Scottish, based on his accent.

he shot the lower jaw off a large polar bear who was intent on eating them for dinner.

"They sure as hell can't chew you without a lower jaw, mate, now can they?" quoted Jim.

Stanley was a rugged mountain man with a huge unkempt beard and body odor that would definitely keep the ladies and bears at bay. He loved garlic and ate it raw to keep the mosquitos off him in the field. The associated flatulence only added to his allure.

Annie quickly understood why "Stinky" was not just a term of endearment, but also an adequate adjective for describing his musky essence.

There's no way I am sleeping in the same tent with that guy. Uck.

The other two members of the mapping team were exploration-field geologists from South America who were on loan from *BEC-- British Exploration Company.*[167]

Jackson Hambey (Jackie)[168] was another friend of Jim, Ed, and Sean's from their college days in New Zealand. It didn't take much prodding to get him to go and spend several weeks in the field with his closest and dearest friends, even if it meant having to endure Stanley's body odor.

Last but not least was *Jacob Bartholomew (Bart) McMillan II.*[169] He was also a kiwi like Sean and Ed. As it turned out, they were all old field mates who either worked together or went to school together, apparently working across the globe in areas like New Guinea too. They were not all specifically igneous specialists, like Sean and Jim, but had experience in all aspects of the geology of economic importance to an exploration company. This included oil, diamonds, platinum group, as well as rare earth metals.

---

167   Fictional company not meant to represent any past or present exploration company.

168   Fictional character Jackson Hambey "Jackie" friend of Jim, Ed, and Sean from college days.

169   Jacob Bartholomew (Bart) McMillan II, fictional character named after friend of the author. Charles Bartholomew a fellow science fiction author and friend.

They were a fascinating team of geologists, and Annie was the only academic other than Sean in the group, as well as the only female. She was intimidated by their credentials and experience but refused to be frightened away from the opportunity to do a job she truly loved.

Because of the short notice, Annie agreed to teach the first half of her field camp with D. During the camp's mid-camp tour, she flew home briefly to see her boys before being gone again for the rest of the summer break.

After securing her boys with their grandparents for the summer, and with the support of Betty, in particular, Annie flew to Billings, where Sean and Jim were both waiting to pick her up. She flew in a few days early to allow herself to acclimate to the higher elevation and to be able to see Sean before his camp officially started.

As Jim and Sean waited together for Annie, they discussed the project goals, the state of the mining business, and, of course, Annie.

"She'll be right, Sean. It's Stinky I am worried about."

Both men laughed out loud at the thought of sweet little Annie having to engage with him.

"Right, what's he gonna do with a *sheila*? [170] He might have ta change some of his personal habits," laughed Sean.

"Like farting all night in the tent. Whew, remember the Atacama?... what a nasty git!"

"Wait, she's gonna be sleeping in the tent with them guys? Geez, I hadn't thought about that."

"If she wants to be safe. I hope it's not a problem for her ... do ya think?" asked Jim.

---

170   A sheila is an informal term for a female. It is also a derogatory term for a female in a group, like babe or chick. Some see it is a term of endearment, like "mate." It really depends on how it is used.

"Naaa. It's the guys who might not be able to keep their willies down. Geez…," said Sean with genuine concern.

"No worries, Sean, I'll give her the .357 and the bear spray. [171]They'll be hating life if they mess with her. I can also pass out rubber bands to pull their diddles to their nuts. That should take care of any of that nonsense."

Both men roared with laughter as Sean uncontrollably shot water through his nostrils and sprayed it everywhere. He had just taken a big swig of water when Jim began to speak.

Even though they were laughing, Sean was definitely jealous at the thought of those guys seeing Annie in her underwear, which would have to be the case on the plateau. There's no way they can remove their clothing for safety and not have the guys see her.

He began thinking about how he could get out of field camp, but it was the next week. Sean thought to himself, *I'll just have to tell Jim to keep an eye on Annie for me. I trust him. Stinky, absolutely NOT!* He wasn't at all worried that Annie would find them attractive, but he certainly hated not to be there with her.

Both men were excited to see Annie exit the doors of the airport terminal and walk toward them in the parking lot.

She recognized Jim's Subaru Outback and of course, Sean's field hat.

Both men stood up from their leisurely positions on the hood of the car.

As she approached, her pace quickened, and Sean reached out and gathered her up in his arms, lifting her off of the ground and holding her above him in the air, as he might do to a child. She dropped her bags and giggled as she slid down his chest. Sean

---

171 The .357 magnum is a weapon used by some geologists because it is easier to carry than a larger weapon. The weapon will kill another animal, but the shooter must be an accurate shot. Bear spray is used by the character Annie and other geologists, along with a loud horn to frighten wildlife in the field.

stopped her face even with his and kissed her passionately in front of Jim.

They both had forgotten that Jim was standing there as they disappeared for a moment in time into their own bubble of space. Jim gulped and laughed at the sight, having his suspicions confirmed as he watched his best friend embrace and kiss his lover.

The couple lingered for a moment or two, with Annie crying tears of happiness in his arms. Sean then realized that he had forgotten his buddy and turned to him and said, "Oh shit, mate. I don't think ya were supposed to see that were ya?"

All three began to laugh as Jim said, "Like I hadn't already figured that out?"

Annie felt her face turn red as she blushed at the thought of Jim knowing their secret, even though she hadn't really considered how they would keep it a secret for long.

Jim took Annie in his arms too and gave her a loving hongi without a kiss or his usual hands-on-her-arse greeting that she was anticipating but hoping to avoid.

"You'll be right?" he said as he kissed her on the cheek before turning to Sean and punching him, hard, in the shoulder, for not telling him sooner.

"Owww…. shit, Jim!" said Sean as he grabbed his shoulder in pain.

"Serves you right, ya sneaky bastad."

Sean loaded Annie's backpack and duffle into the back of Jim's Subaru, still rubbing his shoulder, and the three friends began their trek to the Stillwater Valley.

Annie took her preferred place in the back seat with the hammers and garbage. Ah, she loved the smell of mown hay and dust as they drove with the windows down. As they approached, she recognized Sean's tent. It was in the exact same place it had been before. She felt a bit like she was coming home. Her home and life with Sean.

That evening the three friends sat around the campfire, and Annie listened as the two old classmates told stories of their college days and argued about the details of shared experiences.

She loved sitting there watching the campfire colors of burnt orange, red, and amber flicker on their faces. They were both strikingly handsome men, each different, and each appearing as carefully and skillfully sculpted pieces of art…rugged, muscular, seasoned by the elements, …she marveled at the beauty of the scene in nature…the scents, the sounds. She was also amazed at the love they both obviously had for one another. Annie felt blessed to be witness to such a remarkable sight and experience.

The next morning, Jim had coffee brewing, and Annie rose to see if he had enough to share. She emerged from the tent, wearing only her grey sweatshirt, which was hanging to her knees. Jim was sitting on the opposite side of the fire and facing the direction of her tent and quickly stood up when he saw her emerge.

"Right there?" he shouted. "How did ya sleep?"

Annie rubbed her eyes and extended her coffee mug toward Jim, "Coffee, I need coffee," she sighed.

Jim laughed and took her mug from her, "Yer gonna have to chew coffee beans on the plateau, ya know. Those headaches can be nasty up there."

She moaned and cradled the warm mug in both of her hands, refraining from drinking for a moment, as she allowed the steam to rise and cover her nostrils and eyes.

"Oh Jim, that feels so good. Thank you."

"So, Sean must be *knackered*.[172] I would think," said Jim as he winked at Annie and clearly viewed Sean walking toward them from the tent.

Before Annie could respond, she heard Sean's voice behind her, "Wouldn't ya like ta know?"

Jim laughed loudly and immediately poured Sean a cup of coffee, as though he'd been pouring his coffee for him for years.

"So, what are we doing today, gentlemen?" Annie asked as she sipped her coffee.

"Well, first things first, we are going to go into town and make sure we get all of the supplies that will be needed for a couple of weeks on the plateau."

"A couple of weeks?" asked Annie, "We won't just go up there and stay the entire time?"

"No, we will devote no more than three weeks, that's one week for each section, for the field survey of each area, data collection and field mapping part of the project. We will meet back down at the facilities and spend a few days uploading and entering attribute data into the computer and refining the maps."

"What, no fancy *GPS*?"[173] asked Sean.

This was during a time when accessing the GPS coordinates meant that a team of three would collect the data. One person had to wear the pack with an antenna on his or her head, and another had to carry the recording device, while yet another took the field measurements and placed them in a field notebook, just in case the technology failed.

"Nah, guys. We just need our Brunton's, field notebooks, and surveying tools for this type of work. The data digitizing is done when we put it in software designed to convert our coordinate

---

172 Knackered. British term for being exhausted.
173 GPS, Global Positioning System. A system that uses at least three satellites to triangulate an accurate position on the surface of the earth.

systems. Eventually, data collection will be all computer applications and making our jobs obsolete," Jim said sadly.

Annie felt extremely excited at the prospect of field coordinates and attribute data collection being quickly recorded and remotely sent to a computer somewhere else. She was also very sad that future geologists might not learn how to use the time-honored tools that she and Sean had been teaching students over the years. *In my classes, they will still learn to do it the old way and then apply the new technology,* she thought to herself. She felt strongly about this and would not feel compelled to do otherwise.

"We also have a rock lab with a rock saw and the ability to make our own thin sections. It's old school, but we have everything you need here to produce excellent hand samples and thin sections of your suites you are collecting for your schools.

"The Stillwater Complex area has been mapped pretty well, and there are plenty of core studies. This report will include discussion of the new exploration areas, which may or may not correlate with those here.

"Cores will come later if our preliminary survey and report determine the areas have potential. We hope to improve on the correlations which have already been generated in the past and hopefully extrapolate some new information before actively coring the sites, which is the next phase and another project in and of itself.

"Ph.D. students will be analyzing those cores too. And we have 3D software engineers and geologists on site for the drilling part if we decide to produce them.

"Your assessment goes in my report for the survey of those areas for future mining potential. Sean here tells me that this part is right up your alley."

"I love fieldwork, so it should be a great experience. Do you have the surrounding area surveys for us to study as well?"

"Ah, yes, dear. The previous studies are in our library, so it's all here. This is an exploration survey project. Our team will help to determine if we want to core and hopefully produce those areas. We just do basic data collection, mapping, and analysis here in this exploration phase."

"We have a rock lab and old school stuff like reflecting and petrographic microscopes, as well as computers and mapping software, but none of the experimental stuff. Plus, how else will you and *Seani* [174] get your magnificent suites to take home? You'll want to get nice hand sample sizes of the *reef* [175] too. Sawing them down to size before I have to ship them will help with the cost for sure. The amount of money devoted to this project must include a detailed report of the field data, maps, and I know you understand the amount of work that involves now, don't you?"

"Right," said Sean.

"I look forward to every aspect, Jim. Thank you again for the opportunity to do this work," said Annie.

"So, Annie and I will be doing this part of it mostly?"

"Yes, Sean, this is also yer area of expertise, as I recall. The rest of the team is here for the field measurements, geologic maps, and cross sections. They are pros at getting it done quickly, too, as ya remember."

Sean nodded in affirmation.

"They know exactly what they are doing. I was hoping to have you and Annie here after they leave to do the analysis I need to include in the final report. Both of ya being professors and all and experienced at writing bullshit reports," laughed Jim.

"Oh right," said Sean," snickering at the academia jab.

---

174   Sean's nickname given by his college friends.
175   Reef refers to a suite of rocks that were explored by the Johns-Manville Corporation. The zone, referred to as the JM Reef, is a stratigraphic zone rich in platinum and palladium and other platinum group elements. It is a significant economic section of the banded igneous series, known as the Stillwater Complex.

"So, we will map for three weeks, tops, and generate mapped layers and make sure that our field data matches the mapped data. We will produce a hard copy map, which most of us are used to doing, and we will also generate a digital map, which I know ya teach yer students to do as well? We have a guy who specializes in this stuff, so not too much pressure, but he's not a field person. He needs the field person's perspective and oversight. I know enough to be dangerous about what he is doing, but he has been trained to make maps using *Surfer*[176] and the new technology, *GIS*.[177] We will compare the hard copy and digital copies to make sure nothing was missed."

"That's awesome, Jim! I can't wait," said Annie excitedly.

Sean turned to Annie and said, "Lucky *YOU*. You'll have a whole two weeks of learning on me. You'll have to be my teacher when I return."

Annie smiled, "Imagine that. Me teaching you for a change." Laughing, "Are you sure you can handle that?"

---

176 Surfer was a popular mapping program for mapping data points in the 70 and 80s.

177 GIS, Geographic Information System, where digitized data is published in map layers which can be combined electronically.

Chapter 35—It's Complicated
The Reunion

The campsite, at 6,500 feet, was plenty of elevation to help Annie acclimate.

Jim was also camping there as he drove back and forth to pick up members of the summer team. Members were flying in from near sea level, so there would have to be at least one day of being acclimatized to the higher and drier terrain. All of them, except Annie, had worked at higher elevations in the Andes.

The plan was for everyone to go up to the mine for the orientation, and then take a truck to the nearest accessible point at 9,500 feet, to begin the survey project. From there, to hike with their equipment and set up a base camp, situated on the plateau at an elevation around 12,000 feet. After setting up their tent and establishing the base camp, the idea was to work the areas to be mapped from there.

As everyone began to arrive, it felt like a field camp gathering, except for the presence of a bottle of gin and whiskey.

It is usually not customary for field camps to have hard booze accessible to students who may not be old enough to drink. Typically, as the camp progresses, the older students go out and purchase their own beer, but know they are limited in sharing based on local laws regarding the legal drinking age.

Annie wondered if they were going to drink the scotch and gin straight but soon realized that the seasoned professionals had a variety of packets of lime, lemon, and other flavorings to mix into the glacial meltwater before mixing with the gin. The Scotch would probably be sipped? ...she hoped. *Ewwww*, the mixes for the gin sounded simply horrible, but apparently, it made the transport of booze easier. Bottles of tonic would be just too much extra to carry.

When packing supplies into a remote area, it is prudent to carefully manage any added weight from items not needed for the work at hand. Packing garbage out must also be a consideration.

Sean and Jim seemed to know everyone, and Annie had to meet the new people--all men.

As Stinky watched her shake hands with everyone, he whispered to Jim, "What's a Sheila doing here, mate? You didn't tell me about her."

Sean overheard the query and interjected confidently, "Annie here, is one of the finest field geologists that I've had the pleasure to work with. I can guarantee it, mate," as he reached up to massage his shoulder.

Stinky gave Sean and Jim a dubious glance as he stood back and gave Annie a once over from head to toe.

She felt uncomfortable as he seemed to be sizing her up physically. She wasn't sure if he was looking at her and assessing if she had the stamina for the plateau, or if he thought he wouldn't be able to focus on his work.

Jim then chimed in thankfully, saying, "Ah, come on, mates. She's a college professor, and she teaches students how ta do fieldwork. You might learn a thing or two from her this summer, if ya pay attention."

Everyone laughed at Jim's pronouncement.

"Actually, gentlemen, I am hoping to learn from you how it is really done so that I may train my students accordingly," said Annie.

"Ah well, that settles it then, doesn't it?" said Jackie, removing his hat and politely bowing as if to regard her like royalty, "Well madame, you are quite alright with me."

Leave it to Jim to break the tension and get everyone to relax and laugh at themselves.

Annie was so relieved at the passing of such an awkward moment.

The crew left their tents and traveled to the diner/bar nearby and ate their fill of burgers and chips - thick slices of potatoes - and potato skins.

Annie ordered the potato skins and washed them down with a longneck beer.

The old friends laughed, told stories, and played music on the jukebox. It was a good time had by all.

Sean walked to make his music selections, as he searched his pants pockets for quarters.

"Hey Annie, do ya have any change? There's a great album here. I seem to remember that ya love 'The Band?'".

"You know it." She said, standing and handing him change from her pockets.

Together they selected songs and returned to their table.

"Another round of piss over here! " shouted Jim to the barmaid.

"*And it makes no difference...*" Began to play.

Sean looked at Annie and tilted his head to the dance floor.

"I thought you'd never ask, " she said, as she followed him.

The couple began to dance and became lost in the music and each other. Jim and the guys saw them and shouted, "Hey, no, fraternizing!"

Sean lifted his middle finger to the guys as he turned Annie's back to them.

His gesture only incited them to howl and whistle even louder.

"Is everything okay?" asked Annie

"Oh yes, they are just assholes."

Sean was then a little concerned that the guys might think that Annie was only there because he invited her. He knew, however, that if they got a chance to see her work in the field, they would respect her.

When they arrived back at their campsite, they made a fire and sat near it, allowing the aroma of the lodgepole pine smoke to replace any smells of their meal, or washing.

When camping in bear country, it is best to simply rinse your face and hands with water and not use soaps or scented lotions. Bears love scents that are different from the ordinary smells of nature. Woodsmoke is the perfect mask to cover human odors. In addition to bathing in woodsmoke, it is also a good practice to remove all clothing, except perhaps underwear, before crawling into a sleeping bag.

Everyone disrobed and began handing their outer garments to Jim, who collected their clothing in a large waterproof laundry bag.

Sean strategically blocked any view of Annie as she quickly covered her half-naked body with her large gray sweatshirt.

Jim and Sean, both in boxer shorts, carried the bag away from the campsite.

She sat there for a few moments and averted her eyes from the men remaining, who apparently didn't wear any underwear to sleep at night. She was grateful that Sean and Jim wore undergarments and wondered if Sean had told Jim to please wear them. Feeling uncomfortable, she quickly entered Sean's tent to avoid having to see the nakedness of the men. Annie thought to herself, *How on earth am I going to share a tent with those nasty, naked guys?*

She straightened the sleeping bags and wearily slipped into the warm and comfortable bed where she and Sean had made love the night before. As she lay there waiting for Sean, she could hear the faint sound of men laughing, zipping, and unzipping of bags and also the roar of the river in the distance. Annie loved that sound.

Mother Nature was surely in charge and made sure that they all knew it.

After what seemed like an eternity, Annie heard the zipper on the tent and pushed herself up on her elbows to make sure she could see the opening clearly. Sean's disembodied head pushed through as he stopped and looked around. "Ah, you are in here. I was afraid at first you'd gone off to the river or something."

"Nope, just hiding from the naked guys."

"Ha-ha...I wondered about that," said Sean as he got down on all fours and crawled the rest of the way into the tent. "You are going to have to get used to it, I think. After all, you will be sleeping with them for a couple of weeks, ya know."

"Ugh...I'll just have to pray a lot I guess."

Sean laughed loudly as he plopped himself down next to her on top of the sleeping bags. He pushed up on his elbow and looked at her, saying, "What's a nice girl like you...?"

Annie giggled as he nibbled on her neck. His beard was soft, but she was very ticklish, hypersensitive to all touch.

Sean stopped for a moment and looked at her.

"Whatcha doing, love?" she asked.

"Imagining how those assholes are going to keep their willies down with ya. Yer so gorgeous, a real femme fatale."

"A what?" she asked indignantly.

"You know, a woman who is seductive and eventually brings men to ruin." He snickered as he kissed her passionately on the lips to keep her from being able to promptly respond.

Annie felt hurt by the characterization and pushed him away as she pushed up on her elbow to look him in the eyes. "Now wait a minute! I AM NOT A FEMME FATALE! You take that back!"

Sean giggled and replied in a flirtatious tone, "Okay, I take that back."

As he pushed her to her back, he postured himself above her body so that he could look directly down on her.

"I love ya Annie," he said as he once more kissed her passionately.

"Ya know I'm just teasing ya. You are the furthest thing I can imagine from a femme fatale."

Annie slipped out from under the sleeping bag and reached up to brush his face and said, "I love you too."

As she tugged to pull his face down to hers, he did not release his planked position with his entire body flexed above hers. He slowly lowered his face to hers and began lightly touching the tip end of his tongue to her lips…probing ever so gently, slipping his tongue into her mouth as he kissed her in between circular strokes.

Annie reached up to feel his flexed chest muscles and couldn't help but note his nipples, which seemed harder than usual. She lightly touched them with the tip of her fingers, while Sean moaned and continued to touch her lips with his tongue. Keeping one hand pushing up to his chest, she reached her other hand around to his back and then down his side to his tightened gluteus muscles. His boxer shorts were hanging loosely, and she easily slipped them down to his knees.

As she ran her hand over his hips, she felt him tighten slightly and breathe more rapidly. She then moved both hands to caress his leg muscles, and…oh my he was so firm…he was fully erect with fluid dripping onto her thighs.

Annie, too, felt her own juices flowing and moistening the sleeping bag beneath her.

She continued to kiss his chest and then stomach as she reached her hands further down his buttocks to the opening between his thighs, where she could feel the intense hardness behind his scrotum. Annie had never felt that before and was intensely turned on by Sean's response to her touching him there. She felt him tremble and move his hips forward slightly, squeezing a little, as she gently slid her fingers down to his testicles.

Even though Sean was clearly aroused, he did not break his posture. He wanted Annie to come up to meet him and eventually break his hold.

She had never seen him in this way before. His body was so firm, and he was so erect… For the first time, she felt the urge to explore this part of him. She slid down and stretched herself up to kiss his nipples, flicking them erotically with her tongue as his arms began to tremble.

He now was having trouble maintaining his posture.

Annie slid herself down further so that she could touch his taut testicles.

Sean was not circumcised, and she never truly got to see this part of him aroused. To her amazement, there didn't seem to be much of a difference.

With both hands, she explored his body. She was naive about the male body and had never really felt free or safe to explore in such a manner before.

When she was growing up, "good girls" didn't know such things about the anatomy of men or women's bodies. In the era in which she was raised, sex education was non-existent and considered pornographic.

At the age of ten, almost eleven, she was traumatized by the onset of her menses. She was terrified that she might have cancer and was dying.

Her mother took her to buy the needed items and then told her to wear an awkward, flimsy belt, in which she was to attach a huge, bulky, freely swinging pad.

"How many do I use?" asked Annie.

Her mother's response was, "As many as you need."

Poor Annie thought it was a lifetime sentence and was not impressed with becoming a woman at all. It was disgusting, smelly, and socially awkward. Other girls noticed her belt and would tease her for having to wear one. For a sensitive child, like Annie, the entire experience was embarrassing and traumatic.

It wasn't until her grandmother noted that she was using too many pads and asked,

"Annie, do you really need that many?" She was obviously concerned that she was experiencing excessive bleeding.

"Mom said that I had to wear one every day."

"Ha...ha...No, child. You only use them when the bleeding begins, and you stop using them when it stops.

"It stops?" asked Annie.

"Yes, it only happens once a month."

Annie was so relieved.

Girls of her vintage were raised to think that the boys had all of the information and control regarding sex. She didn't know that she ovulated until she took biology as a freshman in college. It was a revelation to finally understand that menstruation was a cycle and that ovulation occurred at some point.

It didn't make the experience less traumatic for her, but it did finally make sense that she could keep track of the periodicity and plan her own life accordingly. It also seemed logical to assume that it was a way for the female body to get practiced and regulated for pregnancy later on. It made sense, even if it was unpleasant.

Annie was an intelligent woman who was very well educated, but in this area, she was raised to be prudish and to allow men to make the decisions. She had been socialized to be willfully ignorant about sex.

Exploring Sean's body was a new experience for her, and her forensic mind was fascinated by the morphology of this part of her lover's body.

As she left one hand to caress his testicles and continue to touch the mysterious hard place behind them, she slowly worked one hand forward to embrace the full measure of his manhood. Sean's response was a high-pitched whisper of pleasure.

To her surprise and to his even bigger surprise, she began to lick the end of his penis gently and to taste the seminal fluid. It was slightly salty, but not foul in odor or flavor.

As she continued, he began to respond in a breathless, excited whisper, "You don't have to do that. I know how much you don't like that."

He remembered her saying that her husband Robert had forced her to do it and she became sick to her stomach. Sean never wanted her to do anything that made her feel degraded.

"It's okay," she said. "I want to." She then took the entire bulbous end, slowly into her mouth, with a slow circular motion of her tongue. The action seemed natural to her and part of her ability to make love to him. It never once occurred to her that it was the same in any way to what Robert had wanted from her. All she could think about was her intense love for Sean and how much she enjoyed the entire experience of giving him pleasure.

Sean began to vocalize as she moved him deeper into her mouth, "Ahhh…. Ahhh…."

He then released his posture and grabbed her behind her right knee and slid her up so he could kiss her on the mouth as he pushed himself inside of her.

Annie gasped loudly with the penetration, which was effortless. She had a heightened sensation now for the shape of his penis, as it clearly touched her cervix. It was not painful at all. It was as though Sean knew exactly how deep and the precise position to bring her to the greatest pleasure.

They both shouted in mutual pleasure as she felt him spasm inside of her.

"I can feel it. I can feel it." She loudly whispered. "Oh, Sean, I feel it."

"I know, I know." He gasped. "Ah…ah…. oh darling, darling, darling…" His voice crescendoed higher and higher in pitch until he finally screamed out like a woman, over and over, with each squeeze of her vaginal muscles.

Annie breathlessly tried to scream too but could not make a sound. She simply had no air left in her lungs.

Sean was now collapsed on top of her, and their bodies trembled. His muscles were twitching uncontrollably, and he began to weep loudly. "Ahhhaaahhhhhaaa," sobbing," I can't help it."

Alarmed by his emotional outburst, and also fearing that the others might hear him, she began to push him up so she could see his face, but he was just too heavy for her to move. She whispered,

"Sean, love, are you okay? What on earth is wrong?"

"Nothing, nothing," he kept repeating as he sobbed more silently.

"Jesus, Sean, you are scaring me. Please tell me what's wrong."

"Nothing Annie, I just…I just…."

"What? Just what?"

"That was amazing."

She felt like punching him but instead began to cry too.

He pushed his chest up to look at her and said, "Oh, sweetie, I am so sorry. I've never done that before. It was just so…."

He kissed her passionately and then wiped her tears from her cheeks.

"You did nothing wrong. It's all about me. I just love ya so much. I have a lot of feelings right now," and he rolled himself off of her and to her side, pulling her into his arms so she could lay her face on his chest.

"You scared me, Sean. I was afraid I had done something wrong."

"Oh, absolutely nothing wrong. You were amazing. Ab-so-lute-ly amazing."

"So, what emotions are you having? Can I help you?"

"Yer helping me. Yer here with me now and loving me."

"But why were you crying?"

"It's not about you. It's all about me. It's scary how much I love ya…how much I want ya…How much I don't want other men to have ya…but I have no right to ask. I have no right."

"That's hardly a reason to cry, Sean. You know I love you, and you are my one and only. There will never be another for me, never."

"Oh, don't say never, dear. You are an amazing person. Yer a beautiful, smart, talented…woman. There is literally nothing ya can't do. Any man would be crazy not to scoop ya up and want to keep ya to himself. I assure you, there are men out there who would love to do just that."

"Like who?" she said in disbelief, looking at him very seriously.

"Like D. There is no doubt in my mind that the man is in love with ya."

"D!" she whispered loudly, "that's ridiculous. There is no way he's in love with me, and besides, he's married."

"So am I, but that hasn't stopped us." Realizing instantly that he had probably said the wrong thing, regardless of how true the statement.

Annie was quiet for a moment or two, contemplating the reminded reality that he was indeed married to another woman. On a cognitive level, she knew it, but on an emotional and spiritual level, he did not feel married. He felt like they were supposed to be together. She turned away from him and began to cry quietly.

He forced her gently to turn over and come back to his embrace. "Please don't cry. None of this is yer fault. I'm sorry for hurting ya. That is never my intention. I'm the bastard here who is hurting everyone. Let's just forget about all of that and just enjoy this little time we have to be together. Ok?"

"Okay," she whispered through tears that continued to flow onto his chest.

Sean felt like a complete swine, not for cheating on his wife, but for hurting Annie, for making her cry. The last thing he ever wanted to do was to have her hurt in any way. She was his one and only too, even if he was not free to marry her.

His frustration came from his intense desire to want to have her as his own, but not being free to validate their relationship in the way they both wanted and needed. He lay there, holding Annie as she fell asleep, stroking her shoulder and arm and trying not to think about her being alone with all of those men.

He felt so jealous and stupid. *Sean, ya selfish asshole. You want it all, but probably don't deserve any of it, certainly not Annie's love.*

The next morning, Sean woke first, wrapped his towel around himself, and quietly exited the tent. He had managed to get up before Jim, which was a surprise. Jim was always up first.

He walked to the river and stepped down a few feet onto a large, stable boulder where he could sit safely and wash without jumping in all the way. His towel slid off his hips to rest behind him as he dangled his feet and calves into the ice-cold water. *Brrr...*he thought, as he reached down to scoop water up in one hand and pour it over his genitals while rubbing vigorously with his other hand to create a lather with his bar of *Ivory soap.*[178] Looking down, he noted the painful retreat from the cold but bravely pulled his penis out from his body to make sure it was extra clean for Annie.

Unlike Stinky, Sean had always valued being clean, perhaps a habit instilled in him by his own mum, who made him wash his

---

178 The soap brand preferred by those who care about nature. It is gentle with very few extra ingredients. It is versatile and has many uses and the character Sean's favorite soap in the field and at home.

face, feet, hands, and private areas with a cloth every day before getting into bed.

In those days, it saved on washing sheets. Most families didn't have electric dryers and had to hang everything on the line. Laundry days lasted the entire day.

"Hey mate, what the hell?" yelled Jim as he walked up behind him.

Sean turned his head to look and saw Jim standing there, completely naked without a towel.

"Oh, hey, Jim. How goes it? We goin up to the mine today to do our paperwork?" he yelled loudly over the roar of the river.

"Yep. We've got to do the paperwork."

"How's Annie? I thought I heard her screaming last night," he said as he put his weight on Sean's sore shoulder to sit down next to him.

"Ya probably heard me, mate."

Hahaha..." What? That was you? No way. Sounded like a woman being pleasured. Ya bastad."

"Oh, shut it. Stupid..." Sean said as he pulled up his feet and legs one at a time to dry.

"What are you two doing?" yelled Annie as she approached. She could only see the tops of their heads and bare shoulders sticking up over the forest carpet. She immediately realized that they were both naked and sitting on a rock together, "Oh, excuse me."

She shyly turned back in the direction of the tent, giggling nervously to herself. *I've heard that guys do that. It's a male bonding thing, I guess, where they sit around naked with each other. Women sure don't do that, or at least, I don't sit around with other women naked and talking. Come to think of it, I don't sit around naked with anyone.*

Annie returned to the tent and noticed the rest of the members of the team sitting on stones and logs around a morning fire, drinking coffee. She couldn't help but see that the men were all still naked. *How on earth are they sitting on those cold rocks? Wouldn't that be painful?* she wondered to herself.

Bart was stooped over with his back toward Annie, his long male package hanging down between his slightly parted thighs, as he busily turned over pieces of bacon in a cast-iron skillet.

They all waved to her, shouting a variety of morning greetings, all inaudible from that distance.

She grabbed her towel and hygiene bottle and waved to the guys as she proceeded to walk to another part of the river, the same spot that she and Sean had bathed together before.

Sean had delivered the mother lode the night before, and she felt the need to feel fresh and clean for her trip to the mine.

Annie reached the pool and slowly entered the frigid water. She lifted her sweatshirt so that it would not get wet and tied a knot in one corner so it would rest above her hips. She lowered her hips into the water and began to clean herself.

It felt surprisingly good. Her body was so warm that steam rose from between her legs. *Fascinating*, she thought. When she finished washing her face and neck, she slowly removed the sweatshirt so that she could rinse her underarms and breasts.

Brrr...too painful, she thought but continued to rinse her body. She turned to reach for the towel that was behind her and was startled to see Sean squatting there, holding her towel out for her.

"Shit, you scared me!" she yelled as she quickly covered her bare breasts.

He was fully dressed and stood up to open her towel wide for her.

She grabbed her sweatshirt and stepped up into his loving arms.

He gently dried her from head to toe without saying a word. When he stooped to dry her legs, she could see Jim watching from a distance, so she quickly put her sweatshirt over her head and covered the rest of her body.

She felt exposed and wondered what on earth Jim could be thinking about it all. *I hope he doesn't see me as a femme fatale,* she thought sadly to herself.

Annie went into their tent to get dressed and heard the men, who were now all dressed and talking. She couldn't hear what they were saying, but they seemed to be laughing with one another. Their camaraderie was inspiring and brought a smile to her face. She would have to have a positive attitude about these guys and get used to their ruggedness. It was going to be okay.

Chapter 36—The Mine Tour

Later that day, the team was shuttled to the mine for a tour of the facility and to familiarize themselves with the local and regional geology.

The visit included an introduction to field safety, which everyone yawned through, and a filing of paperwork which assured the company of little or no liability should they die or be injured in the execution of the project. The employment was considered temporary and contracted work. In addition to liability, the paperwork included a nondisclosure agreement.

The survey project and report would include proprietary information. The only thing they were allowed to take away from the project was their experience, pay, and the hand samples of the suites for educational purposes.

Jim had already negotiated the salaries with each of his friends. The company included travel to the job and back, plus waived camping fees, and provided a stipend for supplies. Everyone felt happy with the pay and would be focused on getting the job done, as well as enjoying the reunion of old mates.

After the detailed indoctrination, everyone was led on a tour of the facility. The mine itself would be a special tour later in the afternoon and had its own set of documents and instructions before the field trip underground.

Annie remained in the main meeting room and read the journal articles provided by Jim. She had read articles about the geology of the area but wanted to know more about the specific mineral assemblages and rock classification, as well as the magma evolution processes that formed the deposits.

She had seen interstitial plagioclase and individual mineral suites present in igneous and metamorphic rocks, but she had never really seen this specific suite of minerals present in a layered fashion in an outcrop. This banded igneous series had mineral assemblages, which were unique to this type of complex.

Jim indicated that they were different, too, from the banded anorthosites she had seen in the previous field trip. This would be her first time to see these rock types all present in a relatively small area.

The mine tour would give them another look at the rocks and minerals and a 3D perspective of the structure.

Annie was not looking forward to the mine tour. She envisioned a small metal cage as are used in coal mines. Little did anyone know, except for Sean, that Annie was extremely claustrophobic and preferred geology above the surface of the earth. She did not mind interpreting core data and seismic information and transferring structural information *orthographically*[179] to a 2D surface map, but going underground in a tiny little elevator?

No, thank you.

She was determined to just say she did and let it be done with that idea.

---

179 Orthographic projections were done before 3D modeling to rotate 3D subsurface structures to a 2D surface sketch, using geometric manipulation.

Claustrophobia

In her first year as an undergraduate student, she enjoyed exploring caves in *Karst*[180] terrain with her classmates. It was exciting--spelunking had become as interesting to her as mountain climbing, until the fateful day that she got stuck with a mountain of rock on her chest.

During cave exploration, the geologist wears pretty much the same gear as to climb a mountain, except for a headlamp and flashlight and of course, ski poles that are not needed in caves. The idea is to enter spaces in the cave system that have not previously been identified or mapped. As a body crawls through small spaces, air must be exhaled out of the lungs to decrease the size of the chest cavity. This involves holding your breath for as long as a minute while wriggling through a small space to enter another larger area.

Annie's chest was not larger than her geology classmates, but her ability to blow most of the air from her chest to reduce the size and continue to hold her breath without panic was perhaps not as practiced. She found that she had to involuntarily take a breath before completing her movement through a tight tunnel. When she breathed in ever so slightly, it was enough to expand her chest and cause her to be wedged near the end of the tunnel. Her inability to move as she struggled, triggered a major panic attack.

Thankfully, she was with two seasoned cave explorers, *Steve,*[181] and *Bill.*[182]

---

180 Karst terrain refers to areas where sedimentary units rich in carbonate minerals are present. The minerals present are easily weathered both chemically and physically, particularly through a process known as solutioning, where the minerals in the rock go into solution when water interacts with the rock and is subsequently carried away, leaving void spaces in the rocks, cave features.

181 Steve was a graduate student in hydrology and was married with children. Fictional character and not meant to represent any particular person living or deceased.

182 Bill was an undergraduate who was friends with Steve. Fictional character and not meant to represent any particular person living or deceased.

Steve had a broad, muscular chest, and he had gone before her, so everyone thought she'd be fine.

Bill was about Annie's size and was stuck in the room behind her until they could get her out of the space between them.

Anna was stuck with her head sticking out of the opening at the exit of the narrow passage. To everyone's dismay, Anna began to *hyperventilate*.[183] She screamed, just like a woman does during the final stage of labor when she is asked to push.

Steve and Bill also felt panicked as they tried to push and pull Anna, but she wouldn't budge.

The very real fear Anna was experiencing was partly due to her vivid imagination.

"Oh my God, I can't move! I can't breathe. I'm going to die," she screamed tearfully.

"Anna! No, you are not! Shut up and listen to me!" yelled Steve.

"Steve, man. You pull, and I'll push, okay?" shouted Bill from behind her in the tunnel.

"OK, dude," shouted Steve.

Feeling very frustrated by Anna's screaming and frightened for her safety, he yelled, "Anna, for Pete's sake, shut the fuck up and listen to the sound of my voice!"

Apparently, Steve had helped his wife give birth and knew what to do when someone was panicking in such a way. "Anna, seriously, shut up, or I'm going to have to slap you."

She became very quiet and passed out. The two men worked to bring her back around.

Steve knew this was going to be a serious medical emergency if he was not able to get her to be conscious. He slapped her delicately and began shallow breaths into her lungs. He didn't want to expand

---

183 Hyperventilation is when a person is breathing at such a rapid rate, that they have more oxygen in their lungs than CO_2. The author is not a medical doctor, so please consult with a medical professional if you are experiencing this kind of issues.

her lungs too much, but he needed her to wake up and be breathing. Steve got her to breathe again, and Bill poked her in the buttocks and pulled on the hairs on her upper thighs.

When she came to, she kicked at Bill, and Steve had to act quickly to calm her down, or the entire process would begin again.

He spoke very softly to her, saying, "Anna, dear, this is like having a baby. You have to listen to me and do exactly what I tell you so we can get you out of this space. Okay? When I tell you, you've got to give me all the air you can push out of your lungs. I know it hurts, but do as I say?"

"But I've never had a baby," Anna said tearfully as she then began to blow out as instructed.

"No, not yet!" said Steve, "just hang on for a sec. I'll say when."

"Bill, when I get to three, you push hard on your end. Anna, when I reach three, you blow as hard as you are able."

"Ok, here we go… one, two, threeeeeee …"

Bill was reminded of the scene from a movie …" is that on three, or, you know, one, two, three, and then go?" He didn't dare say anything to mess up the process at that point. He would take his cue from Anna, who would be blowing out while Steve pulled. His thoughts would have to wait until later on when they could all laugh together.

On Steve's command, everyone did as he instructed.

The rest of Anna's body, along with Bill, was delivered right there in the dark cavern. Anna was free. She coughed and was offered a sip of water. Her chest was terribly bruised from her own panicked wriggling and the tiny rescue breaths, but she was alive and breathing on her own.

Steve told her to cup her hands and continue to breathe in and out. She had blown too much carbon dioxide out of her lungs and needed to have it replaced. She now had too much oxygen, and this was creating the dizziness, tingling, and fainting. In order for them to continue the trek out of the cave, she would have to be able to breathe freely again.

The trio found an exit to the surface, and everyone lived to retell the story.

Anna, though, vowed never to go underground again.

***

The crew joined her in the meeting room, and everyone enjoyed a sack lunch provided by the company.

As Jim began covering mine safety and procedures, Annie could feel her pulse begin to quicken. She started to sweat in anticipation of the mine elevator. Much to her surprise, there were different types of openings into the mine. One was more like a train tunnel. It was reasonably wide, and the rocks seemed to be reinforced--more like a man-made cave. It had rail cars and tracks, which apparently went down into the mine. There was another entrance to the mine from inside the facility. It looked like a standard elevator, with buttons to push.

They all wore hard hats with the classic cyclops light in the center above the eyes, and for this tour, they were taking the elevator.

Now this I can handle, I think, she thought to herself. She hoped she wouldn't have any issues deeper inside. *Just focus on the mining process... the rocks and minerals and the exotic nature of their formation. Imagine the magma injections, the crystallization from the melt, settling, as well as the density-driven layers...remember how fascinating the railroad cut through the Frazier batholith was at field camp...yes, focus on these aspects.*

To Annie's surprise, her mindfulness worked. As long as they didn't have to crawl through any small spaces, she would be fine.

The entire process from exploration, drilling, mining, milling, transportation to smelting, and producing...was utterly fascinating to her.

She would have much to share with her students after this experience. She hoped that the samples they would collect at the surface would be as nice as the ones she saw on the milling carts. In fact, she wondered if perhaps she would be able to collect from there as well.

Inside the mine, the team was introduced to the process of how the mineworkers knew where to remove rocks.

A geologist examines a sequence of rocks in the mine wall and outlines a section on the wall for the teams to remove.

Apparently, according to Jim and one of the mining engineers, this interaction sometimes leads to conflict when the experienced miner questions the judgment of the geologist.

They all laughed, but Annie was reminded of how this same thing happens in the petroleum industry when geologists and drilling engineers have heated debates about the proper angle or extent of drilling for oil on salt domes.

It had to be a source of great frustration for the one taking the orders, especially if the miner had extensive practical experience than the one calling the shots. Degrees don't always bring the same level of expertise and common sense that is gained from experience and knowledge in application.

Annie was fascinated by the exposed sequences in the mine wall. Layer upon layer of different types of cumulates with interstitial plagioclase. Each igneous rock layer formed when new magma was injected into the magma chamber. New minerals crystallized out of the melt and settled in layers at the bottom, one on top of the other.

"This is magnificent," said Annie. "I assume the area we will be surveying will not necessarily be in layers like this, will they? she asked Jim.

"Probably not, dear, but that is why we are doing the surveys. Who knows what we will find out there? There are other deposits in the Beartooths, other than platinum and palladium."

"The environment which produced these beautiful layers of *cumulus*[184] minerals are quite a different set of processes from those of the *diagenetic*[185] processes I am familiar with. My background is in the formation of clastic sedimentary sequences. I love this," said Annie. "Diagenetic sequences could include different temperature regimes but are relatively lower temperatures compared to those of a magma chamber. The only thing I see that these two processes have in common is geochemical systems, gravity, and time."

Jim sprayed the layers with water so that the minerals could glisten in the light from their helmets. "Annie, these are the ultramafic sequences here. Some beautiful stuff fer sure."

Annie squealed in excitement as she recognized that the interstitial minerals were plagioclase feldspar instead of quartz.

Quartz, in particular, can be found in all rock types and is frequently a cementing agent in sandstones and igneous rocks alike.

She had seen the plagioclase in the anorthosite sequences with Jim on the earlier trip but had not had the opportunity to see them otherwise. Her enthusiasm was endearing, even to Stanley.

"Well, that's not something ya see every day," he said to Jim, with a big smile on his face.

"Yep," said Jim with a chuckle. "She gets excited over plagioclase in particular. Just wait until you get to the anorthosites. Now THOSE are truly exciting."

---

184 Cumulus minerals are those which accumulate in layers on the magma chamber floor as a result of crystal fractionation and gravity settling. In layered intrusions, the cumulates (rocks formed from cumulus minerals) tend to grade from mafic to felsic with each sequence of injection and settling into the magma chamber.

185 Diagenesis is the rocking forming processes that begin with deposition of sediments through the uplift of the rock to be exposed to weathering and erosion.

"Oh, and that is for sure olivine! and is this bronzite?" She asked." This must be the *peridotite* zone?"[186]

"Annie, you will love seeing those in outcrop," said Sean, "The weathering colors are very diagnostic. Olivine will become…"

"Brown," she interrupted, "It will have a brown ring around it! Right?"

"….and lichens will grow preferentially on some of the minerals as well." finished Jim.

"It's all so fascinating, isn't it? I can't wait to see the rest of the series and the new sequences in the field," said Annie.

Sean found himself wishing that he didn't have to miss the first weeks of the project. He would love to see Annie in action with these guys. Ah, well, he had made a commitment to teaching just as Annie had and would have to fulfill that obligation first.

Annie continued to learn about the process and stratigraphy of the area, mapping out in her mind the transects.

* * *

That night in the camp, Jim provided all of the food to be cooked for everyone.

Annie was so impressed at how all of the men worked together to wrap the ears of corn and other vegetables in foil and argued about the appropriate seasonings to use on the baked salmon. They clearly had repeated this scene more than once over the years.

She found herself once more on the outside looking in but also enjoying the performance without being part of the drama. It

---

186 Peridotite is an igneous intrusive rock formed by high temperature crystallization of minerals. It is typically made up of the minerals, Olivine – Si04 – high temp silicate, and pyroxenes – like augite and bronzite- high temperature single chain silicates. Combined with Ca rich Plagioclase Feldspar, this suite of rocks is referred to as Ultramafic in composition. Mafic rocks, like basalts, are typically found in the ocean floor crust directly above such intrusive sequences.

was also nice that none of the men assumed that she should cook anything simply because she was female.

They all seemed to have a combined goal of impressing the woman with their cooking abilities. This didn't offend Annie in the least and in fact, was a source of great amusement. She had to cook plenty in her life as a single mom, so it was perfectly okay to sit back and drink a beer while the men tried to outdo each other.

After dinner, Annie helped to carefully collect all debris from their feeding frenzy and pack up all food supplies in the car.

This time, Jim invited her to help him take it all down the hill to the car and trash receptacles. "You did really good today," he said as they walked through the darkness.

"Really?" said Annie.

"Yes, you were identifying minerals and features that were not that easy. I think you impressed Stanley in particular. He mentioned that 'the sheila might be helpful in the field after all.' I just thought you'd like to know that."

"Thank you, Jim. I guess I am a little bit intimidated by all of the experience you have collected here."

"Well, they are really good at what they do, and they are also crude, but you'll never meet a better group of human beings. There is a reason we have all remained friends."

"I'm honored, Jim."

"The honor is mine, Annie. Seani is like my brother, and I've never seen him happier in my life. He clearly loves you."

Annie was silent, while Jim unlocked the car. She safely stored the plastic containers, while he secured the trash in the trash bins and locked them.

As they walked back up the hill, Jim asked, "Are you going to be alright on the plateau without Seani? I know he is worried about having to leave you. Not because he doesn't believe in your abilities, but because he hates leaving you with the likes of that brood."

"Oh, Jim, they seem okay. The nakedness takes some getting used to, but they seem to be warming up to me, I think. We should be 'right,'" she said as she grinned to herself, and both she and Jim chuckled. She was proud of her picking up on the New Zealand phrasing of "You'll be right," without the "be alright" included in the sentence structure.

"Well, no worries, I'll be with you all, and I'll make sure everyone behaves," he said as he gave her a sideways brotherly hug.

"Thank you, Jim. You're the best," she said as she placed her head on his shoulder and allowed him to hug her as they walked.

"We'd best not let Seani see us being such mates," he said with a big smile as they neared the camp. "I'd hate for him to try to kick my arse."

They both laughed as they crested the hill and entered the clearing where the men were all sitting and laughing around a roaring fire.

"Hey, Jim! That was some good eats!" yelled Stanley.

"Yes, thank you, mate!" shouted the others.

"Annie, what'd you think of the food?" asked Sean.

She rubbed her tummy and said, "It was delicious."

Everyone sat around the fire and shared stories from their different jobs and families, told jokes, and of course, bemoaned the global threat of ignorance regarding environmental issues and human populations, the increasing threat of global climate change, and the future of millions of environmental refugees.

"The prags in governments don't have a clue, and the mine owners only care about the dime," said Sean.

"Right there," retorted Jim.

"It's really not the fault of the companies. They are just delivering what is needed for those living in their ivory towers. It's the miners who live in the communities that see the damage. How do they change it when their jobs feed a village? It's a trade-off, mate. Do we starve, or do we deal with the polluted environment and make the best of the situation?"

Everyone nodded and agreed with Stinky.

"Thank goodness for the work of *Father Rubin*.[187] He's pushing for long term care for victims of mercury poisoning in Peru," said Stinky. "He's a right good mate. Righteously pissed about all the skin rashes and damage to babies."

Annie found herself perplexed by the magnitude of the problems they were discussing. In her mind, she hadn't really considered that mining in other countries was also damaging indigenous populations. Her experience was limited to environmental ethics case studies in the U.S., where mostly Indian reservations were exploited for mineral resources and then abandoned with acid mine water and heavy metal pollution in ground and surface waters.

"So, the companies mining in the Andes are not regulated?" she asked.

Everyone began laughing and shouting at the same time.

"Not on your life!" shouted Stinky.

Annie felt a little bit embarrassed by her naïve statement. It was in her nature to assume the positive until the negative was established. She was a real, "cup is half full" kind of gal.

Jim noted that she looked hurt and added, "Annie dear, the rest of the world will never be as kind and generous of heart as you seem to be. You are truly a dove in a hard world."

Sean nodded in agreement and winked at her.

"Ah, lass, mining outside of the US and Britain is a lucrative business with safety considered for the mining process, some for the miners, but with little thought for the left-behinds," said Stinky, as he raised his cup of coffee.

---

187   Father Rubin is a priest and activist in Peru. His is a fictional character and not meant to represent any particular person living or deceased.

"Even in the U.S., where we have strict regulations on mitigation and reclamation, there are sites which are now superfund sites. Those aren't recent, those are from the early 1900s," said Sean.

Annie replied," Would education help in other areas?"

"No, lass, education has nothing to do with it. It's all about money and squeezing the most you are able out of each process with the least damage to the workers and especially their purses. The ecosystems be damned."

"Of course, there's not much on the *Atacama Plateau*[188] anyway, just rocks and *Abuela's Diner*,"[189] said Bart.

"Ah…. you shit for brains!" laughed Stinky, who lunged in Bart's direction, knocking him over onto his back.

Annie was worried they might get into a fight at first, but then laughed too when she saw them all toss twigs and rocks in Bart's direction and laugh. These guys were clearly trying to lighten the mood.

Later that night, as Sean and Annie lay on their backs looking up at the stars, Annie wondered about the Peruvian Andes.

"Sean?'

"Yes, dear?"

"Have you been to this Atacama Plateau before?"

"Oh, yes, more than once. It is a huge, cold, and desolate place, called the 'Spanish Puna De Atacama.' It's roughly 300 km north to south, and over 200 km wide at elevations ranging from, I'd say, 3,000 to 5,000 meters, maybe? It is quite an expanse. It has desert on one side and Cordillera on the other…"

"Ah, so it's in Peru?"

"No, Argentina and perhaps some of Chile too," said Sean. "It's quite a place. Some areas near the mines have mining company amenities and are quite livable. The work done by these guys,

188 Atacama Plateau is the highest plateau in South America.
189 A fictional diner not represented by any current or past establishments in the Andes.

however, is usually fieldwork first and then identifying deposits within the mines. They usually do the mapping, especially Stinky, and leave the mining geologists to do the inside work."

"Wow, that sounds fascinating. Dangerous?"

"Oh, you bet. Hypothermia,[190] a Yeti here and there..." Sean giggled.

Annie hit him in his sore shoulder,

"Owww!" he groaned.

"No, seriously? What is it like? I really want to know."

Sean pushed up on his elbow and looked thoughtfully at Annie, "Well, it's not much different than the plateau here. Ya have to drink lots of water so that ya don't get dehydrated. Ya have to bury your poop with rocks instead of soil...now that's a trick fer sure. No paper. Ya don't wipe and leave the paper, so ya have to have a baggy in yer pack for the used paper."

"Really, wouldn't you just leave the paper with the poop under the rock?"

"Uh, ya could, I guess."

"Who's going to know?" teased Annie.

"I don't know, I guess the poop police might come along and give ya a ticket," Sean answered, as he gently began to tickle Annie in the ribs.

The couple lay there laughing and giggling.

Jim and Stinky looked at one another, as they were still sitting by the fading embers of the fire.

"I wonder if we'll hear Seani screaming like a little girl tonight?" asked Jim.

"Or crying, one of the two," both men laughed at the thought of Sean having difficulty.

---

190 A condition that occurs when the core body temperature drops below a certain temp. People can freeze to death or at a minimum have extreme frost bite on extremities.

"I'd gladly trade places with him," sighed Jim. "That sheila is one of a kind."

"Aye" said Stinky, as both men nodded in agreement.

"Well," said Stinky, "It's time to put out the fire and get some rest."

Both men stood up...Jim unzipped his fly as Stinky pulled down his pants, and both men began to expertly douse the embers. The smoldering ash sizzled, and a pungent smoke rose and drifted upward into the clear, starlit sky. Urinating on the fire was a very efficient use of fluids, as potable water was a luxury and a necessity for camping in higher elevations.

* * *

Chapter 37—Bears and Mosquitoes, Oh My

The next morning, everyone broke camp and filled their packs for the journey to base camp. Annie helped Sean pack up his tent and supplies and load them into his truck.

"You'll be okay up there, sweetie. I know ya will."

"I hope so. I miss you already," she said with a tear in her eye.

"Now stop that!" scolded Sean. "I will see ya in exactly two weeks, and I will be thinking of ya every single night that I have to lay alone in my bunk."

"Will the bears be a problem, do you think?"

"At this time of year, they should all be down at Yellowstone, digging through garbage cans and feasting on tourists," he said with a chuckle. "No, really. There is always a threat up here, and one must always be diligent, especially since Yellowstone is only eighteen miles, as the crow flies, from the plateau where ya will be camping. The plateau is closer to their winter home than their summer one, so don't worry too much...and besides, Stinky will shoot the lower jaw off the bear so it won't eat you."

"Oh, so I should sleep close to Stinky?" she teased.

"Absolutely NOT!"

"Don't worry, just the smell of him will keep the bears and everything else at bay," she giggled.

"Yer greatest issue will be the damned mosquitoes," advised Sean. "They are out by the millions the minute the sun lips up, and they cover yer entire body until the sun goes down. That's why Stinky eats raw garlic. The bastads do not bother him at all."

Sean then hugged her tightly and nervously kissed her goodbye. "Be safe up there, dear."

"I love you."

"Love ya too, sweetie."

Sean waved to Jim and left his Annie standing there with the crew waiting on her to load the truck. He knew that Jim would take good care of her.

As Sean drove away, he felt a tear roll down his cheek. He reached into his pack and pulled out a towel and wiped his nose. It was killing him to leave her behind. *Ah, well, I'd better focus on my students now. Jim has this. I trust him.*

Annie climbed into the back of the large four-wheel-drive truck and handed her pack to Bart, who shoved it into the back with the others. She sat quietly as the vehicle groaned up the mining road past the mine and on up to the plateau.

It was very early, and most everyone seemed exceedingly quiet as Jim drove. Stinky sat shotgun, and Annie was squeezed between Bart and Jackie.

She could already smell the musty odors of mold, camping supplies, rocks, hammers, dirt, and... mint? *Where is the mint coming from?* she thought.

"Is that mint I smell?" she asked.

"Ah sure, dear. Want some?" asked Jim.

"Sure! Since when do you chew mint gum, Jim?"

"Since a sheila joined our team. Don't want to have bad breath now, do I?" grinned Jim as he winked at her in the rearview mirror.

"Hahaha..." laughed the guys.

She grinned and graciously took the piece of gum. "Oh, so now I have to worry about my own bad breath? I see how it is." It felt good to be laughing and joking with the guys. They were beginning to feel like a team.

The crew arrived at the gate at the end of the mining road, and Jim parked the truck. Everyone exited and began to strap their packs on their backs.

Annie added extra straps on her pack to help secure the almost forty pounds of weight. She knew that she might have as much as sixty pounds on the return trip if she collected any samples. The extra straps were needed to keep the pack tight to her body in the places that were needed, around her middle section and above her hips. She didn't want the straps to pull down too hard on her shoulders. It was a design she learned as a graduate student. Her lower back was strained once, and she adjusted her pack to accommodate the stresses.

After two hours of hiking, mostly uphill, they arrived at the plateau. It was a broad expanse with a lengthy meadow below. Nearby was a glacial melt area for water. Downslope and at the opposite end of the meadow was an area of tall shrubs and large boulders for securing clothing and food for the evening.

"This is perfect," said Jim as he began to remove his pack and stepped downslope slightly and into a space that seemed to have been carved intentionally by nature to accommodate their basecamp. It was a flat area about twelve feet by twelve feet, sheltered by a four-foot vertical drop in contour from the plateau surface above. Jim was right--it was perfect.

The tent was a dome-shaped alpine tent with plenty of floor space. Annie stayed out of the way while the experts erected their home.

Stinky climbed into the tent and shouted, "Ladies first!"

Annie's heart jumped into her throat, *What the heck did that mean?*

Jim motioned for Annie to enter, she stooped down, and Stinky was sitting in one corner.

"Lass, ya may pick yer spot before the rest of us if ya want."

"Oh, I see. Sure. I'll get over here."

She chose the exact opposite corner from Stinky.

"Ok, mates, the rest of ya bastads have to sleep out there. We've taken the tent for ourselves."

The guys all laughed and then began throwing their gear into the tent on top of Stinky.

Annie sat shyly in her corner and watched as the other three men entered the tent and laid out their bags. She unrolled her pad and bag and positioned her pack at the opening, like a pillow. Her spot was set, and to her amazement, they all fit. All five of them. Apparently, Sean would be the sixth man when he arrived.

Jim put his bag next to Annie's and winked as though to let her know that he would make sure nobody bothered her. She was so grateful for Jim. He treated her like he was her big brother, much different than when they first met. She now trusted him with her life.

Annie exited the tent and walked downslope to find wood for their campfire. She entered the small grove of rocks and shrubs and found small pieces of gnarly, gray wood. It was dry and would be perfect. The sun was intense, and she was grateful for her hat and her prescription sunglasses. Her arms looked kind of raw to her through the sunglasses, and there was a chill in the air. It was time to hydrate again.

As she walked back up the slope, she noted a slight discomfort in her stomach and a dull headache. *Perhaps I just need to drink some water and lay down for a minute or two,* she thought.

"Ya doin ok?" asked Jim.

"Well, I'm feeling a little bit of a headache."

"Ah, that's normal. Ya just need to drink more water. Here, drink up."

"I think I'll just go lay down for a while if that's okay."

"Sure, lass, drink up, and rest. We'll check on ya later," said Stinky.

Annie drank a full bottle of water and took an aspirin she had stashed in her pocket. She lay down on her pack and put her hands on her stomach.

Oh gosh, I sure hope I'm not going to be sick. At that moment, her tummy rumbled, loud enough for others to hear.

Lass, "Sounds like yer going to need to pass some air."

Jim stuck his head in the tent and said, "Yes, going up in elevation means that the air in your intestines expands. There's only really one way to remedy that one."

"How is that?" asked Annie.

"Patero," said Jim, "Ya know, uh, break wind."

"Oh," said Annie. "I'm not sure I know how to do that with others listening, without, you know?"

Jim entered the tent and knelt down on his knees and whispered, "Ya see, ya pull yer knees up to yer chest and just…you know…let it out."

"What are you doing in there?" asked Bart.

"Ah, nuttin," said Jim, "just talkin'."

Annie was grateful that he wasn't making a big deal out of her particular discomfort.

"I'll leave ya to it," said Jim as he winked and exited the tent.

"She okay?" asked Stinky.

"Ah sure," just a little headache from the elevation changes.

"Me too," said Bart. "Guess there will be no pissing around up here tonight."

Annie closed her eyes and slowly expelled air a little at a time, trying to be as silent as possible. In the process, she nodded off to sleep.

A short while later, she could hear the men talking and making a fire. After a few moments, she also heard something that sounded like a low, extended, muffled moan, followed by Jim and others, yelling, "Ah, no! glad you didn't do that in the tent."

Apparently, Stinky had let a fart.

"Aye, mate, my eyes are watering!" yelled Jackie. This exclamation was then followed by a long, high pitched, whining noise, much like the sound made when someone blows on a trumpet mouthpiece.

"Ah, damn guys!" shouted Jim. "Jackie! Agh, that is nasty. Did something die inside of ya?"

All of the men were shouting and laughing amidst a period of extended flatulence.

Annie began to giggle at the activity. With each laugh, she began to toot…hers were tiny, little high pitched "pfft…pfft. Pfft…pfft." The more she giggled, the more she tooted. Finally, she dropped her legs down flat and continued to release gas in a rhythmic frumping noise that coincided with each giggle.

Before long, everyone was laughing hysterically.

Annie was laughing so hard that she couldn't sit up and she couldn't leave the tent. She was reduced to a giggling, tooting mess. The sound of her being tickled kept the men laughing too. Her laughter was infectious. She was notorious for once being thrown out of a comedy club as an undergraduate because her laughing interfered with the comedy skit.

"You're killing us out here!" yelled Jackie.

"She must have learnt it from Seani. He does that too, doesn't he?" laughed Jim.

"Come on out and have a cup of warm soup, lass. It's gonna be a beautiful evening."

Annie exited the tent to see the setting sun and a low hanging mist above the meadows far below. "Wow!" exclaimed Annie, "That is gorgeous."

"Nothing better," said Jim reclining against his pack.

Bart pulled a metal cup out of his pack and wiped the inside with his shirttail. "Here, have a sip. It's my famous dehydrated lentil soup.

"Eat this too," said Stinky, as he handed her a garlic clove. "This will keep the skeeters off ya and improve your patero skills ta boot."

Annie peeled the garlic clove and placed it in her cup of soup and allowed the steam to rise and enter her nostrils. "This smells great. Thank you. I feel better already, guys."

The new friends sat around the campfire and watched the stars come out one by one.

"So, tell us about yourself," asked Bart. "You are from Texas, right?"

"That's oil country that is," said Stinky.

"Well, yes. It is oil and gas country, for sure."

"Do you have family there?" asked Jackie.

"Yes, I have two sons. They are great kids, one is seven, and the other is six. They are with their grandparents while I do this job."

"Aye, I have little ones too, but my ex-wife has them. Sadly, I don't see much of em except around Christmas."

"Oh, I'm sorry," said Annie. "I know that divorce is difficult, especially when children are involved."

"You are divorced then, lass?"

"It hasn't been settled yet, but the state of Texas has it in the works."

"Let's talk about somethin less depressin, okay?" said Jim.

"Right, there?" said Bart.

"I guess I'd better take care of a few things before it gets too dark," announced Annie, as she got up and walked upslope and out of the view of the camp.

"It must be rough to be a sheila in the field," said Bart. "Never considered that they can't just stand up and piss on the fire like us."

"She'll be right," said Jim. "She's been doing it for a while now and knows exactly what she is doing."

As Annie walked, she looked down at her boots and listened to the sounds of her own steps on the weathering rocks beneath. This was the highest she had been in elevation. As a young girl, she had always wanted to climb mountains, but just never had the means. Being in Texas, which was very flat, didn't help.

She had driven to the top of Pikes Peak once, which was a higher elevation but only for a few hours up and down. In the first year of teaching field camp, she led a team of students up a Pioneer peak to an elevation of 10,000 feet, but that experience too didn't last very long. They had to make their ascent and descent on the same day.

When they reached the top, the students felt bewildered to discover that a troop of girl scouts had signed the logbook before them. It was a humbling experience for sure, since they felt like they had just climbed Everest.

After taking in the vastness of the Beartooth mountains, she turned her gaze to the northwest, where the sun would not completely set but instead illuminate the sky near the horizon. *I wonder if Sean is at the campus yet? I wonder if he's looking in this direction and wondering about us. Sigh.*

The campfire was now a low glow lighting up the faces of her friends, the tent, and the ground around them. She stopped for a moment, some distance away, and took in the view of the guys all relaxing, talking, and looking up at the sky.

Jackie pointed to the Milky Way, which was just becoming visible.

What a spectacular sight to behold, Annie thought. *I wish I could stay here forever.*

Thank you, Lord, for the opportunity to be here with these extraordinary men. I pray that they will accept me as a friend and a colleague too. Please protect us all as we sleep here and do fieldwork together... Amen

Jim saw Annie walking back and stood up as she approached. To a woman like Annie, this was the sign of respect by a male. She felt honored that she had earned his respect.

"Right there?" he asked.

"Yes, I believe I will turn in now if that's okay with you guys."

"Sure, lass. We'll be joining ya soon."

Annie entered the tent, removed her boots, placing them carefully between her and the side flap. She slipped her clothing and socks into the clothing bag just outside the entrance, as Jim had instructed, and crawled into her bag. She turned with her face to the side of the tent, closed her eyes, and began to pray the rosary, *Please watch over my boys, blessed mother. Wrap your loving arms around them and protect them from all harm. Hail Mary, full of grace...*

When the men entered the tent, they were surprisingly quiet. Apparently, they were hoping that they would not wake Annie with their activity. Jim got in his bag and turned his back to Annie's. The rest of them zipped and unzipped a few times, and then they seemed settled.

A little later in the night, Annie felt Jim move his back up against hers.

It felt good to her, as she was a little bit chilled. She didn't move away and pushed back against him to let him know it was ok for them to be touching one another in this manner. She felt very relaxed and safe with Jim near her.

Jim was relieved because he could rest, knowing that she was okay. Touching her allowed him to be able to keep track of her in a very tangible way.

The next morning, Annie woke but remained silent until all of the men had left the tent. She had decided to wait until Jim retrieved their clothes before getting out of her sleeping bag.

"Annie, got the clothes here if you want to get dressed," Bart said as he put the bag of clothes inside the tent.

She was so happy to find all of her clothing, including both socks. She would not change clothes or socks for a few days.

As she exited the tent, she noted that the men were all dressed. *Well, this is different!*

Smiling at them all, she held out her cup to Jim, who poured her a cup of hot water.

"What's this?" she asked.

"Have a packet of freeze-dried coffee, lass. It's much easier than carrying coffee grounds and having to dispose of them, too."

"But, but," she muttered, pouting with her lower lip out and quivering.

"Don't worry, I have a few coffee beans to chew on too, if that doesn't hold ya," said Jackie.

Annie nodded gratefully, indicating that she would certainly take him up on a bean or two later on.

"Ah, ya don't need those beans. It won't help your headaches up here. It just makes them worse because it adds to the dehydration," said, Stinky.

"Oh?" said Annie. "I thought the caffeine would help the headache."

"Not if the headache is caused by dehydration."

"What about aspirin?"

"Sure, aspirin might help."

"Ouch," said Bart, as he slapped his arm. "Damned vampires are out."

Annie looked down at her own arms to see them covered with mosquitoes, her legs too.

"What the heck? What do I do?" she said as she looked at Stinky and brushed them from her cheeks. They were all over her face.

"Here, I have some organic shit that will repel them for a little while," said Bart.

"Oh, thanks. I have some too. Just didn't believe they would really be this bad."

"Yes, they are awful," said Jim. "But I think most of us are immune to them by now."

"Eat loads of garlic, fart a lot, and keep 'em off of ya. That's what I do."

The team finished up their breakfast, cleaned their dishes, and stowed their gear. Each one packed their day packs with lunch and made sure the water bottles were filled and stowed properly.

Stinky gathered everyone around and discussed the transect for the day and the plan for covering the area. Bart and Jackie would lay out a transect line for them using surveying tools. Jim, Annie, and Stinky were to move along that transect, with two of them collecting data three meters on either side of the center transect line.

"Hmmm, I've never seen this done before," she said. "This seems very efficient."

"Well, it is highly redundant in sedimentary terrain, for sure, as most things don't change drastically, lateral to the transect, but in metamorphics and igneous, in particular, there can be significant changes within a few meters."

"Ok. You are the boss. Let's do this."

After a week and a half of collecting field data and each producing a photogeologic map, the team decided to walk laterally to scout out the next area that they would traverse.

Jim took a higher contour above Annie, and Stinky took a lower one. As Jackie said, "You will be making an Annie sandwich."

With each at a different elevation, they could better see the lateral extent of their mapped features. Bart and Jackie walked along the highest contour, where they could see everyone. Annie was looking at the ground and trying to keep her footing, as well as look for differences on her contour. Jim and Stinky were doing the same.

Bart and Jackie began shouting excitedly and pointing towards Stinky.

Annie looked up and waved at them and then noted that Jim was now very excited, too. They all seemed to be yelling and pointing in the same direction.

Stinky eventually looked up and wondered what was going on.

Annie then heard Jim distinctly say, "Bears." Not Bear, but BEARS!

They all looked toward Stinky and were horrified to see a large tan-colored bear with a smaller one following. Both with their ears flattened to their heads and running down the slope on the opposite side of a down sloping meadow across from Stinky.

Jackie and Bart were sliding sideways down the slope toward Jim, and Jim and Annie were frozen in place.

As the bears got closer to Stinky, Annie covered her eyes. She did not want to see him be attacked. When she heard Stinky shouting and not screaming in pain, she peaked through her fingers to see him doing jumping jacks and shouting something.

After a moment or two, she was able to make out what he was saying…

"I'm a bear! I'm a fucking bear!"

The bears stopped suddenly and looked confused.

Stinky then turned sideways and started moving his arms in an up and down motion, screaming the entire time, "I'm a bear, a fucking bear!"

Annie was so confused. She had been taught to roll into a ball and protect her head, never to scream and yell and jump up and down. *What madness was this?* And it seemed to be working. [191]

After a few minutes of confused stammering, the bears moved away from Stinky, and he continued on his trek, as though nothing had happened.

Later on, after they all rejoined, everyone slapped Stinky on the shoulders and back, congratulating him on his avoidance of the mama grizzly and her cub.

"Aye, she was going to get me for sure."

"I have never seen anything like that in my life," said Annie. "I was terrified for you."

"Well, ya see, the Innuits taught me that trick. Apparently, bears don't see very well, and if you can make yourself look bigger from a distance and if you sound ferocious, sometimes, you can confuse them. It doesn't always work, though. I was pretty damned lucky mainly because I am a big, ugly guy, who could easily be mistaken for a bear."

"But you had a gun. Why didn't you use it?" asked Bart.

"Well, I only shoot as a last resort. She was probably just trying to protect her cub or to teach her cub something. It's their habitat. We are just visiting."

"You don't think they'll visit us tonight in our tent, do you?" asked Annie.

"Ya never really know, lass. Odds are? NO. They don't like to be out, usually, in the heat of the day and don't stray too far from their dens at this time of year. If it were October or worse November, then the odds might be higher."

---

191 This fictional experience depicts a method for evading a bear attack that is not written as an official method. Before hiking in the wild, please consult with ranger stations, access permits, stay on marked trails, and follow the procedures explained to you by national park rangers and officials.

"Besides, Stinky here will shoot their mouths off so they can't chew," teased Bart.

Annie didn't let on, but she was totally freaked out by the experience and would not rest well. That night, Annie asked if she could sleep between Jim and Bart.

The two gladly accommodated her request, and she found herself with Jim's back against hers and Bart's back to her face.

"Ya comfy back there, lass?" asked Stinky. "We are like spoons in a drawer."

Everyone laughed.

Annie felt safe and didn't even mind the flatulence or snoring.

"Annie, you'd better protect me from the bears," laughed Jackie.

"Shut it! Yelled Jim. "Let Annie have sweet dreams, okay mate?"

Chapter 38—The Sixth Man

After almost two weeks of mapping, the team hiked back to their truck, packing out their trash and leaving their base camp and storage area for their return trip.

"Man, I can't wait to hit the river."

"Me, either, mate."

"I can't wait to have a piss."

"Having clean hair…that is what I want," added Annie.

At this point, Annie's hair was feeling a little funky, and she wasn't worried about being naked in front of these guys if it meant getting the salt and dust off of her body. She, too, was more than ready for the river, fresh clothing, real food, and a beer.

As they approached the lower campsite, Annie saw Sean's tent. *Oh shit, I don't want him to see me like this!* she thought.

Jim looked in the rearview mirror at Annie and said, "Just run like hell to the river."

The doors of the truck flew open, and the guys took off to the river. Annie was in the middle in the back seat and didn't see Sean walk up from behind.

"It's about time, you filthy bastads. I was beginning to think I'd have to go up there looking fer ya."

"We are going to the river, mate. All of us," said Jim. "Wanna come?"

Sean waited patiently for Annie to emerge and pulled her into his arms.

"Sean, I'm filthy," she said shyly.

"You taste pretty good to me. Just like I like ya, sweaty, salty, and smelling of garlic."

"Ha-ha, well, I had to do something to keep the skeeters off, don't ya know," she said in her best New Zealand accent.

Sean helped her carry her pack up the hill. After retrieving towels and a bar of ivory soap, the couple walked to their favorite spot in the river just to find all of the guys in their place. They were screaming, naked, and covered in lather.

"It is brutal cold in here, lass," shouted Stinky. "You'd best keep your tits high."

"It's all going in!" she shouted back to him.

Sean was a little jealous of the familiarity between Annie and Stinky, but also happy that the guys seemed to genuinely like her.

"I knew they'd love ya."

"Was there ever any doubt?" she responded as she began to strip off her clothes and walk into the cold water.

The guys all cheered at the sight of her screaming as she entered the pool, totally naked.

Sean stood on the bank and laughed too, as he proudly watched her shed her inhibitions as well as her clothes. He also couldn't help but notice that she looked thinner. *I hope she is eating like she should.*

"Come on in, Sean," yelled Jim.

Sean stripped off his clothes, joined Annie, and began to rub her all over with soap.

"Hey, no fair! Sean needs to lather us all up now," shouted Jackie.

"You wish!" yelled Annie as she splashed water at him and rubbed her suds all over Sean.

The team rinsed and dried and made their way back to camp, where the guys pitched Jim's tent. The sun was shining, and it was late afternoon.

Sean brought Annie's favorite camp chair from his car, and the couple sat and relaxed in the warmth of the lower elevation as the guys collected wood for a fire and brought supplies from the truck.

"Thank you for the brews," said Annie as she sipped her beer.

"That would be what I would want after two weeks up there."

"So, tell me about yer plateau adventure. Did ya find gold?"

"Well, we saw bears! That was pretty terrifying."

"Bears? Like more than one? No way!"

"Oh, yes. Stinky was walking on a lower contour near a drainage area, and here they come."

"There was a mama and her baby, bee-lining it for Stink," interrupted Bart.

"It was pretty intense," said Jim.

"Did he shoot them?" asked Sean.

"NO!" everyone said at the same time.

"The bugger danced," laughed Jim.

"No. He did calisthenics," said Annie. "He literally was doing jumping jacks and …Lord, it was like nothing I've ever seen before."

"How would you know; you had your eyes covered!" teased Jackie.

Sean sat back and laughed at the way they were all talking over one another. He would have to wait and hear from Stinky, he supposed, to get the real story.

"Well…it was pretty interesting geology. I saw some banded iron *(BIF)* [192] that looked almost like a *migmatite*.[193] There is a pretty good unit up there that is easy to track laterally," reported Annie.

"Wow, I bet that messed up the compass readings," laughed Sean.

"Sure did," Annie laughed back. "Seriously, it is beautiful up there. I can't wait to get back up there and finish the next section. It will be great to have you there too."

Her eyes were so full of love as she fixed her gaze on Sean's.

"Yes, sweetie. I have really missed you too." Sean reached his hand over and took hers and pulled it over to his lap, just as he had done so many times before.

They sat there close to one another, holding hands, and watching the sun go down on the flatirons in the distance.

Jim and Stanley were cooking hot dogs and beans, while Bart and Jackie chopped onions.

"I sure hope the bears don't like BBQ beans," said Annie. "Those smell so good."

Stinky rubbed the gun strapped to his thigh and winked as he smiled at Sean. "No worries, lass. We got this."

* * *

After a two-day respite, the team returned to their basecamp, and Sean now took his spot next to Bart as he and Jim made an Annie sandwich in the tent.

---

192 Banded Iron Formation (BIF) is a Precambrian metamorphic rock that is foliated (minerals have a preferred orientation) and is the result of tectonic forces. It is a layer usually associated with the first appearance of oxygen in the atmosphere, hence the oxidized or redness to the layers.

193 A migmatite is a rock, like a gneiss (highest level of metamorphism in a progressive sequence) which is experiencing enough dynamic stresses to raise the heat enough to partially melt the rock. It's a step beyond metamorphism but not yet to a molten state that would produce an igneous rock.

Annie hugged Sean from behind while having her back up against Jim. She felt like she was exactly where she was supposed to be.

As she lay there enjoying the warmth of their bodies, she felt a twinge of guilt as she hadn't prayed or thought of her boys over the last few days. She quietly asked God to forgive her and promised to be less selfish in the future.

The following days were spent in the newest area and mapping the extent of units discovered in the second area. Jim seemed pleased with their work and with the exploration survey results.

As the team sat around the fire, Annie looked at each one of her 'brothers'...yes they felt like brothers to her now. Sean was her one and only and they were all his brothers, and hers too now by extension and shared experiences.

She didn't want it to end. The thought of them leaving made her very sad. The thought of her having to leave Sean...it was almost too much to bear. Annie could feel tears welling up in her eyes, so she got up to walk upslope to take care of her bladder before turning in. When she squatted to pee, she noted that the rocks below her were slightly pink.

"Oh no, not that," she thought. Her period shouldn't be this early, but that would explain her weepy feelings. "Damn it. Oh well," she thought as she pulled a tampon from her pocket and inserted it just in case. *This was at a time when menstrual cups were not as easily accessible.*

She took her hygiene bottle and rinsed her bottom thoroughly and then washed the rocks too. Just for good measure, she walked a short distance beyond, grabbed a few rocks, and placed them on top of the area where she had rinsed everything. There was not much discussion about menstruating females and the smell of blood attracting bears, but it was in the back of her mind. She had been told that it was an old wives' tale--that bears would smell that and attack.

When she returned, Jim and Sean both stood up. It was kind of sweet, Annie thought. Her guys were such gentlemen. She smiled at them both and sat down near the fire.

"Are ya chilled, gal?" asked Bart.

"Just a little," she answered.

"Here, take my jacket," said Sean, as he took his off and put it over her shoulders.

"Guys," she began… "I think I'm getting my period."

"Oh gross," shouted Bart in a teasing manner.

"I think I might be getting mine too."

"Seani, bet you are happy about that, right?" they all laughed.

"No, guys. I'm serious. Will that be a problem for us in terms of wildlife, bears?"

"Well, you're not in the water with a bunch of sharks, lass," said Stinky. "Don't worry about it. Just take care in packing the trash. It goes down and will be in the same area as our other stuff, so make sure it is clearly marked. You can use one of the thick bags that help to mask smells. It will be okay."

"Wow, dude. How do you know so much about this kind of stuff?"

"Well, I've been on camping-fishing trips with sheilas before. We weren't doing field work, but we were in the backcountry," said Stinky. "It can't be too much different."

"Thank you, Stink," said Sean. "I've honestly not read too much about it, either. It's not a topic that is covered in field manuals."

"Delicate subject," said Bart.

"Well, with more and more women entering this field, perhaps it should be something that we all begin to talk about," said Annie. "I honestly feel better now that Stanley told me about his experience, but it still bothers me just a little. I've done field work in other areas and there you could dig a hole and bury your stuff. Up here, it's mostly rock. Kind of difficult to bury anything."

"Well, we cover our poop with rocks. Maybe the same could be done for other stuff?"

"I think I'll just do what I've always done and carry a bag with me in case I need it. I usually try to take care of my bathroom stuff at the same time each day, just like you guys. My concern was for your safety and mine while we slept."

"Ah, well, lass. I'm not worried at all. We are in no more danger now than before. Don't give that another thought."

"Thank you," said Annie, as she walked over and leaned down to give him a hug.

He looked up at her lovingly, "Don't worry. Okay?"

Sean was so impressed at how tenderly Stinky responded to Annie. He wasn't jealous in the least because he could see that he seemed to have genuine affection and respect for her and also for her relationship with him.

None of the guys had asked him once about Sophia or his marriage. It simply didn't matter to them. They loved Sean, and it was obvious that he loved them, too. They also seemed to know that he was not with Annie as a fling. He obviously loved her very much, and they could see that in his body language and their interactions.

In the following days, Annie discovered that she had only had a light period and the rest of the field work and camping went on with no attacks by wildlife of any kind.

Their last night at their camp, Bart pulled out a 30-year-old bottle of scotch. "Aye mates, I was hoping to share this with my missus on our 30th anniversary, but since the *moll*[194] left me, I can't think of anyone better to share a sip with."

"Are you sure?" asked Annie.

---

194 Moll, short for Molly, is a rude term to describe a prostitute or a whore.

"I've never been more sure of anything, love."

Each of them passed the bottle like it was made of pure gold, and "poured a tin."

Bart raised his tin cup and spoke, "To my tribe. To my brothers, and my sister. We will share this bottle again, and I promise ya, it won't be touched until then, *sláinte*."[195]

Annie became tearful as everyone realized that their time together was soon ending.

Jim raised his tin too, "You are my tribe, mates. You did one hell of a good job here, and I can't thank you enough. Until we meet again."

"Here, here!" they all shouted as they raised their tins.

---

195 A Gaelic word that means, "health." It is a drinking toast in Ireland and Scotland, and for kiwi of that descent.

Chapter 39—All Good Things

Jim, Sean, and Annie finished their work on the survey project, and the three friends prepared to end their summer engagement.

As they all sat near the fire, sipping beers, Annie reached over and touched Sean's hand. With a lump in her throat, she asked, "Sean? Is there any way you could come down to Texas and visit? I can't stand waiting until December."

Taking her hand in his, he looked very sad and sighed, "I wish I could, dear. It's just not possible. I'll barely be able to make the meeting in San Francisco this fall. Thankfully, I have a grad student who will be presenting a poster. Otherwise?... It would be difficult to swing." He was clearly worried about being able to get time away and funding to make the trip.

Annie tried not to act disappointed, after all, what did she really expect him to do? He had a family, too. She patted his hand and offered, "It's okay. I understand. We will make it to San Fran. It will work out."

She did not want him to feel bad and realized she had been asking for something that would be clearly impossible, given his situation. *I was just being selfish,* she thought to herself.

"If you are coming out this year, you know I'll do what I am able to help, if you need travel money," he said, "Of that, you can be sure. But that will probably be the only way to see ya before the summer."

"I've got graduate students and fall classes to get settled first, and then I'll see if I can justify a trip without presenting a paper too," said Annie. "Perhaps there is a field trip that I could go on for continuing education."

"Jim? Are you able to come out this year? I think Ed is coming."

"Not sure, Seani. I am stuck here and need to see where the next project takes us."

"Why don't you two come back to the valley and spend some time next summer?" He clearly was going to miss them both very much.

"Annie, ya don't have to bring him, either, if ya don't wanna," said Jim, not even looking to Sean for permission. He loved Annie like a sister, and she would remain important to him for the rest of their lives.

"You've got a deal," she said as she hugged Jim's neck.

Annie didn't want it to end. Her life with Sean in the Stillwater was the time of her life.

Her heart ached for her boys, but the work was so engaging, she barely had time to think of them, and when she did, she felt enormous guilt.

Sean missed his daughters, and he also missed Sophia, but not in the way that Sophia was missing him. He was hopelessly devoted to the mother of his children, but their relationship paled in comparison to what he had with Annie. This reality bothered Sean, but he had no solution that wouldn't destroy his entire family.

As Jim and Annie cleaned up their final meal together, Sean walked down to the river to wash up. His thoughts were of his sweet little girls, who no doubt missed their daddy. He, too, had been so busy with fieldwork, writing, and teaching that he had not had a great deal of time to miss them. There were no cell phones at this time, only radio phones for emergencies and the occasional payphone, but Sean had managed to pen a letter to each of them while at camp and once at the mine.

Sean did not share these thoughts with Annie. It was the one part of his life that he kept to himself. It was his burden to carry alone.

The next morning, Jim and Sean drove Annie to the airport, and once again, Annie and Sean tearfully parted ways.

As the two men watched her disappear into the terminal, Jim asked, "Mate, may I ask you a personal question?"

"Sophia?" answered Sean.

"Ya, what is your endgame here? It's none of my business…"

"Yer right. It is none of yer business," interrupted Sean sharply.

"But, mate, Annie?" sighed Jim.

"I know, I know. I'm a complete and total jerk," Sean said sadly.

"Does Sophia know?"

"No, and if I can find a way, she will never know. Aye, Jim. What the hell am I going to do? I'm in love with em both."

"Yer eventually gonna have to make a choice. Ya know that, don't ya? I don't envy ya, Seani. The guys love Annie too."

"Did they ask about her?"

"Na, it's not their way. It's your business, mate. But Stinky did say he was kicking your arse if you hurt her. So, look out."

"Ha-ha…I'd deserve it that's fer sure."

"I'll kick your arse, too," said Jim in a serious tone. "She's a one in a million."

"Ya. She's my soul mate. I don't want to ever live without her."

"Well, you'd better do what's right. You know what's right?"

The two friends hugged goodbye, and Sean began his long, lonely journey back to California, without Annie.

Annie returned home to her boys, Betty, and MSU. She was particularly proud of the fact that she had made almost ten thousand dollars and had a story about gold and bears to tell her boys.

"Was it a big bear mommy?" asked Ben in a worried tone.

"Of course, it was a big bear!" shouted Bobby. "Bears in Yellowstone can get up to a million pounds!"

"Well, not quite a million," chuckled Annie. "The bears in Alaska are the really big ones and they can get up to 800 pounds I believe."

Ben hugged her tightly and sweetly said, "Mommy, please promise me you won't go back there again. I don't want a bear to eat you."

"Oh, sweetie. I wasn't in any danger. There was a big guy there named Stanley, and Stanley had a huge gun."

The boy's eyes widened. "How big a gun was it, Mommy? Was it bigger than Grandpa's?

His is the biggest in the world!" shouted Ben.

Annie laughed, "It was as big as Grandpa's, and Stanley would have killed the bear

before he would have let it hurt mommy."

"Well, you are not allowed to go again without Stanley and his big gun. Okay, Mommy?"

"I promise," she said, smiling at Betty who was seriously charmed by the entire exchange.

"Anna, you always have such fascinating stories to tell. You also come back from each trip looking thinner and thinner. Let's get you some real food, okay?" Betty gave her a huge hug and led her to the kitchen, where she served pound cake and coffee.

After settling back in with her boys, Anna went back to her normal routine of teaching, grading, mentoring students and being a single mother.

Robert was a good father and spent quality time with his boys. He even came over once or twice and cooked his famous deep-dish pizza for everyone.

Annie found that she enjoyed being friends with Robert again, but made sure she was never alone with him. Even with the divorce looming, he still desired her sexually.

Over the next couple of months, Annie and Sean spoke to each other weekly. It wasn't enough for either one of them, especially for Annie, who had to be without the physical contact of her lover, but she would never complain. She loved Sean and knew the reality and limitations of their relationship. It wasn't fair, but it was what it was, and she was grateful for the time she was able to spend with the love of her life. The song by Patsy Cline, *"I've got your picture, she's got you,"* certainly took on a new meaning for Annie.

Eventually, she saw their relationship as kind of a Hepburn and Tracy relationship. Spencer Tracy was married and would never leave his wife, and Katharine Hepburn was comfortable with living alone and maintaining a relationship with her soulmate and best friend, outside of his marriage.

Katharine Hepburn never married, and Spencer Tracy never divorced, but their love endured. This was Katharine Hepburn's cross to bear, and it seemed that it, too, was Annie's.

Sean loved Annie but had the tougher situation of the two in maintaining their relationship. He had a wife, and she was a very nice person.

Sophia had noticed small changes in their relationship, especially in the more intimate interactions. He was always quiet anyway, but he had become more and more prone to spending time alone writing in his journals.

With his upcoming trip to San Francisco, she noted a quickness in his step and a glint in his eye. He seemed very excited and happy to be going this year. One morning at the breakfast table, she asked, "Sean, would you like for me to go with you to San Fran? It would be fun to go shopping for Christmas there while you go to your meetings... I could leave the girls with Alice?"

Sean choked on his coffee and responded, "What? Really? This close to the end of the school year?"

"Well yes. You've been gone a lot this past year and I thought it might be an interesting trip. Maybe we could spend some time together."

"Um, well, it will be very boring, and I am chairing a session. I'm afraid I wouldn't have much time with ya there, either. You would be so bored. Besides, the girls need ya here, don't they?"

"I suppose you are right."

Sean was thankful that she dropped the subject but found himself feeling paranoid and perhaps a little fearful that she suspected something. *I am going to have to keep myself in check about this trip.*

He in no way wanted Sophia to feel hurt or neglected by his leaving again. Sean felt so guilty and worried but couldn't wait to see Annie.

For the next few weeks, he spent more time on his work, students, grading, and journaling. He was trying his hardest to avoid any more discussion of his leaving.

Sophia found herself at times wondering what was keeping his mind so preoccupied and suggested that they take a family vacation back to New Zealand to visit his parents. In her mind, this might be the perfect time to take his mind off his work and have him reconnect with her and the children.

He attended all ball games, dance recitals and family events for his children and her but was also deeply devoted to his research projects and graduate students. Sean had two wives, and one of them was his work. Sophia had no idea that there was a third love in his life.

With Sophia's insistence and Sean's intense guilt over his upcoming trip to be with Annie, he agreed to allow her to plan a trip for the family to New Zealand. It was settled, the next spring and perhaps even the summer, Sean would take them all home for a visit. He didn't want to take the trip at that time, but he felt he had little choice with Sophia feeling neglected by his work and travel.

Chapter 40—San Francisco

Annie and Sean met in San Francisco and shared a room within walking distance of the conference center. As usual, he paid for the room and food, and she paid for her own transportation and registration fees.

The hotel was built in the early 1900s with French architecture and furnishings. This part of the city had many sidewalk cafes and shops, with an atmosphere that Annie assumed reflected Paris. Even the Catholic church nearby was built in the late 1800s and was of a classic French Notre Dame design.

Annie got up first to get ready for the first day of the conference. She had brought her favorite power suit, which consisted of black slacks, a black jacket, a wine-colored silk blouse, and her favorite dress shoes--black flats.

The shower was a modern design with French décor. Annie selected the rose-scented soap and a soft white washcloth and entered the shower. The water was very cold but warmed up to boiling hot. She squealed out in shock from the cold and then the hot. *This is going to be fun*, she thought.

"Bonjour, ma Cherie," said Sean as he entered the shower.

"Oh, hi," said Annie, as she rinsed her eyes to see his smiling face. "I see you waited until I got the temperature just right."

They both laughed and the look on his face suggested he was immensely happy and, in a mood, to cause trouble...perhaps tickling her or soaping her entire body, not unlike he'd done at the Stillwater. *What on earth is he up too*, she thought.

Sean pulled her away from the water and into his arms as he spoke in a sexy voice, "*Car, vois-tu, chaque jour je t'aime davantage, aujourd'hui plus qu'hier et bien moins que demain.*"[196]

Annie did not speak French and had no idea what he said, but she did remember a phrase from her freshman class that she had hoped to hear one day, "Tu es mon amore," which as she remembered meant, "You are my love."

"Ah, amore de ma vie," he responded. "Love of my life."

Sean kissed her passionately on the lips and then lifted her into the air, almost hitting her head on the ceiling of the bath. He looked up at her breasts as the water ran over her nipples. She was like a sculpture of a Greek goddess with her head back and her back arched.

"Oh, he groaned...what ya do ta me, Annie."

He sucked on her nipples and felt them harden. With this, he lifted her onto his shoulders and pushed her gently against the wall of the shower. Annie wasn't sure what he was doing, but she trusted him.

To her surprise, she felt the warmth of his mouth kissing her clitoris and his tongue began to push upward from her vagina. She gasped and couldn't believe that he was pushing his tongue inside of her. He then began to put a finger on her...oh goodness, why there?

"Sean, Sean, she gasped, what are you doing?"

He then lowered her from his shoulders and positioned her astride his waist as he thrust himself inside of her. "Ah, ah, ah... Sean...Sean." She could feel him becoming harder with each movement. At one point, he held her against the wall while he slowly pulled himself out and then thrust back in...over and over again,

---

196   "For, you see, each day I love you more, today more than yesterday and less than tomorrow." Translation suggestions provided by friend Rose Fabian.

until she felt him spasm. His muscles trembled as he released his pleasure physically and vocally for the entire world to hear.

Annie started to laugh as he weakly allowed her to stand. Kneeling on the floor of the bath, he embraced her around her waist and kissed her stomach. With his head against her stomach, Annie smiled, as she caressed his head and ran her hands over his soft hair. It was as though he was grateful to her for such a pleasurable experience.

He was clearly spent, and it was yet another first experience for Annie. She never dreamed that oral sex would feel remotely that good...and the orgasm a man would have after having done such a thing was incredible.

With his voice shaking, "Annie, oh Annie, Je T'aime, Je T'aime."

"I love you too," she said.

The couple spent the rest of the rainy-day making love. They didn't eat or drink, they just were...

The next morning, they dined in the café on the corner. It was very crowded, and the cups for coffee were very tiny, in fact, espresso cups.

"Bugger," said Sean, slurping the last few drops of his espresso. "When are they refilling the coffee?"

"I don't know, mine is empty too."

A couple next to them, too, were looking into their empty cups and wondering. With everyone looking for the waitress and a refill, Annie shared an old Irish tradition for getting a pint refilled. She lifted her cup and saucer to the top of her head and looked in the direction of the waitress.

Sean whispered, "What the...are ya doing?"

"Do you want coffee?" asked Annie. "Then trust me."

The young couple raised their cups and saucers and placed them on top of their heads, too. They apparently thought it must be an

American gesture for getting a drink refill. After a few moments, other people were doing the same.

Sean was at a loss as he'd never seen such a vulgar display. Certainly, Sophia would never have done such a thing.

To Sean's surprise and dismay, the waitress approached and refilled everyone's tiny espresso cups. Annie smiled smugly as she and the others raised their cups to one another in praise of getting more coffee.

Sean leaned forward and whispered, "Ya truly are a marvel, ya know that?"

"So how long have you two been married?" the young woman asked.

Sean and Annie looked at one another and smiled.

"Oh, Ah..."

"Well, ah..."

"Oh, I'm sorry. You two look like a couple, so we just assumed."

"So, how long have you two been together?" asked Annie, diffusing the tension.

"We were just married and are on our honeymoon."

"How romantic," said Annie. "So, where from here?"

"Hawaii," they both said in unison. "We can't wait."

"Wow! That's quite a trip," said Sean.

"Well, you only do it once in a lifetime, right?" said the groom.

"Sure," answered Sean, looking awkwardly at his half-eaten croissant.

* * *

The rest of the days of the conference, Annie and Sean ate breakfast together in the tiny little French pastry shop and then walked to the conference where they split up and went their separate ways.

Sean was the chair of a session on volcanology, and his friend Ed Smart from the Hawaiian Observatory was a speaker, as well as his buddy *Timothy Bradford*[197] from Brown University. Ed was a geochemist – physical volcanologist, where Tim was a *geophysicist-volcanologist.*[198] Both collected data on volcanoes, and the two disciplines work together in the forecasting of future events.

Annie attended the session and sat in the back of the room until everyone had exited except for Sean and his friends.

"I want you guys to meet a field geology friend of mine from Texas. Dr. Annie Moore."

"Hi, Annie, so pleased to meet you."

"Likewise."

"Dr. Moore, would you like to join us for dinner?" asked Sean.

Picking up on Sean's lead, she graciously accepted the invitation to join the men.

"I know a great sushi place nearby," said Tim.

"There's also a Basque restaurant close too."

"What would you like?" asked Ed, tipping his hat to Annie.

"I'm really not all that hungry. I'll eat something no matter where we go."

"Ok, it's settled then," said Sean. "We're eating South American."

"What?!" laughed everyone.

"Just kidding. You guys pick."

Once again, Annie found herself on the outside looking in. Sean and his friends walked together and shared memories and laughter, while she watched and admired their friendship.

---

197   Tim Bradford is a fictional character. Brown University is used as a place for Tim Bradford, but his character does not represent any personnel from that school present or past.

198   Physical volcanologists study the processes involved in volcanism. The data they collect is physical data that can be mapped and studied in terms of forecasting future eruptions, etc. Geophysical volcanologists study seismicity, gravity, and magnetics. Both used geodesics (movement of the earth at the surface with GPS) to monitor volcanic activity.

At the end of their stay, Annie and Sean shared a ride to the airport and they once again said their goodbyes, each knowing that they would see one another again at the field station in the Rockies that summer.

When Sean returned home, Sophia had planned the trip for their family. The best time for the entire family, including the family down under, was in late June and this would mean that Sean would not be able to teach the field methods course that summer.

After a tearful and heated argument, Sean relented and agreed to give up his summer assignment to spend time with his family. Apparently, his father had suffered a mild heart attack earlier in the week, and Sean's mother was very excited to learn that a visit was in the works. She and Sophia encouraged him to visit sooner than later.

Annie was disappointed, but understood that he needed to see his family, so they continued to talk once a week and made plans, too, for a fall meeting in Montreal, Canada. It would be a while, but they would see each other again. Annie imagined it was not much different than military wives, who had to wait for long periods of time before seeing their husbands. She was resilient and had plenty to keep her busy. Knowing that Sean loved her and needed to hear her voice each week kept her going.

Sean wrote to Annie each month, sharing his ideas and stories about his graduate students. Writing helped him to stay connected to Annie in a tangible way. The phone conversations were short due to the expense of long distance calling at that time. Sometimes he would call Annie, and other times she would call him. Across the miles and the phone lines, their love endured.

* * *

Chapter 41—Down Under

Sean's father, *Ian Michael Anderson*,[199] was a retired Royal Air Force pilot who had been stationed in Auckland during the war. His mother, *Margaret Ann (Maggie) Flanagan*,[200] was a seamstress and homemaker. They had both grown up in the UK and later emigrated to New Zealand after the war.

Ian had fallen in love with New Zealand and vowed to leave the tattered homeland to seek a new beginning with his young bride. They didn't have much money, so he worked with an old war buddy whose father owned a farm. He worked as a farm manager, while Maggie sewed and baked bread. Together, they saved enough to purchase property of their own and begin to farm. Ian was carrying on a family tradition, as his father and grandfather had also done before the World Wars.

Maggie, over the following years, gave birth to Sean and his siblings. He and his brothers grew up helping their dad on the farm. His sister *Mary Ann*[201] helped her mother with quilting, cooking, and sewing, and eventually grew up to become a schoolteacher.

Teaching seemed to be something that Ian and Maggie's children were born to do--that, and farming.

---

199 Ian Michael Anderson, Sean's father, is a fictional character that is not meant to depict any real person, living or deceased.

200 Margaret Ann (Maggie) Flanagan, Sean's mother, is a fictional character that is not meant to depict any real person, living or deceased.

201 Mary Ann Anderson, Sean's younger sister, and is a fictional character that is not meant to depict any real person, living or deceased.

Sean's brother *Richard*[202] returned to the UK to attend college, following in Sean's footsteps, and stayed to become a chemistry professor. He was married to a lovely lady from Wales, and they had three children.

His younger brother *William (Billy)*[203] stayed on the farm with their parents and eventually took over the family farm. Between his sister Mary and him, they made sure that Maggie and Ian were able to continue to live at home on the farm and to continue their work, in a limited fashion, growing old gracefully.

Coming home was an excellent experience for Sean and Sophia's daughters--*Emily and Amanda*,[204] who were in their teens. They were spoiled rotten by aunts, uncles, cousins and, of course, their grandparents.

Mary enjoyed teaching her granddaughter how to sew doll dresses by hand and the art of quilting and making butter and cheese.

Billy's wife Sarah was a Maori woman, who was a devoted farm wife and mother to his two teen sons, who helped to work the farm in between rugby and soccer games.

Both boys, John, and Willy, were sixteen months apart and frequently competed together on the same teams. With the height of their father and the Maori build and coloring of their mother, both boys were very handsome and popular, attracting the attention of the young ladies.

While on their trip home, Sean continued to find time to write in his journal. He also penned a letter that he intended to send to Annie as soon as he had an opportunity to post.

---

202 Richard Alan Anderson, Sean's younger brother, and is a fictional character that is not meant to depict any real person, living or deceased.

203 William Ian Anderson, Sean's youngest brother, also a fictional character that is not meant to depict any real person, living or deceased.

204 Emily and Amanda Anderson, Sean's daughters. Both are fictional characters that are not meant to depict any real persons, living or deceased.

Sophia enjoyed baking with Maggie, Mary, Sarah, and the girls and barely noticed that Sean was still spending time alone and writing. As she walked into the guest room, where they were staying for the three weeks, Sophia noted his journal peeking out from inside of his leather shoulder bag. At that time, Sean was in the barn with Billy, and everyone else was in the kitchen.

She had always valued trust and privacy and had never tried to read his journal, but the opportunity presented itself, and she allowed her intense curiosity to get the better of her. She nudged his journal out of the bag and noted there was also an envelope that was not yet sealed.

The envelope was addressed to "S.A. Moore, USA." and was from S.M. Anderson with his office address at the college. She noted that the envelope felt full and that the pages were handwritten inside. She could feel the cursive letter indentations on the leaves of paper and wondered, *who would Sean be writing such a long personal letter to in Texas?* His professional correspondence was usually typed.

She gently pulled the letter out of the envelope and began to read.

Dearest Annie, we have made it to the family farm, and Mom and Dad are in good spirits, if not in the best of health. Mom baked a million pies and is excited to teach Emily and Amanda how to quilt. Sophia and the girls are both working on being excited about helping with the quilting... Billy has done a great job with the farm.... I will be helping him, and the boys with the mending of fences and we will be going to see the boys play ball over the weekend. They are both extreme athletes, and it will be a pleasure to watch them in action..."

Sophia then skipped to the final page of the very long letter and read the closing, *I miss you terribly and can't wait to put my arms around you again...*

Sophia felt her heart in her stomach. *Love always, Sean.*

Who on earth is Annie? she thought, and *why is Sean writing that he misses her...?*

The reality began to sink in as she read through other parts of the letter. *You would love it here........ The calderas where I did my research....*

Oh my God, she thought out loud, *She is a geologist too?*

She immediately accepted that this was a woman geologist and they shared a love of his field and of each other. Sophia was devastated at the realization. She began to weep and couldn't believe her eyes. He was in love with this, this.... Annie...another woman.

I don't believe this, she said to herself, as she began to hyperventilate. *No, no, no...*

She felt nauseated and overwhelmed with intense emotional pain and a stabbing betrayal. With her hands shaking, she carefully placed the letter back into the envelope and pushed the journal back into its place in the satchel. Thankfully, there was no one nearby to see her fall apart.

How could he do this to the children and to me? What did I do wrong? she thought.

"That SON OF A BITCH!" She would have to confront him, and no one else could know of this--no one.

Later that evening, when she and Sean were ready for bed, she got under the covers as he wrote in his journal. She turned her back to him and began to weep silently.

Sean noted that she seemed unusually quiet and asked, "Sophia? Are you ok? You seem very quiet."

"I'm fine," she replied, but her voice sounded emotional.

Sean loved Sophia and would not want to do anything to hurt her. He felt concerned that she had somehow had her feelings hurt by one of the girls or .... Perhaps he'd not been giving her enough personal attention.

He knelt on the bed and turned her over to face him. Her eyes were red, and the emotional pain was palpable. He whispered in a very concerned voice, "Sophia! My gosh, what on earth is the matter?"

She turned her back to him again.

Touching her shoulder, he again asked, "Sophia, what on earth is the matter? What has happened?"

Sophia said one thing, "My dearest Annie..."

Sean immediately knew that she had seen his letter to Annie, and he felt immediate panic and intense guilt.

"When were you going to tell me about her, Sean? How could you do this to me?" she wept through muffled sobs. "Are you leaving me? Are you leaving us?"

"No!" whispered Sean, terrified, and feeling overwhelmed by his own emotional pain. His mind swiftly returned to his letter. He was trying to recall his exact words. *How am I supposed to possibly explain this?* he thought to himself.

"It wasn't supposed to happen, Sophia. It just did. It is absolutely not your fault," he answered. "We were at camp together, and she was beautiful and inviting. I was weak and should have just walked away. It was all my fault."

They both cried as he explained that he could never stop loving her, she was the mother of his children.

"What about putting your arms around her again?" sobbed Sophia.

"I was planning to end it the next time I saw her," said Sean, as he looked down at the bedspread his mother had made, knowing he was not sure he could ever end his love of Annie. "I promise that I will end it."

Sophia rolled away from him and continued to cry herself to sleep and refused to allow Sean to touch her. He laid on the other side of the bed with his back away from her as well and tried to reconcile what had just happened.

The rest of the trip was filled with lots of activities, and it was easy for Sean and Sophia to avoid dealing with the infidelity, but once they returned home, he and Sophia had a long period of coolness.

Sean gave her space to process her grief and find a way to forgive him, and she gave him space to consider what he was about to lose. Sean had no choice but to somehow end things with Annie. Part of him was relieved because he had hated being dishonest with Sophia. He was overall a sincere and honorable man and living with one woman while also loving another was taking a toll on his marriage and him. She didn't deserve to be hurt, and he couldn't stand her continued pain and his guilt.

Sean had to decide to end one of his relationships and ending his marriage to the mother of his children was not one that he could make. He was too old-fashioned to do anything but the right thing.

Chapter 42—Standing by the road again...

When Sean returned from the trip and finally called Annie, he had no choice but to tell her of the letter and the situation at home.

Annie felt devastated for Sophia and was also understandably concerned that Sean would have no choice but to pull away from her. She knew Sean would probably want to distance himself from her while he worked things out with Sophia.

In the meantime, Annie and Sean had plans to meet at the annual conference, which was being hosted in Montreal of that year. Usually, Sean would get a hotel room, or Annie would, and they would share that room.

This year, Sean told Annie that he had to share the cost of the conference with a colleague or he would not be able to come. Annie couldn't afford a room, but she scraped together enough money to get a hotel room and to go to the conference. No cost was too much to be able to see Sean, even if it was only for a few days.

Each time they had together recharged her, and she left feeling sad but stronger in knowing that she was truly loved. It was the only honest and wholesome thing in her life. She could endure anything if she knew he loved her. He was only a phone call away, and he was her lifeline.

She arrived at her hotel and was excited that Sean would soon be dropping by. He knocked on the door, and she opened it to his smiling face.

They embraced and fell madly into each other's arms, as usual. Only this time, he seemed different. He seemed very distracted and depressed. It was still incredible sex, but she could tell that something was wrong with him. When she asked him what was wrong, he began…

"I have to make a hard decision. I don't want to, but I don't see much of a choice…I feel like I am just using ya and that's not fair…."

His voice began to fade into a muffled vacuum. He was speaking, but she could not hear his words. It was like being in a fog. She felt like someone had punched her in the stomach, and the rest was a blur.

She dressed and accompanied him to the lobby, where he exited in a cab.

Annie went back to her room and stared into space. The hours passed until it was mid-afternoon.

As she lay on the bed, remembering their times together, a beam of light entered through the space between the curtains. It looked like streams from heaven with tiny dust particles highlighting the flow of energy.

Annie thought of Sean and the song she often sang…

"As the morning light stretched in across my bed, I thought of you, hmm. Remembering your laughing eyes and all we said, I love you too …"[205]

She could see his laughing eyes in her mind, and the tears began to flow, as well as the emotions.

The memories of San Diego, San Francisco, Yellowstone, the Stillwater, Denver, the field station in the Rockies …. she and Sean had been together many times for just a few days or even weeks at a time over the past few years, and each time was glorious and beautiful until they had to part again.

---

205 **APA:** Jerry Jeff Walker - Morning Song To Sally Lyrics | Metro lyrics. (n.d.). Retrieved from http://www.metrolyrics.com/morning-song-to-sally-lyrics-jerry-jeff-walker.html

Their time together was not just about having sex. They laughed and shared so many memories and ideas. It was so easy to be together, and it was fun because they were great friends.

The song continued in Annie's mind, *"As two weeks came and went, then you and I were gone, living on."*

Sean was gone this time, and he wasn't looking or coming back. The song spoke to Annie's broken heart as she remembered how his eyes said, *I love you too,* without uttering a sound.

He was there with her.... his scent...his touch...the way he chewed a chocolate bar... She gently sobbed while still hearing the rest of the words in her mind.

Annie was a folk musician and almost always had her guitar at the camp in the Rockies. It was quite fitting for her to reminisce and to relate the moments of her life in poetry, images and in song. This song now represented a small part of where she felt she was at that moment in time, as she tried to process the intense loss, the grief.

"For it seems our love was destined to be caught in other nets. But the love we held so brief, I'd chance again without regret..."

Yes, thought Annie, *without regret.*

How could a love so beautiful and strong be so wrong? It didn't feel wrong. Nothing about it felt wrong. And yet, here I am laying, empty and alone.

Perhaps this was God's plan for her. He had once called her at the age of fifteen to be a nun. She felt the calling and wanted to go, but her parents refused. In their mind, she was too smart and too pretty to waste herself on a life of service and prayer. All that was needed was for her to date boys and not give herself to Jesus. That would be a waste.

But, thought Annie, *How have any of the choices made for me by others been better?... Isn't loving someone with your entire heart and soul a waste, too, if that love isn't returned or cannot be returned?*

This apparently was to be her place, *"standing by the road again, alone"* -- was this her song?

"But now somehow, I'm forced to see me there once more, and that's the song."

That seemed to be her song, alone, and only dreaming of what could have been with the right one to share her love, which would be returned. Now, she would never know for sure, would she?

"For my waking thoughts are but extensions of the dream. Without you here beside me I'll never know all, all that they mean ..."

For two days now, she lay on her bed in the hotel room in Montreal, unable to eat, drink, or get out of bed except to go to the bathroom.

The first few hours after he left her standing on the doorstep of the hotel, all she could do was sit in stunned silence with tears streaming from her eyes. The cab pulled away with the love of her life. A piece of her drove away, too.

It was raining outside, and she would never forget the sound of continuous rain falling on the hotel canopy and streaming to the sidewalk and streets around her. The setting felt symbolic, almost as if she was in a movie or a novel, and she was the heroine left standing with a broken heart. Like a scene, perhaps, from *Dr. Zhivago*,[206] where Lara is left as her love goes off to be with his wife and children. She too was left standing by the road again...living on without him.

She went back to the room where they had shared their last intimate embrace and lay across the bed, which still smelled of their essence.

Eventually, she made herself get up and take a long, hot shower. It felt good to be washing the pain away, but it didn't help. She

---

206 A 1965 movie set during a Russian revolution, where a married man falls in love with another woman, Lara.

couldn't stand up, and just sat at the end of the tub and let the water hit her on the head and shoulders, while she sobbed. Nothing really mattered anymore.

After the long shower, Annie dried her body and changed into the nightgown she had brought with her. She sat on the bed, looking at her reflection in the mirror. All she could see was an unattractive, sniveling shell.

His words were re-running in her mind, his voice, telling her he could no longer be with her. He had to choose his wife over her.

She began to sob uncontrollably. All her memories of losses from her childhood, her failed marriage ...all losses came flowing back. The cumulative pain of a lifetime was right there in a collective moment of rejection and failure.

Everyone she had ever truly loved and trusted had eventually done irreparable harm to her loving heart. This seemed to be the first time, though, she had actively participated in the destruction of her own soul.

She trusted Sean totally. In her heart, she knew she would never trust on that level ever again. This beautiful part of her was dying, at this very moment, dying. She felt dead inside.

Annie had always had such a loving and trusting nature. As a child, she was teased for being so sensitive to everything. She was known for apologizing to flies when she was forced to kill them, saying a sweet little prayer asking for forgiveness for having to take their life.

The love of her life belonged to another woman, and even though she had known that from the beginning, she always believed that the love that she shared with Sean was somehow special and unique and forever binding, not something he would ever give up on. He would never abandon her.

She was so sure of his love for her…. the love that they shared. *How on earth could I have been so stupid, so wrong? I willfully turned from God…gave up the sacraments for our love.*

The hours stretched on as she experienced the emotional pain, covering her face to muffle the screams of despair, which were being released from the very depths of her soul. She feared someone would hear her, so she sobbed and screamed in muffled silence.

When she was physically, emotionally, and spiritually exhausted, she would fall to sleep, only to wake up again with each nauseating wave of intense pain. She was an open, gaping wound, lying across the bed where they had made love, days ago now, before he announced to her that he needed to make a clean break from her.

'He' needed to make a choice because loving two women was killing him. He was suffering. His wife was suffering.

Annie was now suffering too, but somehow, her suffering meant less in the broad scheme of things. Nobody seemed too concerned that she was not sure she could live on.

She had ended a horrible marriage, endured so much… understood that Sean had loved Sophia first and had made a lifelong commitment to her to "love, cherish and forsaking all others…"

Sophia had done nothing wrong and was devastated when she found out about Sean and Annie.

Annie never intended for Sophia to hurt. She would never intentionally do anything to deliberately hurt her, never. When Sean told her that he had told Sophia, Annie felt horrible about the pain that Sophia had expressed to Sean. She felt intense guilt at having hurt another person, especially someone as kind and gentle as Sean described Sophia.

Annie knew that Sean loved them both. She accepted this because she felt that the connection to Sean was different, more profound, cosmic….it was somehow unique and separate from the special love that he and Sophia shared.

Sean struggled with what to do and could not see any positive solution to the current situation. He loved two women and had no right answers or choices. He just knew that his situation at home was unbearable, and something had to be done to ease the stress.

The decision to end his relationship with Annie was the only choice, because he couldn't bear the pain of hurting both women he loved. In his mind, *his* selfishness was hurting them both.

Annie would never move on and find happiness if he continued to keep her in the role of a mistress. He respected her too much to have her continue in that role. Sean wanted to love her entirely, but that was not something he was able to do at this time in his life. Little did he know, she would never love anyone else.

He told her that his relationship was unfair to both women, and he felt he had to make the only choice he could, and that was to deny himself the pleasure of loving Annie totally. His feelings for her would never change. He loved her. But his feelings for Sophia would never change either. He loved her too, and she needed him far more. She had been first and gave her life to him. He knew that both he and Annie would somehow survive, but Sophia, on the other hand, had nothing but her family and her love of her husband, as she was approaching retirement age.

It was not fair to her, as she had done nothing wrong and did not deserve to feel any pain. After all the years she had invested and loved unconditionally, she deserved to feel secure and loved as she grew old.

Annie understood this. Even though her pain was so deep and complete, she couldn't and wouldn't share it with Sean. Sophia's needs were greater than her own. She accepted this reality, but would never truly heal, never truly feel whole again. She had given far too much of herself away. This was a once in a lifetime love, and there would be no other, and in her mind, she had never truly felt worthy of being loved.

Being loved had all just been a dream, and she had to wake up to the reality that she wasn't meant to be loved. She would never be good enough.

Her grandfather didn't think so, her mother didn't think so, her husband didn't think so, and now Sean was confirming it.

Eventually, she summoned enough energy to attend one last day of the conference. Part of her did not want Sean to realize how devastated she had been. Her pride would not allow him to know the depth of her pain.

They spoke briefly, and when he asked how she was, she lied to him.

"Right there? I haven't seen much of ya lately."

"Oh, I was distracted," said Annie.

"Are ya okay?" he asked.

"Oh, sure. I'll be right...right?"

They walked for a short while, and she left him feeling like she was, of course, hurt, and disappointed, but accepted that things must end. It would be okay. As usual, her focus was on the happiness of others rather than her own.

Sean walked away that day feeling like he had also left part of himself behind. His love for Annie would not be forgotten, and he would hold her in his heart forever. In his mind, she was very worthy of all the love in this world. He just couldn't provide the love that she needed and deserved.

He remembered how pretty she looked too as the cab pulled away that day and how it broke his heart to leave her standing there alone in the rain.

As the conference continued, he wondered where she was and was a little bit surprised that she didn't seem to attend any of the presentations that he was sure she would have had a great interest. Her absence was noticed, but he didn't dare go back to her room to check on her. When they were alone together, they were naturally drawn to each other physically, and he knew he would not be able to keep from making love to her. To do that after breaking her heart would be cruel, and he felt like he would only be using her.

He loved her and respected her too much to ever do that to her. Leaving her was one of the most painful things he had ever done in his life. In his mind, he rehearsed over and over again, how he would be able to tell her…dreading it. *I just need to do it and walk away,* he thought. *If I do that, then I won't be able to change my mind. It will be like ripping off a band-aid. The quick jerk, the intense pain, and then the healing begins.*

It seemed better this way. They would remain, friends, right?

Chapter 43—Moving On

Annie returned home to her happy children and her teaching at the college, and Sean returned home to his wife, family, and his teaching and research. It was all as it should be, except neither of them were truly happy.

As Christmas and New Year passed, both settled into regular work and family routines.

Sean immersed himself in his research projects, graduate students, and grant writing.

Time was healing the hurt for Sophia, but nothing was easy about moving on for her or for Sean.

Annie had a difficult time. Not because she wasn't resilient, but because she had always been a fragile and sensitive person when it came to feelings. She had always felt "less" than what she indeed was, and this was her baggage from her childhood, which proved a detriment to her in her adult life and relationships.

They were both raised by parents who taught strength in the face of struggles; no whining, no excuses, don't quit...put one foot in front of the other and face challenges.

Sean was the head of his family and his flock of productive graduate students and projects. He was a strong leader, even though he was also very caring, kind, and loving. His role in life could not allow him to give in to any dark feelings; too many people depended on his strength and stability.

This reality, of course, did not keep him from looking off into the distance and thinking of his Annie. He frequently remembered her smell, her touch, and her loving nature. He remembered their making love together and the laughter. Annie had an infectious giggle. He missed her terribly but could not give in to those feelings.

As the new semester began for Annie, people noticed that she was not her usual happy-go-lucky self. She had lost weight. Her eyes were darkened, and she looked like she was barely engaging socially and physically.

As the days and weeks passed, the department chairman, *Dr. Williams*,[207] called her into his office and asked if she was okay.

"Anna, we are all concerned. You seem to be just limping along."

She replied, "Oh, it's just the divorce and everything. It is all so sad." Her eyes filled with tears.

Dr. Williams suggested that she take some time off from classes, perhaps get a substitute, while she sought a doctor to help her deal with her intense feelings of loss.

Anna was mortified at the thought of being alone with her grief. She had to work and keep going.

"No, I need to teach my classes. That is the one thing that is keeping me going." To stop teaching was out of the question so she instead agreed to go seek counseling immediately and hopefully pull out of the depression.

Dr. Williams reluctantly agreed. "We need you to be 100 percent, Anna. Let me know if there is anything, we are able to do."

Even people at church noticed that she seemed sick. "We are praying for you," is what her friends and church family would say.

She knew she was loved by her children, her in-laws, and by her church family, but she did not feel worthy of God's love at this time.

---

207 Dr. Williams is a fictional character and is not meant to depict any person, past or present.

Annie could not approach the Eucharist--the body and blood of Jesus--with her heart so wounded, weak, and unable to truly focus on the joy, healing, and grace of receiving. She couldn't bring herself to receive the sacrament of reconciliation – confession- either, which is needed before receiving Christ.

Her heart and soul felt dead and she didn't want to be healed, not really, she just wanted to die. The healing would need time and so would her desire to move on.

Without the sacrament of reconciliation, she was separated from the Body of Christ, which was His church and His presence in the Eucharist. To receive the sacrament without repentance would merely be going through the motions, which is considered a sin itself.

God deserved better from her. If there is no joy in your heart and soul, then God is not there. How could she glorify God with her life if she was a burned-out wick with no flame?

Annie wanted to die, but she would not dare ever take her own life. Her children needed her, and she loved them far more than her own life.

One evening after a mass and a communal supper at the parish, *Sister Margaret*[208] noted Anna's demeanor and was compelled to put her arms around her. She began to sob uncontrollably. Sitting Anna in a chair, Sister began to console her, "Anna? Look at me. God loves you. You are beautiful. There is nothing that God can't provide. There is nothing that God cannot heal. There is nothing that can't be forgiven. Nothing."

Sister, like others, assumed Anna was struggling with the loss of her marriage. The nun's words made her think of the song that

---

208 Sister Margaret is a fictional character loosely based on the Carmelite and Benedictine nuns in the author's life. This character is not meant to depict any particular person past or present.

they had sung at mass, *"Nothing can wash away my sin... nothing but the blood of Jesus."*

Anna became very disoriented and collapsed onto the floor of the great hall with tears streaming down her face. She was too weak to sit or stand.

Priests, nuns, parishioners, all came to hug her and love her. Her children were with their father, thankfully, for a court-ordered visitation and did not have to witness their mother's collapse.

It was so apparent to all that she was in great distress. One of the parishioners, who was a psychologist, offered to take Anna to the hospital. She regained her composure and said that it would not be needed. "I am just hungry. I haven't eaten much today. Just please pray for me. "

As each person touched her during prayer, she could feel the anointing of the *holy spirit*.[209] She felt the healing light of Christ, and a smile returned through the tears.

Fr. Michael[210] asked Anna, "is there anything that we can do for you?"

"No, Father," answered Anna. "I am just having a difficult time financially and with the divorce. I miss my boys."

Father offered lovingly, "Anna, I feel strongly that you should seek counseling. You are not well. I also suggest that you engage in a spiritual retreat. Those can sometimes help us all to refocus our priorities. There is a retreat coming up next month that might be beneficial for you as well. There is funding available, too, if you are interested."

The sisters agreed and recommended that she seek counseling for her depression.

---

209 This anointing is said to be spiritual, but some charismatic individuals claim to have a physiological response as well, especially during deep meditative prayer.

210 Father Michael is a fictional character loosely based on Catholic priests in the author's life. This character is not meant to depict any particular person past or present.

It was settled, Anna was to seek help for her depression. Fr. Michael put her in touch with a woman counselor in the area, and she was set to have an evaluation and consultation the following week. He also signed her up for the *spiritual retreat center* in West Virginia. [211]

Anna dutifully attended her consultation and accepted appointments for a counselor, but she was just going through the motions. She deemed herself far too busy to be the one spending time and resources on herself. Being too busy to acknowledge her pain was her own fix for her broken spirit.

With the spring semester in full swing, she was very busy with teaching prep, grading, and research projects and frequently forgot to eat, sometimes becoming sick to her stomach when she did try to eat. Not eating had become a common theme as she immersed herself in work, to avoid the pain in her life.

She rarely cried in front of her children and others, but the late-night shower became her outlet for releasing her emotional pain.

A few days later, while getting coffee in the main office at the college, Anna dropped an armload of papers and collapsed onto the floor in front of the mailboxes. She woke up in the back of an ambulance where she could feel *Adam*[212] holding her hand.

"Shit, Anna! You scared the crap out of everyone. Are you okay?"

"I don't know," she said softly.

Later at the ER, tests were run, and Anna's blood sugar and blood pressure were both dangerously low.

The doctor asked to speak to her privately, so Adam snuck out to call everyone,

"Yes, she is fine, just low blood sugar...yup...probably from not eating. This divorce is killing her, I think."

---

211 Fictional center that is not meant to represent any established center past or present.
212 Adam is Dr. D.

Meanwhile, *Dr. Rogers*,[213] a very slender man with a kind face, questioned her, "When was your last period?"

Anna was stunned by his question and answered, "I have had irregular bleeding since the beginning of the semester, January, I guess? Why?"

"You have a positive lab result for pregnancy. Do you have any idea when you became pregnant?"

She couldn't believe what she was hearing. It had been at least three months since she had last had sex with anyone, with Sean!

"How is this possible?" asked Anna.

Dr. Rogers responded without cracking a smile, "The usual way I assume."

She would have laughed if it hadn't been such a serious turn of events.

Adam returned and scolded her for not eating like she should and asked if his wife could bring her home. He had a meeting to attend and would not be able to stay.

Dr. Rogers shook Anna's hand and wished her luck. Thankfully, he had been professional and did not mention a baby. After what seemed like an eternity, she was released and Adam's wife, Pamela, insisted on taking her for dinner.

"No wonder you are passing out, young lady. Adam says you have stopped eating. You look terrible, just terrible."

Anna was ignoring her as she was processing the news of a pregnancy. She had always been careful, *how is this even possible?* She thought. I *have been having my periods, haven't I?* Each month there was regular bleeding, although very light.

Anna ordered the chicken soup and slowly sipped it from a spoon, as she listened to Pam go on and on about divorce in the church.

---

213   A fictional character, Anna's emergency doctor, not meant to depict any real person past or
present.

"It is truly a shame that people are not allowed to remarry in the church."

Just when Anna began to explain the rules for remarriage, overwhelming nausea hit, and she had to run to the bathroom and vomit. Dry heaves continued with her pulling muscles in her sides. She was clearly sick, so Pam delivered her home to rest.

The next day, Adam called, "you want a ride in this morning? Are you feeling better?"

Anna agreed, and they both rode to work together. As the days and weeks moved on, Anna began to feel a little better and developed a glow about her. Everyone was happy to see her feeling stronger and better.

She continued to meet with her counselor as well as with Fr. Michael, who was convinced she needed renewal and a break from the rigors of teaching and single parenting.

The *Mother of Hope Hermitage*[214] was sponsoring a spiritual retreat that was surely going to help her out of her funk.

---

214 Fictional place not intended to represent any current or past church organization.

Chapter 44—The Loss

The meeting hall of the tiny hermitage was filled with people gathered for the spiritual retreat. After several months of limping along, Anna was finally taking everyone's advice and getting a week of rest and spiritual renewal. Everyone assumed that the divorce was taking a heavy toll on her, especially because she was a devout Catholic and the Catholic Church frowned on divorce.

Twenty years before her divorce, women, and men were not allowed to engage actively in ministries of the church if they were divorced. Thankfully, that practice was replaced with one more suiting to the love and mercy of God and the teachings of Christ.

As it would turn out, her attendance at the retreat that weekend was perhaps a divine intervention for Anna, as she would face one of the most devastating losses of her life. She wasn't at all sure how to handle being divorced, a Catholic, a college professor, a mother to two young boys growing into men, and a soon-to-be mom of a new life growing inside of her, all at one time and alone.

To Anna, there was nothing left but Jesus and at this time in her life, she couldn't feel the Holy Spirit either. The joy of the Lord was gone and truthfully, she had wanted to die ever since Sean left her under the canopy in the rain. Her love and sense of duty to her children, who were saddened by the divorce, and her students were the only things that initially kept her going.

Having discovered she was pregnant had lifted her spirits for sure. The thought of a beautiful gift of life, from her one true love, gave her reason to smile, but it also brought fear of further rejection and judgment.

The tiny little bump on her belly was beginning to show up to her, but she wore loose clothing so that others would not notice. The little angel had been making its presence known for a few weeks and Anna was soon to be faced with the reality of telling everyone. *What will everyone think...Betty, the sisters...Father Steven and Father Michael.*[215] *What will my boys think? Oh my gosh, what will Dr. D. and the department think...my students?*

She was very, very frightened, but at the same time happy because she knew this life had been conceived in love. Anna was already in love with this little person long before she began to move. Yes, she was hoping for a little girl after having boys. This new life was the one positive reminder in her own life that she had to go on. She had to live so that this little one could also live. God would somehow provide the courage and strength needed to persevere.

She was still trying to decide how to approach Sean about it all. He had made it clear that he had to end things with her for his own sanity and for the sake of his own family. Anna never quite understood on an emotional level, but she did accept it cognitively.

Sean was an honorable man, and it only made sense that he would do the honorable thing for his wife and children. She admired this about him and still loved him deeply despite the feelings of abandonment and woundedness.

The absolute last thing that she wanted was to be a part of any other pain for his wife Sophia or for him. She had determined that for now, this was her cross to bear, and she would somehow be blessed for choosing life instead of an abortion.

As a Catholic, abortion was clearly not an option for her, so she had to find the strength to hold her head high and proceed for the

---

215 Both are fictional characters, not meant to depict any living person past or present.

good of the innocent ones in her life, especially the angel inside of her.

The retreat center was nestled in the Great Smoky Mountains and was nothing short of heaven on earth. Trails were abundant and frequently took the hiker past babbling brooks and benches overlooking mountain vistas. It had everything needed for reflection and introspection.

The center was the host too to some very good counselors and provided scripture study and self-help groups to address different aspects of ministerial life. There were lay people of all kinds; priests, brothers and nuns as attendees and facilitating workshops.

For Anna's current situation, she felt isolated in a crowd. Even though there were many wonderful loving people, she felt alone, like she was outside of the joy-filled environment, looking through a glass that needed a good washing.

During the evening praise and worship session, Anna sang out with others and felt joy in singing God's praises. She even smiled as she felt her little one flutter, thinking *she must love music, too.*

Everyone stood and joined hands and arms in joyful praise. It was truly beautiful and uplifting. She noted that she was feeling like she might have an issue with her bladder or perhaps some bloating from eating bean soup with onion. There was a slight discomfort but nothing that wouldn't be remedied perhaps by passing gas in a more private setting.

As the evening went on, Anna laughed and sang, not giving much attention to her physical discomfort. It was time to turn in and everyone filtered to their cells, tiny rooms with one bed, for the evening. She showered and used the restroom. When she wiped, the tissue had a slight tinge of pink.

What could this be? She thought. *Perhaps it is nothing.*

She had experienced bladder infections in the past and this was not that far removed from that feeling and symptoms. *I'll recheck in the morning to make sure things are okay.*

As the night progressed, Anna began to feel greater cramping and the pink was now turning red. She was so frightened.

The next morning, she approached *Sr. Beatrice*[216] and indicated that she had a private issue to discuss. Anna tearfully shared with Beatrice that she had only recently learned that she was pregnant and now feared to lose the baby.

Beatrice consulted with her sisters and *Fr. William,*[217] who oversaw the retreat. The decision was made to take her discreetly into town to the local hospital for an examination. As Sr. Beatrice drove Anna to the hospital in the hermitage truck, she felt every single pothole and her pain increased.

Sister Anne[218] was also with Anna and allowed her to cry on her tiny, bony, shoulder during the hour and a half drive to the local hospital. Sr. Anne led them in prayer as Anna sobbed. "I am so scared," she told the sisters. "I am divorced."

Sr. Beatrice was a short, older lady with a kind grandmotherly face and a blocky frame. Anna felt safe in her presence as she exuded confidence and great authority. Sr. Anne was a tiny woman in her 70s, who was frail and frequently suffered from bouts of pneumonia. Anna felt her love and compassion and was comforted by both the wonderful servants of God.

"Does your ex-husband know of this pregnancy?" asked Sr. Beatrice, in a serious tone.

"No," said Anna tearfully.

---

216   A fictional character named after a close personal friend of the author. The character is not meant to depict any living person, past or present.
217   A fictional character who is the priest who oversees the fictional retreat.
218   Sister Anne is a fictional character loosely based on a close friend who is a Carmelite Sister, but not meant to depict any real person or experience, past or present.

"Perhaps we need to contact him, so he knows what is going on?"

"No," answered Anna, "my husband is not the father."

Both sisters crossed themselves and looked very concerned.

Anna sobbed loudly, "I fell in love with a married man and he loved his wife more than he loved me...I didn't know what to do."

"Of course, he did!" exclaimed Sr. Beatrice. "What the hell did you expect? Men only think of themselves."

To which, Sister Anne spoke softly, "Anna. I'm sure there was love, dear. Who couldn't love you"?

"It hurts so bad, Sister," cried Anna, "I was never meant to be loved, and I'll never love again...not like this."

"God loves you...before you were born and especially now. There is nothing you have done that God won't forgive. You do know this don't you?" asked Sr. Anne.

Beatrice motioned her head in agreement. "This is not a punishment, dear girl. We don't yet know what is going on exactly, so please keep the faith. God would never punish an innocent baby for the sins of the parents, never. And He would not punish the parents for simply being human and failing."

Sister Anne then said in a comforting tone, "You are loved, my dear. Your baby is loved. The man you love is also loved. God loves you all and will not abandon you."

Anna felt great comfort as both held her hands.

When they finally arrived at the hospital, Anna's cramps now felt like full-on labor pains. She had two children previously and knew what contractions felt like. This was labor, and she was hysterical at the thought of losing her baby.

The emergency team collected her in a wheelchair and quickly took her to triage for an evaluation. By this time, Anna's pains were intense, and her tears were not just from fear and anxiety, but from actual physical pain and disbelief at the progressing nightmare.

"Why? Why Lord?! Why!?" she cried. "My baby. My angel."

The emergency room team was swift and professional. They painlessly put in an IV for Anna and began giving her fluids and medications to stop her labor. One nurse put on a rubber glove and began probing her vagina, which greatly upset Anna, who screamed, "No! Don't do that please!?"

She could no longer see the Sisters and began to cry for them to please be with her. "I'm so scared, please let me see the sisters," she cried.

After about an hour, Anna began to calm down. She had been given a sedative and was less agitated.

Sister Beatrice stood outside with a priest that Anna did not recognize, while Sister Anne held her hand. Her hands were so soft and warm. She stroked Anna's cheek as they both listened to what they could hear of the conversation just beyond the curtain and in the hallway.

"Father not involved…. divorced…. probably not going to be a positive outcome…."

As the reality of the loss was becoming clear, Anna squeezed Sister Anne's hand as tears welled up in her eyes and spilled down her cheeks...so much so, that the tears were filling her ears.

Sister Anne took a washcloth, wiped her face, and used a tissue to sop up the tears in her ears. This angel of God had the warmest brown eyes. Anna knew that she was in the presence of God and that it was God who was loving her and suffering with her and her baby in this moment of loss.

A doctor entered the room with a couple of nurses and told Anna that they had done all that they could and would have to allow nature to take its course.

"What does that mean?" she asked weakly and tearfully. "Is the baby going to die?"

"I'm afraid there is nothing we can do, *Mrs. Miller*.[219] I am so sorry."

Sister Beatrice then asked," So does the dear have to go through all this pain?"

"I have given her all I dare at this time and I have left orders to administer more as things progress. We will monitor her, but there is not much more we are able to do."

Anna began to sob loudly as almost everyone, but the Sisters left the room.

A nurse remained for a few minutes and listened to the heartbeat. She looked up at Anna and asked, "Do you want to hear your baby's heartbeat?"

She shook her head no, as she couldn't believe that her baby was going to die, and someone wanted her to listen to the heartbeat of her living baby inside of her.

Sister Anne answered, "I do. May I?"

To Anna's surprise Sister Anne and Beatrice both listened and smiled.

"You really should listen. You will remember that sound for the rest of your life," said Beatrice.

Anna agreed and began to listen. It was fast and strong. She wondered out loud to the nurse, "If the baby can't live, why is the heartbeat so strong?"

"The baby is probably healthy," said the nurse "and there is just something else that isn't working out as it should. These things happen. At least one in four pregnancies end in a miscarriage."

This statistical reality did not help Anna to feel any less devastated and guilty. In her mind, *she* must be the problem. The baby sounded fine, *so what on earth was wrong with me?* thought Anna.

---

219 Anna's married name

As the labor progressed, she cried out in misery and pain, emotional and physical anguish, with each contraction. Sister Anne lifted herself into the bed with Anna and held her as she writhed in pain. Beatrice softly prayed.

After 10 hours of labor, she felt her baby begin to move into her vagina. She could feel the fullness as the small head emerged and the rest of the tiny body slipped effortlessly out into the world. To Anna's surprise and horror, she felt the tiny arms and legs still moving. She began to sob, "Please someone help! The baby is here and needs help!"

Sister Beatrice exited the room while Sister Anne continued to hold Anna firmly and lovingly. Anna could feel the warmth of the fluids and the form of the expelled baby from her body. It was so horrifying to know that this little one had died.

Sister Beatrice and the nurses returned to the room and the nurses lovingly removed the tiny baby and began to clean away the birth fluids and placenta.

Anna was not aware, but Beatrice followed the nurse carrying the baby and made sure that the baby was treated like a baby and not just fetal tissue. She was hemorrhaging from the delivery and could feel the blood flowing from her body as she began to feel cold and dead inside.

The nurses were well trained and began packing her with absorbent gauzes, designed to help stop the flow of blood. The pain was still intense as Anna continued to cramp.

After a few minutes, a nurse, followed by Sister Beatrice, entered the room. She was carrying a tiny little bundle.

"Anna, here is your baby. Would you like to hold her?" asked the nurse.

Anna looked toward the opposite wall and cried, "I can't. I just can't."

"Why not, asked Sister Anne? She is beautiful."

Anna looked surprised and said, "She?"

Sister Beatrice, who rarely smiled, had a huge smile on her face and said, "Yes dear, *she* is an angel. You need to hold her and tell her that you love her."

Anna cried and said, "I'm afraid. What if something is wrong with her? I couldn't bear it. I just couldn't bear it."

Sister Anne then took the bundle and placed it in Anna's arms. "She is beautiful, and she is a gift from God."

Anna looked down at her tiny little heart-shaped face. "Oh my gosh! She has hair," cried Anna as she smiled through tears. "You are so beautiful," she said as she began to cry harder,

"I am so sorry that I failed you. Please forgive me. Mommy loves you. Mommy will always love you."

She held her tiny angel for about half an hour and then asked if she could have a name.

"Of course, she can. What is her name?" asked Sister Beatrice.

Anna stroked her tiny little fingers and arms, her cheeks and hair...she touched her little nose and earlobes. "Her name is *Melissa*."
220

Everyone in the room smiled and fawned over the little bundle named Melissa. The nurse then suggested that everyone leave and allow her to rest. Anna was still bleeding and was very much a patient.

Sister Anne and Beatrice refused to leave Anna's side. She remained in the hospital for another 24 hours and then was released to go home and have bed rest. Anna never returned to the retreat center and as far as she knew, none of the people at the retreat were aware of the exact circumstances of her departure. For this, she was eternally grateful.

---

220 The name Anna chose for her baby. The birth and baby are both fictional and not meant to represent a specific event or person.

As the staff readied Anna to leave the hospital, she asked about Melissa, "Where is my baby? What is to become of her?"

The nurse said, "Well in this state if the pregnancy ends spontaneously before twenty weeks, there is no birth certificate and no death certificate. The standard process is to ask the parents if they want to donate the fetal tissue or perhaps have a private burial, but nothing formal occurs."

The nurse clearly had this document in her hands as part of the paperwork for release. Anna looked, with tears in her eyes, at Fr. William, who had come to offer his support and counsel.

"My baby?" She asked in a choked voice.

Father William then said to the nurse, "We have a special cemetery for little ones like this and those who have been aborted. With your permission, we will take Melissa and give her a proper burial there."

Anna tearfully nodded that this was what she wanted. She knew she really couldn't afford a funeral home and casket and travel back to her home state in her current medical condition. This seemed acceptable.

"We will treat her with great dignity and respect Anna. You may visit her in the future, too, if you'd like."

With this consolation, Anna signed her baby over to be buried in the *"Angel Cemetery,"*[221] with other special little angels who had passed from this life to become cherubs in heaven.

221　A fictional resting place for aborted and miscarried babies. It does not represent a specific place, but there are special cemeteries that are provided and kept by Christian ministries of many difference different denominations.

Chapter 45—Where are you, God?

Anna returned from her trip and was weakened by the loss, but she was so excited to hold her boys and get their hugs.

Ben asked her, "Mommy, why are you crying?"

"Oh baby, I am just so happy to see you. I missed you," she answered as she smiled through her tears.

"Mommy, are you a crybaby?" asked Bobby in an adult voice with his arms crossed. "That's all you seem to do these days."

Shocked at his pronouncement, she said, "Why Robert Miller, I do not cry all the time. I just cry when I am happy to see my boys."

She then started tickling him, which he hated because he would always wet his pants.

"No, Mommy! Stop it!" he giggled.

They all began to laugh, and Anna was so grateful to have her boys. Their hugs took her mind off her intense feelings of guilt and pain over Melissa.

In the following weeks, Anna felt comforted by the love of the sisters and the priests of her parish, as well as the positive interactions with her wonderful students and colleagues at the college.

Sister *Bea*[222] checked in on her throughout the first week to make sure that her bleeding was under control and that she had made an appointment with an Ob/Gyn to be checked out again in a few weeks. She also took time to pray with Anna and to remind her of God's love for her and to not overdo things with her work at the college.

---

222 Sister Beatrice, Bea is short.

Anna, of course, threw herself into her work, her ministries, and her family, so that she would not have time to think about all that had been lost for her in the last few years. She taught her classes, picked up her boys from school and took them to her office for homework and pizza a couple of nights a week and then continued working after they went to bed in the evenings. She was highly focused and productive, having written a paper and was ahead of planning for her classes, but Anna had not begun to heal from her losses. She was simply ignoring them.

She attended church but could still not make a confession and begin to receive sacraments. She sat in the pews with her sons and watched Bobby receive communion every Sunday, but she would cross her arms across her chest, as she instructed Ben to do, and would receive a blessing with him instead. Some people just assumed she was doing it so that Ben would feel better about not being able to receive communion yet, but her confessor knew,[223] and he was very concerned for her frame of mind. He always made sure to find her after mass and look her in the eyes to see if she was doing okay.

"Hi boys," said Father, giving Anna's boys hugs. "Are you taking care of your mommy?" he asked as he looked at her, too.

"Oh yes, Father," Bobby said. "We take very good care of our mommy."

Anna and Father laughed at how darn cute they were and how grown-up Bobby seemed to be.

Father then asked quietly, "Are you eating? Are you seeing your counselor? Let me know what I can do to help you."

"I'm okay, Father," said Anna. "I'm just working very hard. You know, trying to stay busy."

---

223 Priests do not usually remember the sins confessed during the sacrament. In this case, the priest is her counselor which is a different situation. Remember that Anna is a fictional character and so are her priests. None of these experiences are meant to depict actual events.

"Well that's okay, but don't be too busy to care for yourself, young lady," he said with great authority.

She responded, "I promise Father. I'll do better."

She reassured everyone that she was indeed okay, but inside she felt vacant. The place where God had once brought great joy to her soul was now empty, and only the pieces of a cracked shell remained.

Every other weekend, her boys would go with their dad, and she missed having her babies to fill her arms and to make her smile. Those weekends were very difficult, but Srs. Bea and Anne would drive the thirty miles to the south to get Anna and make her come to spend those weekends with them and the other sisters at the *convent*. [224]

Anna was not alone and was not allowed to be idle and feel sorry for herself. There was always work to do, and she helped with the ministries by washing dishes. She especially loved washing the pots and pans. The physical action of scrubbing, the smell of the soap and the warmth of the water, somehow made her feel clean and to have a sense of accomplishment.

The weekends with the nuns reminded Anna of her summers of doing chores with her grandmother *(Martha)* on the farm.[225] While others were older and tended to plow, mowing hay and fence-mending, Anna and her grandmother would spend time together doing the other chores that needed to be done.

Martha taught her how to sew clothes by hand, milk cows, strain milk, churn butter, make soap, peel potatoes, slice vegetables, the art of how to build a fire in the woodstove, to properly cook foods, boil water, wash dishes, roll up biscuits from inside the flour pan, wash clothes, hoe weeds and how to pray the rosary while working.

---

224 The convent does not represent any real place.
225 Annie's grandmother, Martha, is a fictional character that represents the Irish immigrants of the 1800s. Martha is Moira's mother.

The chore of washing clothes was time-consuming and involved, as there was no way to wash clothes in or near the farmhouse/cabin. The water source was the spring, which was about a hundred yards downslope.

Their family farmhouse was rustic and had only one line for water--which emerged as a single spigot in the kitchen sink, no flushing toilet, and only one light from a single electric wire to the house.

The laundry loads consisted of sheets, towels, everyone's underwear, denim overalls, and other assorted rags used in the house. Martha would load up a wheelbarrow, and Anna would pull the wheelbarrow until she reached the downward slope. She would then turn it all around and allow gravity to pull the weight downslope, while she steered the wagon. Outside the springhouse and under a canopy made of sheets of aluminum, there were three large white tubs, which Martha filled with cold water.

The first tub was the washing tub, complete with a rubbing board and a hand-cranked wringer perched above. The water was cold, so Martha would mix a cup of powdered laundry soap into the water and stir it around with her hands.

On the stand next to the first tub were a scrub brush and a bar of lye soap for attacking the tough stains. Martha did the scrubbing and would allow Anna to stand on a box and continue to scrub when Martha's arms would get tired. The two "Women" would work together to get the dirt and stains rubbed out in the first washing.

Anna's job was to catch the clothes as they fell into the first rinse and second scrub tub as Martha cranked them through the wringer. She was not strong enough to crank the wringer yet but enjoyed her job of making sure the clothes didn't flop out and onto the ground.

The second tub also had a scrubbing board. Anna oversaw scrubbing each item as it fell into the clean water, and then Martha would scrub them some more and put them through the wringer and into the final rinse.

On the stand next to the third tub was a jug of vinegar. Martha mixed two cups of vinegar into the cold water and the clothes would go into the final rinse, where they were agitated by hand and then once again fed through the wringer and back into the wheelbarrow.

Annie loved the smell of the clean clothes as they hung them on the line to dry. The clotheslines were strong metal wires strung between two metal poles, which looked like Ts. In the middle of each sagging line was a central pole made of wood, with a metal hoop at the top. Anna's job was to make sure that all the clothes stayed off the ground and to help Martha lift the heavier denim garments onto the line. Together they would lift the central wooden pole upright to lift the wires and clothes above their heads.

Spending time with the sisters was very much like spending time with her grandmother. She became stronger and stronger emotionally each weekend that she stayed, as the work and prayer therapy seemed to bring her peace and contentment.

Even though she still didn't feel the presence of God in her heart and soul, she was part of something bigger than herself and had to serve those less fortunate. The humbling experience of serving others was a great exercise in helping her to begin to heal her own deep woundedness.

Psychologically, she needed to reconnect with a simpler time when she felt safe, loved, and nurtured. The child inside was engaged in humble, tactile experiences which were also benefiting her family--again something larger than herself. This was uniquely therapeutic for Anna.

The sisters were no doubt aware of the benefits of this type of work, as they experienced great joy, peace, and contentment in their own humble lives of service.

Martha, like the sisters, also provided a loving, nurturing environment for personal and spiritual growth.

As the weeks and months passed, Anna continued to recover and to regain her strength and positive outlook on life, but she was far from her old self. She still could not feel the presence of the Lord as she prayed, and it saddened her deeply.

"Where are you, God?" she would ask. "Why have you abandoned me?"

Recalling the words of Jesus in the psalm as he hung on the cross, she sang the Psalm to herself in prayer, "My God, My God. Why have you abandoned me?"

Anna sat in prayerful solitude reciting David's lament to God, with tears running down her face. Her tears were not just because she had lost so much. They were not tears of self-pity, but instead, they were the result of the absence of joy. She hungered to feel God's presence, the anointing of the Holy Spirit. She was a charismatic Catholic who could no longer sense the presence of God in her life as she prayed.

It was as though a multidimensional being had been reduced to only two dimensions. She may as well have been as flat as a topo map, with no expression of relief in the third dimension. She was blind and could not see. She was deaf and could not hear. She was lame and could no longer leap for joy. She was simply going through the motions for others but feeling nothing inside except pain and anguish and an incredible numbness.

Anna had given up doing many of the things that she once enjoyed, such as teaching the field methods course. She didn't seem to lack the energy for her boys, who were a constant reminder to her that there were good things in life and that she had something to live for regardless of her own feelings of low self-esteem.

Adam was particularly bothered by her continued battle with depression and frequently stopped by to give her pep talks.

"Anna, why don't we present a talk together about some of the innovative things we've collaborated on in teaching? ... There's a conference coming up in a few months and you could help me to lead a field trip to the Grand Canyon. There are lots of your favorite rocks there, you know."

She always made an excuse about having to go to the convent to help the sisters or that she needed to be home for her boys.

Adam had been a very close friend and teaching partner, and he truly missed the sweet Anna that he used to teach with in the summers. He couldn't believe she'd be so depressed about divorcing that bastard husband of hers, so one day he asked her, "Annie, what is really going on? You can't be this upset about ending a marriage, can you?"

She answered quietly, "I don't know, D., maybe I just have a chemical imbalance and need some drugs?"

"Well for Pete's sake, get some! I for one miss working with you. Enough is enough!" he shouted in exasperation. "Just get up and shake it off and if you can't, then please get some help."

Annie looked at him with tears welling up in her eyes, "Adam, I'm sorry. I just.....".

He immediately felt so terrible that he had made her cry. He closed her office door and came around her desk and pulled her head into his chest and hugged her tightly, saying, "Annie, you are a beautiful and intelligent woman. You have so much to offer the world. Please snap out of this. If not for your sake, then for the sake of your kids. They need a mom who is going to be okay." He held her face in his hands, looked into her eyes, and said, "You are special, Annie, and I care for you," as he leaned down and kissed her on the lips.

Annie kissed him back and was grateful for his tenderness, honesty, and genuine affection. "Ok," she said quietly, "I will try."

He heard a voice in the hallway and immediately pushed away from her and began speaking about something entirely random. Then he whispered, "I am sorry, I hope I didn't make you feel uncomfortable."

Annie smiled at him and said, "No, D., It was nice. Thank you for caring so much."

He then opened the door and walked out, leaving the door open behind him. Even though Annie was grateful for the tenderness, she did not have the same response or desire for Adam that she had felt with Sean. She was still very numb emotionally and would not be able to move beyond for some time. She also assumed that he was just feeling sorry for her.

She sat there slightly stunned by what had just happened, but realized that she did, in fact, feel something, but it was muted and would not allow her to respond in any demonstrative way.

Her thoughts then returned to her work as she tried to not dwell on what had just happened. *Not again,* she thought to herself. *No, not again.*

A few days later, Adam came back around and acted as though nothing had ever happened, for which Anna was very grateful. She smiled and followed his lead.

"Adam, I've decided to take you up on the Grand Canyon field trip. I would love to do that next spring break. Let's make it happen, okay?"

"Are you sure?" he said excitedly, "You would be great. I will see to putting it on the list of courses to be offered."

Annie didn't really want to do anything but also realized that he was right. She did have to focus on her teaching again and move on. Most of all, though, she felt good about putting his mind at ease. How she felt didn't seem as important as making sure he was not worrying so much about her.

Chapter 46—Seattle
Closure

After a well-planned and successful spring break field trip, things were back to normal for Adam and Anna. They continued to be good friends and colleagues, and there was never a mention of the depression and the awkward period between them.

Adam had hoped that after spring break she would reconsider teaching the field course again, but he was unable to convince her. He did, however, understand that she was still struggling with single parenting and the fallout from an ugly divorce.

Anna still helped in the administration of the field camp course by getting all fee waivers and setting up the housing, scholarships, and the various things that she would have done anyway for Adam. Being able to help with the planning made her feel less guilty about ditching him right before camp. He was joined by an older professor from another school, *Dr. Walter, Walt, Johnson,* [226]who had students at the same camp.

She joined the campers at the vans the morning that they were to leave and felt a twinge of sadness at not being able to go with them. She dearly loved the field camp course, but just needed to be at home with her family and to continue to heal from her losses of that year.

Adam and Walt were grateful for the donuts and coffee that Anna brought as well as the finished paperwork needed for a smooth

---

226 Fictional field camp instructor from another college in the south. His character is not based on any real person, past or present.

trip. She wished them all luck and sadly walked away, realizing that she would probably never be able to teach that course again.

As the weeks of camp passed, it was time again for Sean's camp to arrive. Sean wondered if he'd see Annie there as in summer's past and was hoping that things would not be too awkward for them. He had hoped that they could remain friends. Deep inside, he really hoped to see her again, so he could apologize for his clumsy handling of the entire situation. Even though he had to say goodbye to an intimate relationship with her, he still loved her very much and thought of her often. She was a part of him and always would be.

When they arrived at the Rocky Mountain field station and campus, he excitedly looked for her when he saw the trucks pull in from her school. His heart sank when he saw D., and another man, an older professor, but no Annie. He walked over and greeted Adam, who was genuinely tickled to see him. The men shook hands, and Walt introduced himself.

Sean asked, "So where is Annie this year?"

"She had some health issues this year, Sean, and needed to stay home with her children." answered Adam.

"What the heck happened to her? Is she okay?" asked Sean.

"Well, she went through a horrible divorce and stopped eating. She then got sick from low blood sugar and anemia; we think. She's on the mend now, though. She just needed a break, so she could get herself back on track. She'll be okay."

Sean walked away feeling horrible. When he got to his room, he tried to call Annie. He wanted to know that she was okay.

Ben answered the phone, polite as usual.

Sean spoke, "Hi, Ben, is it? This is Michael Anderson. I'm a friend of your mom's. Is she there? "

"Just one moment, please. Mommy, it's Michael Anderson. Do you want to talk to him?"

"No sweetie. I'm indisposed okay?" said Annie sadly.

"Okay, uh, she is disposed, uh I mean indisposed. So, you will have to call back later."

Sean reluctantly said, "Well, tell her that I called and that I would like to hear from her. Okay?"

"Okay, Mr. Anderson. I'll tell her." Ben hung up the phone and asked, "Mommy, what does 'indisposed' mean?"

"It just means that I am busy now and can't come to the phone."

"But Mommy. You weren't too busy."

"I know," said Anna. I just really didn't want to talk to him and didn't know how to say that without being rude. Does that make sense to you?" she asked.

"Oh, I get it now. You didn't want to hurt his feelings. Mommy you are so nice, aren't you?" he asked.

"Well," chuckled Anna, "Not really. I should have spoken to him. I am so sorry that you were put in that awkward position. Next time, I will speak to him. Okay?"

Sean was disappointed and penned a letter to Annie. *"My dearest Annie...I hope you are okay. Adam said that you have some health issues. Please call me or write me and let me know that you are okay. I still care deeply for you even though I am not able to be with you... I am so sorry for the hurt that was caused. I never intended to hurt you... He told her of his favorite spot in the field and how he missed seeing her at the camp.... A light is missing here for sure. People have been asking about you. You are clearly missed, too, by the town folk who were used to seeing you here each summer...."* He ended the letter with *"Best regards, Sean."*

Annie received the letter in the post and opened it immediately. She loved every word until she read the ending salutation. *"Best Regards, Sean."*

The words cut through her like a knife. It was like salt being rubbed into an open wound. *Best Regards?* She placed the beautiful letter in her bible and swore to never open another letter from him.

Part of her wanted to respond with a letter, but she could not find the words. Annie was honest to a fault and was not able to pretend to just be his friend after all that she had gone through. It was essential to her healing for her to just move on.

He clearly didn't love her and was only feeling guilty about the hurt. Her heart just couldn't take the continuous glaring rejection.

Even though Anna was not with Adam in the summer course, he thought of her often and hoped she was doing okay. He missed having her as a partner and could see that Sean was saddened by her absence as well. She was clearly missed.

Adam wrote to her as well and continued to push her professionally. He knew she still needed to publish or perish. She was not focused on her professional development at the time and he knew all too well that she would not achieve full professor status or tenure if she didn't pull out of the nosedive, she seemed to be in. Their department felt that she was a rare talent, and being a female professor was also a plus for her advancement.

With that in mind, he submitted a paper for possible publication the moment he returned from camp. It was one that both he and Anna had written parts of previously and had been editing for submission. She had agreed to submit the paper before Montreal but had been too distracted to meet any deadlines.

He added his skills as a writer and editor to the process and entered both the paper for publication and submitted an abstract for the annual geology conference being hosted in Seattle the following fall.

Anna was pleasantly surprised and agreed to go to the meeting with him to present their work. It was the least she could do after ditching him with field camp and leaving him to break in a new partner. She knew there might be a chance of seeing Sean again, but felt that Adam would help to buffer the experience if it happened.

The following fall semester rolled around, and Anna used her expertise in photography and graphic design to produce the slides that they needed for their presentation. Back in those days, each view graph was produced on a mapping/drafting table, using mechanical pencils, printed photos, stencils, and rapidograph pens - various drafting tools- much like the maps produced at field camp.

After each viewgraph was produced, a 35-mm color photo was taken of each using a special slide film. The film was then taken from the camera in a dark room, where the film was processed with chemicals and carefully hung up to dry. Each tiny image was carefully cut from the filmstrip and was then placed in square sheaths made of cardboard. The 'slides' would then be carefully placed sequentially in a slide carousel[227] so that the entire carriage could be advanced slide by slide by a specialized projector, designed to shine light through each slide and project each image on a screen for presentation. It was a lengthy process that required practice, patience, and skill.

As it turned out, Anna was quite good at the entire process. Adam felt grateful to have her as the artistic partner in this endeavor.

They were able to get funding for the trip and they both traveled together to the great city of Seattle. The hotel was thankfully just a block from the convention center and would be an easy walk each day.

Anna was worried that she might see Sean this year. Part of her wanted to see him, longed to see him again. Another part of her couldn't bear the pain.

At registration, everyone is given a program with the list of abstracts and authors presenting at the conference.

As they stood in line, Anna looked around to see if she recognized anyone, if she could see Sean. *So far, so good*, she thought, at least until she checked the conference program.

---

227   *a round plastic or metal disk with a hole in the center*

Authors? A…….. her heart jumped. She felt panicked and excited all at the same time. Anderson, S.A., was indeed doing a presentation with one of his students on the rate of magma evolution in the Yellowstone Caldera. She felt like she might faint. *It is a special session and one that I would love to attend,* she thought. *Not because of Sean, as much as the topic.*

Adam noted she was white as a sheet and asked her, "Are you okay?"

"Oh, I am hungry, that is all," she replied.

"I wonder if your buddy Anderson is going to be here," he asked as he perused the program. "Ah, there he is. Mr. Bigshot has a session all to himself on Yellowstone. We'd better not miss that."

"Ah sure that would be great," she said, not wanting Adam to think that it would bother her in the least.

"You know, he asked about you this summer. He seemed disappointed that you weren't doing camp anymore. I told him you were surviving single parenting and he seemed to understand. Are you guys not friends anymore?" he asked.

"I don't have time to really think about it, D. I guess we are. I really haven't thought much about it," she said looking down at the ground.

Adam sensed that something was very wrong but didn't push. He adored Anna and could tell she didn't want to talk about it.

Later that evening, Adam called her room and asked if he could buy her dinner. She graciously accepted and met him in the hotel restaurant downstairs. They were escorted to a small table by a huge window looking out onto the city street.

Adam discussed several of the talks that were of interest to him personally as he skimmed the schedule of events for the next day.

"Have you made any firm choices yet?" he queried.

Annie was looking off into the distance and was not listening to Adam at all.

"I say, did you know that Santa Claus actually lives at the South Pole?" .... "Do you think that the wolves in Alaska will become extinct soon?" he continued. "Annie!?' he said as he raised his voice. "Where are you? Are you sure you are okay?"

"Oh, so sorry D., I was somewhere else. Please forgive me. What were you saying?"

"No kidding," he said in an exasperated voice. "What the heck is wrong with you?"

"I don't know, D. I'm just missing the kids, I guess," she offered in a tone that sounded like she wasn't completely sure what was wrong with her but needed to say something.

"Well, snap out of it okay?" he said in his cute chuckle.

As they were finishing dinner, Adam became animated and started waving at someone who was coming into the restaurant. She turned around to see who was so familiar and made eye contact with Sean.

His face lit up when he saw Annie, but she immediately looked away. He had hoped that they could still be friends.

She felt like she did when she was face to face with the male elk at Frazier Mountain. She didn't dare make eye contact for fear that Adam and the woman with Sean would see that she was terrified. More importantly, she didn't want Sean to see her anguish at having to see him again.

Anna stood up as Sean and the woman approached their table. Sean then properly introduced his wife Sophia to Adam and then to her.

Anna put out her hand before Sean could say her name and said, "Hi, I am Professor Sarah Moore, very pleased to meet you."

Sophia was fair-skinned, had dark eyes and dark hair, with a very petite frame.

Anna felt like an Amazon next to her. She looked into Sophia's warm, brown eyes and knew immediately that she loved her.

She could see her soul and she was a beautiful person. Sophia immediately liked Anna as well.

Adam then asked if they wanted to join them.

Before Sean could decline, Sophia said, "Oh, we would love to. If that's okay with you?" she said, looking up at Sean.

"Sure," he said as he pulled out her chair, so she could sit across from Anna. "I usually only go with him to San Francisco, but this year, it is Seattle," said, Sophia, as she sat and smiled at both Adam and Anna.

Sean nervously sat across from D.

Anna could feel him looking at her, but she didn't dare look away from Sophia. She would not be able to pretend not to love him still and to just be friends. No doubt, Sophia would pick up on the feelings and expressions and that was the last thing that Anna wanted. She just wasn't a good actress and could genuinely focus on Sophia because she saw her gentle soul and wanted to know her and like her.

"So, Sarah? Do you also teach the summer class?" asked Sophia.

"Oh no. I am a single mother with two kids. It is difficult enough to leave to come to a conference, much less to be gone for weeks at a time," she said emphatically.

"Oh," said Sophia. "So, Adam, you teach the summer course then?"

"Ah yes, "said Adam. "I teach with Sean in the summers."

Anna interrupted and asked Sophia about what she did in the summers while Sean was teaching, terrified that Adam would announce that she used to teach the summer course with them.

Sophia and Anna spoke pleasantly as they got to know one another. They spoke of her teen daughters and all the different activities they were involved in during the summers, as well as about Anna's boys and the ranch.

Sophia shared her love of artwork and how much she enjoyed her time in Italy. Anna found that she really enjoyed learning about Sophia and could see why Sean adored her. She was a very sweet, delicate lady who clearly could have done much more with her talents and intellect.

They were both mothers and women who loved the same man. Anna felt a bond with Sophia and could not be jealous of her or hate her in the least. Thankfully she never had to speak directly to Sean. When it was time for dessert or a nightcap, Anna excused herself from the table, so she could go to her room to rest.

"I'm sorry, but I have a headache and need to go lie down. It was so nice to meet you, Sophia," said, Anna, as she shook her hand.

"Oh, it was so good to talk to you too," said Sophia as she stood up and gave Anna a warm hug.

Anna quickly exited and could feel her tears as they flowed down her cheeks. The elevator seemed to take an eternity as she patiently waited with her back toward the restaurant entrance.

"Our Father, who art in heaven, hallowed be Thy name...." she began reciting the Lord's prayer to take her mind off her pain and to keep from collapsing entirely. She managed to get her room door open and lay on the bed staring up at the ceiling.

"Please Lord, spare me this pain. Please, Lord, give me the strength and the courage needed to endure this conference." She removed her clothing and got into a hot shower. Afterward, she crawled into her bed and cried herself to sleep.

When she woke the next morning, she felt a dull pain behind her eyes and mild nausea. She got dressed and met Adam in the lobby. They walked to the convention center and prepared for their talk.

Anna managed to make it through the preparation room set up and everything was perfect for their presentation. While they sat in the dark presentation hall, waiting their turn to present, Anna became overwhelmed with an intensely painful headache and associated nausea. She could not open her eyes, her head hurt so bad.

Adam noticed that she didn't seem well and asked if she needed to go to the first aid station.

She began to cry. "My head hurts so bad."

He helped her into the hall, and she went to the bathroom where she tried to vomit but couldn't. She felt that if she just puked, she might feel better.

Adam was worried and went to a security person who was female and asked her to please check on his friend. She came out of the ladies' room and went to the first aid station and returned with a gurney.

Anna was apparently quite ill and was taken to see the *EMTs*,[228] who had been called to assess her condition.

"Can you open your eyes for me, Ms. Moore?" said the kind fireman.

"No!" cried Anna. "It hurts so bad…" she whispered through the tears.

"I believe she has a raging migraine, so let's get an ice pack across the back of her neck and one across her forehead."

"Ma'am, are you allergic to any medications that you are aware of?"

"Just penicillin," she said weakly.

"Okay, we can transport you to an ER, ma'am or we can give you an injection of a drug called *Imitrex*.[229] Which would you prefer?"

"Please, no ER," she cried.

"Have you had this drug before, ma'am?"

"No, I've never had a headache like this before."

---

228 Emergency Medical Technicians trained in emergency medicine.

229 A drug sometimes given to migraine sufferers to help alleviate the pain. It is a non-narcotic drug known as a Triptan. It is a lot like ibuprofen and is used as an anti-inflammatory.

"This should help relieve the pain. Please follow up with Tylenol. The nurse here has Tylenol that she will give you."

"Call us again or go to the ER if this gets any worse. Okay?" he said to the nurse.

It became clear to Adam that she was too ill to help give their talk, so he left to go to the room for the session.

"Dr. Moore has taken ill and will not be able to join me today, but I will present our findings…" said Adam as he stood alone at the presenter's podium in the front of the room.

Sean was in the audience and immediately got up and left the talk. He walked briskly to the first aid station where he found Annie in the dark and sobbing on a gurney.

"Annie, it's Sean," he said with his voice shaking. "What's going on? How may I help?"

"You can't," she cried while holding a bag of ice across her forehead.

The nurse spoke to Sean and said, "She has a migraine and a really bad one it seems. The EMTs have been here and she has had a pain shot. She just needs to rest now. There is nothing that anyone can really do for her."

Sean felt helpless and very sad. He hated to see her in pain and sat in a chair near her, watching her sleep. Even in intense pain, she looked so beautiful. He wanted to climb on the gurney with her and hold her but knew he could not.

About an hour later, D. arrived, and he too stood helpless and bothered by Annie's state. Both men reluctantly walked away from the first aid station to get a cup of coffee.

"These headaches seem ta be debilitatin," noted Sean. "Has she had em before like this?"

"I've never seen her have one before. She has had some blood sugar and blood pressure issues in the past, but nothing like this. I hope she gets past these issues she's been having."

"Me too," said Sean in a concerned voice.

"Well let me know if there is anythin we can do. I'll check in with ya later to see how she's doing," Sean said as he had no choice but to walk away to meet Sophia.

Anna eventually was able to stand up and leave the station. She had missed an entire day of the conference and felt just horrible for letting Adam down.

He reassured her that he was fully capable of presenting their work and for her to just get better.

"You know, Sean came by to check on you too?" said D. "He seemed very concerned about you."

"I know," said Anna. "That was nice of him."

She spent the next day of the conference in her room unable to do much but take *Acetaminophen*[230] and drink caffeinated sodas to try to alleviate the pain in her head.

Adam came by to check on her and brought her soup from the dining area. He made sure she was not dead and continued his attendance at the varied presentations which were of interest to him, including Sean's presentation on Yellowstone. He took notes to share with Anna.

After the Yellowstone presentation, Sean asked D. about her current condition.

"She's sitting up and eating something, but still looks like hell," said D.

"I have to leave soon but will go by and check on her. Ya think that would be okay?" asked Sean.

"Sure, she is in Room 334," offered D.

Annie heard a timid knock on her door. When she peered through the peephole in her door, she could not clearly see who

---

230 An anti-inflammatory substance found in brand name aspirin free remedies.

was knocking. She walked away from the door and back to her bed. A moment or two later, she heard a louder knock and Sean's voice.

"Annie, it's Sean. I would like to see how yer doin and say goodbye if ya don't mind… Please Annie?"

She reluctantly walked to the door and opened it slightly with the chain in place.

"Annie, are ya going to be okay?" he asked.

She refused to make eye contact with him and replied, "Yes, I think so."

"Did ya get my letter this summer? I'm so sorry. I never meant ta…I never meant ta hurt ya," he said softly.

"It's okay. It wasn't on purpose. I'll be okay. Please don't give me another thought." she said as she closed the door.

Sean, sadly walked away, wishing he could stay, but knowing he could not. He met Adam in the hall and said his goodbyes. "See you at camp this summer, D.?" he asked.

D. chuckled. "You can bet on it."

On the last day of the conference, Anna was able to go to a few talks that she was interested in but was truly sad that she hadn't been able to attend the Yellowstone presentations. She still loved Sean, and it would have been difficult, but she was truly interested in the research and what had been learned from the samples they had collected together there.

As she sat in the dark presentation room, watching a presentation on soil development, she thought of Sean and how guilty she felt not engaging him. *I just couldn't. The pain is just still so intense… and there is Sophia.*

She switched her thoughts from her own suffering to focus on remembering Sophia's eyes and smile. *She is a beautiful woman. I can see why Sean loves her so much,* she thought to herself.

Anna then tried to clear her mind of the couple and focus instead on her sons. She pulled out their picture and smiled once again. "Yes, they are my light. Praise you, God, for their love."

Chapter 47—Seeking Redemption
The dark night of the soul

After arriving home, Anna reflected on her visit with Sophia and realized why Sean had not been able to leave her. She truly was a nice person. Part of her wished that they could have been friends. There was some comfort, however, in knowing that Sean no doubt had to make a tough choice.

Meeting Sophia had brought her the closure she needed to move on and to heal. It was extremely selfish for her to continue an intimate relationship with Sean, knowing that Sophia loved him too and also loved him first.

Her healing continued as she spent every other weekend with the sisters and immersed herself in her teaching, children, and spiritual studies.

Anna's greatest desire now was to find the joy that had been lost. Even though she prayed and served in her ministries in the church, the presence of God, the joy she had once felt, seemed to be missing.

Anna was experiencing a true crisis of faith. She had always believed in the goodness of God and the goodness of others, but the experiences of the past few years had left her feeling confused and empty. *"Why has God abandoned me?"*

It was in her nature to nurture, and she possessed an innate ability to feel the pain and joy of others. Even this experience was muted, lacking the depth and satisfaction it once brought. Father had once told her that her ability was a gift. She now felt it was a curse because she was simply going through the motions without feeling the responses.

During one of her counseling sessions, Anna shared her concerns and feelings. "How can I continue to serve God without also feeling the presence of God? Where is God?"

"It is both a blessing and a curse, dear girl," said Father William. "God uses you every single day. You *are* His hands, His feet, His voice, His love, to others. You do not have to feel the grace to know that God is blessing you and others with each interaction."

"How can that be true, Father," asked Anna. "I don't feel it like I used to."

Father sat and studied Anna as she poured out her heart to him.

"What must I do? I pray the rosary every single day. I sit in the adoration chapel and ask God to fill me and use me for His glory. I do the liturgy of the hours. I fast, pray, and serve. Why doesn't He answer me, Father?" Anna cried. "What is wrong with me that I can't feel loved or joyful anymore?"

"Anna, I think the problem here is that you have not yet forgiven yourself for your failed marriage, the loss of Sean, the loss of your baby… God forgave All even before you asked forgiveness. He has loved you since before you were born."

"I know, Father."

Father William forcefully continued, "*You*, Anna, have not and will not forgive yourself. You blame yourself for all, and *you* carry the burden of all pain on your shoulders. It's not fair. You did not fail your marriage. You tried your best. Your husband failed his family and you. You did not fail in your love of Sean. You have expressed that you gave all, including giving up the sacraments for him. He, in fact, failed you. You did not fail Melissa. You loved her and were willing to face the ridicule of an illegitimate child, to bring her life. You did the right thing for her to the end. You accepted all responsibility for every one of your decisions. You, my dear, have nothing to blame yourself for except being human and having human failings.

"God forgives, showers you with His grace, and blesses you beyond measure, but *you* Anna, *you* are the one refusing His grace and forgiveness.

"*You* refuse God's love because *you* do not feel worthy. Who are you to question God's love and God's mercy!?"

She wept and nodded in agreement, "I truly am not worthy, Father, but I want to be."

Father stood up from his chair and knelt before Anna. He held her hands in his and looked lovingly into her eyes, and whispered passionately… "You *are* worthy, Anna! God made you, and you are wonderfully and lovingly made. Don't ever doubt that. God desires that you love Him, but how can you truly love Him if you hate yourself?"

He then stood and walked to his desk where he picked up the Bible and began flipping pages. "Here, read this passage out loud. Go on," he said as he laid the word of God on her lap.

"Matthew 22:" she began… "*When the Pharisee heard that he had silenced the Sadducees, they gathered together, and one of them (a scholar of the law) tested him by asking, 'Teacher, which is the greatest commandment in the Law?' He said to him, 'You shall love the Lord your God, with all your heart and with all your soul and with all your mind. This is the first and greatest commandment.' The second is like it: 'You shall love your neighbor as yourself.' The whole law and the prophets depend on these two commandments.*"

"What does that mean, Anna?" asked Father.

She was silent and still tearful. "I am to love God and my neighbor? I do that already, Father."

"Is that all it says, dear girl?" continued Father.

"Well…as yourself?"

"That's it! How can you possibly love God and your neighbor if you do not first love yourself?"

She looked down in shame, as she was not even certain she could truly love herself. That was just too much to ask.

Father smiled confidently, "You see…You must first love yourself, as God loves you."

At the end of the session, Father gave her a book and an assignment.

"Here is a book that I want you to read before our next session. Reflect on the words of Mother Teresa of Calcutta. Were you aware that she too sought a holy life, served others and could not feel the love of God in her life?"

"Really?" asked Anna. "No, I never really knew that about her."

"Well, it is true. Learn to love yourself, dear girl, and you may find that the joy of the Lord returns to you. God cannot fill a vessel that is filled with self-doubt and self-loathing. You think your vessel is broken or empty, but I say it is already full, and the pain and self-loathing leave little room to be filled with the joy of the Lord. Just think about that. Won't you?"

"Yes Fr., I will try."

Over the following month, Anna read about the life and struggles of *Mother Teresa*,[231] and also the personal letters she wrote herself, which were published in, *"Come be my light."*[232]

She was shocked to find out that Mother was saddened too by the absence of God, not just in prayer but also in the Eucharist. Her emptiness went on for fifty years and began at almost the very moment she began tending the poor and dying in Calcutta.

---

231 Mother Teresa of Calcutta – catholic nun who served the very poor on the streets of Calcutta, India. She started the order Missionaries of Charity, 1950. She became Mother Teresa and is now a saint in the Catholic Church.

232 A selection of letters written by Mother Teresa to her spiritual advisor. They are published in several smaller books, including "The Dark Night of the Soul," and in the 2017 moving, "The Letters." See the bibliography for further information.

Teresa too seemed cheery in public and positive, but privately expressed "living in a state of deep and abiding spiritual pain." She expressed many of the same feelings that Anna too was experiencing, "dryness, darkness, loneliness, torture."

Mother Teresa expressed her experience as *hell,* and at one point to doubt the existence of God. She went on to state that her smile in public was a mask or a cloak that covers everything. She rationalized the absence of God as a way for her to experience how it must feel for the poor and dying, to know the insecurity and loneliness of poverty as you lack the necessities to live. Teresa thought that perhaps this was God's way of helping her to somehow be more open to their pain and to minister to them more fully.

Anna began to accept what Mother had said but wondered what His purpose was for her. How was she to use this emptiness for His glory?

A few months later, Anna attended a meeting with charismatic leaders of the church and was reminded of the words of Pope John Paul II.

She felt inspired to re-read the *"Theology of the Body,"*[233] which expressly discussed all relationships, including the relationship with the body of Christ through the Eucharist. She hoped to achieve empathy for Mother Teresa, who expressed the absence of God in the Eucharist, and also for the loss that must be felt by those who were denied the sacrament.

The human body includes right from the beginning...the capacity of expressing love, that love in which the person becomes a gift -- and by means of this gift -- fulfills the meaning of his being and existence. St. John Paul II.

---

233 Pope John Paul II, "Theology of the Body," usccb.org/issues-and-actions/marriage-and-family/natural-family-planning/catholic-teaching/theology-of-the-body.

In reading the encyclical and studying it as someone who had been married, in love with a married man, and was now a committed single, she discovered the message of Pope John Paul's teaching of the "integrated vision of the human person."

The human body has a specific meaning, making visible an invisible reality, and is capable of revealing answers regarding fundamental questions for all human persons ...The body shows us the call and gives us the means to love in the image of God.

He also encouraged a true reverence for the gift of one's own sexuality and the challenge to live in a way worthy of the dignity of the human person.

In keeping with the prayers of Pope John Paul II, she increased her engagement in the adoration of the body of Christ in the perpetual adoration chapel at her church and at the convent.

Pope John Paul II had prayed for and encouraged that every parish around the world provide a perpetual adoration for the body of Christ, his people to experience...

Closeness to the Eucharistic Christ in silence and contemplation does not distance us from our contemporaries but, on the contrary, makes us open to human joy and distress, broadening our hearts on a global scale. Through adoration the radical transformation of the world and to the sowing of the gospel. Anyone who prays to the Eucharistic Savior draws the whole world with him and raises it to God.

Over the next few months, Anna continued to pray fervently. Instead of whining that God was not there for her and feeling abandoned, she focused her spiritual energy on the healing of herself. She began praying and asking Mother Teresa of Calcutta and Pope John Paul II to pray for conversion and healing. She had never truly done that before. Her prayers were usually for the healing of others or for her life to bring glory to God, but she had never truly focused her own prayer on the healing of her own soul and heart. It felt selfish.

One day, while she meditated and prayed in the silence of the perpetual adoration chapel at her church, she experienced a warming in her hands as they rested palms up in her lap. She lifted her hands to a prayerful posture and touched them with her lips. "Why are my hands so warm?" she asked.

Being a scientist, Anna was always quick to look for a logical explanation before a spiritual one. She assumed it must have been that they had been resting in one position for too long, and the blood flow or nerves were responding accordingly.

Anna picked up her chaplet of mercy beads and began with an opening prayer from the diary of *Saint Faustina*.[234] ".... O fount of life, unfathomable Divine Mercy, envelop the whole world and empty Yourself out upon us…"

Deliberately and delicately holding each individual bead in turn, she recited "For the sake of his sorrowful passion, have mercy on us and on the whole world." This phrase was repeated ten times in succession. "Holy God, Holy Mighty One…"

What happened next, could not be explained by the physical laws of nature alone.

Anna felt warmth, and intense warmth, not hot, not painful as in burning, but an intense warmth, like being washed or bathed in light. This warmth was followed by what could only be described as a warm breath or wind blowing her hair away from her face. Anna began to whisper, "Have mercy on me and on the whole world. Lord have mercy, Christ have mercy, Lord have mercy."

---

234   St. Faustina was a Polish Catholic nun and mystic, whose visions-apparitions of Jesus Christ inspired the devotion of the chaplet of divine mercy. The prayer is traditionally recited at 3:00 p.m.

Anna then heard an inaudible voice say to her, "Heal me, Lord, so that I may better serve You and bring You glory. Amen."

For the first time since her loss of Sean and Melissa, she felt the presence of God!

She was not hallucinating. It was not a voice speaking to her from inside her head. It was the presence of God instructing and teaching her how to pray for her own healing.

Anna began to sob tears of intense joy as she looked upon the body of Christ, housed in the monstrance and exposed in perpetual adoration.

Where is the light? She thought, *Where is this heat coming from? I want to see the source of this great healing warmth.*

When she opened her eyes, she only saw the bare reality of the physical presence on the altar. She could feel the wooden pew beneath her, her feet on the kneeler in front of her...she was in the real world, but what was happening to her was not of this world. The source was not in the chapel itself.

Anna continued to sit with her eyes closed saying, "Praise You Lord. Thank you, God." Over and over again. "Thank you, Saint Faustina, Blessed Pope John Paul II and Mother Teresa! Praise God for this gift."

After some time passed, Anna could feel the warmth begin to leave. She selfishly asked, "Oh please don't go Lord. Please don't go."

She noted that the leaving was very gradual, but very noticeable. The entire experience had been like the doppler effect, with her feeling the warmth gradually coming and after an extended stationery period, it left in the same fashion.

Anna was so excited, especially about the doppler effect, and a bit dazed. *Who would believe such a thing?* she thought.

She did not walk out of the adoration chapel totally healed of her own self-loathing and doubt, but she once again could feel the anointing of the Holy Spirit and the joy of the Lord was once more radiating from her. In her mind, she had experienced nothing short of a miracle, but she would share it with no one but Father William.

She did feel as though a light; a candle had been ignited in her soul and that light was shining out into the darkness around her.

Everyone noticed it too. Her colleagues at the college, her church family and especially the Benedictine Sisters, who had so lovingly and patiently accepted and loved her through the healing process. The sisters instantly knew that something wonderful had happened. It was obvious that the light of Christ once more filled Anna's eyes. They walked into the chapel for worship and knelt.

As Anna looked up at the corpus hanging from the cross at the front of the church, she began to recite the prayer of St. Francis:

Most high glorious God enlighten the darkness of my heart. Give me right faith, sure hope and perfect charity. Fill me with understanding and knowledge that I may fulfill your command.

When she rose from prayers, she was met by sisters Bea and Anne, who were seated in the back of the chapel. They immediately sensed that she had emerged from *"The Dark Night of the Soul,"*[235] as they embraced and cried together. It was a joyous experience. All darkness had gone away, and she now felt filled with the joy of God.

Over the following weeks and months, Anna could barely contain her happiness. She was singing again. Her soul was singing once more. The infectious smile and giggle had returned, and she felt loved--truly loved--and it didn't have to come from another

---

235 A phrase used in Catholic spirituality which refers to a spiritual crisis one experiences as they move on the path to be in union with God. It is based on a Poem and treatise penned by St. John of the Cross, a Carmelite friar. The story is written so that Anna, a devout Catholic, experiences this darkness.

person, it came from within herself and from the presence of the Holy Spirit.

She took that joy with her and into her teaching at the college and into her interactions with others each day. From that moment on, she never questioned God's love for her again. In this journey from darkness into light, she also found a way to forgive her ex-husband and to forgive Sean, more importantly; she had found a way to forgive herself.

After a year of reflection and healing, Anna asked if she could work to enter the Benedictine Order as an oblate.

An oblate is not a nun in the traditional sense, with vows of poverty and chastity. The role of the oblate is to live in the world, to become holy in the world, and to bring the world to God by being witnesses of Christ by word and example to those around them.[236]

The sisters were accepting of her request, and she prepared by expanding her studies and spiritual advisement.

Anna promised to lead an enriched Christian life, according to the gospel as reflected in the rule of St. Benedict. This included a very active prayer life, by engaging in the liturgy of the hours and by focusing a few times a day to silence. As an oblate, she focused her energy on becoming holy in her chosen way of life, which was as a single mother to her children, a successful college professor, and as a committed single in the Catholic Church.

Her goal was to cultivate an awareness of the presence of God in silence, devoting time daily to the praise of God. It was Anna's greatest desire to be able to experience the full joy of the presence of God in her life. In this way, Anna always had a community, family, and ministry, and she was never alone. She could still

---

236 This experience for the main character Anna does not represent a real person or experience associated with the Benedictine Oblate Order. It is a fictional interaction meant to deepen the healing of the character Anna.

be a loving and devoted mother to her children, which was her sacramental duty.

According to the Catholic church, she was married to their father until "death do they part." She honored that sacrament and the vows she made to raise her children in the Catholic Church.

In the order of Benedict, Anna contributed to the community in service, fellowship, and prayer. She had a purpose and focus in her life once again.

For the next few years of raising her boys, Anna slowly improved her outlook on life and began to heal and move on. She never dated or remarried and left herself little or no time to even consider relationships beyond her boys, teaching, research, and service to God.

Anna found contentment and happiness as a committed single. Professionally, she had earned tenure and the rank of full professor. At her church, she was very involved in the youth ministries and frequently attended youth conferences with her boys.

As an oblate, she enjoyed the opportunities for grace, through self-mortification such as fasting, and humble service.

Anna even began playing her guitar again but found joy only in hymns of praise. When she tried to play folk pieces, she was reminded of Sean, and sadness would creep in. The old songs were not something she was ready to revisit, not yet.

She was clearly happier in general, but there was a perpetual wound that would probably never heal.

* * *

Chapter 48—Living On

In addition to her professional, single life, she also found time each summer to take her boys on camping trips to places of geologic interest. Seeing them and their friends enjoy nature and sharing her own knowledge of the beauty of God's earth, brought her profound joy.

Each summer her boys would usually bring school friends, who would otherwise never have such an experience, and in this way, Anna saw her sacrifice financially as doing God's work too.

The summer trips would usually include a tent site and a day or two in the Stillwater Valley and a yearly visit with "Uncle Jim."

Anna's boys often thought that she should marry Jim and live happily ever after, but she was content with spending time together and making new memories in all the places she had once found joy with Sean.

Even though her love for Sean and the wonderful experiences were not erased, she had found a way to refocus her energy on loving her children and finding her way back to a place inside that was not in shattered pieces.

Jim never asked her about Sean and enjoyed spending time with her and her boys. He looked forward to her arrival each summer and often asked when she would be getting back out into the field.

The valley and the river became a place of rediscovery and contemplation for Anna, as it was always the final stop on all family return trips home.

In the Benedictine tradition, it was a place too where the noise of everyday life was blocked out by the roar of the river, the same river that supplied a focus for her union with Sean. Each quiet period of contemplation brought healing to her brokenness inside.

Anna's boys loved camping in the Stillwater Valley and enjoyed bathing in the river each time, too. They couldn't help but notice that their mom never went in. She just stood on the side and laughed at them as they enjoyed the refreshing water.

Bobby, now in high school, would watch his mother as she walked along the river and sat on the boulders to meditate.

"Ben, do you ever wonder what on earth she is thinking out there?" asked Bobby.

"Your mom just sits out there for hours," said Ben's friend *Wayne*. [237] "She is such a cool and kind lady. You are so lucky to have her for your mom."

"I know," said Ben, looking fondly in the direction of his mom. "She is probably praying. She does that a lot, in case you hadn't noticed. I just wish she would find someone. Bobby and I will be gone one day, and I hate the thought of her being alone."

"What about that guy Jim? He seems to really love your mom."

"Jim?" asked Ben. "They are like brother and sister, I think. I've never quite figured them out. Apparently, they have worked together on projects in the past and have a lot of great field memories."

"Heck, I could come live with her, I guess. I spend more time with her anyway," said Wayne laughing.

"I don't know," said Bobby interjecting, "I'm afraid she will become a cloistered nun and I may never see her again after we all leave."

"What the heck is cloistered?" asked Wayne.

---

237 Wayne is a high school student and friend of Anna's boys. He is sweet, naïve, and a little bit clumsy. His character reminds the author of cartoon character of Shaggy in Scooby Doo. Wayne is a fictional character and not meant to depict a rea person living or dead.

"It just means that they hide behind the walls of a convent, baking bread and praying all day, or something like that," answered Ben.

"All I know is that they leave their families and you are never allowed to touch them again," said Bobby sadly.

"Damn," said Wayne, "I'm going to have to talk to her about that. I don't want that either."

Anna watched the water as it rippled quickly over the stones below. The water was not very deep, but it was moving at a fast rate for sure. Her mind was open to nature, to God, but it was also open to the memory of Sean. She always felt Sean close to her, despite the distance and years of separation.

Selfishly, she kept his memory in a tiny box, stored in a small, secret room in her heart. The secret room was to never again be opened. Trust was the key and that had been lost long ago.

"Hey, Professor Moore," shouted Wayne. "May I come out and join you?"

Anna smiled and waved for him to join her.

Wayne walked toward her, almost stumbling, eliciting laughter from the other boys who were watching.

"Wayne, You are such a clutz," laughed Anna, as he sat next to her.

"Whatcha doing out here all the time? Come on back and let's play a game or something. I can let you beat me at *Scrabble* again,"[238] he said as he gave her a sideways hug.

"Are you serious, Wayne?" she laughed. "Why on earth would you want to lose a game to me? You should always play to win. I certainly do. No mercy, buddy."

"Well, I don't want you to go away and never be touched again."

---

238 Scrabble is a popular word game played by people of all ages.

"What? What the heck are you talking about, Wayne?" she laughed.

"Well, Bobby and Ben said you were going to go be a nun or some such thing, and you'd be behind a wall and we couldn't hug you anymore. I don't want you to do that," he said sadly. "Promise me, you'll always play Scrabble with me."

Roughing his hair with her hand, she said, "Wayne, you silly. I have no intention of being a cloistered nun. Where did those boys ever get that idea in the first place?"

"I don't know, maybe because you won't marry Jim? I sure didn't like the sound of your baking all day and not being allowed to be hugged."

"Well, don't worry about that. I've got plenty of things that I still want to do in life other than bake bread and not be hugged." she chuckled. "Let's go. I hear a Scrabble board calling to us both."

"Alright," laughed Wayne as he managed to fall over his own feet as he got up.

Later that evening, Anna sat and watched her boys, along with Wayne, and Jim, as they sat around the campfire and talked.

One of Anna's favorite things to do was to sit and watch others interact, especially in that setting and with her boys, who were insanely talented.

Wayne always seemed a bit lost in Ben and Bobby's acting skits. He reminded Anna of her own experiences when playing volleyball as a youth. She enjoyed watching the game but was never quite sure what to do when the ball came her way. The awkward experience led her to know that her forte would not be playing sports.

Jim laughed at the boys. Having no family of his own, he genuinely enjoyed the Miller family summer visits. In some ways, he had adopted Annie and her boys as his own and looked forward to taking time off to see them each year.

Occasionally Jim would look over at her and give her a wink, which always brought a smile to Annie's face.

He didn't speak to her about Sean but could tell she had lost her spark. This reality saddened him. He loved them both and knew that they were both hurting. If she asked about Sean, he would tell her about him, but she didn't ask, and Jim didn't bring it up. It just wasn't worth it to open a wound that he could see her clearly trying to heal.

Wayne stood up to get another soda from the cooler and asked, "Want another, Professor?"

"Oh, you know I do," answered Anna.

"And Jim?" asked Wayne holding his favorite Aussie beer in between his free fingers.

"Ah sure, ya know that's right?"

"By the way, it's none of my business, but when are you going to ask Dr. Moore to marry you?" asked Wayne, innocently.

Everyone laughed. Jim looked at Annie and said, "Well mates. I think her heart is already taken."

Annie smiled," Yes, I'm afraid so, boys."

"Who?" asked Wayne.

"His name is Jesus," said Annie, as she looked at Jim, who knew that Jesus was not the only man who had her heart.

"Besides," said Annie, "Jim is like my brother."

"Aye," said Jim as he took a swig of beer. "She be ma sista. That's a fact."

Annie and Jim clanked their beer bottles together and proceeded to drain the contents.

"That I am," said Annie smiling lovingly at Jim. "We are family."

Chapter 49—Holidays

Another year or two rolled by and Jim invited Annie to come to spend the holidays with him in Montana. She knew her family was always welcome in his home, especially during the holidays, but she continued her own traditions of going to the ranch to see Betty and Bob.

This particular year was no different, except that Robert had remarried and had managed to have the first and only baby girl in the family. There was a twenty-year age gap for the couple, but it didn't seem to matter. They were proud parents of a baby girl.

Anna was so happy for him and his new wife, but most of all she was happy for her sons who were over the moon proud of their little sister.

The Millers were like parents to her and the boys always visited, bringing their friends along, too, for the holidays.

Betty was the matriarch of a large loving family and she always provided a festive southern holiday experience, complete with lots of ham, turkey, her famous mashed potatoes and of course, the pies--lots and lots of pies.

The kitchen and dining areas were always noisy and filled with the smell of coffee, cinnamon and nutmeg, and tables with a family of all ages and sizes playing games.

Anna loved to just sit and take it all in... the laughter and yelling was so much fun. Watching her own sons and their cousins play games was the height of entertainment.

Her favorite place to be, though, was in the grand living area, near the fireplace, which was huge, about six feet by four feet by four feet, with a large, warm fire. It reminded her of the fireplaces in the Montana resorts and restaurants, only larger. There was plenty of space for roasting chestnuts and even making s'mores with the grandchildren.

Anna liked to sit in the brown rocker to the left of the fire, where she could see the fire as well as the festivities across the room where a large spruce tree, handpicked by Bob Senior, was brought in fresh the day after Thanksgiving.

When most folks were recovering from the food and watching football, Betty had everyone jumping to get the place decorated for Christmas, especially the tree. It was a celebration for her boys, herself, and the grandparents. Anna felt so blessed to be part of such a loving family.

Robert and his new wife arrived, and all activity seemed to come to a standstill. Everyone made over little Mary, including Anna and the boys.

Bob and Betty beamed with pride as they promised to make sure that she would have everything and anything that a little girl might want. The plans were already being laid out for the tiny little heiress.

"Oh yes, she will be barrel racing by age ten," said Bob, grinning at Betty from ear to ear. He was obviously trying to get a rile out of her.

"No, Bob. She will learn needlepoint and how to bake pies first."

Robert's wife, Beth, just looked at Robert worriedly as she was beginning to see that her baby was not just going to be hers to spoil, it would seem.

"No, Pops," yelled Ben. "I'll teach her how to chop wood, so I'll have a replacement."

Everyone laughed. It was a tradition in that family that the youngest had to chop wood in their spare time...so they always tried to stay or at least look busy.

"No," said Anna, "She will be a princess and wear ribbons in her hair."

As she reached down and touched her tiny little hands, Beth looked up at Anna and smiled. Yes, that one seemed more like what she wanted for her little girl.

Betty was very perceptive and could sense that Anna felt melancholy about Mary, but she just assumed that she was wishing that she and Robert had also had a little girl. She had no idea about Melissa and how seeing Mary rekindled those feelings of loss.

Betty put her arm around Anna's waist and asked, "Can you help me with the coffee for a minute?"

Anna dutifully walked down the long hall to the kitchen with Betty and started drying the coffee cups from the drain rack and putting them on their pegs.

"So, Anna. What are your plans for the summer this year? Do you have a group going north again?"

"I'm not exactly sure yet and haven't planned a trip for this summer. I'm thinking of just taking some time off to travel and rest, but it will depend on the student interest, I suppose."

"That sounds like a great idea, dear. Where do you plan to go?'

"I'll know when I get there, I assume," Anna said in a sad voice.

Betty poured them both a cup of coffee and motioned for them to sit down and chat.

"Anna, I don't mean to stick my nose in where it doesn't belong," she said as she stirred cream into her mug, "but, you really should start dating again, don't you think?"

Anna let out a little giggle as she sipped her coffee, causing a dribble down her chin and onto her shirt. "Well," she said, wiping her chin," I don't really see much point, do you?"

"Of course, I do. You are still attractive, and you are secure financially. Retirement is coming sooner than you think, and … well, I just wish you had someone to love you the way you deserve to be loved, that's all," she said as her voice choked back tears.

Anna reached over and took her hand, "I love you so much, Betty. It's just not what God intended for me."

"What the heck does God want you to do? Grow old and die alone?" Betty said angrily as she blew her nose, "That doesn't sound like a loving God to me. You deserve better."

"Well…"

"Well, what? Your marriage has been annulled. You are free to date…aren't you?"

"Yes, I suppose so."

"If you ask me, you spend far too much time with those sisters at the convent. You need to get out and meet someone before it is too late. Promise me you'll think about it. Please."

"I will. I just need my life to slow down a little bit."

"Well, find him soon. If you wait for time to slow down, you may be dead! What about that guy Jim that the boys are always talking about? Ben thinks he's in love with you. He's also buying a ranch. Sounds like he might be a good catch."

"Betty!" laughed Anna, "I don't want to 'catch' anyone. If God intends for me to find love again, then God will make that happen. I won't hold my breath, though. I am truly at peace with whatever God has planned for me. Being alone doesn't bother me."

"Anna," Betty whispered, "That's a cop-out and you know it. You are just afraid of being mistreated…or failing again. Please consider that you are free, and you need to find someone. Your boys are worried about you, too. Bob and I both want the best for you."

"Okay," said Anna.

"Just be open to the possibility," said Betty as she gave her a big hug and a kiss on the cheek.

Chapter 50—Once Again

After the boys were off to college, Anna continued to sponsor field trips and take students to camp in the Rockies and in the Pacific Northwest. Just as with her children, she would always make one of the final stops at the Stillwater Valley in Montana, and a visit with Uncle Jim.

Jim was retiring from the mining business and had cut back his hours, but still made time for college groups who wanted to tour the facility and the local geology. He had saved enough money to purchase a small ranch home in the valley and was well set for a peaceful retirement.

Deep down inside, he hoped that Annie might one day come and live there, too. Not as his wife, but so he would not be alone, and he could see that she was always okay. She would always be special to him.

He graciously offered his home to Annie's camp each summer, but she was determined to give her students a genuine camping experience. So, he camped, too. He enjoyed her visits and the new faces each summer as well as the annual tour of the mining operations and the local geology.

During one of the summer camps, Jim introduced her to a friend of his who was visiting the Stillwater mine. They had worked together in the early days of Jim's career in the Bushveld in South

Africa. His name was *Dr. Johann Burmeister, III*[239] and he too knew Stinky, Ed, and Sean.

Apparently, Dr. Burmeister was a premiere expert in geochemistry and igneous petrology. His work with a Ph.D. and post-doctorate at Cambridge University in England involved the study of cumulate minerals from the world's known banded igneous complexes. He had brought a graduate student with him to collect samples from the Stillwater Complex. The idea was to compare to the *Paleoproterozoic age*[240] - *Bushveld intrusion of South Africa.* [241]

Economic geologists were especially interested in the abundance of platinum group elements[242] *that appeared as layers in the banded igneous complexes of both sites.*

"It's a small world," he said in a very polite, polished British accent, as he extended his hand to shake Annie's.

"She's ma mate," said Jim nervously. "Family, really. We see each other every year, and I plan to have her come live with me one day," he said, winking at Annie.

Jim wanted them to meet but didn't want her to be taken in by his eloquence or charm. He had been friends with him for many years and would not want his sister to date him--*ever.*

---

239 A fictional character who is a friend of Jim's from south Africa. He has a PhD and is an expert in banded igneous complexes of the world. His character does not depict any living person, past or present.

240 Paleoproterozoic Era refers to a specific time period in geologic time, 2.5 by to 1.6by, within Proterozoic Eon. The Paleoproterozoic is thought to be the time of continental shield formation. See image in appendix

241 Both the Stillwater Complex of Montana and the Bushveld Complex in South Africa contain banded igneous sequences that represent a wide range of magma chemistry and cumulate minerals. The identification and classification of igneous rocks, using cumulate minerals, was a huge research venture for many PhD candidates in the 70s and 80s.

242 Platinum Group Elements of the Stillwater and Bushveld are magmatically derived sulfide deposits (sulfide minerals that are created from the movement of magma). These deposits are mined for metals such as Iron, Chromite, and Platinum. Steel production requires both Iron and Chromite and Platinum is used in catalytic converters and other devices of use by the human population.

Johann towered over both Jim and Annie. He was a very distinguished-looking gentleman who was well over six feet tall, with pale skin and light-colored hair that he had slicked back. He wore suspenders, which she would later learn was his signature dress.

Annie thought he looked like someone out of the 1800s and didn't find him attractive in the least. He was too thin and seemed much too pretentious for her taste. This didn't keep Jim from being nervous about their meeting.

"Right there," said Jim. Indicating that the introductions were over. "Let's go have a piss, shall we?"

"Oh right," said Johann, not wanting to release Annie's hand from his grip, as he was obviously intrigued.

"I need to settle my kids first. Can you wait?"

"Ah sure, we'll drive up there and get ya here in about an hour. How does that sound?"

"Sounds like a plan."

Annie hadn't been to the bar in years. She had always intentionally skipped the place because of the memories she was trying to avoid. Her time was spent mostly meditating, hiking, and communing with nature.

When she arrived back at her camp, she found her college students building a fire and getting ready to relax for the evening.

"Hi, guys. Do you mind if I join Uncle Jim and his friend for a brew this evening?"

"Just be home before ten o'clock," shouted Michael, who was sitting in the center camp chair and clearly in charge at the moment...or at least in his mind.

"Now, does this mean we can drink, too, while she's gone?" ...whispered a voice that she didn't recognize.

"Now guys." Said Anna, in her best professorial voice, "Not happening, especially if you are not old enough to drink in this state. Got it?"

"Michael, I'm holding you personally responsible," she said, as she pointed her finger at him and postured herself in a very serious stance.

"Yes ma'am, Dr. Moore. I'll make sure they are good."

"Aww, man!" whined one of the other students.

"No whinging now," she said, stopping for a moment to acknowledge that she was using Sean's words. "I mean, no whining. Got it?"

"You gonna get all gussied up, Professor?" asked *Nathan*[243].

"No, just getting my ID. That'd be pretty embarrassing if I were to get carded."

They all laughed at the absurd notion that she would look young enough to be carded.

"Hey, you never know," she said. "Besides, I want to take my own money. None of this having strange men pay for my drinks. Right guys?"

"Yes, ma'am. You can't be too careful."

A short time later, a pair of headlights appeared at the bottom of the hill, and Dr. Moore made her trek down the slope to meet her ride for the evening.

"Hi, doll," said Johann, sitting with his elbow hanging out of the passenger side window.

"What's a sheila doin' out at this time of night by herself?" laughed Jim from the driver's seat.

"Oh, shut it," said Annie, as she opened the back door and climbed in with the hammers and trash in the back of Jim's truck.

As Jim drove down the bumpy road, Annie enjoyed the cool breeze blowing her hair in all directions. She particularly loved the dust on her face and hair. It didn't feel dirty, but instead was clean...

---

243 Nathan is a post doc student who had always loved Dr. Moore's summer trips. He was along to collect rocks and network with industry geologists. He is a fictional character named after one of the author's favorite students.

fresh. She wondered if it was the same feeling that some animals have when they roll in the dirt.

The salt would occasionally get into her eyes and make them tear, but she loved the taste when she licked her lips. Even the tears that ran down her cheeks smelled like fresh summer rain.

Johann and Jim talked the entire journey, but Annie couldn't really hear what they were saying. Their combined accents made it difficult to recognize phrasing, so she just focused on the scents in the air and the sound of the gravel beneath the tires.

An occasional rock would dislodge and fly up to hit the undercarriage, with a pow or a ping. She couldn't help but notice the differences in the sound of the tires on clay minerals versus rocks and gravel; smooth rolling, then crunching and clicking.

Fascinating, she thought, as she listened to the differences, but as usual, she didn't feel compelled to share her observations with others.

As they approached the bar, Annie felt her heart racing.

Jim could sense her dread and knew she hadn't been in the bar since she was last there with Sean, Stinky and the boys, years ago. He opened her door and took her hand, "Hey, just relax and have some fun. I'm here with ya, so ya know it's all going to be okay. Right?"

"Yes, "she whispered. "I'm okay, really I am."

Annie noted that the place hadn't really changed. The same checkered red and white curtains on the windows, the same jukebox, the same smells of greasy chips from the fryer, fresh-cut onions, and fresh bread...oh and the sounds... Music and conversations in the background, and bottle caps hitting the floor. It smelled and felt like home in a way.

"The lady will have a Moose Drool, I'm having your draft, and … whatcha havin', mate?" asked Jim.

"Ah, yes, well...would you have any Beefeater gin, my good lady?"

The barmaid turned and pointed to her top shelf of liquor. "We have both kinds of gin here and none are Beefeater. Sorry"

"Ah, right then, I'll have what the lady is having then."

Jim rolled his eyes at Annie, who giggled a little at his obvious jealous behavior.

They sat down and talked for several hours.

Annie found herself daydreaming and not really paying attention to their conversation about mining and geochemistry. She was relaxing, listening to music, and wondering if her students were behaving.

"Now, Annie here. She's a hell of a good field geologist. I bet she'd be perfect for your northern expedition."

"Oh, what?" asked Annie, embarrassed that she was clearly somewhere else and not listening to their conversation.

"Yes, I am taking a group, fully funded of course, ..."

"Of course," said Annie.

"...to the *ultra-mafic - mafic*[244] Border Ranges and metamorphic *Chucagh ranges*[245]. I have Ph.D. students working on *K/Ar*[246] geochemistry and we will need folks to help us collect pristine samples. It will be hiking and camping for about two weeks."

"Wow!" said Annie. "That sounds fascinating and a lot like pack mule delivery?"

---

244 Ultramafic is a compositional classification based on the abundance of high temperature minerals in igneous rocks - rich in minerals like olivine and Ca rich plagioclase feldspar – Ultramafic rocks tend to be rich in Ca, Mg, and Fe as well. Mafic is the compositional classification for rocks that contain pyroxenes, like augite, as well as plagioclase feldspar that has some Na as well as Ca in the silicate structure. Both Ultramafic and mafic rocks tend to be dark in color and rich in Fe, Mg, Ca, and Si.

245 The Chugach Mountain Range is a Pacific Coast Range in southern Alaska. They are made up of metamorphosed rocks.

246 K/Ar stands for Potassium/Argon – geochemists use the radioactive isotopes in rocks and compare their ratios to determine age dates of minerals in the rocks. Radioactive isotopes have known decay rates and those can be measured and then compared.

"Fraid so, *dear*,"[247] said Johann. "We need good field people, but we also need someone who is physically able to pack in and out...if you know what I mean."

"You should do it," said Jim, looking at Annie. "She needs to get back out into the field."

"Well, that's good enough for me. I've heard a lot about you from Jim, Stinky too, and if you can pass the Stinky *smell test*, then you are good to go with me."

Haha...smell test, thought Annie. *This guy has a sense of humor, at least.*

"Well, okay. Why not? When will this expedition occur? If you are serious, then send me all of the information and paperwork that I know you need to fill out."

"I'll need your vitae, and I may ask Sean, Stinky and/or Jim to write you a letter of support."

Annie could feel the blood run from her face. "No, let's not do that."

"Won't my recommendation be enough, mate?" asked Jim. "She's got one hell of a resume and many years of experience--lots of publications too."

"We'll work it out. I look forward to working with you, Annie. It's a deal?"

"Sure," she said as she shook his hand.

Jim was immensely proud to have introduced Annie to Johann, and most of all to have been a part of getting her back out into the field. He was pretty sure that Annie could handle herself with Johann too.

Her love for Sean was forever and he knew that.

---

247 Dear, is a term of endearment used by many older men, especially those socialized in Europe. It is more respectful than sweetie or honey, but still meant to subjugate the female intellectually.

Just the same, he intended to have "that talk" with her about Johann before she left for the summer.

They drove Annie back to her camp and said their goodbyes.

"I'll be up tomorrow evening to see ya on your last night here. Ok?" Said Jim, giving Annie a hug and a kiss on her cheek.

"It was so good to meet you, Johann. I look forward to hearing more about your work in Alaska."

Kissing the back of Annie's hand, he said, "The pleasure was all mine, I assure you."

Jim leaned in and whispered in her ear, "Slick git."

They both chuckled as Jim ran around the truck to get in.

Annie hiked up the slope to her campsite while Jim showed his truck lights up the path. She turned and waved goodbye to them and was very proud to see that the fire was out and that her students seemed to be in bed for the evening.

"Wow, good job, Michael," she whispered as she entered her tent.

✳ ✳ ✳

In the next few months, she received packets of information and documents from Johann, and the trip was set for the following early summer.

Annie enjoyed the research into the metamorphic terrain she would be visiting. She was intrigued by the wealth of research being done on argon isotopes and the role of garnets in the geochemical processes. It was not her area of expertise, but she found the mineralogy and geochemistry very stimulating.

Chapter 51—North to Alaska, Chugach

Annie flew into Anchorage and was taken by the beauty of the mountains to the east. For the first time in years, she was truly excited to be doing something other than taking students on a tour.

The sage advice and words of concern from both Betty and Jim were playing in her mind as well. She would be open to whatever God had planned for her in this trip but would be cautious of the advances of Johann the third, who seemed to be a big flirt and interested in her for more than her knowledge of geology.

Johann and his students met Annie in the hotel meeting room where they would plan the expedition. There were three students, two males, and one female.

That's convenient, she thought. *I will share a tent with the gal, and the guys will be together?*

"Hi, Dr. Moore. I've heard a lot about you. My name is *Tiffany Swift*." [248]

"Oh, very nice to meet you. Now, you are a Ph.D. student, is it?"

---

248 Tiffany Swift is a female undergraduate student who is hoping to get into the graduate program and work with Dr. Burmeister. Her character is fictional but definitely meant to depict her, like the geobabes, as women socialized through tv and a growing social media culture, to pretend they weren't as smart as they seemed. If the men wouldn't respect their intellect, or if the female lacked the intellect, perhaps she could at least use the fact that she is female to get ahead. This depiction is not meant to demean the women, but instead to highlight how men and women in positions of power in the sciences have and still do exploit women and men sexually.

"Ah, no ma'am. I'm a senior undergraduate. Dr. Burmeister invited me because I am thinking of joining his graduate team next spring."

"Oh, so about a year from now. Well, I'd say you have a few options, then, don't you? It's good to get experiences like this on your resume for sure."

"Yes, ma'am. I'm hoping it will help me with acceptance into the program too."

Annie met the two others, *Ronald Post and Victor Newman*, both Ph.D.[249] students who would soon be looking for postdoc positions, something she definitely did not envy them.

At this particular time in the field of academia, it was virtually impossible to get a job right out of a Ph.D. program. Everyone needed postdoc publications and help from their mentors to even get a foot in the door.

Interestingly enough, it seemed that women had a better chance than men with most universities who were looking to meet diversity quotas. The sad truth was though that they would be paid less for the golden jobs and pushed perhaps harder than their male counterparts to publish or perish, or at least it often seemed that there were no accommodations for women who had children or might have a pregnancy.

She had talked to many women who left academia to stay home and be mothers while seeking other positions in STEM.[250] The rigors of tenured faculty positions appeared to be set up specifically to weed out anyone who had an interest beyond doing research, seeking grants, publishing papers, and putting out graduates. It was a grind for all, men included, but at least the men were compensated financially.

---

249 Ronald Post and Victor Newman are fictionalized characters who are both PhD students with Dr. Burmeister. Their characters do not depict any real person present or past.

250 Science, Technology, Engineering, and Mathematics

Victor pulled out a topo map and placed it on the conference table. The map had two areas of interest. He then proceeded to do a slide presentation where he outlined his plan for getting to "his" research area and the types of samples he was intending to collect.

Annie took notes and asked questions. She couldn't help but notice that Tiffany seemed more interested in her shoelaces which were bright pink.

Oh, God! She thought, *Not another geobabe type.* She clearly felt that Tiffany would be her special project on this trip. *What the heck was Johann thinking, anyway?*

Ronald didn't use slides but did a fine job with his low-tech presentation using his maps and a large writing pad. He also seemed to be quite the comedian, making them all laugh throughout the discussion. In some ways, he was easier to understand and more entertaining, but Victor's certainly was more aesthetically pleasing.

That evening, Annie learned more about the interrelationship between metamorphism, deformation, and magmatic intrusions in the *accretionary prism*[251] where they were focusing their work for that week.

Vincent was quite a handsome young man of Italian descent. He had dark eyes, olive complexion, and a well-sculpted muscular frame. Apparently, he had come from a family of volcanologists, so Annie found conversations with him quite enjoyable.

If she had been about twenty years younger, she might have given him a run for his money. He was "easy on the eyes."

"So, guys, how do garnets figure into this equation?" she asked.

---

251 Metamorphism refers to the type of a rock after the pre-existing rock has been altered due to dynamic pressure of temperature. A magmatic intrusion is molten rock material (magma because it is beneath the earth's surface) that has intruded into pre-existing rock. Usually there is a melting or baking of the pre-existing rocks. An accretionary prism is a mass of pre-existing rock and sediments which has been scraped off of a subducting (one plate moving beneath another) oceanic crust onto an overriding tectonic plate during a collision of land masses.

"Well, you see, dear, the temperature modeling of *garnet*[252] growth helps one to evaluate the process for how the deposits were able to reach *greenschist*[253] facies heating. Was it from the increased load of thrusting of metamorphosed sequences or from advective heating from aqueous fluids and conductive heating from subjected oceanic crust? That's what Victor here is trying to sort out."

"Right--what he said," said Victor.

Ronald and Tiffany laughed, as they probably had noticed that Johann liked to show off his immense knowledge in front of his students and others.

Annie thought it was a bit rude, *mansplaining*[254] at best, and continued to ask Victor for details of his research.

The evening was cool, and the fire was sizzling, crackling, and popping, probably from the mostly green wood being used at the site.

I miss the smell of lodgepole pine, she thought.

"What type of wood is this?"

"I believe this one is called hemlock?" answered Ronald.

"Yes, that explains the popping. It may not be fully dried out yet though," said Annie.

"The smoke should keep the mosquitos off though, regardless," said Johann.

As the tents were being put up, Annie noted that there were only two tents.

"So, what is the tent situation? Who am I bunking with? Or was I supposed to bring a tent?"

---

252 Garnets are high temperature silicate minerals that are used to help determine the degree of metamorphism in regionally metamorphosed rocks (regionally, meaning tectonic processes with dynamic pressure).

253 Greenschist is a classification for low to medium metamorphism in metamorphic rocks.

254 Mansplaining is when a person, typically a man, proceeds to explain the obvious to another person, typically a woman - pedantic explanation = excessive detail only included to either boost the ego of the person telling or to insult the intelligence of the listener.

"Ah...I guess you are bunking with us," said Ronald, seeming a little bit unsure about his answer as he glanced in the direction of Johann and Tiffany.

"Well, that works, I guess there is plenty of room in there for four?"

... silence...

Then she noticed that Tiffany was helping Johann with his tent about ten feet away from the others.

"Oh," said Annie, looking at Vincent and Ronald. "Don't worry, guys, I don't bite...but I do fart."

Both Vincent and Ronald laughed.

"Oh no! I do too," said Vincent. "Sorry, guys."

"I may have to sleep out here by the fire," said Ronald," just kidding, of course. I assure you I can hold my own. Be scared. Be very scared."

"This is going to be fun," she said, "What's a little H2S among friends anyway?"

After they had settled in their tent, she couldn't help but notice that Tiffany kept carrying box after box into their tent.

Turning to the guys, Annie asked, "my goodness, what is in all those boxes? I thought we were supposed to pack light for this trip...and, what about bears? Should we be putting everything into the truck for the night?"

"Johann has his own way of doing things," said Vincent, with a sigh. "He's not the least bit worried about bears."

"Well, I hope they eat him instead of me, then," said Annie, realizing immediately how horrible that sounded. "Of course, I hope the bears don't eat any of us, but if they are going to, they should eat the one that isn't putting their stuff in the truck."

Ronald laughed, "It's okay, Dr. Moore. We feel the same way. He's always done this. One year, undergrads actually put meat on his tent."

"That is horrible! I hope they got expelled for that."

"Nope. He never noticed."

"Good grief."

"Be back soon," said Ronald.

Vincent climbed into his sleeping bag and put his back to Annie. "G'night, Dr. Moore."

"Good night," she said as she climbed into her bag and faced her favorite side of the tent, away from Vincent and opposite Ronald's spot.

It felt so good to be sleeping in a tent again. She loved the smells and the sound of the wind in the trees above them. In the distance, was the distinctive call of an owl. Not a hooting sound but a rapid firing, soft undulating almost yodeling quality, high pitched "whiiiipppet, whiiiipppet, whiiiipppet." The sound began low in volume and pitch and then increased through a long call, at least a minute in duration.

Annie couldn't recognize the other call, which seemed to be more of a small screeching sound, perhaps an immature of the species. *Gosh, I wish my daddy was here. He would probably know these bird calls.*

Drip, drip, drip...splashed delicate drops on the canopy of the tent. It was droplets falling from the branches above. The humidity was quite high there, not much different than the Pacific Northwest in the Cascades at that time of year. Evenings were prime time for condensation beads to form and for low hanging mists to develop above the land and water bodies.

It was at times like these that Annie could feel her age creeping up on her. The damp contributed to aching shoulder joints, hips, and knees. Was it just old age or was it that she hadn't slept on the ground in such a place for some time? *Sigh...the exercise will no doubt loosen things up this week,* she thought to herself. She briefly said her prayers and drifted off to sleep.

The next morning, there was a scratching noise on the side of the tent near Ronald.

"What the heck do you suppose that is?" he said, sitting up in his bag and rubbing his face with his hands.

"Don't know," said Annie. "Sounds like a little critter...too small to cause much of a fuss."

Victor threw his shoe at the side of the tent, and it scampered away.

"Guess you showed him, didn't you?" said Ronald.

"I hope you didn't hurt him," said Annie.

Outside the tent, they could hear Johann asking, "Where is the coffee pot? You find it while I get some kindling."

"If we wait a few minutes, there may be coffee brewed for us," said Ronald, winking at Annie.

"Sounds like a plan, but, nature calls, so..." she exited the tent and waved at Tiffany, who was digging through one of the plastic boxes,

"Did you hide the *loo*[255] in one of those boxes?" she asked in a teasing tone.

"No, but I sure hope I find the *camp press*[256]."

Both laughed as Annie walked off to find her spot.

The rocks were covered in moss and quite slippery that early in the morning, but Annie managed to walk an appropriate distance from the others.

She found a spot where it looked like she could easily dislodge a section of rock and soil, like a lid and gently place back with little damage to the surroundings. As she squatted, she couldn't help but notice the fine mist that was hanging just above the surface of the river. There was a clear separation between the cloud

---

255   An informal British term for a toilet
256   Press is an informal term for a French press used to compress or squeeze the grounds – filter water over grounds to make coffee.

forming and the water below. *Fascinating,* she thought. *Temperature inversion,*[257] *no doubt. It will burn off during the morning sun.*

---

257 A temperature usually decreases with height above the ground. Inversion is where the air temperature is actually cooler near the surface, overlain by a layer of warmer air, and it creates a cloud.

Chapter 52—Coffee Beans and Badgers?

She continued to take in the smells of morning dew and organics of the forest, breathing in deeply the humid, earthy essence, and wishing she could just stay and linger for a while.

The very next moment, the serenity was rudely disrupted by a commotion that seemed to be coming from the direction of the campsite. Tiffany was squealing, the guys were shouting, and there was a clatter of aluminum pans and metal spoons.

What in heaven's name was going on? thought Annie as she moved quickly in the direction of the screams, careful not to roll an ankle on the slippery stones.

As she entered from behind the tent she shared with the guys, she could see Tiffany bent forward clanging a spoon on a metal pan. There was something going on between the back of Johann's tent and the bank of the river. The guys were laughing with a full roar by now and pointing. Annie was beginning to see that the fuss was not a major indication of a life-threatening emergency.

She came directly to Tiffany, to see if she could help, and was surprised to see a large, furry rodent of some kind, standing on its hind legs, barking.

"Oh, my Lord! Is it rabid?" asked Annie.

Before anyone could answer, the beast turned toward Johann's voice coming from the tent and launched the full weight of its body onto the side of the tent. It apparently had claws because tears were visible in the side of the tent as the animal shredded the fabric.

"What the hell?" shouted Annie.

"It's attacking Johann!" cried Tiffany.

A few moments later, a scream came from the tent, much like you'd expect to hear when a martial arts master is trying to karate chop a piece of wood.

"Eeee ya!" Johann punched the animal through the side of the tent and sent it rolling, head over heels, toward the riverbank.

To everyone's amazement, the creature got up, shook itself, stood on its hind legs for a moment, snarled and hissed before returning to all fours. It then ran full force right back into the side of the tent.

Things were beginning to take a serious turn when the guys noticed the claws and teeth and the ripped fabric. All were standing now and gathering sticks and stones to defend themselves if needed.

The guys were shouting, Tiffany was crying, Annie was yelling, and Johann once more punched the critter and sent him rolling.

This time, Johann emerged from the tent with only one suspender holding his pants, and said he'd had enough.

Annie decided to name the creature *Barnie*,[258] and walked toward him, offering to help him in some way. Barnie turned toward Annie and looked confused before he once again attacked the side of the tent.

Johann picked up a rock that was approximately two feet in diameter and walked toward the charging animal. Barnie turned and met Johann head-on, "Hisssss, yip, yip, growl."

"Die you *blardy*[259] bastard!" shouted Johann as he launched the large rock right on top of him.

To everyone's horror, Barnie could be heard wheezing from beneath the rock. He was stopped for sure, but the rock had only

---

258 Barnie is the name that Annie gave to the creature, not sure if it is a badger, or some other large rodent. It is a fictional creature.

259 Blardy is Australian slang for the British, 'bloody.' Which means, 'very.' Most people would agree that it is used as a pejorative.

caused him to sink into the moist soil left from the melting of the permafrost.

"Wheeeza...silence... Wheeeza...silence... Wheeeza," was the sound that everyone heard coming from under the rock.

"Oh my God! The poor thing! I don't think he's dead," said Annie.

"Ya think?" asked Ron, expressing total disgust with the situation.

Johann went back into the tent and didn't seem to have a care in the world about poor Barnie. He was bigger, he was smarter, and he had clearly won the battle.

Inside the tent, Tiffany could be heard crying, "Johann, how could you kill the little thing?"

"Little thing? The bastard was attacking me. Look what he did to my tent! He was after my coffee beans, no doubt."

"What the heck was that thing?" asked Vincent. "It wasn't a badger, I don't think."

"Definitely a badger of some kind," said Ron.

"Hey guys, could you help me with this?" asked Annie, as she began trying to dislodge the rock from on top of Barnie. "Let's see if it is dead. We should take him away from the campsite. His body will begin to smell and attract flies and perhaps other animals."

"Right there," said Ron.

The two struggled to pull up the side of the rock, but the suction from the mud was too great. Vincent stood up and walked over to lend his strength. The three of them managed to move the rock back and forth together until it began to raise up on one side. They rolled the rock on end towards their feet, expecting to see a squished, bloodied body beneath.

To their surprise, Barnie began to hiss and wheeze and scampered off from the opened side of the tomb and quickly disappeared into the forest.

Annie dropped her hold and ran back away from the rock, not wanting to have her legs clawed by an injured animal.

"He's gone," said Vincent.

"Was he okay? I couldn't see him very well."

"He was running pretty fast. I'd say he's okay," said Ron.

"He will probably die somewhere, but thankfully not here."

"So sad," she said, looking down at the vacant hole shaped like the dislodged stone.

Even though Annie was excited about the geology, she was no longer looking forward to spending time with the mansplaining, pompous, selfish, murdering ass, named Johann.

Jim was right. He is a slick git.

As they drank their coffee, Ron, Vincent, and Annie all looked silently at each other. It was clear that none of them were happy with the events of the morning.

Annie was very concerned for Tiffany, who seemed to feel she had to please Johann to be accepted into a graduate program.

Did she know that there was no guarantee of acceptance?

Ah, perhaps she is very talented and has great grades, too. I shouldn't judge her just by her behavior.

She watched Tiffany and Johann walking together back to the truck and found herself wondering about other male professors that she'd known over the years. Were they all subject to abusing their positions? Sure, many men were *misogynists* [260]and made passes, but with so few women in geology, Annie could only truly speak for her own experience, where she was the only woman in so many cases.

She had not seen this blatant behavior with Dr. D. or her department chair at Mondavi State, but had seen a few undergraduate females flirt with the male professors in hopes of getting a better grade. *Ugh*, she thought.

---

260 A man who doesn't respect the dignity of a woman. He sees her as being out of her role which is in the kitchen, pregnant, and subservient to a man.

Men like Johann, who are in positions of power, should never take advantage of a female or male student that might be in their program.

In Annie's mind, he was behaving in a very unprofessional manner. She wondered if there would be an opportunity to discuss the subject with Tiffany. Perhaps as they got to know each other better in the field?

As it turned out, the geology was much more interesting to Annie. She wanted to learn as much as possible from her tent mates about the complex metamorphic and tectonic processes of the area.

Not every injustice requires my intervention, she thought sadly to herself. *Tiffany will have to learn on her own. All I can do is model proper behavior.* This was a lesson that had taken her a great many years to learn.

After the Alaska field trip, Annie semi-retired from classroom teaching but continued to serve on graduate committees and to accompany graduate students in their fieldwork. She loved leading field trips and continuing her role of mentor and guide. It was much preferred to having to maintain grants through endless reporting and politics. In particular, she loved the freedom to travel and camp as she pleased.

With her boys both away at school and living their own lives, she had her summers to herself. With this freedom, she also retired from taking students on geo-trips. It was time for her to focus on her own future.

Chapter 53—St. Helens

Annie lay in her tent writing in her field notebook. She noted the sound of the breeze and the motion of the tent as it oscillated in and out. She wrote, *it's almost like the tent is breathing... The crackling of a nearby fire and the gentle murmuring of voices...the air is just cool enough to require a blanket...* then with the call of a bird, her stream of conscious thought was redirected to nature, in that moment.

The light was growing dim, and Annie decided to lay her notebook down to her side and continue to sense the world around her. *I had forgotten how peaceful camping could actually be. Thank you, Lord, for the earth and all the experiences afforded by Your creation...*

With each camping-geology experience, Annie would write more and more, interspersing her own thoughts, prayers, and ideas among the sketches and geologic information she chose to record. She had hundreds of yellow field notebooks, some of which had very little written in them. It seemed practical to take a couple with her to record experiences--perhaps a memoir one day?

It was late May, and Annie had joined a planned field trip, sponsored by the *International Association of Volcanologists.*[261] The trip promised ten days of camping and hiking in the Cascade Volcanic Range of North America, and included expert field guides from the USGS, as well as the University of Oregon and Washington. After the eruption of Mt. St. Helens in 1980, those

---

261 A fictional organization not meant to depict any group present or past.

who had been studying the area had become the experts in volcano monitoring and hazards.

The main attraction for this excursion was a planned hike to the forming mammalian plug (dome) in the crater of St. Helens. *A lava dome [262] is a sign of a period of relative quiescence after an active and destructive eruptive phase. No other volcano in modern history had been so closely monitored prior to, during, and after a major event.* For those who were interested in volcanic hazards and monitoring, this was to be one of the best field trips of the time.

The eruption of Krakatoa in 1883 [263] is reported to have been one of the first series of volcanic events in history to have its activity recorded with a variety of scientific instruments. Barographs and tide gauges were widely used in the 1800s to help with monitoring and forecasting weather systems, particularly in marine settings. Even though these instruments were used for weather and atmospheric research, they captured the shockwaves created in the atmosphere, as well as ocean and land surfaces. (National Centers for Environmental Information, 2017)

Unlike Krakatoa, where populated and busy marine traffic areas were able to capture the events as they occurred, Mt. St. Helens had the most advanced monitoring devices of that time, including tilt-meters, laser interferometers, seismic sensors, gas chromatographs, and advanced computer systems programmed to analyze the wealth of data being recorded. (Volcanoes.usgs.gov, 2016) Lives were being saved because of the information collected at this one volcano--the significance of St. Helens could not be overstated.

---

262 Lava domes, and in this case, a mammalian dome, is a natural consequence of a post destructive eruptive phase for a stratovolcano like Mt St. Helens. It signals a period of quiet in the eruptive sequence. It does not mean that the volcano will not erupt again in the near future but does signal an end to a recent effusive event.

263 Krakatoa is a dangerous stratovolcano located in Indonesia and has erupted periodically over geologic history, as recently as 2018. Stratovolcanoes form their classic cone shapes from the layering of volcanic flows over geologic time. The layers are what give it the name Stratos – from 'strata' meaning layer.

The field trip began with Lassen Peak, in Northern California, which erupted in 1915 and continued until 1917. The eruptions were some of the first to be caught on film in modern day U.S. It seemed a logical place to begin as it demonstrated the transition from Sierra Madre mountain building and cascade volcanism. Four distinct types of volcanism were also available in the Lassen Volcanic field; Stratovolcano, shield, cinder cone, and large volcanic plug. (United States Geological Survey, 2020) In addition, there were hydrothermal springs, volcanic structures, and stratigraphy to examine.

The first evening of the trip, Annie set up her new tent. It was her gift to herself for semi-retirement. She was getting too old to lie out in the moist air and soggy ground of the cascades.

The tent was one of those that was advertised to work like an umbrella. She scoffed at the reported ease of use and especially the inflated price but was going to try it anyway. To her amazement, it sprang open and only needed to be shaken slightly and then pegged into the soft soil.

"Wow, isn't that something?" she asked out loud.

"It certainly is," said a young woman holding a sledgehammer with an extremely long handle. The expression on her face also implied that she was judging Annie as a novice for choosing such an easy set up.

"Yes, I think I might like this," said Annie as she unzipped the front and crawled inside of her new home.

"It's just enough room for one person in here, and I love it," she said as she stuck her head out of the opening and smiled proudly at the young woman.

"What's your name?" she said as she stood up out of the tent and extended her hand.

"Um, *Alice Boyd.*"[264]

"Are you a trip leader?" asked Annie.

"Oh, me? No. I'm here with my prof. He's one of the leaders. *Dr. Mark Spencer. U of O.*" [265]

"I've not met him," said Annie. "You'll have to introduce us later, okay?"

"Sure. Nice to meet... you?"

"Oh, I am Sarah Moore. I'm a retired professor from Texas. I love volcanoes and now that I have more time, I've decided to take advantage of learning."

"Cool," said Alice with a smile. "See you around."

The next morning, campers secured their campsites and proceeded to take their place in one of three vans. Each van had room for fifteen, so the participants were squeezed in like sardines.

At one stop, Annie was particularly pleased with an *ash fall*[266] deposit that seemed to be limited to a small layer exposed in a road cut. She picked up a piece that had broken off the formation and noted how light if felt. The sample was pristine, white, and very fragile. Annie crumbled a piece in her hand and noted that the texture was almost like that of a clay mineral, like *Kaolinite.*[267] *This feels like clay,* she thought. *Is this a clay, or just microcrystalline shards of rock and minerals? Probably shards, but I'll check.*

---

264 Female student from U of O, who has a very long handle on her hammer. This is seen my Annie's character as a phallic symbol, representing a woman who feels she must be more male like to be taken seriously.

265 Dr. Mark Spencer is a fictional character not meant to represent any living geology professionals. The use of U Of O, is meant to represent a possible college program in volcanology, perhaps University of Oregon. This field experience and personnel do not represent any program or personnel past or present associated with U of O.

266 Ashfall deposits are ejected from the volcano as pyroclastic plume (fiery pieces of ash). The ash falls to the surface and produces a layer of ash which hardens. Some of these are referred to as Tuff if they are found in lenses rather than in broad layers.

267 Expandable clay from the weathering of an igneous rock rich in feldspar minerals (aluminosilicates).

Annie picked up her hand-lens which dangled about her neck and examined the grains. It was very fine grains, probably ash. *Ash of course is pulverized rock that is either in a flow deposit, like a pyroclastic flow, or an ash-fall, better known as a tuff or tephra.*

Just as she touched her tongue to the sample, she heard a female voice, a British accent, say, "What on earth are you doing?"

She looked up with her tongue still on the sample, to see a beautiful dark-skinned woman with a colorful bandana tied around her neck and a safari hat upon her head.

"Oh," said Annie, as she removed her tongue. "I was just testing it to see if it was an expandable clay."

"By sticking your tongue on it?" asked the woman as she laughed.

"Well, of course. How else do you test an expandable clay?"

"I certainly wouldn't taste it!"

"Excuse me. Hi, my name is Annie. What is yours?"

"My name is *Elsinore Ledbetter.*"[268]

"It's so good to meet you."

"Yes, sorry for teasing you about eating rocks."

"It's okay. I once had a professor who spit on every rock he found and just grossed me out."

The two women laughed and quickly became friends.

Elsinore was a PhD student at UW in Seattle and was from a small village in Africa. She was an older student who was married to a professor of engineering.

Later that evening, as the two women were discussing their families and backgrounds, Elsinore shared with Annie about how women in her homeland were not always lucky enough to go to

---

268 Elsinore Ledbetter is a fictional character who becomes friends with Annie. She was born in Africa and is a PhD student at the University of Washington (UW) in Seattle, WA. She is an older student and does not represent any real person past or present associated with UW geology. Her character is meant to represent the struggle of women in the sciences, not just in the US but elsewhere in the world.

school or to college. Missionaries were allowed to take children to learn at a private school. Elsinore had been fortunate enough to be selected to attend the school.

Annie learned that women the world over faced challenges greater than misogyny or sexism. They endured genital mutilation, rape, and human trafficking.

"You are an amazing person," said Annie. "You escaped such hardships to be able to go to college."

"I was also fortunate enough to have met my husband. He was allowed to teach at the *Colorado School of Mines*,[269] and I was allowed to be with him. With his support, I have been able to also seek advanced degrees."

"So, no children?"

"No, my husband and I do not want children. We agreed that the world was overpopulated, and we could better serve the world by not contributing to the problem."

"Wow," said Annie. "Good for you."

It was the beginning of a unique friendship between the two women.

Bigfoot?

The night seemed to drag on as Annie tried to sleep. For some reason her thoughts were with Sean. *He is an expert in this field, so why isn't he part of this trip?* She did not want to see him, or did she? Still, it was a bit of a mystery as to why someone of his status would not be in the midst of St. Helens.

Annie decided to exit her tent and sit outside for a little while. Perhaps seeing the night sky would help her to get her mind off of Sean and allow her to become sleepy.

---

269 The Colorado School of Mines is located in Boulder, CO and is a premier institution of learning in engineering, physics, and the geosciences.

She sank down into her chair with a thin blanket across her lap. Looking at the night sky was always one of her favorite pastimes, but it only seemed to remind her, too, of Sean. She imagined him sitting right there beside her and holding her hand. Annie closed her eyes and for a moment allowed herself to remember his tender kiss, his smell, his warmth, their lovemaking…his smiling eyes…" God, I miss him," she whispered.

To her surprise, there was movement in the distance. She continued to sit in her chair and did not move as she watched a large shadowy figure as it walked between tents and even stopped periodically to seemingly look down to the ground where people were sleeping under the stars.

The large form walked back and forth as though it were confused, or perhaps lost. It seemed to also be covered in hair.

In the darkness, Annie could not make out any of the features of the creature or person, but she knew the behavior seemed odd.

"My Lord in heaven," she whispered out loud. *I hope it's not Big Foot[270]. What the heck is it doing? Wait, is it coming this way? Shit!!!*

As the form lumbered in her direction, she quickly launched herself into her tent and lay perfectly still. She didn't dare breathe. *What if it is a murdering madman?* Annie's thoughts raced with scenarios of Big Foot dragging women off into the forest or a crazy mountain man abducting men and women for companionship.

"Crunch, crunch, stomp, stop, sniff loudly… Crunch, crunch, stop, stomp, sniff loudly."

It was right outside of her tent!

Annie was frozen with fear and the experience reminded her of her childhood, when someone would enter her bedroom and stand at her bedside. She would call out and ask, 'Is it you, Mom? Dad?' Just to have no answer. She did what she had done as a little

---

270   A large, fictional ape-like creature that is a myth in many areas across the globe.

girl, she lay as still as possible, holding her breath, and eventually falling asleep.

The next morning, Annie woke up to the sound of voices being raised. She sat straight up and listened closely to see if anyone was discussing the creature that walked through the camp the night before.

"What? Where is the coffee?"

"Who needs coffee? Here, have a coffee bean," said another voice with a thick accent.

Her heart almost stopped as she was sure she recognized the voice of one of the men. She leapt up to her feet and bent over to glance out of the mesh screen window near the top of her tent.

"Stinky?" she yelled excitedly. "Is that you?"

"That it is, lass," he laughed.

"Oh, my goodness, what the heck are you doing here? Come on over and help me out of this tent."

The two began unzipping her tent and he reached inside and delivered her as though she were a baby emerging from a womb. With one swift tug, he lifted her body so that her legs would wrap around his waist and her arms around his neck.

She didn't care how it appeared or how bad he smelled; her heart was filled with joy as she embraced him once more.

He was an enormous man of six feet five inches and very near three hundred pounds, none of which was fat. Stinky was a mountain man, physically intimidating, and very strong. But when it came to Annie, he was gentle and loving.

Annie cried and laughed as she kissed his cheeks. "I am so glad to see you, my friend."

"Well, where ya been, lass?" he asked as he laughed in a deep bellowing voice.

"How are you here for this field trip?"

He released his hold so she could slide down his body with his hands still holding hers.

"Well, ya see…I like volcanoes too."

"Really, I knew you were an economic field geologist, but had no idea that you had this much interest in volcanics."

"It sounded like a fun trip and besides, Jim said you'd be here, so how could I stay away? Didn't want to miss a chance to see Annie, now did I?"

"Jim? I asked him to come on out and he said he had some work to do in Montana."

"Who needs Jim, lass, when ya can have me?" he said with a wink of an eye and a fist pound to his chest.

"Right there," she said as she laughed out loud.

"When did you get here?"

"Well I got here late last night. Everyone was bunked down and I didn't see a clear spot, one, to lay ma bag."

"That was you last night? I was scared to death. I thought perhaps Bigfoot was in the camp to kidnap a mate."

"I suppose so, and aye, I could use a mate too."

"Oh, you!" she said as she slapped his chest.

"I saw one person who was sitting out, but they disappeared right quick when I approached."

"Oh my God. That was me, Stink. I'm so embarrassed. If I'd known it was you, we could have squeezed you into my tent last night."

"That tiny thing?"

"Yes, it might be big enough."

"Don't think so, lass. I might roll over on ya."

They both laughed and walked off together along a nearby trail.

"So, How are ye lads?"

"My boys? Oh, they are great. One is finishing college and will probably get married soon…"

"Ah, grans you'll have then, granny," he said as he playfully pushed her shoulder.

"Oh yes, I assume I'll be a grandmother soon enough."

"The other lad?"

"Oh, he's floundering in college, but his grandfather is funding his education, so he'll be right, eventually. He will not be letting his grandparents down."

"Well, he will be grateful for college when it is all said and done. What will he do when he finishes?"

"He will work on the farm. His major is agricultural business. So, I know his grandad and father will be very happy."

"The older one?"

"Ah, well, he is going into teaching. History, I believe. My ex says it's a worthless endeavor, but I am supportive of anything he wants."

"History, huh?" said Stinky, raising his left eyebrow in doubt. "He'd better do something else if he's gonna raise a family."

"Well, we'll see what happens. His girlfriend teaches kindergarten, so together they will both be teachers. And you, Stinky? How about you, mate?"

"Me back is giving me a worry, but I'm still working. Not like that sissy Jim. There's always work for me."

"I know, so what are you doing out of the field at this time of the year?"

"It aint summer yet, lass. This trip was perfect timing. I was supposed to see Seani, but he had a family emergency in New Zealand."

"Oh?"

"Seani lost his pops. Didn't know if ya knew that."

"Oh no!" said Annie, shocked at the news.

"He is there now, working with his sibs as they try to sort out what to do about their mum. She is ..."

"I'm sure she is not doing well with losing her life partner."

"Aye, she's around the bend fer sure. That be a deep sad. Figured Jim had told ya. Sorry lass."

"It's okay, Stanley. I don't talk to Sean, and Jim doesn't talk to me about him either."

"Jim says that he tries, but you don't oblige."

"Well, let's talk about something else, okay: I'm sorry he lost his dad. That must be why he's been on my mind lately."

"Ya sure, that's the reason? You two surely belong together, ya know."

Annie was deep in thought and quiet.

Stanley did all the talking, but she barely heard a word of it, as she felt such overwhelming sadness for Sean.

Looking down as they approached camp, Stinky pointed to what appeared to be an animal footprint in the moist path. They both looked at one another with surprise as it was huge and didn't look like a bear.

"Aye, lass, you may have seen 'em after all."

"No way," said Annie as she got down on her knees to examine the print with her hand.

She followed the ridges along the outside to where the toes should be, "That's a really big person for sure." She glanced at Stinky's boot size and then up at him. "Did you venture out barefoot, mate, to take a pee?"

"That's a personal question. don't ya think?" he laughed. "A gentleman would never tell."

After breakfast and coffee, the trip leaders gathered everyone for a presentation and discussion of the trip to St. Helen's. Stinky leaned over toward Annie, "Ya, they'll be a pissing contest amongst that brood, fer sure."

"Really? Why do you say that?"

"Seani told me about the guys leading us into the dome tomorrow. They be big shots or so dey tink they are."

"Oh, okay," and she raised her finger over her lips to indicate that they needed to listen and stop talking.

Stinky rolled his eyes and whispered, "Aye, lass."

After the presentations, everyone packed up for the trip to camp near St. Helens. The hike was scheduled for the next day if the weather permitted, and the USGS said it was safe for them to enter.

That evening, Annie sat in her camping chair and watched as Stinky laughed and drank beer with some of the *fellers*. [271] Elsinore walked over and sat down to talk to her.

"Hi there. Are you enjoying the trip so far?" asked Annie.

"I see you've picked up a man for this trip."

"Him?" laughed Annie, "No, he's just an old friend. We have done field work together in the old days."

"Oh, so you're not…"

"Heavens, no!" said Annie. "We are just friends."

"Well, I never judge," said Elsinore. "Where I come from, if the wife doesn't mind, a man may lay with whoever he wants."

"What? That's horrible," said Annie.

"This is why the women are stronger than the men in our village. The women all stick together, and we take care of our sisters. It's us against the men."

"Wow," said Annie, as she took a swig of beer. "…and I thought things were bad here."

"Here, the woman may choose the man. Where I come from all men choose any woman they want."

"That's just not right," said Annie, watching the men all posturing themselves around the campfire.

---

271 Fellers is a common slang for fellows and common in the Australian and New Zealand parlance.

"Look at them over there with their chests pushed out like gorillas," said Elsinore.

Both women laughed out loud.

"Annie, I need to go to the stream and bathe. It is dark. Would you go with me and carry the torch?"

"The what?"

"A torch. I need the light for washing," as she pointed to the flashlight.

"Oh, flashlight," said Annie, "Okay?"

As the women walked away from the campsite, Annie found herself feeling uncomfortable with the venture, especially after feeling that huge track with her hand earlier. The sun was down, and it was probably not the best idea to walk anywhere away from the campsite. Elsinore almost fell twice.

"You okay there, Elsi?" asked Annie.

"Elsi? That's what my husband calls me."

"Is it okay if I call you Elsi, too?"

"Sure."

"I hear the water over here," said Annie as she aimed the flashlight at the stream. It was tiny but flowing.

As Elsi began to unzip her pants, Annie turned her body away to protect Elsi's dignity.

"Please bring the torch closer," she said.

Annie looked back briefly to see where the stream was and moved the light closer. She still turned her body away.

"Annie, do you find my body unpleasant?"

"Oh no. That's not it. I'm just not someone who is comfortable with such things."

"We are just women. As women, we must watch out for one another in a tribe of men. Right?" asked Elsinore.

"Sure," said Annie.

The women walked back to the camp and each went their separate ways.

"Miss Annie, thank you so much for helping me."

"No worries" she said as she crawled into her tent.

"Good grief, that was uncomfortable," she whispered.

Annie was not the type of woman who ever needed other women to do such things. She had been naked with men but had never had that experience with women.

"Lord help me," she said as she turned on her lamp to write a few words for the day.

The men shouted and laughed into the night, but that did not keep Annie from sleeping soundly. Perhaps she was able to sleep well because she knew Stinky was there too?

The Throat of the Dragon

The next morning, Annie woke to the smell of bacon and coffee.

"Now that's what I'm talking about," she heard Alice say.

Annie stuck her head out of her tent to see Stinky wearing an apron and cooking in a cast iron skillet over a fire. "Is that bacon I smell?"

"Aye, lass, get over here and get some before the fellers eat it all."

"We have to leave here in about an hour, everybody, so finish up, pack up, and let's get to the vans by 0900," said a small man with glasses and a big bushy mustache.

She had no idea who he was but assumed he must be from the USGS[272] because she hadn't seen him before that morning. He was clearly leading them to the crater that day.

"Hey Stink. Who is that guy?" she asked quietly.

---

272 United States Geological Survey

"He's the bigshot from the USGS. *Martin Short,*[273] I believe is his name...or is it Tall...Geez, I can't remember. He actually knows what he is talking about, though...not sure about the rest of 'em," he said, chuckling.

Everyone was loaded up, including Stinky in his rented truck, and they all rolled off to drive as close to the crater as they could get in vans. It was a bit bouncy, but they managed to get within six miles.

"We've got a little bit of a hike today. Sorry we couldn't get any closer, so make sure you have plenty of water, your sack lunch, a good hat, long sleeved shirts and pants, ...there is fumarolic activity up there and the gasses may etch your camera lenses and oxidize your body parts...so just be mindful of the environment. It is an active volcano, so you may see rocks and pebbles rolling down the sides. We've checked the emissions and seismic activity and we should be okay, but one never knows for sure with a volcano, now, do they?" [274]

Elsinore and Annie exchanged concerned looks.

"Oh well," said Annie, "Perhaps today is a good day to die."

Elsi laughed nervously and said, "Speak for yourself, woman."

It occurred to Annie at that moment that Elsi had never watched Star Trek Next Generation and had no idea about *Klingons and Worf's*[275] battle phrase.

---

273 Martin Short is a fictional character that is not meant to represent any specific person working for the USGS in the past or present.

274 This hiking experience is loosely based on the author's hikes into Mount St. Helens during the late 80s and 90s.

275 Worf is a fictional character in The Next Generation Star Trek series. His character is Klingon and they are a warlike group of space travelers who value honor and death in battle.

She just laughed at her own clever nerdiness as they began their trek through the *lahar*[276] and pyroclastic flows, and ash fall deposits.

The consistency of the deposits that they were walking over was that of a fine flour. Much finer than a fine sand. The challenge was to maintain footing while trying to move upslope. It was very much like "take one step and slide two steps back," but they all managed to make it to the scar rim (what was left after the collapse of that side of the volcanic cone) of the northwest side of the crater.

When Annie reached this point, she saw that they still had a distance to go to the dome. She stopped for a few moments to catch her breath and turned around to look out toward the valley and the path they had just hiked.

"Oh my God!" she gasped.

The vast destruction in front of her eyes was like nothing she'd ever seen before in her life. It was more than she could process. So much utter devastation. Such horrific beauty. There were no words to describe the scene. Her legs were shaking with emotion, as she also imagined the experience of David Johnston[277] and others who perished that fateful day. *What must that have been like, to know it was happening, to see it coming, and to not be able to do a thing to stop it?*

Annie felt she was looking at a cemetery.

Stinky came up the slope toward her and also turned around. "That's a mess fer sure, lass."

Annie just stood there, speechless.

"Let's keep going," said Stink, as he put his hand on her shoulder and pushed her gently along. "We'll be there soon."

---

276 Mt St. Helens had active glaciers at the time of its 1980 eruption. The pyroclastic material that was ejected combined with the water from the glaciers created a fast-moving debris flow filled with pyroclastic debris and mostly ash.

277 The USGS volcanologist who died monitoring Mt. St. Helens and was killed in the pyroclastic flow which covered his position on a hillside six miles away.

The closer they got to the dome area, the more the air smelled of sulfur.

Stinky turned to Annie and said, "Twasn't me, lass."

Annie punched him in the arm and said, "You're right. It was me!"

Stinky's laugh was so loud that it echoed through the crater. "Can't take ya anywheres."

The group finally reached the dome, and Annie took off her pack and sat down to get a swig of water.

"Here, lass, have some sardines."

"No, thank you. It smells bad enough up here as it is. I'll stick with my PBJ."

Elsinore was in the last group to arrive and took a spot near Annie on a large rock.

"What took you so long?" said Annie in jest.

"Some of us have shorter legs," said Elsi, breathless. "This is absolutely terrifying, don't you think?"

"Yes. I'm ready to leave now," said Annie. "I've seen it. It's great, now let's go."

"Exactly, let's leave them if they insist on staying."

As the two ladies sat eating their lunches, they watched as one of the professors from the colleges stood on the top of the dome and discussed magma mixing.

"Would you like some tea?" asked Elsi.

"What? You brought tea? Of course," said Annie as she accepted the tiny lid from Elsi's thermos. "Yummy. This is...?"

"It's Darjeeling, dear," said Elsi.

"Mmmm... very good!"

The two women sat and watched as the men debated why St. Helens is not on the same linear track as other Cascade volcanoes.

"I never really thought about that, did you?" asked Annie.

"Yes, it is too far west, I think," answered Elsi, as she sipped her tea from a second thermos cap.

"So, what do you think?"

"I think it is a piece of a broken plate."

"A subducting plate that just broke off, you mean?" asked Annie.

"Yes, the magmas suggest a different source, perhaps."

"Who knows for sure?" said Annie.

Stinky leaned over to the ladies and said, "They don't know, now, do they?" pointing at the men all posturing themselves as the one with the correct hypothesis.

The three laughed as they finished their tea, sardines, and PBJ sandwiches.

As they sat there waiting, Annie could feel a sort of rumbling beneath them as pebbles trickled down the sides of the crater.

Annie whispered to Stinky, "Are we safe here?"

"We be sittin on a beast, lass," said Stinky.

"Nothing like looking down the throat of a dragon," said Elsi.

It became very clear that the volcano was alive. It was breathing, and there was something going on not too far from the surface... tiny little seismic events beneath them.

Annie couldn't help but remember the story that Sean had told about his close call with a volcano. She was also reminded of the team that was surprised at Galeras in Columbia where so many were killed and gravely injured. *What the hell were you thinking?* she thought, as she had no choice but to sit and watch the geochemists argue.

With every tiny tremor and every little slide of debris down the side, Annie felt her anxiety level growing. It would not be good for her to have an anxiety attack inside of an active volcano. Also, she didn't want to appear weak in front of all the brave men, and the girl with the long-handled hammer.

"Volcanoes are just as unpredictable as bulls or buffalo," said Annie. "So, why are they still standing up there?"

After two hours of discussion and debate, the team leaders decided that everyone needed to get back to the vans so the group could make it to camp in time for a grilled salmon dinner.

Another professor and his wife had volunteered to feed them all and the grilled salmon was a Pacific Northwest favorite.

* * *

That evening, after dinner, Annie retreated to her tent and wrote in her field notebook, "*Mt. St. Helens was beyond anything I had imagined. I can safely say that I will NEVER hike into an active volcano again. EVER. It was frighteningly beautiful, exciting, and awe-inspiring. As we approached the volcano in the trucks, I gasped at the size, and how it filled my entire field of view. The dome was sitting, exposed from the northwest by the scar from the collapse of the cone on that side. It sat majestically in the center with small bits of white showing from the active glaciers that are growing within and on top of the dome.*

As we hiked through the debris flows, through the lahar deposits and ash, my legs and ankles felt heavy, and keeping my balance was a challenge. It was much more difficult than running in dry or wet sand. The deposits ranged from being filled with unsorted debris with some pieces very sharp--I assumed volcanic glass--to being homogeneous mixtures of ash and in some places, tiny bits of pumice.

The soles of my boots were warm from the heat of the day warming the silica rich ash and debris. As we ascended the flow deposits to reach the lip of the scar, I turned to see the devastation and the expanse of the pyroclastic flow that destroyed everything in its path. It looked as though a huge mower or razor had shaved off all the trees in the distance, leaving flattened, gray toothpicks, all lying in the direction of the fiery flow.

The remnants of Spirit Lake could be seen beneath the material from the collapsed section of the cone. I wanted to fall to my knees, I felt so weakened with emotion at the thought of David Johnston seeing an entire mountain collapsing and having a huge pyroclastic flow moving toward him at hundreds of miles per hour.

When we arrived at the dome, I touched the rocks with my bare hands and could feel that the volcano was alive beneath us. Much like a city has a 'beat' from all of the cars driving on the freeways and overpasses, the mountain also had a beat, maybe a heartbeat. It was alive and you could feel it within your entire body. I wanted to run but could not. I was afraid of looking foolish.

As a geologist, I have always loved volcanoes, dreamed of visiting an active one, but I had no idea it would be like this. So intensely beautiful--it filled my senses. I experienced the volcano almost as a living being, magnificent in sight and potential for destruction."

Annie, Elsinore, and Stinky all said goodbye after the Mount Rainier tour. Stinky had a job in South Africa, Elsinore had a PhD to defend and a husband, and Annie had the rest of her summer to ponder the experiences of that May field trip.

Chapter 54—Final Journey

That following summer, Annie embarked on her first summer trip alone. She needed the time alone to process her feelings and to discover some direction for the rest of her life. As Betty said, she was still relatively young, she had some health issues, but she could still hike into active volcanoes, so she wasn't too far gone.

Jim was a little bit concerned about her making the journey alone, but he knew that she could take care of herself. She assured her sons, Betty and Bob, and Jim that she had books on tape and plenty of CDs for entertainment.

As she drove across the high plains toward the Rockies, she sang along with each song that played and even had percussion instruments to keep her engaged. The tambourine was for sixties and seventies. The shake-it was for all Latin rhythms and other genres that the tambourine didn't quite fit. Truckers sometimes did a double take when they saw her rolling down the highway singing and playing percussion instruments, but Annie didn't care--she was enjoying it immensely.

Some of the music was from the late 50s and 60s and reminded her of her parents and growing up. Other songs were from her teen and early 20s (70s and 80s) where she remembered her marriage to Robert and sharing his life. The 80s and 90s brought memories of the songs her children and their friends liked and how much she missed the summer trips with her boys and their friends. Then there were the songs that reminded her of the love she shared with Sean and the summers she spent with Dr. D. and all the students from the years of field camps.

Annie laughed when she remembered one summer camp where Dr. D. lost his mind and sabotaged the speaker system in the van he was riding.

The T.A. for that year had installed a tape player so he could listen to his favorite music as he drove. He particularly liked "Acid Rock/Heavy Metal."

One day, Adam had had enough of the music and ripped the speaker out of the passenger door of the van.

The crime remained a mystery for the rest of the field camp. It was only after Anna and D. were entering the final grades that he admitted that it was his work of vandalism.

She laughed and cried as she reminisced. Twenty-plus years of joy and pain had passed, and she was reliving all of them through the music from her radio and CDs. Taking a road trip by herself was a great catharsis for her soul.

She returned to the small town in the Rockies, where the field station and campus were located, and where she had taught the field methods course, and also had fallen in love with Sean. She had tried to get back each summer, but some summers it just wasn't on the way to the features that she needed to show her students.

This particular summer, she reserved a cabin at a campsite, where field camps still gathered for their summer courses. The thought of seeing young geology students once more excited her greatly. She couldn't wait to see them as they engaged in learning the time-honored skills of field geology.

Annie couldn't help but be surprised and feel proud to see that half of the students appeared to be female. What a wonderful sight to see! She remembered how difficult it had been for her at their age as usually the only one or in the minority for sure.

They seemed to be just the same as she remembered her students; Tevas, a specific kind of sandal worn by those who enjoy outdoor activities, bandanas, socks hanging on lines stretched between trees, ah...it was so good to be back "home."

One of the professors from another school thought he recognized her, and approached excitedly, "Oh my God! Is that you, Annie Moore! Are you here with your students?" asked *Walt Smith*,[278] a professor from a neighboring school in the south.

"No, I stopped teaching the field methods course years ago, but I do love coming back here and seeing all the new students you have."

"Ah, Annie, they are very much the same, but also very different. They are by far lazier than our students used to be."

"Really, that's hard to believe. Ours were pretty lazy too, you know," replied Annie. "I also see lots more girls. That's a good thing. So, some things seem to have improved. Right?"

"Haha...Annie, you always did have a way of seeing the good in situations, didn't you? Giving her an unexpected hug, "It is so darn good to see you. Would you be free to come over to our campsite this evening and join us for a brew and old times?"

"Oh, I'd love that."

"You'd better bring your guitar too," chimed Walt, as he walked back to talk to his students.

She couldn't drink like she used to, but she gladly brought some hummus and organic chips to share. She also brought a six-pack of her favorite brew, "Moose Drool" beer, which is only brewed and sold in the northwest. Draped across her shoulder and back was her famous old guitar, which had seen more than one campfire in its forty years of being played by her.

---

278 Walt Smith is a fictional character, not meant to depict any person living or dead.

Walt could see Annie walking to their campsite in the firelight and stood up to shake her hand and offer her his chair. He was a gentleman and was demonstrating proper manners for his students.

"Everyone?" he said, "I want you to meet Professor Annie Moore. She is a retired field camp instructor and one of the finest field geologists in the business."

She felt herself blush at his very nice introduction.

He went on to say, "And she has a very nice folk voice and is a heck of a guitar player as well."

She felt a little bit insecure with all the buildup, as she had spent the last fifteen years not actually touching her guitar or singing very often, so the expectations may have been a little high for her in this circle.

"I haven't played for quite some time. I only just pulled it out again really for this trip. Is there anyone else here who plays and would like to use my guitar? I'd be glad to sing along," she said modestly.

None of the faculty were interested, but luckily a student approached out of the darkness at that moment and was excited to see a guitar,

"Wow! Is that a classical?"

"Yes, it is," said Annie. "She has nylon strings and metal strings and is well seasoned. Would you like to play?"

"May I?" asked the student.

She gladly handed him her guitar and he began to play. To her surprise, he was a blues guitarist who was unable to bring his guitar to the camp.

"You are so good," she said.

He played her guitar for over an hour and everyone was highly impressed and entertained.

Annie asked, "Are you familiar with pieces by 'The Band?'"

He looked up in the dark sky for a moment and then began to play one of her favorite songs of all time, "It Makes No Difference."

She felt a wave of emotion flow over her as he played the musical introduction. How did this young man know? As she sang, tears filled her eyes, as the song made her think of Sean and the times they had spent there together in that very place.

"It makes no difference, where I turn. I can't get over you and the flame still burns...

Annie began harmonizing.... *"The sun don't shine, anymore. And the rains fall down on my door."*

Everyone clapped at the end of the song.

Annie wiped tears from her eyes and apologized for her emotional expression.

"You are a gifted musician," she said to the student. "I hope you never give up that gift.

Thank you so much for sharing it with me."

He seemed genuinely flattered and handed the guitar back to her.

"I think granny here should go get some rest." She excused herself to return to her cabin.

"Hey Annie," shouted Walt, as she began to walk away. "Why don't you join us in the field tomorrow? We will be at *Montgomery mountain.*[279] You remember that place, don't you?"

"Oh yes, I certainly do," said Annie. "We'll see, Walt. Thank you for a very nice evening. It was just like old times."

The next morning, Annie was sitting, drinking warm tea, and working the crossword in the paper when she heard footsteps stomp onto her porch, followed by a rather startling knock.

What the hell? She thought, as she slowly opened the door.

---

279   Fictional field area not meant to depict a real place in this story.

It was Walt, grinning widely with his field hat on and sunglasses hanging on a cord around his neck. "Hey granny, wanna come out to the field with the kids?"

She reluctantly agreed and collected her water bottles, backpack, hat, and a huge scarf to wear around her shoulders and head. She climbed into the front seat of their van and was introduced to the students, who all seemed ready for a day of work.

As they drove out to the field, past the Pioneer Mountains and the glacial deposits, Annie remembered her days of running over gophers. The memories were flooding back. She was a little bit excited and intimidated, as she hadn't been out in the field like that in some time.

To her surprise, it was just as she remembered it; very hot, dry, and dusty, with sagebrush and cactus everywhere, and the scent of dust, evergreen (cedars), and sage filling the hot desert air. There was even a dead cow formation to complete the experience.

She particularly enjoyed finding the teams of students in the field, who were just full of questions. Annie easily slipped into her field camp professor role and didn't tell them anything, but instead asked them questions in response to their questions.

It was so fun. She couldn't help but note that they seemed to be in larger teams--groups of four to six, instead of twos, and they had "WALKIE TALKIES!" *What the hell?* she thought.

Each team was spreading out over the area, in what didn't appear to be a transect at all, just mindless wandering, from what she could see. They also didn't have any sense of contours, going up one steep slope and then down to the lowest contour next. It reminded her of a Monty Python skit, where cartoon cutouts followed each other in a linear fashion up and down.

Sigh … they clearly didn't have her as an instructor, or there would be some order to this madness.

As she walked a dirt path within a drainage area--arroyo--in the desert, she couldn't help but notice the fine clays that she remembered being such a challenge when they were wet. She reached down and collected some in her hand and felt the texture as it slipped through her fingers and was swept into the air by a gentle breeze.

Annie was reminded of just how much she loved field geology and missed it. The smell of clay and dust was so pleasing. She even hoped to see a bull snake slithering partially beneath the dirt on the path. Maybe she would consider coming out of field retirement to join a field camp the next summer. It might be something she would once again enjoy.

On the path coming towards her, she saw a team of all girls. She waved at them and they waved back, smiling as they approached.

"Where are you ladies heading?" she queried.

"We still have to cover this slope over here, and then maybe we will be finished for the day," answered one of the young ladies, as she pointed to the top of a ridge in the distance.

"Well, let me see your map. Do you mind?" asked Annie.

"Sure, we are here and need to cover this area," said one of the girls, as she pointed with her dirty finger.

"Ah, I see," said Annie. "May I suggest?"

"Sure," they all said excitedly.

"Go down here to this fault zone, see that in the distance?" Annie pointed to the feature in the distance, also showing them on the map. "Take that fault zone and then make your way up to the higher contour. Since you have walkie-talkies and are working in teams, one group can take the higher contour and the other two can take a lower one... you know, *you take the high road and they'll take the low road and I'll get to Scotland before ye*" she sang, and they laughed.

"You can communicate that way, instead of having to go up and down and up and down and…. Lord I'm tired just watching you guys do that," she said laughing with them.

"Whose bright idea was it for a group of six to all walk up and down like that anyway?"

"We hadn't really thought about it, Dr. Moore," said one of the girls.

"Thank you so much. We have heard so much about you and it is a pleasure to get your advice."

She seemed intrigued, "What exactly have you heard about me?"

"Our instructors told us that you used to be the only female instructor at these camps. You paved the way for the rest of us, it seems."

Annie wanted to cry. That was the nicest thing she'd ever heard. "Who said that?" she asked.

"Dr. Walt, he said you were a legend in terms of female field camp instructors."

"What happened? Why did you quit?"

Annie then said, "Well ladies, it's like this. I wasted my life on children and damned men."

They all laughed together.

Annie continued, "I tried to do it all and all at one time. It didn't work out so well for me. You don't have to do that." She hesitated to continue but noticed that they were all very focused on her words. "So, do you really want my advice?" she asked.

They all nodded their heads, affirming that they were indeed interested.

"1) Don't get married, ever, it's a waste of your time, energy, and talent, 2) don't have babies, they too can be a waste of time, talent, and energy, but not as much as the men, and 3) seek your own career and life goals before seeking the other two.

"Men will always be there, and they are simply not worth what you will give up for them, and babies can be adopted. Your youth and ability to do what you are doing right now is limited.

"Enjoy your life before settling down. I tried to do it all at once and it was just too hard. I know that may not be what you want to hear but take it from this old lady. I DO HAVE REGRETS.

"I wish I had my youth back and the knowledge I now have. I would not have wasted so much of my life on trying to please others and especially on seeking the love and security I needed from men.

"I have been alone now for about twenty years, and I've learned that 'I' am the only person on which I am able to rely. Nobody is there for me, not really. At this point in my life, I have good friends and some family, but for the most part, It's just me. It is just me, and I am okay without a man. I don't need one to be happy with myself."

She looked at their faces and realized that she may have allowed her own bitterness to seep into her advice and said, "I apologize ladies. That was perhaps a little too negative."

One of the girls said in response, "No, not really," looking at the other girls in the team, "We've basically come to that conclusion ourselves. Hearing you state it validates it for us."

Annie then backpedaled just a little bit, "Well, don't get me wrong, marriage and babies are great, if that's what you really want, but I didn't. It was a choice that I feel society made for me. I would have been much happier as a committed single person with no children, even though I love my own children very much. I wouldn't send them back for all the world. So, don't let the bitter rantings of an old woman jade your desires for love and happiness. I'm sure it is out there and in great abundance for most people. It just wasn't for me."

They thanked Dr. Moore for her insights and advice and seemed to be very pleased to have met her and received her unfiltered comments.

She continued away from them in the other direction and thought, *Damn, Annie. Where the hell did that come from? That was not very sweet, nice, or Christian, was it? Oh well, it was honest, and that is perhaps the best that anyone can share from a life of experience.*

She walked on and passed some familiar structures. One was a tight fold embedded in rock. She struggled up the slope to the folded area, sat down, and looked out across the valley floor in front of her to view a volcanic ridge in the distance.

"Thank you, God," she whispered, "for this opportunity to revisit the field. I have missed it so much. Please forgive me, too, Lord for my bitter words of advice. I should have been more measured, and kind. Amen."

Before leaving, she placed her rock hammer in the middle of the tight fold and snapped a picture of the structure. Smiling to herself, she said, "It is so much easier to capture these moments with cell phone cameras now. Praise God for technology, too," she added.

She saw the vans in the distance and decided to go seek refuge from the sun and refill her water bottle. The vans were even different. They were higher, blockier, and just ugly compared to the Fords of the old days.

Annie opened the door and pulled herself up into the van seat, so she could take off her scarf, hat, and perhaps even her boots. The breeze blowing through the van brought back such fond memories of the days when she used to do this in the summers. It was heaven. It felt like home.

She then realized that she missed Adam and also Sean. She hadn't talked to Sean in years and was saddened by the reported loss of his Pops.

Adam was retired and living on a ranch somewhere in Wyoming.

Perhaps she should stop in on him and his good wife on her way back home to see how they were doing?

Revisiting the field was refreshing and exactly what she needed at that point in her life. She felt revitalized, alive again.

She thanked Walt and the students profusely for allowing her to go with them that day. It was their last day of mapping on that project, so she would not be going out again, but it was just as well. There was only one more day in the area before she would be moving on to her destination of the Stillwater Valley.

Chapter 55—Now and Forever

The next day, she packed up and drove most of the day, stopping for supplies, and of course an espresso or two. She had reserved a cabin in a less remote area of the Stillwater but was still very near the river. This campground was one where field camps would bring larger groups to visit.

The campsite coordinator remembered her and gladly rented her a cabin for a ten-day stay. She was older now and didn't feel as secure in a tent, in bear country, as she had when sharing tents with her students and children in years past, and especially with Sean.

Annie was so happy to have this time to relax and do nothing. She brought her radio, too, to help pass time and enjoyed the oldies hippie station from a mountain community nearby. She had her own cookstove and a comfy chair, just like the one she had taken on her field trips with Sean. The evening air was filled with familiar scents of lodgepole pine wood smoke, evergreen, sage, organics, the smell of the river, and the crisp dryness of the mountain air.

She watched the stars pop out one by one against the darkness of the night, as she lightly strummed her old guitar. It was so relaxing, and she knew she was home.

"Perhaps I should just retire here," she thought to herself.

Ten o'clock came, and it was time for everyone to get quiet and settle in for the evening. She picked up her chair and her things and entered the cabin and lay on the bed to say her prayers. "Let there be peace in this troubled world. May my children be protected from all harm. And, please be with Sean and his family... Amen"

In the breeze of the opened windows, Annie felt the whispering touch on her bare torso. She found herself remembering Sean – his smell, his skin -- and longing for his touch.

"Lord, forgive me," she whispered. "I still love him."

The next morning, she got up and took a long walk along the river, listening to the roar and sitting quietly in silence so that she could hear the voice of God in her heart. As she sat there with her mind free and open, she could feel the anointing of the Holy Spirit within her.

"Praise You, Lord," she uttered, but couldn't even hear her own voice over the river. *"Praise You for the beauty of the earth,"* as she began to sing the hymn to herself, *"For the beauty of the earth, for the glory of the skies..."*[280]

Annie was so grateful for the ability to sit there without fear, comfortable with being alone and not fearing being eaten by a bear. She was one with nature, her God and at peace with herself.

As she sat in this special place, she once again couldn't help but think of Sean and reflect on how things had turned out in her life. So many questions had been answered through the years. Annie had gone from being a young girl and woman, who felt she had no choices in life, to a mature self-actualized person, who accepted responsibility for her own happiness and security.

In reflecting on her relationship with Sean, in particular, she had come to accept that he had not done anything to her. She was not a victim of a lost love but was a willing participant in a shared love relationship.

Annie understood that she chose to give her heart to him, forsaking all others. It was her choice to give her life to Jesus, as well. All things that had transpired since her meeting Sean were

---

280 "For the beauty of the earth," Author, Folliott Sandford Pierpoint (1864), tune written by Conrad Kocher, Germany, 1786.

ultimately of her own choosing. She only had herself to blame for the emotional pain and guilt that she carried for decades.

God had warned all of humanity about the reality of "free will." Sin was not some punishment imposed by God Himself but was the result of our own willful choice to deny God. Sin is, by definition, the "absence of God." This absence, though, is not God's abandoning us; it is our willfully rejecting His love in our own lives through the choices we make. God does not make good or bad things happen to any of us. WE do that to ourselves. The cosmos, nature, ...things just happen, but how we choose to respond to these things, is what defines our own happiness and our own character.

Annie continued to speak to God, "I will always love him, Lord. I will never accept that the love I hold for him in my heart is in fact sinful. But I do accept that it was my own choices which opened me up to the ultimate pain of life's experiences. This was and is MY choice. He is forever in my heart and that will never change." In this moment of personal responsibility, she began to pray,

"I pray dear Lord that my love for him and the grace I have received from living my life as a committed single will somehow bring him closer to You. Please Lord; let any grace I have, be given to him. I do not know why he is so heavy on my mind and so full in my heart at this time, but for whatever the reason, please let your will be done, and if the grace I have to give can bring peace, joy, healing or love to him, then please anoint him as he needs according to Your will. Amen. ...

Thank you, Lord, for the blessings of this life and for the love I hold in my heart for my one true love. Amen

Being a deeply sensitive person, Annie had come to realize that she could sense when friends, family, and others needed prayer. She seemed to know when something was wrong or when there was an imbalance of some kind. Some call it a sixth sense.

She wondered if all the times Sean was heavy in her mind if those were times in his life that he needed her extra prayers, like her knowing his pain when his "Pops" passed.

The ancients would have been afraid of it and may well have burned her for being a witch. Whatever the gift, she was certain it was not magical, but indeed came from God in heaven. She had a cosmic, spiritual connection with nature and with animals and people. She accepted this role and embraced the gifts of the Holy Spirit in her life. Annie learned to love herself and to praise God for all things in her life, good and bad.

Annie stood up and walked to the stream's edge. The water was crystal clear and smelled fresh and crisp. Leaning down carefully, kneeling as if in prayer, she put her hand in the stream and felt the force of the flowing water against her fingers. The current was strong but didn't feel frightening. It felt inviting as her memories took her back to the day, she had bathed in the same river so many years ago. It was cold and invigorating as it washed past and between her fingers, seeking to pull her hand downstream with the current. After a few minutes, she noticed that her skin was beginning to turn blue, so she pulled her hand back and held it with her other hand. It felt numb and lifeless.

As she walked back toward the cabin, she massaged her cold, lifeless hand with her warm hand. As the blood began to flow back into her fingers, they felt hot and prickly, like needles were being pushed into them. It was very painful.

She thought to herself, *Well that's quite a metaphor I think for how it feels when we become numb to the experiences of this world and then begin to reawaken and feel again. There can't be renewal without some kind of pain, I suppose.* She chuckled to herself as she walked and began singing....

"In the morning, when I rise... give me Jesus...."[281] This was one of her absolute favorite songs of praise, and she sang it almost every day of her life.

After returning from her morning reflection and prayer, Annie was sitting in her cabin, enjoying a fresh cup of coffee and the crossword from a paper she had bought in town a few days earlier. She heard footsteps approaching, crunching the forest carpet and then steps on the porch of her cabin. The footsteps stopped and there was a pause.

She wondered, *who might that be? Are they there or did they just walk on my porch and off again?*

She rose to peek out of her window and was startled by a soft knock on her door. She thought, *Oh my goodness. Who would be coming to see me?* She assumed it was probably the camp director coming to check on her. He and his wife knew that she was alone and had some health issues and had promised to keep her in mind if they hadn't seen her each day.

She cracked the door slightly and an older man was standing there wearing field attire. He had a hat and sunglasses and she couldn't see his face very well. She heard a voice that sounded very familiar,

"Annie?" the man asked.

Annie looked confused and a little bit surprised.

"How are ya Annie?" he said with a voice and an accent that she recognized.

"Sean?" she asked. Not really believing it could be him, but it sure seemed like him.

"I couldn't believe it when Linda (the camp director's wife) said that a retired field camp instructor named Moore was staying here!" he said breathlessly.

---

281 Sang during the Civil War, words written by Frances Jane (Fanny Crosby" 1820, Music written by John Robson Sweney, 1899.

"I am here with some students and just wanted to see if it was really you."

She stood there in stunned silence and finally said, "Yes, it's me."

Before she could say another word, Sean reached for her and she moved right to him. They hugged, kissed, and held each other.

Annie breathed in and immediately felt "home" again. Sean's sunglasses fell from his face during the embrace.

As he cradled her face in his hands, she looked into the same smiling eyes that she had grown to love so many years ago, and he said, "I have missed ya so much."

Annie looked up at him with tears in her eyes, smiling and replied, "Me too."

Chapter 56—This is not goodbye

Sean and Annie stood embracing for what felt like forever, both crying.

He lifted her face and combed her hair back with his long fingers and looked into her tear-filled hazel eyes. The pain he saw hurt him to his core. Overcome with emotion, he pulled her head into his chest, to his heart, and stroked her head and shoulders, as if she were a small child.

"Annie, I'm so, so, sorry," said Sean through his tears. I never meant ta hurt ya, and I have missed ya every day.

"It's okay, Sean. I understood," she whispered softly.

"Please say that ya forgive me," he said as he looked once more into her eyes, hoping to see a glimmer of resignation and forgiveness.

"I forgave you years ago, love. You would never intentionally hurt anyone. I know this."

She pushed him away from her so that she could better see his face because she could still barely believe that he was there with her.

His face was older, clean shaven, but the eyes, oh those beautiful smiling eyes, were so sad. The sadness she saw broke her heart. She could hardly bear the pain he seemed to be feeling at that moment.

"After all these years...I can't believe I've found ya again. What are the odds, right?" he said as he trembled and wiped tears from his eyes.

"May I come in and we can chat for a few minutes?"

"Sure, said Annie," as she opened the door wider so he could enter.

Sean was shaken to see that her cabin looked just as he remembered her dorm room from so many years before. The same blanket on the bed, the guitar in the corner, the French press on the table, and her rosary. The only addition was a rather large crucifix with a Benedictine cross which stood in the center of the shelf, perhaps like an altar or shrine of some kind. He clutched his stomach for a moment as though he thought he might become sick as emotion flowed over him.

"Sean, are you okay?"

"Yes," he said, sobbing uncontrollably. He couldn't help it. He was finally free to release the pent-up guilt and pain that he'd been carrying around for so many years.

"God, I'm sorry, Annie. I don't know what's come over me. I just can't seem to stop."

"It's okay, love," she said gently. "You apparently need to get this out." She placed her arms around him as she had done in the corridor of the field station dorms. Her head was on his chest, his arms around her and resting on the small of her back, both swaying gently back and forth as Sean wept. The aroma of woodsmoke and a hint of jasmine filled his senses.

Sean pushed Annie back to arm's length so he could get a good look at her.

She was older, not trim, and healthy as she had been in her 30s. The years had been hard on her physically, spiritually, and mentally. Even with the imperfections, she was still Annie. Her hair was shorter and had streaks of gray, but oh those eyes, unyieldingly kind and full of love. She was simply beautiful, just as he had remembered her.

He bent down and kissed her forehead," Yer so beautiful, still."

"Oh, good grief," she said and laughed. Slapping him familiarly on the chest, "You know that's not true." She released her embrace and moved to sit at her little chair seated at the collapsible table that she always took with her for camping.

She looked at him, too. He hadn't changed much at all. He was still tall, muscular, not quite as tanned, but still very, very handsome to her. His hair was completely gray, and his beard was gone. His face was as smooth as a baby's behind, lacking the rugged appearance that she remembered so well.

"You haven't changed much, Sean," she said. "You seem to have lived a good life and have retained your good health and physique. In fact, you look younger without your beard."

"Oh, we've all changed and not for the better, I can assure ya that."

Sean moved toward her sitting position, moved the table to one side, and knelt before her. Taking her hands in his, tears still streaming down his face, "I have never stopped loving ya, Annie. I sent letters, tried to call, talked to D., and there was no response. He suggested that ya had become a nun or some such ridiculous thing. Is that true?"

"I've never stopped loving you, either," she said with tears welling up in her eyes. She looked away and choked back her own tears, "Always and forever, Sean. I never stopped loving you, and I won't. You have always been and will always be, 'my one and only.'"

"So, ya never remarried?"

"No."

"Did ya join a convent or somethin?"

"Kind of, but I'm not a nun. I just live like one."

They both laughed as he pulled himself up to her so they could embrace once more.

Sean stood, taking her hands into his. He led her to the bed where he sat down in front of her, placed his forehead on her stomach, and put his hands on her hips, as though he had always done so.

She felt the same to him. She was rounder and fuller, but it still felt the same. He moved his hands to her waist and up her back where he could feel she wasn't wearing anything underneath her old gray sweatshirt. He then moved his hands around to explore her breasts, which were not as firm and supple as they once were, but certainly warm and very soft. He cupped her right one in his hand and began to lift her shirt as he touched the nipple of her left breast.

Annie shivered as the touch caused her to become moist and warm. She quickly withdrew. She felt insecure and was embarrassed for him to notice the changes in her body.

He sat there looking at her as she turned her back to him.

"No," she said. "I just can't. That part of my life is over, Sean."

Sean stood up and put his arms around her from behind. She could feel his penis against her as he pulled her closer. He gently turned her around to face him and kissed her passionately on the lips. He reached down and lifted her sweatshirt so that he could see her breasts.

Annie resisted and pulled the shirt back down, "No, Sean, please, I'm so ugly."

Sean stood upright, looked her in the eyes, and sternly said, "Yer absolutely NOT ugly." Taking her hand in his, he lifted her hand to his mouth, and he kissed the back of her hand gently as he continued to look her into her eyes, "Yer beautiful, especially ta me." He lifted her sweatshirt over her head and threw it to the floor as he gently laid her back on the bed.

Annie closed her eyes as he closed the shades, locked the door, and removed his own shirt. She was so scared and so insecure... unsure if she were in a dream or had perhaps died.

"Annie, look at me, please."

"She opened her eyes to see him standing totally naked in front of her."

"I'm old, dear. I have man boobs now where I used to have a firm chest. My willie can't decide if he's up or down. I have *erectile dysfunction* – E.D.[282] My prostate gland is swollen all the time, and I can't sleep for having to pee all night long.... but one thing hasn't changed dear. I love ya, and I want ya."

"I'm so afraid," said Annie.

"Me too," he said as he climbed onto the bed.

Together they removed her pants. She wasn't wearing underwear, which was usual for her when camping. He tossed her pants to one side and began to kiss her stomach and move down to....

"No!" Annie said sternly. "Please, no."

"Are ya sure?" he asked softly.

"Yes, I'm sure. If you are going to kiss me, then kiss my mouth, please."

"He moved her legs apart with his knee as he leaned down and kissed her passionately. She could feel the dampness between her own legs and moaned gently as he sucked on her nipples.

Annie reached down and touched his nipples and then his penis and said," Oh my, some things have not changed."

"Oh, believe me, it hasn't seen any action in years, so who knows what will happen."

"Me too, didn't you see the 'Out of Business' sign?" They both giggled.

---

282 E.D. Erectile dysfunction is common in men as they age. The causes are varied and range from enlarged prostate glands to a reduction in their natural testosterone.

Annie ran her hands over his chest. To her, he still felt strong and sexy. She put her arms around him as she licked his nipples.

He moaned, "Oh, ya bad girl," as he lifted her legs and pushed inside of her.

Annie gasped, "Oh..."

"Is it okay? Are ya okay?" asked Sean.

With a firm lift of her hips, she once again embraced him and squeezed. Her pelvic muscles were still firm, and she was amazed at how good it felt to have him inside of her once again. She forgot about her body image and the extra weight.

Nothing had changed that mattered to them as a couple. All was right with the universe, and the sex was just as mind-blowing as it had been when they were younger. They both screamed out in pleasure as they were once more together.

Sean was not having any problems with ED at that moment, and she was just as she had been so many years ago. They moved together, and Annie climaxed first. She was so amazed that she could still feel anything. He screamed over and over again as he too ejaculated for the first time in years.

"It's beautiful, Annie. It's beautiful," said Sean breathlessly, as he pushed up with his arms so he could look down at their bodies moving together and look at her face.

Annie had died and gone to heaven. She didn't even feel her bad hip, which had caused her nothing but pain since an injury years earlier. She felt complete again--like she had been reborn somehow.

Sean collapsed on her, and she could feel him slip slowly out of her vagina. When they were younger, his penis would have remained regardless, but some things simply had to change for two people who had not been sexually active for what was years for them both.

"Oops," said Sean. "Guess that's that for the moment."

Annie chuckled, "How disappointing."

Sean moved to lie beside her, as they both lay on their backs, laughing loudly.

"Well at least we're not crying anymore," said Annie, continuing to laugh.

Sean pulled her to his chest as he held her. "It's so good to be with ya, again..." rubbing her shoulder and arm.

"What just happened, Sean?" asked Annie.

Sean pushed up on his elbow," I think we were meant to find each other again and correct the mistakes made, especially mine."

Annie began to cry, "I don't know what to think, Sean."

"Don't right now. Just relax here, and let's just be for now."

After a long silence, Annie spoke, "I was so sorry to hear about your Pops."

"Yes, poor mum. She seems so lost without him." He said, wiping a tear from his eye.

"Stinky told me about your trip to St. Helens. I'm sorry I couldn't be there with ya both for that trip."

"I'm so sorry for your loss, Sean."

He pulled her closer and said, "Ah well, it was his time, I guess. He had suffered quite some time with prostate cancer. The bastad disease just keeps on until it finally does ya in."

Sean began weeping again, "I'll never understand such things, Annie. It makes no sense to me that we haven't found a cure for such maladies."

Annie pushed up on her elbow and wiped his tears from his cheeks, "I don't understand it either, Sean. I lost my dad to lung cancer, and I would never wish that on another person."

As she lay her head back onto his shoulder, she couldn't help but wonder about Sophia and the girls.

"I'm sure you were blessed to have Sophia and the girls to help you through this painful time."

Silence....

"So, what of your family and Sophia, Sean?"

Sean sighed as though he really didn't want to talk about his wife and family.

"The girls are grown, and Sophia is still Sophia."

"So, you are still married?"

"Nope," he said as he patted her shoulder with his hand.

"I see," said Annie sadly.

Sean paused, "It was all my fault. All of it. I hurt you. I hurt her. I hurt my children. I was a selfish bastad who tried to do the right things but failed miserably. Sophia never truly forgave me, and I simply threw myself into my work and wasn't a very attentive father or husband. I was a piece of shit who was just trying to manage through somehow."

He paused briefly and looked down to make eye contact with Annie. "I wrote you letters, and they came back. I attempted to call, and you wouldn't answer."

Annie looked away and refused to respond to him.

"Sophia was not to blame. I was distant and selfishly pushed her away rather than have to tell her that I couldn't get you off my mind. She knew that when I was sitting on the back porch looking out at the sunset on the ocean, I was somewhere else, and it wasn't with her. Each night, Annie, I just knew that ya were also looking at the sky and somehow, we were together in that way. Sophia insisted that we go to counseling, so I went, but resented every minute of it."

"Yes, men tend to think they are not to blame for anything," said Annie. Understanding all too well the pain of a wife who is struggling to save a marriage and the man is merely going through the motions to please everyone.

"I figured you'd take her side," he said with a chuckle.

"Yep, men are all swine."

"I'm afraid that I have to agree with both of ya on this one," said Sean in resignation, as he pulled Annie closer, patting her on the arm.

"So, what happened, Sean? How are the girls? Where is Sophia?"

"When the girls left for college, Sophia decided to go home to Italy and visit her family. She has dual citizenship and all, anyway, a few weeks. She decided to stay with her family and returned to her first love, art. We eventually divorced when she met and fell in love again."

"Oh?" asked Annie.

"Yes, she met a filthy Frenchman, a winemaker, who swept her off of her feet. "

"Oh, I'm so sorry, Sean."

"Ah, well," Sean sighed," she is no doubt happier with him than she ever was with me, I suppose."

"Sophia got on with her life and has decided to forgive all. I, unfortunately, was not/have not been able to forgive myself at all. I've dated a few graduate students over the years, but never felt fulfilled in those relationships, either."

He paused briefly and looked down at Annie again, who was looking at the breeze blowing the tree outside the window.

She would often become very quiet when he was talking, and he sometimes wondered if she was asleep.

"You still with me, dear?" he asked.

"Yes, I was just imagining Sophia happy and you sleeping with graduate students."

"Well, ya shouldn't dwell on my sleeping with graduate students. There weren't that many, and it was quite dangerous to my own position, to say the least. As it turns out, *Willie* hasn't seen much action in years."

"What have you been doing, then?"

"I climbed a few peaks…finished a few bucket list projects, especially ones that took me to New Zealand, so I could see my daughter who still speaks to me. I have tried to stay busy and out of trouble."

"Hmm…. The girls? One of them doesn't speak to you?"

"Ah, well, that's a love-hate thing. The older daughter understood about the infidelity, but never really forgave me for not being there for her during her difficult years in high school. I was always at work. My work seemed more important to me than her in her mind. She and her mother fought a lot, and of course, I wasn't there to do my part in supporting her mother. The younger daughter is a schoolteacher and has moved to New Zealand to live near her aunts and uncles. I do hear from her, and of course, I go out of my way to see her every couple of years."

"I'm so sorry, Sean. I had no idea."

"What the heck are ya sorry fer, Annie? It wasn't exactly your fault, now, was it?"

"Well, yes. I was a participant in the destruction of not just my life, but yours, too. I have asked God to forgive us both, and now…." Her voice trailed off as she was still in shock from the reunion.

"Ah Annie, I am so sorry for the hell I put all of ya through. Please forgive me, won't ya? And please, please, please promise me you will stop blaming yourself."

Annie rested her cheek on his chest as tears streamed from her eyes.

Sean could feel her tears and gently touched her cheek with his other hand.

"Please, dear. Please don't cry. I am so happy to be with ya. I want ya to be happy, too. Please don't cry."

The couple fell asleep and slept for hours.

Annie still snored, only much louder now.

Sean woke and brushed her hair with his fingers as she slept, remembering every detail of her beautiful shoulders and arms. He was beyond happy to find her there and didn't want to ever let go of her again, but also knew he would have to get back to his camp soon to check on the students before everyone bedded down that evening. He had spent the entire day with her, not wanting to move a muscle to disturb their reunion.

Annie woke and looked up at Sean, who was looking at the ceiling of the cabin. "Whatcha thinking, love?"

Sean looked down at her, smiled, and said, "I'm thinkin bout not ever leaving this spot for the rest of my life. That's what I'm thinkin. But, ...," looking back at the ceiling, "I guess I'd better go check in with the kids who might be wondering if I've been eaten by bears or some such nonsense. Oh, they wouldn't believe what the *codger*[283] had really been up to all afternoon, would they?" he said, snickering to himself. "Do ya want ta come back with me and meet the kids?"

"No, love. You go do your work, and I will stay here. I'll be here till the end of this week. I'm sure you have plenty to keep you busy." Annie then sat up in the bunk and began putting her shorts back on and crawled over Sean to retrieve her sweatshirt.

"Where ya going?" he asked in a concerned tone.

"Well, old people have to pee a lot, don't they?" she answered chuckling.

"They certainly do!" laughed Sean. "Too bad, going for me is such a challenge. It seems ta take days just to get a trickle. Damned irritating, ta say the least."

"That sounds terrible. So, you literally can't go?"

"Oh, I go, but I have to stand there forever till it happens, one drop at a time."

---

283 Old man

Annie opened the door and exited the cabin.

Sean listened to her walk a few steps behind the cabin, and then he heard a steady stream.

Lucky you, Annie, he thought as he looked down at his willie and said, "Now it's yer turn, buddy," and rose to get dressed, too.

Annie stood for a moment looking up at the setting sunlight through the trees, "God, what am I supposed to do now?" she asked, as she crossed herself and began to walk back around the cabin to the front porch. When she rounded the corner, she spotted Sean by a nearby tree with his head resting on the trunk and his willie dripping urine to the base of the tree. She sat on the porch for a second, watching him and wondering if he was indeed having a struggle this time.

Sean turned toward her with a smile on his face and said, "I think, being with ya helped?" He zipped his shorts and strolled toward her. She stood up to greet him and put her arms around his waist.

"I don't want to leave ya, Annie. Please come with me. I know ya would love to meet the students."

Annie looked at his sad eyes and said, "I love you, too, but I need to remain here."

"Please?"

"Sean, I have the cabin here…and you have your students. I'm not sure that I want to ….to. I just need to stay here, okay?" she said through choked tears.

Sean reluctantly turned to walk away. After walking about ten feet, he turned around to see Annie still standing there. As though drawn by a magnet, he ran back to her and took her in his arms. She held him tightly, too. They both cried and kissed.

"Annie, I'll be back. I promise."

"Okay," she said.

"I promise," and he jogged down the path away from her.

Chapter 57—It makes no difference...

Sean walked into the small camp office, which was thankfully empty, and snuck around the back of the building through the laundromat and into the men's restroom. He had hoped that none of his students would notice, but he was spotted immediately.

"Where have you been, man?" *Ahmer*[284] said. He had noted his entrance and ran to greet him.

"*Ami*[285] was going to organize a search party if you weren't here by dinner."

"Oh, I was scouting out places for us to go tomorrow. No worries."

"Well, you'd better find her quick. She may have the authorities out soon if not."

The two entered the restroom and were met with the shouts and laughter of half-naked young men getting their evening showers.

"Dude, you had everyone worried," said *Andy*. [286]

"No worries, guys," said Sean. "There is lots to see in the next few days and lots of rock samples to collect."

They all laughed at how silly it was to worry about Professor Anderson. Although the young men would never admit it, they too were a little bit concerned. He wasn't a young man, and he hadn't told anyone what his plans were for the day.

---

284 Ahmer is a fictional character, an international student attending the field trip. His character does not represent any real person past or present.

285 Female student on the field trip who had great affection for Professor Anderson. Her character does not represent any real person past or present.

286 Andy, PhD student who was helping to lead the field trip. His character does not represent any real person past or present.

They were going to allow Ami to take the drama award though. Ami was an undergraduate geology major who had sort of a crush on Sean. She followed him around like a puppy, annoyingly asking questions. Everyone just rolled their eyes, but Sean thought it was kind of cute.

Sean collected his towel and toiletries and walked to get his shower too. He felt totally knackered after his physical workout with Annie earlier that day and wondered if she too was exhausted. The water was so cold that he had to stand outside of the stream and wet his entire body with his hands. *The river would have been worse*, he thought, as he cupped his hands to collect water.

He reached for the bar of Ivory soap that he always carried in his bag and recalled bathing in the river with Annie, and wished that she was there with him now, so he could lather her entire body. He felt his penis harden with the memory.

"Oh, Geez, I'd better stop thinking about her, or I'll have to stay in here for a while."

The experiences of the day had left him drained emotionally and physically. He wasn't up to an evening around the campfire but knew he would have to make an obligatory appearance and drink at least one beer before turning in for the evening.

His students were so excited to be able to see Yellowstone and the Stillwater with the men who were considered legends and leading authorities on the geology of that region; Sean, Yellowstone, and Jim, the Stillwater.

Jim had retired by now but was still associated with the mine and agreed to help Sean lead the group through the upper and lower banded series.

The students were there as part of their summer field camp, which had invited Sean to join them for a few weeks. Most of them had taken his igneous and metamorphic petrology course or the volcanology course. He wasn't retired from teaching but had taken on fewer graduate students.

Jim would arrive the next day, and Sean couldn't wait to tell him about Annie.

The Stillwater was their last stop before going back to the field camp for the next two weeks. Sean knew he only had until the end of the week to see Annie before she left the area. His heart sank with sadness as he remembered her eyes.

The group had already gathered around the campfire by the time he had dressed. They were riotous and apparently having a great time. The night air was crisp, and the mosquitoes had bedded down for the evening, so it was no doubt going to be perfect.

As he walked toward the group, he wondered if he should walk the trail in the dark and be with Annie for the evening.

"Annie, what would ya have me do?" he asked softly to himself.

"Hey professor, come on over. We have hot dogs!"

"...and s'mores..."

"...and beer..."

"Well, how can I turn those down," he said, with a forced grin on his face.

"Where were you today, Dr. Anderson? I was so worried about you," chirped Ami.

"Oh, uh, I was just looking around at stuff for our outing tomorrow. No worries, okay?" he said, and slapped his bare knee.

He could see their faces in the light, and he was reminded of all of the times gone by as a student himself or on trips with others. Oh, to be that young and experiencing everything for the first time. Either he was getting older, or they were getting younger. One thing was for sure, they made him feel young.

I wish Annie had come. She would have loved these kids, he thought as he took a swig of beer. *I promised her I would see her again. How will I keep that promise on this trip, if she won't come along?*

Annie cried herself to sleep after Sean left and didn't wake up again until much later that evening. She hadn't eaten lunch or dinner. It was too late to visit the river for prayers, so she rose and warmed water for organic tea with her electric kettle. A protein bar and tea would help the shaky feeling.

As she sat there with the windows open, a breeze was blowing through. The curtains appeared as sails, and Annie removed her sweatshirt so the night air could envelop her body.

"Here I am Lord...sinful and sorrowful. What am I to do now?" she said.

She lingered for several minutes, allowing the coolness to distract her from her conundrum. A tune began to run through her mind. It was inaudible but clearly experienced...

"I am constant...I am near. I am peace that shatters all your secret fears..."

"Praise you, Lord," she said, as she allowed herself to feel worthy of love, and to be at peace once again. In her experience, God spoke to her heart and soul when she was still and listened. As a blessing, images, song lyrics, and music would often come to her during deep prayer or meditation. Somehow, she knew that God loved her despite everything, and this reality made all the difference in the world.

"I pray, Lord, that You will guide me with Sean. He is no longer married, but I still feel intense guilt for my part in hurting others. If it is Your will, I will walk away once more. I know that I can do this with You at my side. If it is Your will that we are together, please give me a clear sign. I love you, Lord, ...my strength. I also love him with all of my heart. Whatever Your will, Lord, I surrender to You. Please let my actions bring You glory. Amen"

She sat and drank her tea, which was now tepid, feeling a resignation to the will of God. She had placed all in His hands, and she was at peace.

The next day, Annie rose and went for a walk along the stream, dipping her hands periodically in the ice-cold water. She found herself at the bathing pool she had shared with Sean. The memory of his soaping her all over and the afternoon they spent making passionate love came flooding back. At that moment, if he had been there, she would have resigned all to him.

"Is this just lust, Lord?" she asked. "Do I really trust him with my heart, my body, …. Will I ever trust him again?"

She found herself feeling hurt and jealous, too, that he had been with *graduate students.*

"That is clearly more than one," she spoke aloud indignantly.

She then imagined him *in their pool* with one of them. *Ugh!*

"Dear God! Help me to not have these feelings of jealousy. He clearly isn't still doing this. Is he? I hope? Oh, Lord! ALL MEN ARE SWINE!" she screamed loud enough for the wildlife nearby to hear her. She felt so angry that she kicked moss into the air and far enough to make it almost to the other side of the river. If he'd been right there at that moment, she might have kicked him instead.

"Bastard!" she cried. "I hate you! I hate all men!"

She removed all of her clothes and dipped into the pool. It didn't matter that she hadn't brought soap or a towel, she wanted to immerse herself and be cleansed by the flowing water.

The flow was swift, and she could barely stand, so she sat down on a rock that rose above the water. As she sat there, the current flowed down the outside of both legs. She slowly lowered her buttocks and eased her entire back into the water in front of the rock so that the water could flow over her shoulders and down over her breasts. It was so invigorating. The cold numbed the pain, anger, and lust that she had been feeling. She tipped her head back and slid under the water so that her entire body was immersed.

After the water therapy, she gathered her clothing and slowly walked back to her cabin, totally naked, without care. Her shoes were barely on her feet, as she didn't bother to put them on and lace them. Each foot was slipped in just enough to protect it from the forest carpet.

Sean and the field camp students met Jim at the mine where they would begin their trek in trucks up to the plateau. The two geezers met with a chest bump and a hongi, which entertained the students.

"Some things never grow old, do they?" asked Jim as he then greeted everyone else.

"Nope," said Sean. "Especially YOU! Ha-ha!"

"You're looking fit, mate," said Jim as he searched his face and eyes for some indication of his current level of happiness. "I think I've seen that look before," he said in an accusing tone.

"We'll talk about it later," said Sean as he looked over the top of his glasses to meet Jim's gaze.

"Ah, geez, mate!!! Did you find her?!" he shouted loudly and excitedly.

Sean grinned from ear to ear, "Shhhhhh.... not here," he whispered.

Jim could hardly contain himself until they got in the truck.

Sean felt his spirits lifted by Jim's extreme positivity regarding Annie. Perhaps they would be together. He had hope.

The men entered the truck, and Jim began, "So, what is it? Is it Annie? For real? Did you find her? Did she talk to you? ..." He was so excited that Sean thought he might never stop talking.

"Yes!" said Sean, with a big smile.

"I knew it!! She said she was coming soon, but I wasn't exactly sure. I've been out of the country for a few weeks."

"You are not going to believe this. She is actually here at the Stillwater."

"Are you kidding me? Where? When is she coming?" asked Jim.

"Well that's a bit complicated, I think. She's been alone for a very long time, and I'm not sure she will ever trust me to not hurt her again."

"So, you've seen her and talked to her?"

"Oh, ya."

"You DOG!" barked Jim.

Sean couldn't help but smile to himself. He was inordinately proud of the fact that he could pleasure any woman, especially Annie, at this point in his life.

"Yes, Jim. We had a fond... reunion."

"So, how is she, mate?"

"She is, of course, older, but she is still Annie. I love her, just the same."

Jim ceased his excitement and spoke in a more serious tone, "So, is she right, mate?"

"Ya, she seems to be okay. She just didn't seem to want to come along with me."

"Oh, Seani," said Jim sadly. "You broke her heart. Give the gal a minute to sort out how she feels. I am certain that she loves ya... over the moon. Yep, over the moon. It will be right. You bet it will. After all these years, the two of ya were meant to find each other again. To be sure mate. The gods have willed it."

"I just hope her God has," said Sean sadly.

The truck meandered up the bumpy mountain mining road and pulled in behind the other trucks. Jim reached up and touched Sean's shoulder as they came to a stop,

"Don't give up. I know she loves ya. I can feel it in here," he said as he pointed to his heart. My heart knows such things."

"Thanks, mate," said Sean. "I won't give up."

Chapter 58—Mosquito Glen

The field trip group spent the entire day on the plateau stopping for lunch at the famous *Mosquito Glen Campsite*,[287] which had been the site of many a geology group in the past, including the tour with Annie and the boys from South America.

"What the fuck?" yelled Ami. What is with these mosquitoes? You could hang a license plate on some of them. Everyone laughed as she swung her arms around madly like a propeller trying to get them off.

"Well this camp is called Mosquito Glen, you know. Perhaps it is aptly named," laughed Ahmer.

"You need to eat more garlic, *doll*,"[288] said Jim in his best New Zealand accent. "High mountain glaciers attract the beasts in the summer. Even the bears leave to get away from them," he laughed. "Here try a sardine," he said as he handed her an open can and a packet of crackers.

She declined the food and continued to sit there with her knees pulled up. Every inch of her exposed body was covered in a layer of mosquitos...some just hovering above the others because there was no place to land. Ami was miserable and was ready to go home.

---

287 Fictional campsite not meant to represent any real place.

288 In this case, doll is used as a term of endearment...a sign of respect. It is also seen as insulting to many women as it once again places the female in a subordinate position, lesser than... diminishing their intellectual prowess. One might argue that the female is also socialized to behave as lesser too and that is why it is so normalized in many cultures.

Sean felt sorry for her as he remembered his first experience in that area too. Sadly, the entire plateau was mosquito haven during the day, so it was not just the spot where they were sitting.

"Ya mind if I give it a go?" he asked as he pulled out a bottle of organic insect repellent.

"Smells like shit, but it might do the trick."

She nodded and extended her white arms, now covered in red bumps.

"You are going to need to calamine tonight for sure."

"Thank you, Professor. I think they don't like that," Ami said as she rubbed the oils more evenly over her skin. "Whew, that stuff really smells." she said, gagging slightly. "What the hell is in that stuff? Is it time to leave yet?"

"Nope, not yet. We still have a few cumulate minerals to identify first."

"If we must," she sighed.

"She'll be right," shouted Jim as he waved for everyone to get packed up and get back to the cross-section.

At the end of the day, the group was dehydrated and pretty tired. The next day, thankfully, would be in the mine, where they could walk through the reef.

They met at the parking area where they had left their trucks and discussed the plans for the evening and the next day.

"Sean, aren't ya going ta take these kids to the Chrome Bar?" shouted Jim. "It's not right to end a field day without havin a shot of piss, mate."

"He means beer," said Ahmer as Ami looked disgusted at the thought of urine.

"I learned that from an Aussie roommate I had once. They say all kinds of weird shit."

"Yes, let's go, man," shouted Ami. "I've never had piss before."

The students chimed in with shouts of agreement and laughter.

Well, that settled it. Everyone wanted to go, so Sean had no choice but to relent to the collective cheers.

As the group caravanned down the slope, Sean thought of Annie and how he would manage to see her that evening. He was knackered, and if he drank a beer or two, he would not be able to do anything but sleep.

"Ya want me ta babysit, while ya go see your love?" asked Jim, as he lightly punched his buddy in the shoulder.

"Nah, I probably need to go with the gang and then think of something later on."

"Maybe I could give you a lift to where she is staying?"

Sean looked at his friend and replied, "Would ya? I hate that I haven't been back since...., you know."

"I would love to see her again too mate. It's a date," Jim said with a huge smile on his face. "Where is she exactly?"

"She is at a cabin up where we used to camp years ago...almost the exact spot in fact."

"Oh yeah, I know that place well. Ya shouldn't be walking up there after dark, fer sure."

"I am definitely takin you."

"Thanks, mate," Said Sean, relieved.

Chapter 59—The Chrome Bar
We'll be right

The *Chrome Bar*[289] hadn't changed a great deal from when Annie, Jim, and Sean had last been there years ago. The music on the jukebox was the same classics with some country mixed in for good measure. Beer was now on draught instead of just bottles and cans, but the burgers and fries were outstanding.

As Sean and Jim walked in the door, they noticed that the establishment had hung new curtains and had added booths along the perimeter of the main room. The center of the room still had what looked like the original tables and chairs, with plastic tablecloths for an elegant finish. It felt the same, though, especially with Jim there with him.

A tiny dance floor still remained in the southeast corner directly to the left of the jukebox. The sound of pool balls colliding with each other could be heard over the laughter and talking of the rather large group. An additional game room had been added some years before to accommodate large numbers of tourists with families that seem to drive through the valley each summer. After a meal, the kids could play games while the parents drank a few rounds and listened to music.

Everyone ate, and then the students took their beers to the game room to play games for a while. Jim and Sean were left sitting in a

---

289 The Chrome Bar is a fictional diner based on the popular "Nye Bar" in the Stillwater Complex of Montana, Nye, Montana. All characters and personnel associated with this fictional place do not depict any real persons, past or present.

booth together reminiscing about the good old days and discussing the changes to their lives over the past few years.

"Looks like we are going to be here for a couple of hours," said Jim.

"I may have ta go soon. I'm just not as young as I used to be, ya know," said Sean.

"I'll go check with the others and see how long it is going to be, okay? Be right back."

Sean leaned against the wall and closed his eyes. He could see Annie from long ago, trying to teach Jim how to do a Texas two-step. She was so beautiful, and Jim was so pissed.

"Haha," Sean laughed out loud at the memory. He got up and went to the jukebox, just as he had done many times before and began searching the list of songs and albums.

"Patsy Cline? Geez, don't want to cry all over Jim."

His eyes then settled on old favorites, many of which always made him think of Annie. One song stood out, "It Makes No Difference," by The Band. His heart leaped in his chest. This was their song! It must be fate. He searched his pockets for enough quarters to play the album, which included favorites, like "The Weight."

Sean could hear Jim laughing loudly from the game room as the album began to play. He stood facing the jukebox as the collection played. He was the only one left in the dining area and could feel the stark absence of Annie as the album began to play.

"Ah, Annie, damn it. I wish ya were here with me, love."

Annie had decided to drive into the bar to avoid being home if Sean stopped by. She hadn't eaten much the past day and was also afraid of allowing herself to feel vulnerable. Waiting endlessly for him to return or not return was driving her crazy. She couldn't pray...all she could do was think of him and imagine that he really didn't love her.

As she drove up to the parking lot, she could see that there was quite a crowd inside.

Should I go in? I hate crowds, she thought to herself.

The smell of burgers was enticing, so she got out of her car. As she approached the glass door to the dining room, she could see the back of a man who looked like Sean at the jukebox. She almost fainted at the sight.

"Oh no, I can't go in there now. Sean might think I came here looking for him. Oh Lord, what should I do?"

Before she could make an exit, Sean turned around and saw her standing there.

He melted in the spot. Their eyes were locked as he walked to the door and opened it wide with his arms extended to embrace her.

Instead of falling into his arms, she paused just outside the door for a moment, and looked away from him with tears in her eyes. In the distance was a glorious sunset peeking through the clouds. A silver lining was showing at the top of the cloud just in front of the setting sun.

Annie stood and looked at the glorious display. The cloud moved slightly and allowed a burst of sunlight to open up and shine on her face. At the same moment, she felt a puff of wind blow her hair back out of her face, as the sun once more bathed her entire body in light.

She turned back to face Sean and saw that his smiling eyes were lit up.

The love he displayed was without question.

He took her hand and led her inside the room to the tiny dance floor.

She melted into his arms as their favorite song played, *"and it makes no difference, where I turn...The flame still burns..."*

They both began to sing as they swayed to the sad guitar and saxophone solo.

"Annie," Sean whispered. "Please don't let go of me. Please don't go,"

He pulled her so close she could barely breathe. "I can't ever let ya go...I think I'd rather die."

"I won't, love," said Annie, "I won't. I have always been yours, and that will never change."

"I love ya, Annie," said Sean as he pushed her away so he could see her eyes.

"I love you too, Sean," she said with tears of happiness flowing down her face.

The song ended, and the couple still stood there embracing and kissing.

"Hey, you two get a room!" shouted Jim, as he stood by the bar smiling.

Annie looked shocked in his direction and ran from Sean to embrace her old friend. The three stood together in a group embrace.

"Annie and Sean," said Jim, "Don't you dare put me through this again. You two are meant to be together, now see here...he choked back tears...get on with it!"

Annie looked at Sean, and Sean looked at Annie..." We'll be right," said Annie.

"We'll be right," said Sean.

The End

"Every failure, every triumph, every experience,
only serves to make me who I am.
I need my pain. I need my joy.
Experiencing life means having both."

C. D. Phillips

Field Camp—What do the students do?

To a geologist, the field is where knowledge gained in the classroom is applied. Skilled field geologists work outside and spend their time collecting detailed information about the geology in given areas. The kind of information gathered and reported on is usually dependent on the type of environment and the specific information that is required. Fieldwork also includes taking physical samples of materials collected in the field for analysis in the laboratory. Not all field geology involves volcanoes and dinosaur fossils.

The field geology instructor is typically a seasoned field geologist who has honed the art and science of field mapping. The field geology camp is a transformative, capstone experience for undergraduates seeking a Bachelor of Science in geology.

For field geology students, the challenge is to endure a six- to eight-week boot camp where they must engage in the survey and mapping of sedimentary, metamorphic, and igneous terrain. It is physically and academically grueling work and requires that they apply knowledge and skills developed in a series of final summative assessment projects

They hike a two and a half square meter mapping area in four to five days. As they walk through the field, they record the geologic information about the rocks present at the surface. A *topographic map*[290] is used as a base map for analyzing, planning, and navigating the mapping area, and for data collection.

---

290 Topographic maps are maps of the earth's surface which have lines of equal elevation. They are 2D representations of the 3D surface. They include elevation, roads, …natural and man-made features as well.

Typically, the geologist determines a *transect line*[291], sometimes multiple lines, depending on the size of the area and the specific information needed. The transect is selected to cross any structures present and cut across as many different *outcrops*[292] as possible.

The student creates a cross-sectional view, where information recorded at the surface is translated vertically beneath the earth's surface and also horizontally across broad areas, along the transect line.

This process allows the geologist to reconstruct the geologic history of an area, from the deposition of sediments through all changes to rocks up and to the present. It is a sort of forensic study of the geologic processes and the history that created the formations seen at the surface.

The student is required to generate a map of the distribution of geologic features, a *Geologic Map*[293], and to write a report where they connect the geology of the area to the regional geology. The map should include colors, symbols, and a legend, which explains the mapped information. Colors are correlated with the age of *rock strata*[294], and symbols are used to denote the rock types present as well. The map is created as an overlay to a topographic base map, which is used in the preliminary survey.

It is also necessary to see if the rock strata are flat lying or have been folded or faulted from their original position. To determine

---

291 The transect is a line selected to allow for the collection of optimum data points across features in a mapping area. This line is usually determined from the careful examination of a topo (topographic) map and aerial photos of the area.

292 Outcrops are rocks which are present, exposed at the earth's surface.

293 A geologic map is one that is generated using a topographic base with the distribution and orientation of rocks exposed at the surface.

294 Strata refers to the layer of rock present; stratigraphic units are specific layers of rock that have been described and classified by a geologist during the mapping process.

this, a three-dimensional orientation (*strike and dip*[295]) of the rock layer is also denoted by universal symbols, used by all geologists, to indicate the general trend of the outcrops.

In the beginning projects, the student is given instructions on safety, regional geology, and guidelines for behavior when walking on terrain that is owned by others, particularly federal lands.

Many field camp professors prefer that their students have a minimum of high-tech tools to begin their experience. Each student is provided an aerial photo of the area, a topographic base map, a Brunton compass, a hand lens, and an assigned learning partner for physical security, but also for the learning process. It's usually better if a student has a fellow student learning with them. Ideally, they are a support for each other in the process.

Much like the kids who attend 'Hogwarts,' geology students are provided a list of tools and materials that will be needed for the six- to eight-week course. The student has the responsibility to purchase the necessary items for the living arrangements, which might include camping in wilderness areas, living in rustic camps with limited amenities, or residing in a dormitory setting. Each housing arrangement has its own set of challenges, especially for the novice at camping or the student encountering and experiencing a different culture; like cowboys, cowgirls, bars, saloons, and gambling.

Each student is also responsible for acquiring the proper tools needed to be productive in finishing their project reports and to produce accurate and professional looking maps. In the old days, twenty-plus years ago, that meant light tables, vellum, drafting tools

---

295 Strike and dip refer to the orientation of a geologic feature. It is also referred to as the attitude. The strike line is associated with the azimuth system along the horizon with due north being 0 or 360 degrees with cardinal points at each 90-degree interval from due north. The dip is the measured angle that the bedding plane or other linear facets within the rock strata, dip from the horizontal downward toward the center of the earth.

- including mechanical pencils, and *rapidograph*[296] pens, as well as various shaped rulers. Of course, colored pencils were needed, too, for annotating the maps. Modern tools make these obsolete but learning to use the low-tech devices before the high tech is a time-honored teaching best practice.

After the teams of students are oriented in the field area, meaning the instructor makes sure the student knows where they are challenged to determine a transect line for their project. Groups of students move along the designated path collecting information on the rock types and orientation present in each outcrop.

In sedimentary terrain, it is generally easy to determine the direction and orientation of the *bedding plane* [297] and to record general descriptions of the grain size, texture, and composition of cementing agents.

When Anna first visited the camp as a new professor, she literally sat on the top of a ridge and mapped the entire valley, using aerial photos and a topo map. She then walked transect lines to *'ground truth'*[298] her *photogeologic*[299] map. It took years of remote sensing experience to be able to map an area accurately only using a photo. She understood well that the photo-derived map meant nothing without checking her work in the field.

Geologic information gathered by the students in the field is typically written in a field notebook and denoted as an identifying mark on both the topographic and photogeologic maps, point 1

---

296 Professional stylized ink pens, used in art, and all science and engineering, where drafting of final products was a necessity. They were popular before computer graphics software and hardware.

297 A bedding plane refers to a layer of rocks, strata, which can be clearly delineated from rock layers, above and below.

298 Ground truthing is a process used when someone has made a geologic determination of an area. Going into the remotely mapped terrain and confirming the assessment made virtually improves the accuracy of the interpretation.

299 A photogeologic map is one where the geologist places mapped information on an aerial photo. The photo is then considered a map as well.

in the journal, corresponds to point 1 on the topo and photo. This exercise requires that the students be able to find themselves on a topographic map. Each student should have the experience of having to be able to do this at least once, without the aid of high-tech devices, such as a *GPS*.[300]

A hand lens[301] is used to examine the features of the rock very carefully. This allows the students to see how the minerals, grains, are distributed in the *groundmass*[302] and to identify the grain shape and size. Each student is also given instruction or should already know how to use the *Brunton compass*[303] to measure the strike and dip of bedding directly

Each compass has bubbles, much like a carpenter's level, to help students to measure angles of inclination and geographic orientation accurately. It has characteristics which allow it to be used to triangulate position as well. The Brunton compass is used by forest rangers, military personnel, geologists, and many other professions who need to measure the orientation of features in nature.

In addition to understanding how to use the tools of the science and general behavior and safety guidelines for the field, students also must be aware of the climate and elevation of their physical environment. In the heat of the summer months, which is typically when camps are conducted, many fail to hydrate properly and end up with dizziness and perhaps a visit to the infirmary.

Anna, Sean, and Adam were seasoned field camp professors and were aware that despite all the warnings regarding heat exhaustion

---

300 GPS is a global positioning system, which uses satellites to triangulate a position on the surface of the planet.

301 A hand lens is a small optical instrument used to magnify objects.

302 Groundmass is the fine-grained material of a rock in which grains are framed. It can be a cementing mineral in sedimentary rocks or very fine mineral assemblage with larger grains present, such as in Igneous and Metamorphic rocks assemblages.

303 A Brunton compass is a specialized compass which includes leveling bubbles, a mirror, azimuth, and degree markings to measure the orientation of rock strata.

and heat stroke there would always be one or two students who would suffer, usually mild, but on occasion requiring a visit to the local hospital and administering intravenous fluids.

Anna would not allow students on her van to the field unless they had everything they needed. No hat, no water, no lunch...just like their mom, she would order them back to their dorm or bunk to get what they needed. Adam thought they should be left behind to teach them to be responsible, but on this, Anna would not budge. She would rather be a hag about it in the beginning than to deal with the problems that would result in a student getting in trouble. In Adam's defense, he had never had the experience of being a parent. His children were all adults, and he had little patience for nonsense of that sort.

Like Anna, Sean was also a parent and sort of a fatherly figure in his concern for his

"kids," but he was very strict when it came to safety and etiquette in the field. Although the mapping areas are typically in BLM (Bureau of Land Management) land, many of the local ranchers had been granted grazing rights, so there were herds of cattle wandering around as well. Most of the time, the cows kept well clear of the students. He made sure that his students understood that interfering with any of the indigenous wildlife was strictly forbidden and rock rolling was a big *No.*

In one field area, a beautifully preserved dinosaur bone, embedded in a wall of sandstone, was strictly *look but don't touch.* Sean enjoyed showing this locality to some of the local ranchers, in future years, who never failed to be impressed. Good relations with the ranchers was critical to the success of each field camp, and every year Sean would write to all the landowning ranchers asking for permission to cross their land. He loved the physical challenge of hiking and enjoyed mapping his own research projects each summer, always finding something new each time.

There was a great deal of socialization and instruction for Sean's new campers. They were green, but he couldn't wait to get them out to the first couple of mapping projects, which would lay a foundation for all other projects they would explore.

Creating a geologic map of the area traditionally required a large sheet of *vellum*[304] overlain on a topographic base map, which allowed for the transfer of information from the field maps, cross sections, and aerial photo maps. A mechanical pencil was used to annotate the map and to transfer contour intervals.

Modern technology now includes the use of *GIS*[305] programs to generate maps. Both high- or low-tech maps must clearly show the transect line and contain structural features describing the folding, faulting, and general orientation of all outcrops.

Field geology instructors are typically seasoned field geologists and are drawn to teaching senior level students the tools and methods used in the field. In the case of these three instructors, each had to learn the new tools of the trade in their own continued education. Teaching the ancient skills was basic best practices, any technology used beyond that was added value and skill building for the future of any geologist. Everyone should be able to create a map using online data, but they should also understand how to ground truth that information. These truths were part of the best practices for teaching in any reputable field geology course.

For the field geology professor, like Sean, Adam, or Anna, there was a great sense of satisfaction in seeing the progress of students. To see once nervous, tentative young men and women, many of whom had led somewhat sheltered lives, evolve into confident and knowledgeable practitioners of the science and art was rewarding.

---

304 Velum is a thin sheet of translucent plastic used in drafting and mapping.

305 GIS refers to a geographic information system, which is a computer program, software, that renders the attribute data collected in the field and creates a layer of information that is stacked one on top of the other to generate a final mapped image of all digitized data information from layers below.

Even students, who were reticent at first and didn't think they belonged in the field, almost invariably described the experience at the end of the course as the highlight of their undergraduate career.

Revisiting the field each summer becomes a yearly pilgrimage for many instructors and former students.

Bibliography

Kelley, V. C., & McCleary, J. T. (1960). Laramide Orogeny in South-Central New Mexico: GEOLOGICAL NOTES. *AAPG Bulletin, 44*(8), 1419-1420. Retrieved 6 21, 2019 from https://pubs.geoscienceworld.org/aapgbull/article-abstract/44/8/1419/34781/laramide-orogeny-in-south-central-new-mexico

Lavender, G. (2013). 'Imposter syndrome' shown to drive women away from physics. *Physics World, 26*(10), 10-10. Retrieved 6 21, 2019 from http://iopscience.iop.org/article/10.1088/2058-7058/26/10/13/pdf

Paull, R. A., & Paull, R. K. (1993). *Stratigraphy of the Lower Triassic Dinwoody Formation in the Wind River Basin Area, Wyoming.* Retrieved 6 21, 2019 from http://archives.datapages.com/data/wga/data/055/055001/pdfs/31.pdf

Zen, E.-A. (1983). Geology of North End of East Pioneer Mountains, Beaverhead County, Montana: ABSTRACT. *AAPG Bulletin, 67*(8), 1362-1362. Retrieved 6 21, 2019 from http://archives.datapages.com/data/bulletns/1982-83/data/pg/0067/0008/1350/1362b.htm?q=+textstrip:la+textstrip:luna+textstrip:formation+textstrip:middle+textstrip:magdalena+textstrip:basin+textstrip:colombia

Billing, N. (2003). *Nut - The Goddess of Life in Text and Iconography.* Retrieved 7 19, 2019 from http://uu.diva-portal.org/smash/record.jsf?pid=diva2:162294

Knappen, R., & Moulton, G. (1931). *Contributions to economic geology (short papers and preliminary reports), 1930, Part II, Mineral fuel. Geology and mineral resources of parts of Carbon, Big Horn, Yellowstone and Stillwater counties, Montana.* Retrieved 7 22, 2019 from https://pubs.usgs.gov/bul/0822a/report.pdf

Phinney, W. (n.d.). *Science Training History of the Apollo Astronauts.* NASA SP-2015-626. Retrieved 7 22, 2019

Stillwater Complex trip. (2016, August 25). Retrieved from http://minerva.union.edu/hollochk/teaching_petrology/stillwater.html

bat'leth. (n.d.). Retrieved 8 4, 2019 from Star Trek.com: http://www.startrek.com/database_article/batleth

Nakata, J. S., Tomori, A., Tanigawa, W., Okubo, P. G., Mattox, T. N., Heliker, C., . . . Keszthelyi, L. (1998). *Hawaiian Volcano Observatory, Summary 92.* Retrieved 8 5, 2019 from https://pubs.usgs.gov/of/1998/0147/report.pdf

Rao, N. V. (2014). Petrology: Principles and practice. *Journal of The Geological Society of India, 84*(6), 739-739. Retrieved 8 5, 2019 from https://paperity.org/p/53767000/petrology-principles-and-practice

Phillips, C.D. (2020) All **footnotes** are provided by the author who is a geoscientist and college professor. Course notes and a lifetime of learning and teaching in the sciences.

Acknowledgements

Special Thanks to the friends, colleagues, family, readers, and editors, for their unyielding support and encouragement in the writing of this novel.

Assistance with editing:
- *Jerry H. Moore*
- *Charles M. Bartholomew*
- *Karla W. Caraway*

Reading of rough drafts - feedback, character development, and content area advice -
- *Jerry H. Moore*
- *Charles M. Bartholomew*
- *Karla W. Caraway*
- *Karen Hyatt*
- *David Fuccillo*
- *Travis Jenkins*
- *Carol Fuccillo*
- *Lisa Mabry*
- *Yanick St. Jean*
- *Karen Hyatt*
- *Dorothy Cardiel*
- *Jeanne M. Pichoff*
- *Amy Haskell*
- *Juanita Lamb*
- *Caroline Cashmen*

- *Leighanna Guillet*
- *James White*
- *Denise Richards*
- *Dominic Fuccillo*
- *Esther White*
- *Rose Fabian*

Epilogue

"Stillwater" is a work of fiction based on the life and professional experiences of a female geology professor. The characters are developed based on real and fictional people with embellishments for the sake of the narrative. Settings are also based on actual and fictional places.

This work is not meant to be autobiographical, but is instead a fictionalized characterization of real-life experiences, through the eyes of the main character, Annie.

Annie is born in the mid-1950s, raised in a devout Catholic home where she dreamed of being a singing nun, the first woman to climb Mount Everest and perhaps walk on the moon. Her dreams were deeply rooted in her fascination of the cosmos and planet Earth. She was in love with it all and perceived the divine nature of everything.

Growing up in the 60s and 70s, Annie was introduced to the concept of the *superwoman*.[306] Her character is a wife, mother, college professor, and professional geologist.

The character of Annie is an amalgam of three different women, one living, one deceased, and one fictional. She is intelligent, yet shy, somewhat prudish, obedient, spiritually mature, and a Catholic woman, who married young and began a family as society and her religion expected. Her world is challenged as she meets a man with whom she discovers a profound metaphysical connection.

---

306 Superwoman - This term applied to women, who could marry and have families as a society and the church expected, but also pursue their careers as they stretched societal and religious boundaries.

The character of Sean was developed as a love interest for Annie and is not meant to depict any specific living individual. His role is loosely based on a variety of male professionals, many in geology. The primary inspiration for Sean was a cowboy from New Zealand, who was working a summer job at a ranch in the Rocky Mountains. The physical attributes for this character were inspired by a chance meeting of the New Zealand cowboy, as he sat on a barstool and chatted with his co-workers. His rugged good looks, tall, athletic frame, and unmistakable accent made him very appealing to the author as the perfect love interest for Annie.

Sean's professional dossier was provided by a friend of the author and real-life volcanologist, who does not want to be acknowledged, but gladly contributed to the factual presentation of the character.

Stillwater is written for women, by a woman, with input and editing by male and female friends of the author.

All characters are fictional and not meant to represent any real person past or present. The likeness to actual persons or places is not intentional, and considerable effort has been expended to fictionalize each character.

Annie has been an inspiration to me as a writer. I am happy to have made the journey with her to self-actualization.

C. D. Phillips, aka Sarah Anne Moore

Dedication

This book is dedicated to my grandmother, Sarah Anne (Annie) Moore. She was the inspiration for the main character and the writing of this novel. She taught me everything I know about hard work, pride in a job well done, the spirit of adventure, and how to be a kind person in a cruel world. She modeled strength of character and courage in hard times. *C.D. Phillips*

"You only fail if you don't try. Can't never could do anything."
Annie Moore

The Author

C. D. (Dianne) Phillips, is a Professor of Science and Mathematics at Northwest Arkansas Community College, in Bentonville, Arkansas, where for sixteen years she has been teaching geology, honors geology, environmental geology, astronomy, physical science, and undergraduate design and technology in STEM. Before that, she was an adjunct professor and lecturer in Physics and Geology at the University of Arkansas in Fayetteville and Fort Smith, AR.

Her life-experience, including her roles as wife, mother, grandmother, scientist, field geologist, science communicator, mentor, and educator have provided the knowledge base for her writing of this novel. She has written and published several articles in her field of study and has participated in and supervised geology field trips for over thirty years.

A very important factor reflected in this book is her involvement in the community where she promotes social justice, women's issues, and an awareness of needed educational reform for equal status of other women in the Sciences. Her strong belief system and well-developed survival skills are expressed in the adventures and experiences of the characters of her book. Over and over again the inspiration she receives from her students reinforces her will to achieve her goals, for this inspiration is the means by which her dreams soon become her reality. Stillwater is only the first installment of this series, with more to come.

Stillwater—Description

Stillwater will make you laugh, cry, and perhaps lead you to look at rocks, maps, volcanoes, and yourself in a different way. The story includes geology field experiences and adventures, field mapping, lots of hard science, romance, sex,[307] and spirituality. Annie is a woman of passion for her career as a geologist and professor, her students, her family, and her faith. She finds her worldview, spirituality, and morality challenged as she struggles with an extra marital relationship with her one true love, Sean. Together they share a love of volcanoes and each other but must deal with the social and religious boundaries established for them in the 50s, 60s, and 70s. Annie's experiences with systemic sexism in geology and academia will be recognized and appreciated by women and men of all ages, as her character blazes a trail for other women to follow.

The reader will be intrigued by the main character's romance, but also by the camaraderie of the characters and by the worlds they inhabit: their families, their workplaces, their hang-outs, and the sub-worlds of academia and field geology. You will be drawn into the love story that is woven into the tapestry of science, nature, and spirituality.

> *"As you glance into the Stillwater, you see a reflection of Annie and Sean that is embedded in your mind through the entire book. ...Stillwater runs deep and cold through the valley and along the cliffs and becomes an everlasting waterfall." Jerry H. Moore*

---

307 Contains material that may not be suitable for children or prudes.